The Healer's Legacy

Helen Pryke

Pink Quill Books

Copyright © 2022 by Helen Pryke

Pink Quill Books

Cover by Francesco Valla

The poems *Imagination* and *Dawn Will Rise* reproduced with kind permission from Sarah Northwood.

The characters and situations in this book are entirely imaginary and bear no relation to any real person or actual happenings. All rights reserved.

No part of this book may be reproduced in any written, electronic, recording, or photocopied form without written permission of the author. The exception would be in the case of brief quotations embodied in the critical articles or reviews and pages where permission is specifically granted by the author or under the United States Law of Fair Use.

Although every precaution has been taken to verify the accuracy of the information contained herein, the author assumes no responsibility for any errors or omissions. No liability is assumed for damages that may result from the use of information contained within.

For all the readers who have welcomed the Innocenti into their hearts.

We are the daughters of the women they burned.

I rest beneath a wide space like dark land after sunset,
Listening to the beat of horses' feet beneath my ribs,
Which thrums and hums and moves in certain movement,
Precise and subtle as it chimes to sense the
Void between the wait and motion.
I am not myself like hail is not rain,
And wish upon the stars to be waiting in
The time before the sun rises.
So within this heavy pause, I can rest,
Assured the dawn will rise again,
And with it so will I.

Dawn Will Rise by Sarah Northwood
(taken from *Poetry of the Heart and Soul*)

Prologue

Tuscany
October, present day

THE MUSTY SMELL OF damp hung in the mist-laden air beneath the trees. My feet stirred up clumps of mushy leaves, revealing hidden mushrooms and blades of grass as I passed. But my mind was on my manuscript, and the stories I was writing. Stories that might never be seen by others' eyes, but that I had to write down, to unburden my soul.

I knew the woods off by heart, having traced each healer's steps along the ancient paths surrounding the cottage. Further along to the left was the place where the villa had once stood. There was nothing there now, only an irregular rectangle shape in the ground, covered by the trees and bushes that had grown over the last two hundred years.

I had visited the site of the old stables many times, trying to imagine the villa as it had been throughout the centuries, slowly changing as time passed. It was hard to believe that there had once been carefully tended gardens and an ornamental pond with ducks and herons beneath the wild tangle of undergrowth. The souls of the Innocenti who had lived there were long gone, but an echo of their tortured pasts remained, forever bound to the land where they had lived.

Each time I witnessed a healer's story, a sliver of me remained in the past. Luisa, Agnes, Sara, and Morgana; I had watched their lives while under the influence of my great-grandmother's cordial, an impotent observer as their histories were revealed. It had given me a greater understanding of where I had come from, of the terrors my ancestors had gone through in order to carry out their calling as healers.

Morgana's story had been the hardest to bear. The torture, the suffering she had endured, the hatred spread by the witch hunters, the betrayal by not only the villagers she had tended but also her husband, had broken my heart. I'd vowed never to learn about another healer again, never watch their tragic stories. My book would have to finish there, with Gemma's story untold.

But then I had discovered the place where Gemma had eaten the poisoned honey, not far from the tomb that lay forgotten at the heart of the woods. I often visited Bob's grave in the silent clearing. The weathered headstone was harder to read, but the inscription was still there. And sometimes, when there was no breeze and everything was quiet, I heard a whisper.

Something was calling to me, a sweet song tinged with notes of darkness that made my skin tingle. Something that wanted me to bring the past back to light. There was another secret to unravel, answers I needed to quell an itch that wouldn't go away.

I had one more story to write.

Gemma

1631-1637

Chapter One

France, January 1631

She was lost. Gemma dismounted from Ombra and looked around, miserable, exhausted, and starving. A light drizzle that she'd welcomed at first had drenched her to the skin, adding to her wretchedness. The mare snorted, and nudged her with her nose.

'I know, I know. We need to find some shelter.' Gemma didn't look down at her leg; she couldn't bear to see the gash in her breeches, soaked in blood. Her head spun, and she swayed. 'Let's go a bit further under the trees.' Ombra stayed close by her side, letting Gemma lean against her so she could stay upright. In the two months they had been travelling, they had developed an even closer bond, and she was sure the mare could read her mind.

The horse led her under the dripping trees, treading carefully, until they reached a thick canopy of branches. Gemma sank gratefully to the ground, her thigh throbbing, and curled up on a bed of fallen leaves. Even though she knew that she should tend to her wound, she felt too exhausted. Her stomach ached from lack of food, but it didn't take long for the constant drip of water to lull her to sleep.

It was dark when Gemma awoke. Ombra lay beside her, shielding her from the cold wind with her body. The rain had stopped, and a patina of ice covered everything. The moon glowed in a cloudless sky, millions of stars glittering dots in a distance too great to comprehend. Her grandfather had been eager to learn about astronomy, ever since he heard about something called a telescope. He'd been determined to buy one, but then the witch hunters had come, and all their plans had come to nothing.

Gemma wiped away a tear. Memories of her grandparents, the villa, and her life at the cottage with her parents threatened to overwhelm her, bringing a wave of grief. Her mother, Morgana, had died, burned at the stake for witchcraft, so that Gemma could flee and carry on the work of the healers. She felt the weight of the burden on her shoulders, a burden she had neither asked for nor wished to carry.

The night she'd left Gallicano was still fresh in her mind: the mad gallop through the sleeping village, Ombra's hooves making barely any noise on the grassy verges, past the shops and houses she knew so well, their inhabitants dreaming peacefully with no guilt at what had happened earlier that day. She'd gone through the meadow where she and her mother had planted the oak tree a few years earlier, little knowing how their lives would be turned upside down.

The stone shack where they had imprisoned her mother stood, abandoned, at the edge of the meadow, and the wooden hut that had been hastily built for Morgana's trial looked as though someone had thrown rocks at it. Bits of splintered wood lay on the ground, and its door hung crookedly, the building abandoned when the witch hunters had moved to Lucca. Resembling a slovenly hovel, it was hard to believe that it was the place where her mother's guilt had been decided. Riding past, Gemma had refused to look at it, anger making her shake at the thought of how her mother had been treated by the people she had once cared for.

She knew it was all her uncle's fault: his obsession with Teo had been the cause of Morgana's suffering, and had ultimately led to her death. She would never forgive him. Fury raged within her, a deep, dark hatred, her mind set on what was right and wrong, with no room for nuance, no space for doubt. She would travel to Avignon, to her uncle's villa, obtain a place as a maid, and then make him suffer for everything he had ever done to her mother. A few belladonna berries tucked in the pouch around her waist would suffice for what she intended to do. And she would make sure that he knew exactly who she was as he lay in agony, dying.

The first few days of her travels were a blur, with Ombra taking her wherever the terrain was easiest. As they neared the coast, she'd got her bearings and turned towards Genoa, and its port. She'd thought to take a boat to France, using the little money she carried in a pouch around her waist, but the hustle and bustle of the crowded streets, and the possibility of running into the witch hunters, frightened her, and she'd changed her mind. Travelling across the country had been a long, hard ride, where she'd begged lodgings and food when she could, and slept rough and hungry if no village was in sight.

And then news of the plague had arrived. The towns and villages shut themselves off from the outside, refusing to allow strangers in, and she could find shelter only on the most isolated farms. Every town she passed through spoke in hushed tones about the plague raging through Milan, with the sick locked up in their houses to die a horrific death, or taken to the *lazzaretto* in the church of San Carlo to die among the stench and filth of thousands of others. Gemma had avoided the towns after that, terrified of falling ill. Her mother had told her the story of Agnes, and how she had fought to save her friends and loved ones during the plague of 1348, only to watch each one die. Gemma had no desire to end her journey in that way, not before she had the chance to see her uncle die with her own eyes.

So she had kept to the forests, using the hidden tracks that only the deer knew, and slowly made her way north. Food was scarce during winter, and she had to rely on people's goodwill at the occasional cottages she encountered to continue her journey. If it hadn't been for Ombra she would surely have perished; the mare had a knack of finding sheltered crevices where bushes still had berries she could eat, and burrows of small creatures hidden beneath the layers of leaves. It wasn't much, but it was enough to keep her alive.

She'd rejoiced when she found a cave; it was somewhere dry to stay and the animal tracks she saw in the area were promising. But she'd awoken in the dark of night, struggling to emerge from a nightmarish dream where she was crawling to reach her mother's body, the rock walls closing all around her, burying her beneath their weight, dirt and dust choking her as she tried to scream for help.

Shaking and crying, she'd remained huddled at the entrance, her cloak wrapped tightly around her, while Ombra stood behind her, shifting restlessly and occasionally blowing through her nose. Sleeting rain soon soaked her through to her skin, but she couldn't bear to go back inside to the warmth and fire. She'd left the morning after, her mood grim, and it had taken several days to shake off the feeling of dread that had settled on her.

The sun had come out briefly the day before, drying her damp clothes and bringing hope back to her soul. Her mood lifting, she'd made good progress, until the disaster happened. She'd been walking up a steep hill, holding onto Ombra's saddle, the mare's muscles straining under her velvety coat as she planted each foot firmly on the ground before taking her next step. Gemma had felt the ground slip beneath her boot, the rock coming out of the earth as she put all her weight on it, and had slid downhill a fair way, twisting her ankle. Something sticking out of the ground had sliced her leg open, her scream echoing around the mountainside as she desperately reached out to clutch onto a branch, a trunk, anything to stop her fall.

A boulder had stopped her descent, bruising her shoulder and ribs as she crashed against it. Winded and shaken, it had been almost dusk when she'd found the strength to get up on her feet and try to find shelter. Holding onto Ombra's saddle, they'd clambered awkwardly along the side of the mountain until they'd come to the grove of trees, where she fell asleep.

Gemma knew she had to clean and bind her wound, and she desperately wished she had her mother's remedies with her.

Clenching her teeth, she pulled down her breeches, holding back a scream as the material tore away from her skin, making the wound bleed once more. Thanking the Healer that she hadn't been wearing a skirt, she used her water bottle to clean out the cut as best she could, the cold water numbing the pain a little. Ombra nudged her shoulder, snuffling in her ear.

'That tickles.' Gemma snorted and pushed the mare away. The wound was clean, but still bleeding, and she needed something to tie around it. Using her teeth, she ripped a wide strip off her shirt and wrapped it around her thigh. Blood soaked through the cloth, and she pulled it tighter, grunting as she tied a knot.

'That will do for now,' she said to Ombra, 'but we need to reach a farmhouse or a village soon so I can tend to it properly.' Thinking of her mother had stirred up memories of the Grove, with its sweet-smelling plants, and the brightly coloured dragonflies flitting around the fountain. Gemma could almost smell the pots of lotions and creams in the pantry, the cauldron boiling over the fire, filled with the herbs that had cured so many of the locals. She brushed away some tears and sniffed loudly.

'Thinking won't bring her back.' Gemma had never felt so alone. Travel-weary, cold, dirty, and lost in a foreign land, her heart ached to be back with the people she loved. She lifted her head and screamed, a raw, feral sound that carried her pain and anger up into the sky, to the stars far above.

Ombra snorted and stamped her foot, her ears flattened against her head. Gemma stopped screaming and leaned against the horse, taking deep gulps of air and breathing in her comforting scent.

'I miss them so much,' she whispered. 'I miss *her* so much.' She hauled herself up into the saddle and clicked to Ombra. 'Let's find food and a warm bed, eh? I don't think I'll survive many more nights outdoors.'

The mare carefully picked her way down the slope, and by morning they were on a well-worn path. Gemma let the horse decide their route, while she drifted in and out of sleep, her fevered dreams riddled with images of vengeance and death.

Chapter Two

Gemma raised her head when Ombra stopped outside a cottage, but was too weak to call for help. Slumped in the saddle, her head thumping in time with the horse's heart, she felt the world spin around her as her body succumbed to the fever burning through it.

Calloused hands gently pulled her from Ombra's back, holding her when her trembling legs threatened to spill her to the ground, and voices spoke words she didn't understand. Gemma lashed out, struggling to escape her captors' grip, only managing feeble gestures as her limbs refused to collaborate. She spat and hissed, determined they wouldn't take her without a fight, until the darkness overwhelmed her and she fainted.

Gemma awoke to find an elderly man sitting next to her on a low wooden stool. The intense aroma of a rich meaty stew filled the air, making her mouth water, and her stomach contracted. The man had his back to her, so she took the opportunity to look around.

She was in a stone-walled cottage with low ceilings, lying on a pallet not far from the fireplace. The only furniture was a small table and two stools, but there was a wall with a doorway across the room, which she presumed led to their bedchamber. Blackened pans hung from hooks on the wall, and clay pots stood lined up on a rickety shelf.

A woman stood before the fire, stirring one of two pots hanging above the flames, her sturdy figure clothed in a black woollen dress, a grey shawl around her shoulders. She turned and spoke to the man, a thick, heavy dialect that Gemma couldn't understand, but her smile was kind and her wrinkled face showed no displeasure for their visitor.

The pallet rustled as Gemma shifted her weight, already tired from holding her head up for so long. The woman hurried over, concern on her face as she shooed the man from his stool. He got up slowly, grumbling, and rubbed his back with a grimace.

'Marguerite.' The old woman leaned over, pointing to her chest, and repeated the word, nodding. Then she pointed to the man. 'Jean.'

'Gemma.' She struggled to sit up, but Marguerite put out her hand and shook her head.

'*Reposez.*'

Rest. Gemma was so weak, she obeyed without a murmur. The old woman shooed her husband away, and he stomped out of the cottage, muttering loudly, while Gemma lay back and closed her eyes.

Marguerite made little noise while she worked; all Gemma could hear was the soft swish of her woollen dress as she moved. The noise lulled her into a half-sleep, and she felt as though she was in a waking dream as she listened to the woman pour boiling water into a glazed bowl, the familiar scent of herbs wafting around the room. Her eyelids were heavy, too heavy to open, and she drifted away into the night.

Movement brought her back again as Marguerite lifted Gemma's shirt to check for other wounds. Gemma tried to grab the hem and pull it back down, sweating from the effort, but Marguerite easily prised her fingers from the material. She hesitated a moment when she caught sight of the birthmark, and Gemma tensed, waiting for the old woman to shout at her to leave. But Marguerite merely narrowed her eyes, then continued her careful examination. Evidently satisfied that the bruises didn't hide broken bones, she unwound the bandages from Gemma's leg. From her gasp, Gemma imagined it wasn't a pretty sight.

When she saw the old woman take a bent needle and some catgut from a basket, she tried to move away.

'You must clean the needle,' she said, her voice dry and raspy.

Marguerite ignored her and threaded the needle.

'No. Put it in the hot water!' Gemma caught hold of the woman's hand and guided it to the bowl, then mimed dropping the needle. 'Eau. Clean.' She searched desperately for the right words, but was relieved to see that Marguerite had understood. Her mother's teachings had been drummed into her from an early age, and the thought of the dirty needle going near her already infected wound made her feel faint.

Marguerite wiped the deep cut with a clean square of cloth, then removed the needle and thread from the bowl. Hunched over Gemma's leg, she stitched the edges of the wound together with deft movements and tied a knot at the end. With a grunt, Marguerite rose and fetched another bowl where some ingredients had been steeping. Once she had squeezed out all the liquid, she took the remaining paste and spread it over another clean cloth. The still-warm poultice stung when it touched the wound, and Gemma had to clench her jaw to stop herself from yelling.

'*Reposez*,' the old woman repeated, making a downwards movement with her hands.

Gemma lay back on the mattress and closed her eyes. The throbbing in her leg subsided, and she fell asleep.

Her dreams were filled with fire. Hungry orange flames, devouring everything in their path, laying waste to meadows and forests. Animals and humans fled from their devastation as fast as they could, only to be overtaken and consumed until they were no more than charred ashes on the ground. Rina, Fredi and the children, their sheep, all screaming in agony as the fire swept over the mountainside. Gallicano was no more; its people burned as they ran from their homes, seeking safety in the valley.

A man writhed on his bed, sweat pouring from his body as he clutched his stomach. Gemma watched from a distance, detached from his suffering, as the poison worked its way through him. The belladonna berries had been meant for her mother, but Morgana had used them to make sure the Witchfinder William Hopkins went to his grave shortly after her own death. His face contorted into a ferocious sneer and his limbs thrashed wildly, until he suddenly fell limp and moved no more. The fire roared over the house where his body lay, dragging the Witchfinder's soul down into the depths of hell.

Only the cottage and the Grove remained, untouched in the midst of all the destruction, a haven for the healers and the dragonflies. Morgana stood beside the fountain, young and healthy as Gemma remembered her, not the tortured skeletal woman she'd last seen in the prison, surrounded by healers from the past, the dragonfly on her outstretched hand. Gemma stepped towards her, joyful at seeing her mother once more, and their fingertips touched. A breeze blew over the Grove, cooling Gemma's skin, and broke the fever that had besieged her for days. The Grove, and Morgana, faded into a misty whiteness, her mother's smile the last thing Gemma saw before she woke up.

Tears coated her cheeks as she lay shivering, the last vestiges of her dream dissipating with the fever. A calm fell over her, as though a great burden had lifted from her shoulders. The Witchfinder was dead, of that she was certain. But she knew others would take his place, and the Innocenti wouldn't be safe for a long time yet. She couldn't return to Gallicano, that much she knew.

'The healers will have an end, but also a beginning. Your future awaits.' She had not forgotten Bob's words, nor the damselfly's promise to accompany her on her journey, wherever it took her. But she often wondered if he had seen the dark hatred within her that wouldn't give her peace, that insisted she get her vengeance on those who had wronged her family. And if he had, would he ever let her go back? Was that why the damselfly had yet to appear?

The old woman placed a cool, damp cloth on Gemma's forehead. '*La fièvre a disparu.*' She smiled, creases crinkling at the corners of her eyes, her worried frown lifting.

'My horse!' Gemma sat up with a start. How could she have forgotten about Ombra?

'*Ne vous inquiétez pas, elle va bien.*' Marguerite passed her a small cup of warm liquid and gestured to her to drink.

Gemma sipped the willow bark tea, its bitter flavour chasing away the residue of her dreams and waking her fully. She glanced down at her leg, but it was still covered with a bandage. Relieved to see that there was no sign of pus, she tentatively moved it.

Marguerite put her hand out. 'Non,' she said firmly.

Gemma sighed, but lay back down. Marguerite berated her, speaking too fast for Gemma to follow, but she understood the gist of her words. *Rest now, heal sooner.* It was what she would have said to one of her patients.

It took a week for Gemma's leg to heal enough for her to hobble around the cottage. Each day she grew stronger, as the old woman's pots of stew gave her body much-needed energy, but her slow progress was frustrating. Every day spent healing was a day longer that her uncle spent in exile, living his life while her mother was dead.

Jean found a stick for her to lean on, and she took to walking round and round the room, building up her strength. The day he brought Ombra to the door, she cried, tears rolling down her cheeks as she caressed the mare's nose. She was pleased to see that Ombra's coat was shining with health, her rounded flanks and bright eyes showing that she was well fed and looked after.

'Don't get too lazy,' Gemma admonished the mare. 'We won't stay here forever.' Ombra nuzzled her hand, searching for treats.

Gemma turned to Jean. 'Merci.' She couldn't find the words to thank him properly, but he merely nodded and brushed away her attempts with a wave of his hand. Marguerite pointed to the door and made a shooing gesture.

'I can go outside?'

'*Oui. Allez.*'

Gemma stepped outside, and took a deep breath of cool air. After the stuffy heat of the cottage, it was a delight to feel the cutting coldness of the wind on her skin. Ombra trod beside her, their feet leaving tracks in the frost-covered grass. The sun hid behind low-lying grey clouds, and there was the scent of rain in the air, but Gemma felt as light-hearted as if it were a balmy spring day. Ahead lay Avignon, her uncle, and her future, and while she yearned for the cottage and the Grove with all her being, she couldn't help feeling a shiver of excitement at the thought of the adventure that awaited. All her life she had felt as though there should be more, and now was her chance to experience it.

Chapter Three

February 1631

Although her leg still hurt too much for her to ride Ombra, Gemma enjoyed her daily walks. Much as she appreciated everything Jean and Marguerite had done for her, she craved time alone, out among nature and its honest simplicity. Time to get the thoughts in her head straight, to suppress the darkness that was ever present, threatening to erupt at the slightest provocation. Her feelings of mistrust hadn't passed with the kindness of the French couple, even though she knew she had nothing to fear from them after Marguerite's reaction to the sight of her birthmark.

Speaking haltingly, she held stilted conversations with Marguerite and Jean. They'd drawn her a map of how to get to Fréjus, the furthest they'd ever been, and reassured her that she would find someone to direct her to Avignon from there. The thought of the journey ahead terrified her, but at the same time she couldn't wait to see new things, meet new people. The restless spirit inside her rebelled at having to remain at the old couple's cottage, and she was eager to get back to her solitary travels across the country. Now that spring was on its way, the days were slightly warmer, the harsh cold of winter finally over.

The wound in her leg had healed well, though slowly. Marguerite's garden lacked the variety of plants in the Grove, but her cures were effective. When she'd found out Gemma was a healer, she had been willing to learn anything she could; and in return, Gemma discovered skills the old woman used, which she wrote down in the recipe book before going to sleep at night.

When she'd seen the wooden chest in the stable, together with her other belongings that had been attached to Ombra's saddle, she'd cried with relief. The loss of the book, after everything she and her mother had been through, would have destroyed her. Every day she was grateful that she had come across Jean and Marguerite; their kindness and acceptance had saved her life, of that she was certain. The old woman had never mentioned her birthmark, or treated her differently, and Gemma wished she could speak French well enough to ask Marguerite about her past. She suspected they had been through similar experiences.

She felt full of vitality that morning, the crisp air and brilliant sunshine lifting her spirits. Everything in the French village was so different from Gallicano, the smells and sounds, the trees, the plants growing in the meadows, even the birdsong, and yet there were so many things that reminded her of home. The sight of a group of women gossiping by the well, the sound of the farrier's hammer striking metal, the aroma of fresh bread wafting from the bakery, made her ache for her friends and family.

'Good morning, Gemma.' Michel, the butcher's son, interrupted her thoughts with a beaming smile. At twenty, he was four years older than her, and betrothed to Pier Lapin's daughter, but this didn't stop him from talking to her whenever he could. Marguerite delighted in telling her all about the villagers and their lives, using hand gestures and voice tones to help her tell her stories, and Gemma smiled at the thought of what Pier would do should he see Michel; the burly farmer could lift an ox, as he had proved many times during village festivals, and would have no qualms in showing his future son-in-law how to treat his daughter properly. But Michel was one of the few people she had met who could speak Italian. For the chance to hear her own language, albeit spoken with a heavy French accent, she put her misgivings aside.

'Good morning,' Gemma replied, with a hesitant smile. She kept a respectful distance, her eyes lowered, aware that other people were nearby.

'You are looking well. How is your leg? Good, yes?' Michel scratched at his thick, bushy beard, his fingernails rasping against his cheek.

'It's almost healed. Marguerite is good at healing the sick.'

'I hear you will be leaving soon.' He shuffled his feet awkwardly, glancing at her.

'Yes, as soon as I can ride. In about a week, I would imagine.'

'You have a... er... husband to get to? A lover?'

Gemma flushed. 'You know I don't! I'm travelling to Avignon. I have a place of work waiting for me when I arrive.'

'My apologies. I will miss seeing you every day, and the chance to speak Italian, that's all.' He leaned forward and lowered his voice. 'I wish you didn't have to go, my dearest Gemma.' His hand brushed hers.

She jerked backwards as though his touch had stung her. A sudden vision overwhelmed her of the two of them, locked in a passionate embrace, his hands entwined in her hair as he lowered himself on top of her, their desire possessing them. She staggered slightly and stared at him, wide-eyed, her heartbeat loud in her ears, as she tried to gather herself.

'Gemma?' He leaned forwards, his eyebrows raised. The odour of onion and stale sweat wafted over her, making her feel nauseous.

'I... Sorry, I felt faint for a moment.' She had to get away, before any damage was done. If the vision came true, if that was the path she chose, she would never go back to Gallicano. Living her days as a butcher's wife in this small village was not how she'd envisaged her life. After everything her father had done to her mother, she had vowed that no man would have the chance to decide her future. The image she'd had, while touching her mother's hand in the prison at Lucca, of being on a ship, protectively holding her hand on her swollen stomach, would be a constant reminder whenever temptation lay in her path. That, and the desire for vengeance.

Another feathery touch on her skin made her glance down, an angry retort on the tip of her tongue. Her words faded away when she saw the damselfly, its blue and black body as long as her hand, wings folded along its back. Gemma lifted her arm, smiling.

'You found me.' It was the damselfly from the clearing where Bob's grave lay, she was sure of it. 'You promised, and you came.'

Michel cleared his throat. 'Er, perhaps I should go. My father is waiting, he sent me on an errand...'

Gemma barely noticed him. A swarm of damselflies rose from some nearby trees and flew over to her, surrounding her, creating an elegant dance to soundless music. She stood in their midst, arms outstretched, laughing as their wings brushed against her. They had found her; she was no longer alone.

The damselflies flew up into the air, circling and whirling as they disappeared among the trees, leaving Gemma standing there, watching. The giddy joy of rediscovering her friends dissipated as she looked around and saw the disapproving stares of the villagers. Michel had fallen over as he backed away from her, and sat on the ground, a bemused look on his face, which was rapidly replaced by an expression she knew only too well. Fear.

Chapter Four

Marguerite passed Gemma a sack full to the brim with food, enough to last a week if she was careful. Tears ran down the old woman's wrinkled face, her pale blue eyes rimmed with red.

'Merci beaucoup,' Gemma said, tying the sack to Ombra's saddle. The wooden chest was already in place, hidden beneath some rolled-up blankets. 'Oh, please don't cry,' she added, turning and giving Marguerite a hug. 'I'm going to miss you both so much.'

Marguerite wrapped her in her arms, then kissed her on the forehead and let her go. Gemma turned to Jean. He was not a man who showed his emotions, but he pulled her into a tight hug, clapped her on the back, and muttered something, before gesturing to her to mount her horse.

Astride Ombra, Gemma flexed her leg. It wasn't perfectly healed, but she would be able to ride a good way before having to stop. Enough to get far from the village, and the suspicious locals. She'd been lucky to stay this long, she knew; not everyone was as kind or welcoming as Marguerite and Jean. If it hadn't been for them... She shuddered at the thought of lying in the open, her wound festering, easy prey for the wolves that roamed the countryside.

'I know you can't understand me, but I want to thank you for your kindness and help. And for looking after Ombra. It means so much to me, and I hope that one day I can repay you.' She smiled down at them and lifted her hand, then clicked her tongue. As Ombra made her way down the track, Gemma heard Marguerite say, in broken Italian, 'Be safe.'

Gemma let Ombra set her own pace, and the mare galloped along the well-worn track. She had been eager to leave the confines of the stable, unused to staying in one place for any length of time. Gemma crouched forward, the wind whipping the horse's mane across her face, and laughed at the sheer exhilaration of the new day. Soon Jean and Marguerite's cottage was far behind them, and Gemma slowed the mare to a steady canter.

She passed village after village, avoiding the inhabitants and the crowded markets. After seeing the expressions on the villagers' faces when the swarm of damselflies had left, she was wary of going near people. While the days gradually became warmer, with the first flowers casting sprinkles of colour across the landscape, the nights were still cold, but she managed to find shepherds' huts to shelter in, or lonely farmhouses far from anywhere. With the occasional day's work in exchange for a barn to sleep in and a hot meal, she slowly made her way across France to Avignon.

The nights she had to stay out in the open, she barely slept. The sound of wolves howling in the distance, the snap of a nearby branch, a flutter of wings as an owl passed overhead and the shriek of its prey as it snatched the poor creature up in its talons, kept her awake. Shivering beside a small fire, she would wait for dawn to break and then leave, half sleeping as Ombra carried her.

The damselfly often hovered near them, or settled on the mare's head, between her ears, its long, thin body quivering with the horse's movement. Gemma hadn't seen the swarm since the village, but hoped it was close by. They made her feel safe… or as safe as she could be, travelling alone.

There weren't many other people out and about; the cold, and the sudden thunderstorms which turned the tracks into rivers of mud, deterred anyone who had no urgent reason to travel. Still, she kept off the commonly used roads as much as possible, preferring the cover of the trees. The forests reminded her of home, of the clearing with Bob's grave, and the river where she'd often swum. Lonely, cold, and hungry, she cried bitter tears, her heart aching for everything she had lost.

For the first time since she'd left Gallicano, she allowed herself to think about the people she'd left behind. Poor Rina, who had spent three years in prison with Morgana, tortured, raped, and starved until the witch hunters had let her go, a mere shadow of her former self. Gemma wondered whether, now she was back with Fredi and her children, Rina could sleep through the night, or if she woke, screaming, from nightmares of that terrible time. Would she ever be able to return to her normal life, or would she be forever on the watch for strangers arriving at the farm, her blood turning to ice in her veins at the slightest glance in her direction?

And the others – the washerwomen, the labourers, the shopkeepers, and the poorer people her mother had always helped;

did they spend their days bearing the burden of guilt for not having spoken up for Morgana, or did they go about their chores without another thought about the woman, their friend, they had condemned to death? Gemma had to believe that deep down, most of them had some remorse for their actions, but in her darkest moments she wondered if she would ever have the strength to return to the cottage, and all the memories it held.

She often thought about Tullia. From the moment she'd seen her standing outside the hut where Morgana was held prisoner, whispering her poisonous words into the Witchfinder's ear, Gemma had been consumed by an overwhelming hatred for the woman. Not only had she recognised her as the 'fairy' who had lured her into the forest when she was ten and encouraged her to eat poisonous honey, but she'd later found out that Tullia had forced her father to betray Morgana, and was responsible for her mother's death.

Gemma knew that to contemplate killing someone went against everything a healer believed in, unless it was to save them from unnecessary suffering and help them find peace. To take a healthy life was unheard of in her family; even her grandmother had been unable to let Gemma's father, Teo, die at birth, although she knew he would be responsible for the tragic events that eventually followed.

But Gemma had already started down that path, from the moment she decided to go to her uncle with the intention of poisoning him. And once she had carried out that act, once she had gone beyond the calling of a healer, then surely she would be able to do it again.

She had always felt that she was different from her family, a damselfly rather than a dragonfly. A desperate longing to travel and see the world had always been inside her, although she would have preferred to leave in different circumstances. But she knew she would return, one day; no healer could withstand the pull of the cottage and the Grove. And when she did, she would have no qualms about killing Tullia.

Chapter Five

Avignon, March 1631

AFTER WEEKS OF TRAVEL, Gemma could see church spires in the distance and the glimmer of the waters of the Rhone sparkling in the sun. The road was crowded with slow carts pulled by oxen, solitary riders like herself, families with squabbling children and bawling infants being shouted at by fraught mothers. She pulled her hood over her head, hiding her matted hair, hoping her bright green eyes were in shadow. Her mother had loved their vivid colour, but in these times of witch hunts and plague, Gemma preferred to attract as little attention as possible.

Shouting came from ahead, and the crowd slowly drew to a halt as everyone reached the banks of the river. Men gestured towards the city on the other side, waving their arms, responding heatedly as the people in the crowd tried to push forward. Ombra snorted at the confusion, and edged sideways, away from the noise. Gemma shushed her, stroking her neck to calm her down while she tried to understand what was happening. Her French had improved during her travels, and she could follow a conversation if she concentrated hard.

'The bridge is down!' a man said, stomping across her path. He threw his arm out, almost hitting Ombra's nose. The mare jerked her head, and half reared. 'Keep your damn horse under control!' he snarled. 'Like we 'aven't got enough problems 'ere, without that bloody creature kickin' out.'

Gemma pulled on Ombra's reins and urged her away from the crowd, desperate to find somewhere quieter. Their shouts rang around her head, hurting her ears, unused as she was to so many people at once. She headed for a copse a little way away and stood Ombra beneath the shade of the trees as she decided what to do.

Watching the crowd on the riverbank, she saw that there were two ferryboats taking people across. Packed to the seams, they lay dangerously low in the water, while the passengers stood crammed on the deck, some hanging over the outer rail. Gemma looked at Ombra.

'I can't see you getting on one of those ferries. Nor me, come to think of it.' She wanted to cry. All that way, only to be halted at the last.

The number of people wanting to cross didn't diminish all day; if anything, it grew larger. Gemma resigned herself to staying where she was, and hoped it would be easier the next day. Perhaps if she made sure that she caught the first ferry, there would be fewer people. With that thought, she wrapped her cloak around her and lay down on the soft, springy grass. If she slept, the morning would arrive more quickly.

A noise awoke her. Sitting up, instantly alert, she pulled her hood over her head and kept as still as she could. She heard Ombra shifting behind her, and put a hand on the mare's shoulder.

'Ssh.' Someone was there, she could sense them. There was little light; the sun was just beginning to rise over the horizon, and there were dark shadows beneath the trees.

A twig snapped, followed by a cough. Muffled footsteps thudded over the thick layer of leaves on the ground. Gemma silently got to her feet and moved to Ombra's side. Reaching for the saddle, she slipped her foot into the stirrup and hoisted herself up.

'No you don't,' came a voice in her ear. Stale breath wafted over her, accompanied by the smell of many weeks' worth of sweat, and the dank, musty stench of urine. A hand grabbed at her cloak and pulled her to the ground.

Gemma twisted violently, leaving her cloak in his grasp, and turned to leap onto Ombra's back. Another hand gripped her arm. She wriggled, trying to escape, but they surrounded her, leering and grabbing, hands clutching, fingers scraping. They were shouting, but they spoke a dialect she didn't understand, strange, heavy words that filled her with fear.

'No!' she screamed, kicking out at them.

They moved, faster than she could have imagined, pinning her arms to her side, grabbing her legs, an arm braced around her neck, forcing her to the ground. She twisted and wriggled her body, scratching and biting anything within reach, but it was no good. The three of them were stronger than she was.

'Italiana?' One hovered above her, close enough for her to see the pock marks on his face.

She could see! The sun was higher now, surely the first people would be arriving for the ferry. This was her chance. She spat at him, teeth bared, her body taut as she prepared to scream.

The punch to her face almost knocked her unconscious, and as she lay on the ground they fell upon her.

'She wears breeches, but she's no boy!' one crowed in delight as he tore her trousers down around her knees.

Her head felt hazy, and her limbs were too limp to stop them ripping at her clothes. Her throat was dry, and no sound came out, however hard she tried. Ombra neighed, a desperate, terrified sound. It rang through the copse, and Gemma listened as it soared out above the trees into the morning sky, willing it onwards to someone, anyone, nearby.

It was no good. She couldn't move to save herself from what would surely happen next. The men's breathing grew heavier, their movements becoming more frantic as they tugged and ripped and grabbed. Somewhere in her mind, she knew she had to lie still, let them do what they wanted, and pray they would leave her alive after.

A shout penetrated the fog in her mind, bringing her back to the surface from the place deep inside where she'd been hiding. The hands suddenly let go of her, hot, stinking breath gave way to the cool morning breeze, and pained grunts filled the air. Gemma slowly lifted her head, dreading what she would see.

A man stood nearby, brandishing a thick branch. One of her attackers was clutching his arm, his face white, the elbow sticking out at an awkward angle. Another had blood streaming down his face from a deep gash on his brow.

The man raised the stick above his head and yelled something, too quickly for Gemma to catch it. The other men shuffled nervously, obviously unwilling to enter the fray again. He took a step forward, teeth clenched, his expression furious.

They glanced at each other, then scarpered off through the trees. In a few seconds, silence returned. Gemma sat with her back against a trunk, hugging her knees to her chest, her whole body shaking.

'*C'est fini*,' the man said, crouching beside her.

Gemma clasped her hands together, trying to calm the trembling. She vaguely heard the man speaking, but there was a dark fog all around her, muffling every sound. And then Ombra was there, her nose snuffling against Gemma's shoulder, the familiar aroma of grass and sweat and horse making the fog dissipate. She grasped Ombra's reins, clutching onto them as though her life depended on it, and took several deep breaths.

'Merci,' she said, keeping her eyes on the ground. He spoke again, but too quickly. She shook her head. 'Italienne.'

'I speak some Italian. Are you all right? Your lip, it's bleeding.'

His voice was soft and kind, and she finally found the courage to look at him. A mop of unruly brown curls framed his tanned face, a concerned smile on his lips. Gemma noticed that his grey shirt had numerous patches, and his leather jerkin was scuffed and worn in places. She struggled to her feet, still clutching onto Ombra's reins, and wiped the blood from her chin.

'No, they didn't... hurt me. Y-you arrived just in time. If not, I don't know what might have happ–' She let out a deep, juddering breath and tried to compose herself. Now was not the moment to fall apart, not when she was so close to her purpose. She needed to keep her head for a while longer, so that she could reach her uncle's house. 'But I-I'm keeping you from your labours. Please, I must get to the ferry and cross the river. My aunt secured me a place as a maid at a villa, an Italian conte's house. I can't afford to lose the work. If you could just help me get to Avignon...' She hated how panicked she sounded, but couldn't bear the thought of staying there a second longer. *What if her rescuer left and the men came back?*

'Whose villa is it? There are many Italians here in Avignon, but perhaps I know him.'

Gemma hesitated. If she wanted to find her great-uncle, she would have to be honest. 'The Conte de Gallicano, Leandro Innocenti.'

Chapter Six

The man raised his eyebrows and whistled through his teeth. 'Leandro Innocenti. I have heard of him, almost everyone in Avignon has.' The man held out his hand. 'I know someone who can take you and your horse to his villa. I imagine you are impatient to be somewhere safe, out of harm's way. Come.' He must have seen her hesitate. 'This person is a trustworthy man, he will look after you. I guarantee it.'

Gemma ignored his outstretched hand and gestured for him to lead the way. The crowd was already gathering on the riverbank, and she felt a moment of apprehension. Her rescuer cut through a group of chattering merchants and headed directly for a small, dark-haired man standing slightly apart from the crowd, his brows furrowed as he glared at everyone around him.

'Hey, Albi!' her rescuer called. The man turned and a grin lit up his face.

Gemma hung back while they spoke, fearful of going too close. She couldn't get the image of those men out of her mind, and of how close they had come to defiling her. She shuddered, and hugged her cloak more tightly around her, hiding her bruises and torn clothes.

After a few minutes, the two men approached her.

'I must leave now, I'm already late,' her rescuer said, 'but Albi here will take good care of you.' He clapped the man on the back and strode away before Gemma could say anything.

She suddenly thought that she hadn't asked her rescuer his name and opened her mouth to call after him, but he was already gone, lost among the crowd. She shrugged, and turned to the man standing nearby. His weathered face was half-hidden beneath a loose-fitting brown felt cap, his baggy breeches tucked into worn leather boots, and a stained jerkin covered a grimy doublet of uncertain colour. He frowned as he caught her looking at him, thick black eyebrows almost meeting in the middle. But Gemma had noticed a slight creasing of the skin around his eyes, as though to herald a smile, before he realised she was watching him.

'Thank you, it's very kind of you to take us across. I didn't mean to impose, it's just that he…' She waved her hands in the direction the other man had taken, embarrassed that she didn't know his name. 'He insisted,' she finished lamely.

The man stared at her and grunted. 'Damn bridge collapses every time it rains. See, three of the arches are down, an' another one's on its way. Been like that forever, bloody Pope doesn't want to spend a florin to fix it.'

'Do you have a boat? I wanted to take a ferryboat, but there's so many people waiting already.'

'You'll be lucky, with that 'orse to take across as well.' He coughed and spat a ball of phlegm on the ground. 'There's another ferry to that island there, but then you'd have to go up some stairs to the rest of the bridge and pray it doesn't collapse as well while you're on it.' He snorted, and wiped his nose on his sleeve.

'No thank you.' Gemma looked around at the restless crowd, and the slow-moving ferries arriving across the river. She huffed, frustrated. *Did he have a boat or not!* She couldn't spend another night on the riverbank.

'Look at them, all pushing and shoving to get across to that shithole.' The man spat again, more vehemently this time.

'I thought it was supposed to be a beautiful city,' Gemma began.

'Beautiful! Pah. If you live in the *Palais des Papes*, or have a villa in the centre of the town like them Barberini, then you would consider it beautiful. But for the rest of us commoners, it is a sewage-filled pit, and stinks right down to its rotten core.'

After her experience, Gemma was inclined to agree with him. 'So why do you live here?'

''Cause of this.' He stretched out his hands, palms up. Rough and calloused, with dirt ingrained in the creases, they were the hands of a man who had worked hard all his life. His right forefinger was cut off at the first knuckle, the skin puckered over the top of the stump.

'How did that happen?' Gemma pointed at his injury.

'Workin' on the bridge. I was an apprentice to a mason, and learned the trade. When he moved on, I stayed here, at the request of the Pope, to work on his palace. Then I chopped my bloody finger off, an' I couldn't work no more. It's hard to hold a hammer.'

Gemma hesitated, then leaned over and peered more closely at his hand. 'The skin's been sewn too tight, you can hardly move it. I'm not surprised you can't hold a hammer.'

'What d'you know about it? You some sort of witch?' He snatched his hand away and stared at her.

'I'm a healer,' Gemma hurried to explain. 'I use herbs – I *used* herbs to make people better. And stitched up wounds when necessary. But that was before...' Her voice faded as she realised she was talking too much.

The man narrowed his eyes. 'You're a bit young to be travellin' alone. You runnin' from something?' He held up his hands. 'Don't answer, I don't need to know. But you don't want to be roamin' the streets of Avignon all by yourself, it ain't safe.'

'So I've seen.' Gemma found it hard to keep the bitterness out of her voice. 'But I must get to the villa, before I lose my place of work.' Tears pricked at Gemma's eyes and she blinked them away, angry at this show of weakness. Now that she was so close to carrying out her plan, she couldn't let her emotions stop her. Since the attack, she could feel her resolve waning.

'I come here every mornin' and spend my day cartin' rich people across the water to the city. A quick word in a finely dressed man's ear and they're more than happy to pay extra just so they don't have to wait for the ferry and cross with the commoners. An' never a kind word when I do it.' He grunted. 'My barge is over that way, I'd be happy to take you. And your 'orse.'

Gemma shook her head. 'I've little money, I can't accept your offer. I'll wait for the ferry, if you'll just tell me where to find the conte's villa once I'm in the city.'

'What sort of man would I be to let you wander about alone? Look at you, you wouldn't last half a day on the streets of Avignon. What with the pick pockets, cutthroats, and lowlifes, you wouldn't make it till nightfall. I'll take you across, no more will be said about it.'

Gemma was touched by his kindness. 'Thank you. I don't know what to say.'

'Then say nothin'. I prefer it that way. Name's Alberto Fornari,' he said as he gestured for her to follow him.

She felt a slight pang at deceiving him, but forced herself to ignore it. 'Rina Galli.'

The barge was hidden among tall grasses and bushes further down the riverbank, a good distance from the crowd.

'Here. The 'orse should fit, if it'll go on. If not, you'll have to leave it behind. Might be gone when you get back, though. Nice beast, that, bit unusual for a maid.'

'She was a gift, and she's coming with me,' Gemma said firmly.

'I get it.' He winked. 'Your previous master very generous, was he?'

'It was my mistress, if you must know,' Gemma retorted.

'All right, no need to get upset. I was only jokin',' he muttered.

Turning her back on him, Gemma took a strip of cloth from her bag and tied it around the mare's head, covering her eyes. With gentle shushes and encouraging words, she led the horse forward. Ombra's ears flattened against her head as she felt the ground shifting beneath her hooves, but eventually she stood on the barge, legs splayed, snorting heavily.

'Best get going.' Alberto pointed at the road, where several people were clambering along the riverbank towards them. As he pushed off with a long pole, someone shouted, and the people picked up their pace, determined not to be left behind. Alberto made a shrugging gesture with his hands, and turned his back on them, grinning. He winked at Gemma. 'What a pity, eh? There was space for them as well. Just keep the 'orse still, though, or we'll be swimming across!'

Chapter Seven

The putrid smell of the city rose to greet them as they left the riverbank and headed through the streets. Gemma had never seen so many people in one place before, not even on market day in Lucca. The stench of sweat mingled with the pungent odours of garlic and spices, while a steady stream of murky-looking water ran down the sides of the roads, the smell of human waste making Gemma's eyes water.

A woman stepped out of a low-roofed house, holding a chamber pot.

'Oi, look out!' she shouted, and threw the contents into the channel of muck. Several people jumped backwards and swore as the filthy water splashed their boots and cloaks.

'See. Shithole,' Alberto remarked.

'This wasn't quite what I was expecting,' Gemma admitted. The narrow streets were lined with houses of all shapes and sizes, squeezed together until you could barely tell where one house ended and the next began. Some children sat outside on their doorsteps, while others ran around, bumping into passers-by or throwing rotten food at them.

She hurried after Alberto, holding on tightly to Ombra's reins. The mare's nostrils flared, her eyes wide open, unused to the noise and confusion, and Gemma walked by Ombra's side, her presence helping to steady the horse's nerves.

'It'll get better soon, after we reach the piazza,' Alberto said. He walked with his shoulders hunched, his sturdy boots trudging through the filth on the ground.

He was right. The square was wide and spacious, with white-washed buildings around its edges, brightly coloured flags hanging down from the windows, and flowers in large ceramic pots. It was a warm spring day, and people sat outside, laughing and talking while drinking flagons of beer or sweet-tasting wine.

Gemma glanced back at the street they'd just walked down, the dark, grimy walls in stark contrast with the brilliant white piazza.

'Hard to believe, isn't it?' Alberto gestured behind them, scowling. 'Down there, squalor and poverty; here, fine food and wine, clean clothes and pretty houses. Come, it gets better as you go further in.'

There was still a slight odour of poverty that not even the heady perfume of the rose bushes could cover, and Gemma noticed that many of the people carried scented squares of fabric, which they kept dabbing at their noses. Several stopped and stared as she passed, and she suddenly became aware of her travel-worn appearance. Ombra's coat was no longer sleek and shiny but splashed with mud, her mane and tail knotted with burrs. At least she looked the part of a housemaid, she thought morosely.

Once they were past the square, the streets grew wider and the houses larger. Light-coloured façades with ornate balconies and glass windows were set back from the road, leaving a wide gap for people to walk. Here no one emptied their chamber pots onto passers-by, and everything was cleaner. Carriages passed them, some open, others closed, the occupants staring at them, curious. Alberto remained silent until they reached an enormous building.

'Here lives our beloved Pope,' he muttered, jerking his head.

The Palais des Papes. Gemma had been curious to see it with her own eyes, ever since she'd left the cottage months earlier. She hadn't expected to see a building badly in need of repair in parts, a shadow of its former glorious self.

'The bridge, the palace, everything is rotten at the core, just like the rest of this city.' Alberto spoke with contempt. 'The rich enjoy their depraved pastimes, throwing their money away, while the poor drop dead working for them.'

'Did you lose someone you love?' The words left her mouth before Gemma could stop them.

He turned brusquely without speaking and walked away, not bothering to see if she was following. Gemma sighed and tugged on Ombra's reins, hurrying after him.

Alberto didn't stop until he reached a modest, yet elegant, brick-walled house at the end of a quiet street, surrounded by trees.

'This is where the conte lives.' He placed a hand on the wrought-iron gate, then hesitated. 'We were to be married, but she fell sick last year. We couldn't afford to call a physician, or even buy something from the apothecary. We barely had enough for food. She died a few weeks before our wedding.'

'I'm so sorry.' Gemma could see the pain in his eyes, it reflected her own.

'A few months later I inherited the barge and now I make just enough money to survive. It's a pity it was too late for both of us. I swore I would never marry again, not if I can't take care of my family.' He shrugged. 'But we mustn't talk of this, not now. Come, I've been here before, we must go round to the back.' He strode down the path along the side of the house and she followed with Ombra. When they arrived at the back door, he knocked loudly, and Gemma envisioned the staccato raps disturbing the peace of the house. She straightened her back, readying herself to convince whoever appeared that she had been hired to work there.

Quick footsteps rang out on a tiled floor, and a woman opened the door, smoothing down her dress. There was flour in her hair and on her nose, and her cheeks were flushed. She dabbed at her nose, only managing to spread more flour on her face, and sighed. 'Albi, what a pleasant surprise! Sorry, I look a mess. Our housekeeper is in bed with influenza, and we're running around doing all her work as well as our own. I was preparing the dinner.' She glanced down at her hands and gave a rueful shrug. 'I think you can see that.'

'You look as beautiful as ever, Paola,' Alberto said, his gaze openly admiring.

'Oh, get on with you.' Paola flushed, her cheeks red beneath the flour.

'It looks like we arrived just in time, then,' Alberto said, turning to Gemma. 'Here's your new housemaid, as promised.'

Paola looked confused. 'House–?'

'My aunt sent for me,' Gemma interrupted. 'She assured me there was a place for me here. I've travelled a long way.'

'It appears you need another pair of hands, and I've brought you a maid,' Alberto said cheerfully.

'A maid with a horse.' Paola peered out of the door at Ombra, who was cropping the grass.

'She was a gift,' Gemma said, starting to feel desperate. 'Without her, I wouldn't have been able to get here.'

Paola ran her hand through her hair, spreading even more flour over herself. 'Well, we do need some–'

'Paola, who is it at the door?' a voice shouted from the depths of the house. 'I had just got settled in my chair to read, but that damned draught is making my neck ache!'

A portly man walked down the hallway. The ends of his long, black curly hair, too black surely for a man of his age, fell over a delicate lace ruff, which hid the rolls of fat on his neck. A neatly trimmed moustache complemented his pointed beard, and he held a piece of white linen to his nose, an embroidered *L* clearly visible. Gemma barely remembered her great-uncle, he had left Tuscany for a tour of Europe when she was little, but she instantly knew it was him.

He drew nearer, his dark-green satin doublet shimmering in the sunlight streaming through the door, slashes in the puffed sleeves showing the white shirt he wore underneath. His dark grey breeches were tucked into white satin stockings, but the whole effect was quite spoiled by the beige *pantofles* he shuffled along in. The backless slippers had lost their shape, and were a complete contrast to the rest of his elegant outfit.

'Yes?' he snapped. 'What are you selling? Don't keep me waiting here all day, I'll catch my death.' He coughed, and hastily made the sign of the cross.

Paola curtsied. 'This is... I'm sorry, who are you?'

'Rina Galli.' Gemma began to curtsey, then remembered she was still wearing breeches under her cloak, and stopped.

'This is Rina,' Paola resumed. 'She says her aunt promised her a place here, but–'

Leandro peered down his nose at them, his lips pursed. 'Mme Dupuis is still unwell, is she not?'

Paola nodded.

'And we need a maid, do we not?'

Paola clasped her hands in front of her and looked at the ground.

'Well, Rina, it would appear that your aunt, however fortuitously, sent for you at the right time. Paola, see that she knows what to do. The nag can stay in the stable with mine until we decide what to do with it. And get the girl some decent clothes.' He turned and made his way back down the hallway, grumbling under his breath.

'I must admit, it's a relief for me, havin' an extra pair of hands.' Paola smiled at Gemma. 'The conte is kinder than he first appears, you'll see. Come, I'll take you up to the attic.' She turned to Alberto. 'Ask Gianni to see to the horse.'

As Gemma followed her to the back staircase, she silently marvelled at how easy it had been to enter her great-uncle's house. He wasn't what she had expected at all, his gentle tone and flamboyant clothes at odds with his title. He had almost seemed... kind. *Enough of that!* a little voice warned. *You're not here for a family reunion*. She touched the pouch at her waist, and hardened her heart to the task ahead.

Chapter Eight

The ornately decorated parlour was symbolic of Leandro in every way, with its sumptuous chaise longue covered in dark-blue velvet, and gold-framed mirrors lining every wall. A huge chandelier hung from the ceiling, a wide gold rosette spreading out from its centre. Gemma rubbed wax into the surface of the cabinet, the rich hue of the dark walnut wood coming through as she polished. Her mind drifted as she moved her arm.

Two weeks had passed since her arrival, and she'd spent that time learning her duties as a maid in her uncle's house. Her room was a small space up in the attic, enough for a narrow cot and her meagre belongings. Every morning she rose at dawn, when the cockerel began crowing, and was kept busy all day long by the convalescing Mme Dupuis.

But she always managed to sneak out during the day to visit Ombra. She was pleased to see that the mare was well cared for, although Leandro's remark about 'deciding what to do with it' troubled her. Gianni was happy to talk to her about anything and everything, and she came to find out much about her great-uncle and his life in Avignon.

However, the more she heard about Leandro, Gemma mused as she polished, the more difficult it became to reconcile her image of him as someone hateful that she had to destroy, to the person she saw before her.

The one thing that had kept her going through her long journey from Tuscany, through the dark, cold nights and the rain, snow so deep that it had reached Ombra's belly, biting wind that cut to the bone, up steep mountainsides and down slippery paths, so hungry that she'd resorted to chewing on bark to trick her stomach into thinking it was food, was her desire for revenge upon those who had caused her mother's death, starting with her great-uncle. She had ridden to Avignon with that thought only in her mind, the one reason for continuing her travels when others would have given up.

Until she had seen Leandro standing in the hallway. He couldn't have been further from the dark-haired, leering villain she had imagined him to be. Leaning on a cane, his breath coming in wheezing gasps, dressed like a man twenty years younger, his soft, effeminate voice had been contradictory to his grandfatherly figure. She had also seen the bare patches on his head, before he had swiftly shifted his wig to cover them once more, and the red sore inside his nose. His carefree life abroad had not been without a price to pay. To her annoyance, she'd felt pity when she saw him, not anger. She'd wanted to make him suffer for what he'd done to her mother, but she saw that he was already suffering enough.

The longer she stayed in his house, the more difficult it would be to go through with her plan, she knew. Looking down as she polished, she saw her face reflected in the wood. Unblinking, she stared at her reflection, the ceiling of the room far below her, as though she was gazing into a deep pond. Something rose from the depths, a small point of light getting steadily larger, until she saw what it was. The damselfly.

She spun round with a gasp, sure that she would see it hovering over her shoulder, but there was nothing there. The room was as silent and empty as before. She put the cloth down, her hands trembling slightly, and sat on a nearby stool. Muffled sounds came from other rooms, Paola giving orders in the kitchen, Lucie, the chambermaid, running up the stairs with fresh linen, Leandro calling for more wine. Gemma wiped her hand across her brow. She had to do it, soon, before she became too attached to the other members of the household, before she lost the courage to poison her uncle.

Gemma sat on the edge of her cot, her head bowed beneath the slanting ceiling of the attic. She held the pouch in her hand, her fingers rubbing the worn leather. Slowly, carefully, she opened it and peered inside. The belladonna berries were shrivelled and dried, their glossy sheen now a dull black, but they would still be effective.

Leandro always took a tisane in his chamber before going to sleep, and Paola had passed this duty on to Gemma a few days earlier. 'It'll save my legs on those stairs, an' I can get on with cleaning up the kitchen,' she'd said, red and flustered from the intense heat coming from the fireplace. 'I did ask Lucie, but the lazy wench kept forgetting.' She raised her eyes to the ceiling and huffed. 'His lordship doesn't require much cosseting, but he does insist on his evening tisane.' Gemma had merely nodded and carried the conte's tray upstairs, forcing herself to hide her elation.

She tucked the pouch into her sleeve and made her way down to the kitchen. The tray had already been prepared, steam rising from the wooden cup next to the plate of biscuits. Paola stood at the back door, gazing out into the garden.

'I'll take this up, shall I?' Gemma called.

'Everything's ready, Rina, you just need to strain it,' Paola replied. 'His lordship will be eager to drink it this evening, his gout was so bad he could barely walk.'

Gemma quietly took out the pouch, opened it, and let a few berries fall into the cup. She busied herself while the berries steeped, then strained the tisane and threw away the herbs. Satisfied all was as it should be, she picked up the tray.

'I'll make sure he drinks it all,' she said as she left the kitchen.

'Ah, my tisane! Thank you. Here, put it on this table.' Leandro cleared some papers from a small table by his bed and gestured to her to place the tray there. He grimaced as he moved, and gave a small laugh. ''Tis more painful than usual today.'

'This will take the pain away, I'm sure of it.' Gemma took a couple of steps back.

'Such a wonderful aroma,' Leandro said, breathing in deeply. 'It's the only way I can get to sleep, you know. Otherwise the nightmares come and–' He paused. 'You don't want to hear an old man's fears.'

Gemma remained silent, her head bowed. Leandro sighed.

'Never mind.' He reached over for the cup and winced. 'It hurts to move. Would you mind passing me the tisane, Gemma?'

She was already handing him the cup when she realised what he had said. She paused, her arm trembling.

''Twas the eyes.' Leandro grimaced. 'And your mouth, so similar to hers.'

'How long have you known?' The words were barely a whisper.

'As soon as I laid eyes on you the day you arrived. I wondered why you wouldn't tell me who you were and pretended to be a maid, and could only come to one conclusion.' He nodded at the cup in her hand. 'Did you prepare it?'

Gemma couldn't reply.

'Come, child, give me the tisane. Perhaps tonight I will sleep better than other nights, hmm?' He took the cup from her unresisting hands and raised it to his lips. '*Sogni d'oro, cara.*'

The months of hardship, her long journey through the bitter cold mountains and across France, the days and nights she had gone hungry, her stomach screaming for food, had all led her to this moment. Her unrelenting desire for revenge had driven her on when she had felt like turning back, it had been her whole life, up until now.

And then she saw the shadow above him and she shivered, as though a goose had walked over her grave. As he tilted his head back, she grabbed hold of his hand.

Chapter Nine

A TUMULT OF IMAGES crashed around Gemma's head, one blurring into another. The cup, lying on its side, spilled liquid seeping into the coverlet; her uncle, head thrown back on the pillow, his eyes rolled up so that only the whites were visible, his back arched as convulsions shook his body; his clawed hand reaching out to her, seeking solace in his final moments; and herself, falling to her knees, pleading forgiveness to the healers, to the damselfly, to the grave in the clearing, as Leandro drew his last breath.

The pain she felt inside was like nothing she'd ever experienced before, not even when her mother died. Every part of her body burned with the shame of what she had done, her skin crawled with self-hatred, and in that moment she knew that she had done wrong. Leandro had been a victim of circumstances, just as she had, just as her mother had. All those months of nurturing thoughts of revenge had made her into someone she didn't want to be, someone who didn't deserve to call herself a healer.

She lowered her head and let go of his hand, refusing to look at the dead man lying before her. A tear ran down her cheek, but she didn't brush it away, even though it tickled her skin. She felt numb.

'Gemma?' His voice was tentative, his tone gentle.

She looked up to see Leandro, visibly shaken, but otherwise unharmed. The wooden cup lay tipped on its side, the puddle of spilled liquid soaking into the coverlet. She saw the shadow still hanging above him, and turned. Hovering near a candle on the wall was a dragonfly, its body a brilliant gold colour in the flickering flame.

Gemma turned back to her great-uncle. 'Forgive me.'

'I might. If you help me change this wet bedding.' As she hurried over to him, he added, 'And I believe we need to talk, niece.'

Leandro pulled the sheets up around his chest and took the cup Gemma offered him. Steam rose from the freshly made tisane, so he balanced it on his lap. His hands trembled, and his eyes glittered with unspoken emotion.

'Now that we are comfortable once more, perhaps you could tell me why you tried to poison me.'

Gemma blinked. 'A little forthright, but no more than I deserve, I suppose.'

He clenched his fist. 'I think you deserve a lot more, but I'm willing to listen to you before I decide what to do.'

'Decide what to do?' Gemma asked hesitantly.

'I *should* go to the authorities, any man in his right mind would. However, I'm curious to know why you went to all that effort to hide your identity, to pretend to be a servant. And the nag? A top-quality mare from the Innocenti stables, I presume.' His face grew red with suppressed emotion, and sweat beaded his brow. His hand shook, and some drops of tisane spilled, scalding his skin and making him yelp in pain. He glared down at the cup, then hurled it at the wall.

Gemma watched the liquid drip on the floor, the white-washed wall stained with the herbs of the tisane. Footsteps sounded in the hallway outside, dull thuds getting heavier as whoever it was approached.

'Go away!' Leandro thundered. 'Leave us be!'

The footsteps stopped, then beat a hasty retreat. A door slammed in the distance, and there was silence.

'Well? Cat got your tongue?' Leandro snapped. 'Did Morgana send you? Does she hate me so much that she sent you to poison me?' His shoulders sagged, and he suddenly seemed to age ten years before Gemma's eyes.

Gemma shook her head, and was dismayed to find tears pouring down her cheeks. She wiped her face and managed to regain her composure, while Leandro waited, his cheeks flushed with anger.

'I-I had to leave. The Grove, the cottage, Gallicano... nowhere in Italy was safe for me any longer. The witch hunters came from England.'

Leandro held up his hand. 'The witch hunters?'

Gemma nodded.

'I heard they were in Europe, but–' He gave a frustrated sigh. 'Why did my parents not tell me? I might have been able to do something, talk to the Pope, perhaps...' His voice trailed off. 'Perhaps not.'

'It would have been too late, even if they had written to you. They took Mamma, kept her shut up for months, then when a reprieve arrived from the Medici, they moved her to Lucca.'

Leandro's face drained of colour as she spoke, and he put his hand over his mouth. 'They accused Morgana of being a witch?'

Gemma swallowed hard before replying, tears threatening to spill again. She hoped he felt as miserable as she did. 'They took another woman at the same time, Rina, her friend. But they let Rina go, and I found her in the mountains, trying to make her way home. She told me some of what she and my mother had been through, the torture, the starvation, the violation of their bodies... It will haunt her dreams forever more.'

'And Morgana?' Leandro whispered. 'She came home, didn't she?'

'I saw her, one last time. I rode Ombra to Lucca, and made my way through the city to the house where they were keeping her prisoner. She was so thin, so weak, but she defied them to the end, refusing to confess that she was a witch.'

'To the end? Is she–?' He turned away, his hand over his mouth as he gave a cry of distress.

'Dead? Yes. They burned her at the stake. I don't know the details, I didn't see her, but I was in the Grove when they did it. The dragonflies knew, and I felt it, the very moment she died, in my heart.' Gemma knew she had been brutal with her words, but she didn't care. All the hurt, anger, and hatred she had been holding onto for so long finally found its way out, and she felt the burden lift slightly.

Leandro put his face in his hands, sobbing. 'Morgana and I had our differences, but I would never have wished that on her. She was a good woman, your mother.' He wiped away his tears with shaky hands. 'How did they find her? I mean, why did they think she was a witch?'

Gemma shrugged. 'My father.'

'Teo?' Leandro blurted. 'What does he have to do with anything?'

'He told them.' Gemma watched as Leandro's expression passed from incredulity to anger. 'Does that surprise you, Uncle?'

'Of course it bloody surprises me! Your father, betraying her. I never would have thought him capable of it.'

'He had little choice, as he was being threatened.' Gemma's voice sounded cold even to her own ears.

'Threatened? Who by? And why?'

'A woman with a grudge against our family. Why? Because of you. And him.' Gemma sat straight in her chair, and watched as realisation dawned on her great-uncle.

He slumped back against his pillow. 'You know.'

'My father told me. Not all the sordid details, thank goodness, just that he has a weakness for men. In particular for you. And my mother paid for that with her life.'

Chapter Ten

The room fell silent, the only sound the crackling of the logs in the fire. Gemma waited for Leandro to start wailing, for his empty excuses and a pathetic attempt to make reparation for the devastation he'd brought to her life. But none of that happened.

'I understand now why you came. I imagine you hate me,' Leandro said, staring at the flames. 'And you should.' He looked up at her, his suffering plain on his face. 'I didn't care about who I hurt, I was selfish and spoilt and careless, and gave no thought to anyone else. Until the day Morgana came to me and begged me to give her marriage a chance.'

It was Gemma's turn to look astonished. 'She did what?'

'It was the day after Renata died. I was desperate with grief, as was your mother. She loved Renata and felt responsible, even though I assured her she wasn't to blame. But she thought I didn't care, that I was glad my wife had died and I was free, and she pleaded with me to stop meeting Teo.' He swallowed, avoiding her eyes. 'I didn't. I couldn't. We continued to meet in secret, until the day you ate the honey.'

'*Ten years?* You kept on seeing each other for ten more years?' Gemma tried to control the tremor in her voice.

'I know it was wrong, but at the time…' He broke off and sighed. 'She loved him, and I hurt her, I know that now. When she came to me the second time, so desperate, I begged Isotta for some money and left, took off on a tour of Europe without even saying goodbye to Teo. I visited many places, Italy, Germany, Spain, and finally I arrived here and decided to stay. I wrote one letter to Teo, shortly after I left, asking him to forget me and be a good husband and father. I never heard back from him.'

'I hated you,' Gemma said, the bitterness creeping up on her again. 'The night I left the villa and rode for the coast, I had only one destination in mind. Avignon. And you. I wanted to hurt you, like you and my father hurt my mother.' She studied Leandro. 'But I see before me an old man who is clinging on to his long-lost youth, dressed like a peacock, living a lonely, empty, frivolous life. I have travelled all this way for revenge, and find I no longer have the taste for it.'

'If it pleases you, I wish I had died in place of your mother.' Leandro sniffed, and wiped his nose on the back of his hand. 'Everything you have said is true. When Morgana came to me the first time, I told her I would wait for her apology. I was furious with her; how dare she tell me how to live my life! Ever since I was little, my every whim was catered for. I was a miserable excuse of a man – my mother and grandmother dealt with the business of the villa while I sat and snivelled in a corner, unwilling to take on the responsibility.

'When I met Teo, nothing else mattered to me. The villa, the Innocenti, the horses, I didn't care. I never wanted to be the Conte de Gallicano. But my mother died, and our cousins discovered my secret. I was forced to marry Renata, and Morgana had to marry Teo.' He stood, leaning heavily on his cane. 'I have ruined so many lives, Gemma, just so I could be happy. Morgana told me Renata wanted me to love her, but I couldn't give her that, I couldn't give her the one thing she wanted. And she died, because of me. If I'd loved her, she might have fought more to live, she might have survived giving birth. I didn't realise that until many years after, when it was too late.

'I eventually did the one decent thing I've ever done: I left, so that your mother and father could have a normal marriage. But even that wasn't enough. I put my past behind me, convinced I was doing the right thing. But, like the selfish bastard I am, I thought only of myself. And now–' His voice broke. 'And now it's too late.'

Gemma heard the pain in his voice, and believed he truly regretted the past. She wanted to hate him so much, even now, but knew that he had paid the price for his behaviour. The death that awaited him was far longer, and much more painful, than that of her mother.

'How long do you have left?' She tried to keep the compassion out of her voice, but found she couldn't.

Leandro jerked his head up, a look of surprise on his face that quickly turned to resignation. 'I should have known you would notice. Your mother was the same.' He shrugged. 'The physician says it could be months, or it could be years. No one knows with the *mal francese*.'

'Syphilis.' Gemma knew little about it, and there was hardly any mention in the recipe book.

'Once I dined with princes and popes, but when the sores appeared on my face I was shunned by all. Very few people want me as a friend now, and to be honest, I prefer it that way.' He hesitated, then added,' I don't suppose you have a cure? You're a healer, there must be something.'

When she shook her head, he leaned forward, his shoulders shuddering as he sobbed. Gemma stayed until he fell asleep, then quietly made her way back to her own room. As she closed his chamber door, she noticed that the dragonfly had gone.

Chapter Eleven

THE NEXT MORNING LEANDRO was already in the parlour when Gemma went downstairs. His face was tired and strained, his cheeks sunken, as though the news of Morgana had caused his bones to decay. He raised a hand and called Gemma inside.

'We must tell the others who you really are. Although perhaps we will not tell them everything.' He held up his hand as she opened her mouth to speak. 'It is not appropriate that they believe you to be a servant. I will also make sure you are given other clothes.'

'Yes, Great-uncle.'

He winced. 'Call me uncle if you must, but great-uncle... no. I may be sick, but I have a little dignity left.'

Gemma smiled. 'I imagine Mme Dupuis will have something to say about all of this.'

'She will be more upset that she is losing a good worker.' Leandro chuckled. 'I overheard her saying how happy she is to be able to rest her legs since you've taken over so many of her chores!'

The servants all took the news in different ways. Mme Dupuis, as predicted, narrowed her eyes and pursed her lips, and merely tilted her head as a sign of respect. But Gemma heard the elderly woman muttering under her breath whenever she passed her in the house, especially when going up the staircase.

Paola appeared first confused, and then hurt, and only spoke to Gemma when absolutely necessary. This upset Gemma more than she cared to admit, as she had liked the warm-hearted Italian woman from the moment they'd met. She knew she had betrayed the cook's trust, and she desperately wished she could turn the clock back.

Lucie, on the other hand, had stared at Gemma with wide eyes as Leandro briefly told them about her journey across France with Ombra, and how fear of persecution had made her lie about who she was. He hadn't elaborated on who was persecuting her, and they would never have dared to ask, but Gemma could see that Lucie was full of questions.

'I think we shall put Gemma in the Peacock Room,' Leandro glanced at Gemma, who suppressed a smile, 'and she will need some new clothes. Lucie, you will assist her.'

The young girl led Gemma to her new chamber, which boasted tapestries in flamboyant blues, golds, and greens, and a coverlet embroidered with peacock feathers. A fire crackled in the grate, banishing the damp chill that seemed to permeate the Avignon air.

'I almost preferred my old room up in the attic,' Gemma said, looking around. 'Oh, that reminds me, I have some things I have to collect–'

'I will go, milady.'

Gemma protested, but had to give in eventually. She sat on the edge of the bed, absentmindedly stroking the coverlet as she wondered what would happen next. Now that Leandro knew who she really was, would he allow her to stay? Where would she go if he didn't? And did she want to stay?

Lucie returned with the wooden box. 'That's a beautiful dragonfly,' she said, pointing at the carved top.

'It's been in our family a long time,' Gemma replied, smiling as she took the box. She ran her hand over the dragonfly, then sighed. 'We've travelled a long way together.'

Lucie started to speak, then closed her mouth again.

Gemma took pity on her. 'Help me find some clothes to change into, and I will tell you a little about my travels.'

Lucie gave a squeal of delight and rushed out of the room. She was soon back with an armful of garments.

'Milady, his lordship apologises for the lack of fine clothes befitting his niece. He promises he will remedy that as soon as possible, and begs that you will find this suitable.' The girl held out a plain linen dress, with a sash to tie it around the middle.

'I don't need fine clothes, this is perfect.' Gemma took the dress, the material cool and crisp on her hands.

'Yes, milady.' The girl curtsied. 'May I help you with your hair? His lordship asks if you will join him when you are ready.'

Gemma smiled. 'Only if you don't call me "milady" anymore.'

'Oh no, milady, that wouldn't be proper!' Lucie pulled a comb through Gemma's hair, tugging at a stubborn knot.

Gemma sighed. 'It's going to take a while to get used to this.' She winced as Lucie tugged harder. 'So, shall I tell you about my journey across the mountains?'

It rained for a week. No one ventured outside if they didn't have to. The streets flooded, torrents pouring along the sides of the roads, carrying detritus down to the riverside, and the waters became a churning, turbid mass of rotting food, excrement, mud, and dead animals.

Gemma took to passing the time with her great-uncle in the parlour, where they talked for hours about almost everything. Out of their conversations grew a mutual respect, and Gemma was glad of this time to get to know each other. After a few days, she felt confident enough to ask him a favour. It had been on her mind since the day she had arrived, after seeing how close Alberto and Paola were. She had lost the cook's friendship since revealing the truth about herself, and wanted to somehow make amends for her betrayal.

When she arrived in the parlour that morning, Leandro was lying sprawled on the chaise longue, a book on his lap, and his leg elevated on a pile of cushions.

'Come, Gemma.' He gestured to a nearby velvet-covered chair, its seat padded with feathers. 'I apologise for not getting up, my gout is bad again today.'

'I'll make you a tisane later, and a poultice to put on your foot. Do you have some nettles I can use?'

Leandro snorted. 'You'd best talk to Paola about that, I have no idea. If there aren't any, go to the apothecary, tell him to add it to my account.'

'Thank you.' Gemma clasped her hands on her lap. 'I wanted to speak to you about Alberto Fornari, Uncle. You probably don't remember him, but he brought me across the river, then showed me the way to your house and made sure I was safe.'

'Yes, of course I remember Alberto. He has been here before, I've seen him talking to Paola. What about him?'

'Alberto is – was – a stonemason before he was badly injured. He worked on the bridge, but had to stop when he lost his finger. He's a good person who has had much bad luck. I have the feeling he would like to marry, but won't until he earns enough to look after his family properly. Could you not find work for him, either on your own house or a neighbour's? This part of the city is beautiful, but the buildings are old and looking the worse for wear.' The words poured out of her so fast she hardly stopped for breath.

Leandro held up his hand. 'You remind me of your mother when you speak so passionately about these things. That's not a bad thing, I assure you.' He smiled, and thought for a moment. 'I will see what I can do. My good friend Lady Grey has many contacts, I'm sure she will know someone who needs a stonemason.'

'That would be perfect.' Gemma relaxed, the tension leaving her shoulders.

'Speaking of Lady Grey, I was thinking of introducing you to her.' Leandro picked up his book and opened it. 'Once this infernal rain stops, of course!'

Chapter Twelve

A few days later Gemma was eating her breakfast alone in the dining room when Leandro bustled in. He was dressed in dark-green velvet breeches and a scarlet doublet, but in place of the *pantofles* he wore leather boots, the tops turned neatly down just below his knees, the heels high enough to keep his feet from getting wet in puddles.

'Good morning, *cara*. Lady Grey has invited us to join her for lunch today, I told her servant we'd be delighted to pay her a visit. She is a wonderful woman, full of *joie de vivre*, but so irreverent.' He winked. 'Just the thing we need to cheer us up, I think.'

'That sounds wonderful, I would love to meet her. Do I have time to see Ombra before we leave?'

'Oh yes. She's never up before noon, and lunch is always a late affair. We have plenty of time.'

Gemma brushed the crumbs off her fingers. 'I won't be long.'

Ombra greeted Gemma with a snort, the horse's soft mouth snuffling against her hand in search of food.

'Here. Don't say I never give you anything.' Gemma held out a crust of bread on her palm. The mare shook her head, chewing the bread methodically.

The stable was clean and airy, a comfortable bed of straw in one corner and a bucket of water in the other. Someone had brushed Ombra's coat until it gleamed, and her mane and tail were free of tangles and burrs. Gemma noticed her saddle and bridle hanging on the wall nearby, the leather freshly oiled.

'At least they're looking after you.' She stroked Ombra's neck, breathing in the horse's familiar scent. A damselfly flew in through the stable door and landed on her hand. 'I wondered where you were,' Gemma said with a smile.

A sudden noise startled her. Ombra jerked her head up, and the damselfly darted away. A young lad, about her own age, looked at her sheepishly.

'Sorry, milady. I was bringing some oats for the 'orse, I didn't mean to disturb you.'

Gemma felt a blush warm her cheeks. Had he seen her talking to the damselfly? 'Thank you. I was just leaving. Are you the one tending to my horse?'

He hunched his shoulders. 'Yes, milady. Is there something wrong? She's a beautiful beast. I brush her every day, and give her the best oats–'

'No, no,' Gemma interrupted. 'You've looked after her perfectly, she seems very happy. I just wanted to thank you.'

The boy reddened and scratched his head, then lifted the bucket. 'Can I feed 'er now?'

'I think you'd better,' Gemma replied as Ombra scraped her hoof on the floor. 'I'll be back later,' she promised the mare, who ignored her and stretched out her neck towards the bucket of oats.

As she headed inside, Paola opened the kitchen door and threw a handful of breadcrumbs out for the birds. Gemma gave her an uncertain smile, wishing for the thousandth time that they could sit and talk over cake and milk, like before.

'Good morning, Lady Gemma.' Paola avoided looking at her, but Gemma saw a smile twitch on the cook's lips.

'Good morning, Paola, it's a beautiful day,' she replied.

'That it is. Just what we needed, after all that rain. Alberto was glad it stopped, it's his first day today. He's that happy to be working on buildings again, you have no idea.'

'I'm pleased he found work doing something he loves,' Gemma said. 'Give him my regards.'

'I will, Lady Gemma.' Paola hesitated, then said, 'Perhaps you would like some cake later, if you're passing the kitchen.'

Leandro was waiting in the hall for her, wearing a wide-brimmed hat adorned with long white ostrich feathers that bounced with every movement he made.

'Your clothes are very plain, *cara*, but they will have to do for now. Tomorrow the seamstress will come and measure you for some beautiful dresses, fit for the great-niece of a conte!'

Gemma glanced down at her sturdy leather boots, plain black dress and grey cloak, borrowed from the housekeeper, Mme Dupuis.

'Please don't go to any trouble. I'm quite comfortable dressed like this.'

'Nonsense. If you are to stay here, you will be invited to dinners and parties, and you must have suitable clothes!' Leandro waggled his finger at her. 'No argument. Come, let us go to Lady Grey's.'

It was only a short walk to the yellow-walled villa surrounded by blossoming cherry trees, but Leandro was puffing heavily when they arrived. A man with a shock of white hair and deep wrinkles on his leathery face opened the door, a broad grin breaking out when he saw who the visitors were.

'Good morning, Conte,' he said breezily.

'And good morning to you, François,' Leandro replied, handing him his cloak.

The servant ushered them in, snapping at a boy to call her ladyship, then took them through to a parlour that was even more sumptuous than Leandro's. Feather cushions covered in richly coloured brocade filled every space on the chairs and chaise longues, and paintings covered the wall. Gemma blushed when she saw the subject of the paintings: a young woman in various stages of undress, some barely acceptable for a bedroom, let alone a parlour! Her pale skin was porcelain-smooth, with hardly a blemish, and long, blonde curls trailed down a slender neck. The painter had given her a haughty expression, but Gemma could see glimmers of a mischievous sparkle in the woman's blue eyes and a slight upturn at the corner of her mouth that hinted at a more vivacious character. She was looking at a picture of the woman's breasts spilling out of a tightly laced bodice when Lady Grey entered the room.

'Leandro! What a pleasant surprise!' She held out her arms and enveloped him in a perfume-filled hug, kissing him on both cheeks.

Gemma turned, expecting to see a dowager similar in age to her uncle. Shocked, she found herself face to face with the woman in the pictures. Trying to regain her composure, Gemma's first thought was that Lady Grey was even more beautiful than her pictures, and only a few years older than Gemma herself, although she was relieved to see that she was dressed more sombrely than in her portraits.

Slightly breathless, Leandro extricated himself from his friend's embrace. 'This is my niece, Gemma.'

'How wonderful! It's lovely to meet you, Gemma. I saw you were admiring my paintings.'

Gemma blushed. 'They are extraordinarily detailed, the artist is very talented.'

'Not everyone is as polite as you about them.' She chuckled. 'But they hold treasured memories for me, and I refuse to hide them away. Dearest Giorgio taught me much in our time together.' She winked.

'Did he teach you Italian? It's just... you speak it very well.' Gemma stumbled over her words as Lady Grey laughed.

'She is so sweet, *caro* Leandro!'

'Yes, well...' Gemma caught him glancing at her red face. He coughed. 'I thought she could do with some female company, rather than a *vecchietto* like me.'

'You're not that old, Leandro,' Lady Grey exclaimed. She spoke an excellent Italian, but had a pronounced English accent that added an odd eccentricity to her words. 'But are you sure you want someone like me taking her under my wing?'

'She's travelled alone all the way from Tuscany to Avignon by horse, I'm sure she is more than a match for you, *cara*,' Leandro replied.

She raised a delicately plucked eyebrow. 'You rode here? How on earth...? You must tell me all about it.' With a flurry of skirts and curls, she ushered them out of the parlour while issuing orders to her servants. Bemused, Gemma followed her uncle along the hallway to the dining room, hoping there wouldn't be any more paintings of their hostess in there.

Chapter Thirteen

Wall-length windows gave a spacious, airy feeling to the room, and orange silk curtains added a touch of warmth. They were pulled back and fastened with a cord to let in more light. A pristine white linen cloth covered a long table, its edges draping over the padded velvet seats of the high-backed chairs.

To Gemma's relief, there were no paintings at all on the walls. As she took her place to Lady Grey's right, opposite her uncle, servants silently placed plates and forks before them, and filled their venetian-style glasses with white wine.

Lady Grey held her glass in the air, the sun filtering through the green, red, and blue swirls, reflecting a rainbow pattern onto the tablecloth.

'Here's to new friends, and old.'

Leandro and Gemma raised their glasses. Gemma cautiously tasted her wine, and found it tasted a lot better than she'd imagined.

'This is a chianti, imported from Italy. Your uncle has taught me to appreciate only the best things in life.'

'You must have a very rich husband, Lady Grey, to be able to live like this.' Gemma wished she could take back her words as soon as she'd said them, but the woman merely laughed.

'Please, call me Katherine, if we are to be friends. I have no husband, yet,' she winked at Gemma, 'but my father is happy to pay for me to live here, if it keeps me far from the family home. I was not the perfect, obedient, quiet daughter he wished for. Luckily he has my sister, who is more than happy to take my place while I live in exile.' She laughed. 'Don't look so shocked, my dear, I am enjoying my life here much more than I ever did in England. So tell me, do you have brothers or sisters? Why are you so far from home?'

Gemma waited while a servant put a large platter of sliced cold meats on the table, accompanied by bowls of olives, pickled vegetables, a pie of some kind, and a basket of bread. Leandro gestured to her to take what she wanted.

'Katherine's cook is one of the best in Avignon, you must taste a little of everything,' he urged.

Gemma put some slices of meat on her plate, together with a few olives and vegetables, the aroma making her mouth water. The meat had a crust of sage and rosemary, and was sprinkled with salt and pepper, the flavours combining to make every mouthful a different experience.

'I haven't tasted anything like this since...' Gemma faltered. 'It reminds me of the Grove.'

'The Grove?' Katherine asked.

Gemma swallowed the last of the meat before replying. 'Our herb garden, back in Tuscany. The Dragonfly Grove. Mamma is – was – a healer, and we grew all kinds of plants which we used in our remedies.'

'And your mother…?'

'She died.'

Katherine reached over and patted Gemma's hand. 'I'm very sorry to hear that. How did it happen?'

Gemma hesitated. She had spent the last few months with only her own company, distrustful of anyone she met. She remembered the look of fear on Michel's face when she'd danced with the damselflies, and remained silent.

Leandro leaned over and patted her hand. 'You can tell Katherine, I would trust her with my darkest secrets.'

'As you have, *caro* Leandro,' Katherine said with a low chuckle. He flushed, and dipped his head in acknowledgement.

Dreading Katherine's reaction, Gemma took a moment to reply. 'The witch hunters came and took my mother away. They kept her in prison; we thought they might let her go, as her friend Rina came home, but sadly, they didn't.' She put her fork down and pushed the plate to one side. 'It was very good food, thank you.'

'I despise the witch hunters. Whoever's work they are carrying out, it isn't God's. How many poor women have perished because of their lies and tyranny?'

Gemma brushed away a tear and sniffed.

'I'm sorry, I didn't mean to upset you,' Katherine said. 'But perhaps it would help to talk about it.'

Her expression was so kind, her voice so gentle, that Gemma found herself telling Katherine the whole story, from when she and her mother had run through the forest to the villa, up to the moment they had said farewell at the prison in Lucca.

'I wasn't there with her at the end, but I knew when it was over. The dragonflies knew as well.'

Katherine frowned. 'This talk of potions and herbs and dragonflies is all very well within these walls, but you must not speak of it to others. Not everyone is as understanding as I am. And your witch hunters have some very influential friends. It wouldn't do to be overheard, not at all.'

'What do you mean, influential friends?' Gemma felt the familiar anger rising in her, and clenched her fists beneath the table.

'She means the Pope.' Leandro had been silent up until then, eating while listening to Gemma's tale. 'Almost two hundred years ago, the *Malleus Maleficarum* was approved by Pope Innocenzo VIII and he gave its authors full power to find and destroy witches. Even though the Church never officially accepted the text, it has turned a blind eye to its use during the last two centuries by priests and laymen alike.' He glanced at Katherine. 'The Papal Palace is only a short distance from here. What if the witch hunters should return?'

She nodded, her face grave. 'I fear we must see what awaits us, before it is too late.' She stood, pushing her chair back, and beckoned to Gemma. 'Leandro, I will tell François to bring your favourite dessert, and some more wine. Gemma and I have much to talk about.'

Gemma followed Katherine from the dining room, mystified. They hurried along the hall towards the back of the house, and Katherine opened a door. A musty smell came from inside, as though it was a little-used room, and heavy curtains blocked out the daylight. Katherine took a taper from her pocket and lit it from a candle in the hall, then guided Gemma into the room and closed the door. The flame flickered, casting shadows around the dark space, and Gemma caught glimpses of glass cabinets, a desk strewn with strange objects, and rolls of parchments scattered over the floor.

Katherine lit several candles, then blew out the taper. 'I do not have many talents,' she said in a low voice, 'but I recognise a witch when I see one.'

'I'm not a witch,' Gemma protested. 'I am a healer, no more, no less.'

'Hush.' Katherine glanced around, as though fearful someone was in the room with them. 'The walls have ears.' She clutched onto Gemma's arm. 'What you are is not important right now, your powers will be revealed to you eventually.'

She moved the curtains aside and picked up a silver bowl full of water from the windowsill, then placed it on a small table. 'This is called scrying; it is one of my few powers, but a useful one. It will enable us to see the future.'

'You're...' Gemma's head spun as it dawned on her.

Katherine smiled at her. 'Yes, my dear. Like you, I'm a witch.'

Chapter Fourteen

Gemma stared at Katherine. 'You can see the future?'

'Yes.' Katherine rummaged in a cupboard, making cups and bowls rattle as she searched for something. 'As can you, I presume.'

'Not always. My mother could – she could see a person's moment of death, just by touching their hand.'

Katherine stopped and turned to face her. 'She could see their deaths? What an extraordinary talent.'

'She didn't think so, she hated it. She saw spirits too, in the shadows of the cottage.'

'Aha, found it!' Katherine held up a piece of white quartz, the candlelight shining through it and creating a rainbow of colours on the surface of the water. 'Sorry, I am listening. Imagine that, seeing someone die just by touching their hand. What a useful power to have. I presume you can't do this as well?'

'No, but–' Gemma hesitated.

'But...' Katherine gave her an encouraging smile. 'I've heard most things, you won't shock me.'

'I hear the voice of a man who's been dead for three hundred years. He gives me advice, in a vague sort of way.' Gemma closed her eyes, and for a moment she was back in the clearing, standing beside Bob's grave, listening to his words once more.

'What else?' Katherine lit another candle, and a strong scent began to fill the room. Smoke drifted from the tip of the flame, threading its way through the air, winding around their heads. The atmosphere grew heavier, the air denser, and Gemma felt as though she were floating in a shadowy realm of nothing, with no floor, or walls, or ceiling.

'I-I think I saw my future. The last time I touched my mother, we both saw a vision – not of death, but of me, on a boat, some years from now, and heavy with child. I cling to the hope that this means I will return to Tuscany one day, however unlikely that seems right now.'

Katherine nodded. 'I can only see the future in the next few weeks, two months at the most, not years ahead. But let's see what we can find out.' She clasped the crystal to her chest for a moment, then placed it in the water and glanced at Gemma. 'This is my altar, where I scry, or cast spells, or I come here to clear my mind. First, we must cleanse the room.' She held a bundle of sage to a flame until it caught light, then moved it over the table, backwards and forwards, a slow, gentle rhythm that mesmerised Gemma. With the dark room, the heavy perfume from the candle, and the familiar aroma of sage, she found she was drifting away, to another place, another time...

'Stay with me.' Katherine's voice broke through the fog in her head. 'Look at the crystal in the water, focus on it. You are a traveller, that much is clear, but now is not the time to journey to different realms. I have much to teach you.'

Gemma's mind cleared, and she reached out to touch the wall behind her, taking comfort from its solidity.

'Good. Keep your eyes on the crystal and concentrate on your breathing. Slowly in, slowly out. Look at the surface of the water and let your mind wander, but focus on the crystal.' Katherine's words faded as the water rippled, the crystal softly glowing in the candlelight.

Gemma watched the ripples, tiny shivers at first which grew in ever-wider circles, the crystal at their centre. Shadows passed across the bowl, through the reflection of the candles' flames, and figures began to form. She narrowed her eyes and peered more closely, but couldn't make anything out from the confused jumble of shapes.

And then she was far away, in a room streaming with light, dragonflies flitting all around, dazzling her with their vivid colours. The marble floor was streaked with black and gold veins, and pictures adorned the white walls. Gemma looked at them, one after the other, marvelling at their beauty and detail. They were paintings of women, each one dressed differently from the others, some with their hair pulled up in elaborate styles, some with long ringlets falling over their shoulders, others with simple braids. All were different, but they all looked familiar to her. And as she stared, the background in each painting came into focus, and it was always the same: the Grove, with its trees and bushes and plants, every woman holding a sprig of the silver-leaf plant in her hands.

Gemma walked along the wall, her heart filled with love as she looked upon the healers that had gone before her. A bright light shone at the far end, so bright she had to turn her head, and then she saw her.

'Mamma,' she whispered.

The woman in the portrait was her mother, she knew that, but somehow she was different, more ethereal, even more beautiful than Gemma remembered. Morgana smiled at her, and reached out her hand. Gemma lifted her arm, fingers stretched out, and their fingertips almost touched. Just a little further and she would be reunited with her mother...

'Gemma!' Katherine's voice echoed around her head, and she jerked her hand back. The room suddenly went dark, as though someone had snuffed out all the candles at once. A horrific shriek shattered the quiet, full of desperation and hatred, and something grabbed at her hair. Gemma screamed, her head throbbing as hair was pulled from her scalp, and she lashed out, kicking and hitting.

'Gemma, it's me, Katherine. Please wake up.'

Gemma heard quick footsteps, then light flooded the room as Katherine pulled the curtains back. Smoke drifted up from the candles, their wicks blackened, melted wax dripping over the edges. Dust motes floated in the air, creating golden clouds that billowed and gusted in the draught.

Gemma put her hand to her head, and was stunned to see droplets of blood on her fingers. 'What happened?'

Katherine came back to her side, distraught. 'I have never felt anything like it. There was a presence here, something dark and bad. I saw you were struggling, but I couldn't move to help you. You were fading away, leaving me, and I feared you would disappear completely. You would never have found your way back.'

'Your voice,' Gemma murmured. 'I heard you calling. You saved me.'

'It was only thanks to your friend here. He arrived, and somehow broke the incantation holding me still.' Katherine gestured to the altar.

Gemma looked up to see the damselfly staring back at her. Whatever had happened to her had something to do with the curse on her mother, she was sure of it. She sat up, rubbing her sore head, wincing at the patch of raw skin where her hair had been ripped away. Katherine stared at her, her face pale, her eyes wide with fright.

Gemma held out her hand to the damselfly. It flew over and rested on her outstretched palm. 'I have something to tell you about my family,' she said.

Katherine finished fussing over Gemma's hair and stood back with a satisfied air. 'There. I've managed to cover it, you can't tell anything's amiss now.'

Gemma looked in the mirror Katherine was holding. 'Thank you.' Her eyes filled with tears. 'What do you think happened?'

Katherine sat down on a stool, her shoulders slumped. 'I've never seen anything like that before. But from what you've told me of your family, there are stronger powers at work here. Tell me what you saw in the water.'

'Nothing.'

'Nothing? Are you sure?'

'Just some shadows and vague shapes. I was concentrating on the crystal.' Gemma paused. 'I was in a room with portraits of the healers on the wall, and there was a bright light that called to me... Mamma, my mother's hand reaching out to pull me into an embrace… and then I saw a darkness behind the light, a face snarling at me, its hands grabbing me like claws, trying to drag me into the shadows.' She covered her face with her hands and sobbed in fear.

'Gemma.' Katherine pulled her hands away. 'Look at me.'

Gemma lifted her head, still sniffing.

'I don't think this had anything to do with scrying. I saw images in the water, of us travelling by carriage somewhere. Our destination was about to be revealed when I noticed you were in trouble.'

'What do you think it was then?'

Katherine thought for a while. 'After everything you've told me about your family, I believe you healers have a special connection with the spirit world. Your mother saw shadows and death, and you can see far into the future. I am actually quite envious of you, my dear.'

'But the darkness?' Gemma insisted.

'Did you not say the land where you lived is cursed?'

'Yes. Agnes, the first healer, tried to remove it from the ground, but only succeeded in lessening its power. We have seen its effects on people throughout the centuries: it attacks their weaknesses, their anxieties, and makes them act in horrific ways. My own father betrayed my mother, even though he knew it would lead to her death, so that his own secret would remain safe.'

'And you believe it was the curse that made him do it?'

'What else?'

'Is it possible he acted out of fear? If his secret had got out it would have meant a terrible death for him.'

'As it was for my mother.'

'Sometimes we don't think beyond our own fear, or of the consequences to other people.'

Gemma remained silent.

'You have a lot of anger in you, Gemma. I can see it all around you, a shadow whose weight you bear.'

'I came here for revenge,' Gemma whispered. 'I wanted to hurt my uncle, to repay what he did to my mother. Now I only pity him. But I *will* return to Gallicano one day and seek out the others who did us wrong.'

'I understand your reasons for that. However, I believe you should think carefully. Once you no longer have so much anger and hatred, perhaps the darkness will recede and you will be able to live more peacefully.'

'And how do I do that?'

Katherine stood. 'I don't know. Revenge gives us something to live for, to keep going when times are hard.' She gave her a sad smile. 'I will see what I can do to help. But in the meantime, you can let me take you to buy new clothes, and accompany me to some dinner parties before we leave.' She held out her hand and helped Gemma to her feet.

'Leave?' Gemma asked, bemused.

'In my vision we were travelling somewhere by carriage. That could mean we will be leaving Avignon, at least for a little while. So, let us have some fun before!'

Chapter Fifteen

KATHERINE'S IDEA OF FUN was very different from her own, Gemma mused, as the seamstress took her measurements and made a note on a sheet of paper. The woman held several pins in her mouth, her lips pursed to keep them in place, her face severe as she concentrated on her work. This was the third morning in a row Gemma had suffered this torture, while Katherine carefully chose the colours and material for the new dresses.

'I'm quite fine with the dresses Mme Dupuis gave me,' Gemma had tried to say the first morning, gesturing to the plain black linen dresses laid out on the bed.

Katherine had clasped her hand to her breast, eyes wide with horror at the sight of the clothes. 'You can't wear these to a ball in Avignon! You couldn't wear them to a parish dance in England, if it came to that. No, you must have new dresses suitable for your standing in society.'

Gemma sighed. If she'd known it would have been this long and torturous, she would have refused to go ahead with it.

'I definitely think this cream satin,' Katherine said, holding up a luxurious fold of cloth, 'together with this green. It matches her eyes.'

'Just the cream,' Gemma said quickly. Katherine frowned, but nodded.

The seamstress stood back and removed the pins from her mouth, stabbing them into a velvet cushion which she stowed in her bag.

'I have everything I need, milady. The dresses will be ready by the end of next week; three, just like you asked. I'll have them sent to the house.'

Gemma sank onto a chair as Katherine escorted the woman out of the room, their voices fading as they walked down the stairs. She leaned back, her head against the wall, and closed her eyes. Since Leandro had introduced her to Katherine, she'd hardly had a spare moment to herself, what with being measured for dresses, long meals together, and leisurely walks around the safer parts of the city.

The day before, they had come across Alberto, working on the outside of a neighbour's house. Covered in plaster, his dark hair grey as ash, he'd slid down the ladder and rushed over to thank her profusely.

'This is the work I was born to do, not ferrying spoilt rich people across the river,' he'd enthused, then flushed, embarrassed. 'I'm sorry, Lady Grey, I didn't mean–'

'Don't worry,' she'd replied, flapping her hand. 'I know quite well what you meant, and I agree that they're nasty, selfish arsworms.' Ignoring his shocked expression, she'd offered her arm to Gemma and bid him good day with a wide smile. They had giggled all the way down the street, and Gemma smiled again at the memory of the look on Alberto's face.

'She may charge more than the rest, but there's no better seamstress in all of Avignon,' Katherine said, bustling back into the room in a rustle of silk skirts. 'Wait until you see the dresses, and you'll wonder why you ever said you'd wear those awful black rags!'

'I came to ask if your visitor would be staying for lunch, milady,' came a stony voice from the doorway.

Gemma opened her eyes to see Mme Dupuis glaring daggers at Katherine, her hands clasped before her as though to stop herself from lashing out.

'Oh, not today, Mme Dupuis,' Katherine replied airily. 'I'm glad to see you're feeling better, Gemma told me you were indisposed a couple of weeks ago.'

'I'm quite well, thank you,' the housekeeper said stiffly. 'Would you like me to take the clothes away, milady?'

Once Katherine had left, Gemma sought out Mme Dupuis, but she was nowhere to be found. Sighing at the thought of having to apologise profusely to the offended woman, Gemma went to the kitchen in search of sustenance before having to carry out her task.

Paola looked up as she entered and flushed bright red. Alberto leapt to his feet, furiously chewing on something before swallowing it down.

'Milady.' He bowed, and surreptitiously wiped at his mouth with the back of his hand.

Gemma held back a laugh. 'Alberto! How lovely to see you. Have you come to sample some of Paola's wonderful biscotti again?'

He choked, and it took him several seconds to regain his composure.

'I told him to drop in whenever he was passin', nothing like a good broth or some freshly made cake to put some weight on those bones. Can't have him wastin' away now he's workin' with the stones again.' Paola bustled around the kitchen, tidying up spilt flour and sugar.

Gemma thought Alberto looked less gaunt than before. His skin was rosier, and the dark shadows under his eyes had faded to a grey smudge. He glanced from Gemma to the cook, and stood abruptly, grabbing his cap from the table and twisting it in his hands.

'I'd best be going,' he mumbled. 'No rest for the wicked.' He practically ran out of the kitchen, leaving Paola staring after him, perplexed, and Gemma desperately trying not to laugh, and failing.

'I'm sorry, I shouldn't have intruded,' she said, wiping a tear from her eye.

'Oh, don't worry about him, he'll be back again soon.' Paola winked at her. 'He's always poppin' in for a warm milk and some biscotti. Typical man, follows his stomach.'

'I'm sure seeing you has a lot to do with it.' Gemma winked.

'Do you think so?' Paola smoothed her hair, a wide smile on her face. 'I must admit, I look forward to his company at the end of a long day.'

'He seems very happy in your company as well. I'm sorry I scared him away.'

'Like I said, he'll be back tomorrow, don't worry. Can I help you with something, milady?'

'I'm looking for Mme Dupuis. I've searched all over the house but she's nowhere to be found.'

Paola looked out of the kitchen window. 'This time of day, she'll be at her mother's. She goes every afternoon, makes sure she eats something warm, then tucks her up into bed. She'll be back before we lock up for the night.'

'Thank you.' Gemma turned to leave. 'I know a couple of love potions, if you're interested.'

'I don't think that will be necessary,' Paola replied, blushing.

Gemma opened the door with a smile. 'Neither do I.'

Chapter Sixteen

April-May 1631

THE HARMONIOUS NOTES OF a lute, viol and harpsichord filled the house, competing with the guests' lively chatter as everyone left the dining room and converged in the large room across the hallway. The furniture and rugs had been removed, and chairs placed along the walls, together with small tables to rest drinks and plates on. The marble floor had been polished until it gleamed, and the guests glided effortlessly as they danced a slow pavane.

'I can see trouble when they start the gaillarde,' Katherine said, chuckling, the upper half of her face hidden behind a velvet mask. 'With all that leaping and jumping around on this floor, I'm sure a few limbs will be broken by the end of the evening!'

'I hope not,' Gemma replied, adjusting her own mask. The string was too loose, and it slipped whenever she spoke. She felt sick after the rich food they had just eaten, and wasn't in the mood for either dancing or setting broken bones.

'Here, let me do that.' Katherine deftly made a tighter knot. 'Come, let's meet our fellow guests. And act mysterious!'

Gemma followed slowly as her friend moved among the crowd of dancers and spectators, feeling out of place in her new silk gown. She hated the way it rustled as she walked, the way the bodice and stomacher restricted her movements, and the way the stiff lace collar around her neck scratched at her skin. The hours of standing still while it was being fitted had been agony, only made bearable by Paola's biscotti and Katherine's constant chatter. She yearned for her comfortable riding breeches and jerkin; indeed, she wished she were with Ombra in her stable, curled up against the mare's warm body.

Stopping to catch her breath some time later, Gemma leaned on the back of a chair, trying to ease the weight off her right foot. She was sure she had a blister, though her slippers were made of the softest leather.

'Where have you gone now?' she muttered, searching the crowd for some sign of Katherine. Annoyed at her friend's disappearance, and keen to avoid being asked to dance again, Gemma slowly walked around the edge of the room towards the open doors at the far end and went outside, breathing in the cool night air with relief.

While pulling at her collar, she heard voices carry across the garden, a woman's shriek, then a muffled 'Hush'. Thinking perhaps someone was in trouble, Gemma stepped lightly over the lawn, holding her skirts so that the silk wouldn't make a noise. The grass was damp with dew, and she shivered at the chilliness in the air. The spring days were warm in Avignon, but the nights were still cold, and she wished she'd brought her shawl.

Lanterns dotted around the garden lit up the path, casting shadows among the trees and bushes. A tall hedge surrounded the lawn, with an archway of roses leading through to a paved courtyard with an arbour made from willow branches in the middle. A curtain of honeysuckle covered the arbour, but Gemma could hear voices coming from inside. Just as she was about to run over, someone pushed the honeysuckle aside and a woman stepped out, fanning herself with her hand.

It was Katherine. Her cheeks were flushed, and her hair was in some disarray. Gemma suddenly realised what was happening and tried to draw back into the shadows, embarrassed. Katherine took a step forward, then turned as a man emerged from the arbour.

He grabbed Katherine's wrist and pulled her back, his hands clutching at her waist, his mouth capturing hers. Katherine arched her back, pressing her body against his, giving herself to him. He grasped a handful of her hair and tugged, making Katherine cry out, then shoved her back into the arbour.

Gemma froze. Was Katherine in trouble? Or was it all part of making love? Uncertain, embarrassed at the thought of what Katherine would say if she was wrong, Gemma crept slowly backwards, desperate for them not to see her. When she reached the rose archway, she turned and ran, heedless of her dress dragging along the damp ground.

Not looking where she was going, she careened straight into someone and had to grasp their arm to stop herself from falling.

'I'm s-so sorry,' Gemma stammered, still agitated at what she had seen.

'Is something wrong?'

Gemma looked up then, his voice penetrating through the turmoil in her mind. A familiar mop of unruly brown curls greeted her, although the man standing there was dressed in fine clothes fit for the evening, rather than the labourer's garments he had been wearing the day he had saved her from her attackers.

'You!' they both said at the same time.

He gave a low laugh. 'I never thought I would see you again, though I desperately hoped I would.' He held out his hand towards her, then frowned as she shrank back. 'Something *is* wrong. You're trembling.'

'I…' She couldn't speak, the words stuck in her throat. She wished she was more like Katherine, more knowledgeable of such things. 'I'm not sure.'

'Has someone tried to hurt you again?' He turned abruptly, peering into the darkness.

'No, no, nothing like that,' Gemma said hurriedly. 'A friend… but it's nothing. I'm sure everything is all right.'

He looked at her, concerned. 'Come inside, I will get you a drink. A glass of wine will make you feel better.' He gestured to her to follow, and led her into the ballroom. 'Sit here, I will be back soon.'

Gemma sank onto the chair, and hid her shaking hands among her skirts. The musicians had been joined by someone playing a flute, its playful notes ringing out above the chatter, and the dancing had become livelier. Women shrieked with delight as their dresses swirled when their partners lifted them into the air and swung them around, hands daring to go higher, or lower, than was deemed proper in the confusion. The music grew faster and louder, the dancing more frantic, the shouts and laughter adding to the general melee of decadence and impropriety. The beat of the drum began, the rhythm entering Gemma's blood, stirring emotions she'd never felt before, the image of Katherine and the unknown man still in her mind.

Her rescuer came back with a glass of wine and passed it to her. 'Drink this, it will help,' he urged.

She breathed in the fruity aroma and took a sip. The wine tasted sweet, and bubbles tickled the inside of her mouth. The man sat next to her, his hands clasped together.

'We keep meeting, but we haven't yet introduced ourselves,' he said with a gentle laugh. 'I'm Claude Auclair.'

'Gemma Innocenti,' she replied shyly. Then she realised who he was. 'This is your family's home!'

'And you appear to be related to Leandro Innocenti, not a maid as you originally claimed. I'm pleased to make your acquaintance.' He smiled hesitantly, his blue eyes framed by long black lashes, his brown hair curling over the shoulders of his embroidered linen jacket. Yellow-brown breeches, and boots of black, high-quality leather, completed his outfit.

'I thought you were a labourer,' Gemma said, mortified. 'I had no idea you were a nobleman. I apologise for misleading you about my uncle.'

'I haven't seen Albi since then, so I had no idea what happened to you. I'm glad you made it safely to your uncle's house.'

'You were both very kind that day.' Gemma fell silent, unsure what to say next. 'I didn't see you at dinner,' she said eventually.

'My father's gatherings bore me, I rarely attend them. I was taking a walk out in the gardens to get away from the incessant noise.'

'I apologise for interrupting your walk.' Gemma took another sip of wine, a larger one this time. Her hands no longer shook, and her agitation was fading away. 'Please, don't feel that you have to stay with me. I will be fine.'

'No, I shall remain by your side until you want to leave,' Claude said. 'That is, if you don't mind.'

Strangely enough, she didn't. 'I prefer to sit here and watch the dancing, though,' she told him.

'Then we shall do that,' he replied.

The frenzied music of before became slower, and the dancers glided with impeccably timed moves as they weaved in and out among each other.

'How do they do that?' Gemma said in wonder.

'Are you sure you don't want to try?' His eyes sparkled in the bright light from the chandelier above their heads.

'No. Believe me, your feet will thank me for it,' she said with a laugh.

'Then perhaps we can go for a walk in the garden.'

Gemma bit her lip. 'No, thank you.'

'No, perhaps not.'

'If I could choose, right now I would like to be with my horse,' Gemma blurted, then put her hand over her mouth. 'I apologise. I didn't mean to be so rude.'

'I prefer spending time with my horses as well,' he said, grinning. 'Perhaps you would like to see our stables one day. We have a few brood mares, sometimes I travel across Europe looking for new stock.'

Gemma stood, smoothing down her skirts. Perhaps it was the wine, or the fact that he had saved her once before, but she felt safe with him. 'What if we should go now?'

'But your dress...'

Gemma lifted the bedraggled hem with a sigh. 'I believe it is already rather the worse for wear. Mme Dupuis will have something to say tomorrow.'

Claude got to his feet and held out his arm. 'Well, if you're sure, let me accompany you to the stables.'

Chapter Seventeen

Gemma breathed in the familiar sweet aroma of hay and horse as she followed Claude into the barn. He had picked up a lantern from the garden, and its flickering flame lit their way. Soft neighs greeted them as several horses looked sleepily over the half doors of their stables, curious to see who was disturbing them.

Claude stopped beside a handsome grey and rubbed its nose. 'This is my stallion, Lumière. I've had him since he was born, his dam was my mother's horse. Until she had her fall.' He wrinkled his nose.

'Fall? Is she all right?'

'Only her pride was hurt, but it was enough to make her lose interest in the horses.' Claude shrugged. 'I wish you could have seen the stables a few years ago, we had some beautiful animals.'

'You must miss them. I know I would.'

He looked wistful. 'I dream of building up our stables again, perhaps with a breed I saw during a trip to Spain last year. They were beautiful animals, I'd never seen them before.'

A vibration of wings close to her ear made Gemma turn, but nothing was there. Out of the corner of her eye she saw a blue blur as something – *the damselfly* – darted out of sight. She would have thought it a trick of the light if she hadn't seen Lumière startle and jerk his head. Her mother had taught her never to ignore a sign from the dragonflies.

Gemma hesitated, then blurted, 'You should come to our villa in Tuscany to see my family's stables.'

'I have heard much about them during my travels. Careful, I might well accept your invitation.' He laughed.

'I would like that.' She felt reckless, as though she were teetering on the edge of an abyss, where one step could decide her future, for better or for worse. Emotions surged within her, pulling her one way, then another. The precipice loomed before her, deep and dark and endless, daring her to jump. She crossed her fingers behind her back and made her choice. 'I could show you the place I grew up, the cottage, the Grove, and the dragonflies...' She dared to glance at him, and was relieved to see him smiling. 'I wish you could have met my mother, she was a wonderful person.'

'She died?'

'A few months ago.'

'I'm so sorry.'

'It's hard to talk about it.' Gemma gestured to the next stable. 'Will you show me the rest of the horses?'

Claude nodded and led her along the stable block to the far end, stopping in front of every stable. Gemma stroked each horse, their velvety noses snuffling at her hands in search of treats.

'You are limping,' he said, frowning.

'It's these boots. Lady Katherine lent them to me, she said they would be perfect for dancing. But they pinch so!'

'Here.' He pointed to a dusty wooden stool behind a partition. 'Sit down for a while and rest.'

Gemma sat gratefully, heedless of the dust on her already ruined dress, and Claude pulled another stool over for himself. He set the lantern down on the ground, making sure it wouldn't fall over.

'Tell me more about your villa and the horses,' he said. 'I've never been to Tuscany, although it's something I've longed to do.'

'It's beautiful, especially at this time of year with the trees just coming into leaf,' Gemma said. 'I–'

The barn door burst open and two men staggered in, shouting as they fell over each other. Gemma and Claude peered around the edge of the partition, then Claude pulled her back and put his finger on his lips. He bent over and blew out the candle inside the lantern, so that the only light came from the moon outside.

'That's Bishop Castelli,' he whispered. 'He's very close to the Pope. A man to avoid at all costs.' He pulled Gemma further into a corner, and kept his hand on her arm as the two men stumbled around the barn. She continue to watch the drunkards through a crack in the wood, intent on listening to their conversation.

'As I was saying, before you so rudely interrupted me–'

'I did not interrupt you!'

The bishop harrumphed, then belched loudly. 'You did, Giovanni, but that is neither here nor there. As I was saying, Cardinal Ricci is a greasy little weasel who has his tongue so far up the Pope's arse that he could lick the man's tonsils.'

The other snorted. 'Be careful what you say. Cardinal Ricci has ears everywhere.'

'Well, unless he's lying under a pile of horse shit, I doubt very much he's in here!' the bishop replied. 'Or can he speak to the animals now, like San Francesco?'

'You have such a wicked tongue, Lorenzo.' The other man giggled, then hiccupped. 'Speaking of the Pope, what do you think of his latest guests?'

Bishop Castelli spat on the ground. 'The benefactors? Damn heathens, the lot of them. They come straight from the crotch of Satan, and fester in the armpits of God while they spread their poison throughout Christianity. Witches are the scourge of society and must be eliminated in any way possible, before they destroy everything we have worked for. Why should men suffer being led astray by these whores who fornicate with the devil? Instead they go crying to the Pope that the church shouldn't allow the hunting of witches, that these women are innocent of any crime. They've all been bewitched, the lot of them!' He leaned against the wall, panting heavily, his face red and sweaty after his lengthy discourse.

Gemma put her hand over her mouth, desperate not to make a sound. If the two men caught them spying, she dreaded to think what they would do.

'Soon the witch hunters will arrive, they'll put them in their place,' Giovanni said, a sneer on his face.

'I look forward to hearing their news. Apparently their hunt in Italy was a great success. Got one of the most dangerous witches they'd ever met.' Bishop Castelli leaned forward, almost losing his balance. He grasped onto Giovanni's cassock and managed to stay upright. 'Although it's a shame about William.'

'William? William Hopkins? What happened?'

The bishop shook his head. ''Twas a sad business. The same day he burned the witch on the pyre, he fell sick and died.' He put his mouth next to Giovanni's ear, then said loudly, 'They say she cursed him just before she died.'

'No! Well, if that isn't proof, I don't know what is,' Giovanni replied, rubbing his ear and shuffling backwards.

'Exactly. Apparently they found him frothing at the mouth, in the throes of death, his face frozen in an expression of horror. I dread to think what the poor man saw before he died. At least they burned the witch, they say she died in agony. They searched everywhere for the daughter, but she'd run away. The locals wouldn't talk. 'Cept for one. She told them everything she knew, said the family was famous for its witchcraft. Told them they'd recognise the daughter by her green eyes, a witch's eyes, she said, and her familiar, in the shape of a horse which she rides through the sky at night. If they ever find her, she'll wish she burned at the stake with her mother!'

Gemma felt her world collapsing around her. After everything she had been through, they had found her. She stared at the two men, fear rendering her immobile. Claude clutched at her arm, the sudden movement startling her out of her trance. A sob burst out of her, and she clasped a hand over her mouth.

'What was that?' The bishop spun round, peering frantically into the dark shadows.

'Probably just a rat,' Giovanni said, staggering after him. 'Or the devil 'imself, come to tell us witches is innocent.' He giggled.

'Shush.' The bishop took a few steps forward, then Lumière stuck his head over the stable door and whickered.

'Shit!' Giovanni sat down with a bump, his legs splayed in front of him. He started laughing, great, gasping snorts that echoed around the barn. 'We're in a barn of horses, one o' them probably farted!' He struggled to his feet, still laughing.

The bishop held out his hand to help him. 'It's more likely it was you than a horse! Let us go, before Cardinal Weasel comes looking for us and we have to explain what we're doing in a stable.'

''T'ain't nothin' he ain't done with the Pope,' Giovanni said, and the two men burst out in raucous laughter as they left the barn, clutching onto each other.

Gemma slid to the floor, tears streaming down her face.

'Did you know William Hopkins?' Claude asked.

'Oh yes.' Gemma stared up at him, unable to keep the bitterness from her voice. 'He's the reason my mother died, and why I had to leave my home.'

'Your mother was the dangerous witch they burned?'

'No. She was a healer. All she ever wanted to do was make people better, using the plants from the Grove.'

'I see.'

'She wasn't a witch!' Gemma snapped, angrily wiping away the tears. 'And neither am I.'

Claude sat down next to her. 'I believe you,' he said gently. 'My great-grandmother lived until she was ninety-one, and swore that the plants in her garden kept her healthy. Your mother must have been a very wise woman.'

'She was. But I do know why William Hopkins died.' Gemma looked down at the ground, twisting her hands in her lap. 'I gave my mother some berries. Poisonous berries. I meant for her to eat them before he put her to death. I imagine she found another use for them.'

When he remained silent, she put her arms around her knees and huddled against the wall, fearful that she had said too much.

'I'm glad she killed him.' Claude clenched his fists. 'At least he can't hurt anyone else now. But they are after you, Gemma. If what I've heard of them is true, they won't give up searching for you.'

'They won't find me here, it's the last place they'll look.'

He touched her cheek with his fingertips. 'People are already talking about your green eyes, and how many know you arrived with a horse? It won't take long for the witch hunters to find you.'

'So I must leave. Again. For months I slept under blankets of damp leaves, suffered the snow and ice in the mountains, dreaming of hot baths and a full stomach, just so that I could escape the witch hunters' persecution. I'm tired of running, of being scared, of suffering for these evil men and their twisted ideas of moral justice.' Gemma stamped her foot in frustration. Would she never be able to stay in one place for more than a few weeks at a time?

'I can't imagine what you've been through.' Claude's face twisted with anguish. 'But you must leave before they arrive. It may be only days. We have to plan your departure as soon as possible. Tomorrow I will come to your uncle's house and help you make preparations.'

Gemma raised her head, surprised. 'You'll help me?'

'Of course. Why wouldn't I?'

'Perhaps because we hardly know each other.' But she felt something between them, she had felt it that day he had rescued her: a sense of belonging, a feeling of old souls destined to be together throughout eternity, the knowledge of a fate that was meant to be.

'I feel like I have known you forever.' Claude tucked a strand of her hair behind her ear, his touch as light as a dragonfly wing. 'I will do everything I can to keep you safe, so that we can be together again one day.'

Chapter Eighteen

Gemma made her way around the room, searching desperately for Katherine among the masked dancers. Silk skirts twirled as men swung the women up in the air, hands on corseted waists, sly smiles beneath velvet masks, the music a sensuous rhythm all around them. She and Claude had parted at the door, fingertips touching briefly before he disappeared into the crowd. Gemma wished they could have had longer, could have at least had more than a whispered promise of an uncertain future. But the thought of the witch hunters was too strong, a deep, throbbing anger that filled her whole being and rendered her incapable of thinking about anything else.

Pausing for a moment, she stood in front of a curtained alcove to catch her breath. There were too many people, all unrecognisable with their masks. She would never find Katherine.

A hand clasped her arm and pulled her back behind the curtain. She turned, fist raised, ready to hit out at whoever it was, then lowered it when she saw who was there.

'Katherine! I've been looking everywhere for you. Where have you been?' Her voice faded as she took in the sight of her friend. Katherine's carefully styled hair was unpinned in places, curls tumbling over each other. There was a streak of dirt on her chin, and she had a red patch on her cheek, while her dress was ripped at the shoulder.

'What on earth?'

'Shush. Don't attract attention.' Katherine pulled at the curtain, making sure it was completely closed.

Gemma remembered the man kissing Katherine, her body pressed against his, then looked at her friend's pale, tear-streaked face and understood. 'I think I had best get you home.' She took off her shawl and put it around Katherine's shoulders. 'Here, this will cover your dress. And if I rearrange your mask, like this,' she tugged it until it covered the mark on her cheek, 'and tidy your hair, no one will notice.'

'Thank you.' Katherine clutched the shawl and straightened her shoulders. 'Is he out there,' she whispered.

'Who?' Gemma peeped out of the curtain, but couldn't see anyone nearby.

Katherine shook her head, appearing confused. She lifted her hand and wiped away a trickle of blood from her forehead, then stared at her finger in dismay.

Gemma put her arm around Katherine's shoulders and spoke gently to her. 'I need to get you home. Come, I'll ask someone to bring your carriage.'

Gemma settled Katherine in a chair near the fire, then took a stick and stirred the smouldering embers in the fireplace. When small flames rose out from the wood, she stood, straightening her back.

'Bring Lady Katherine a warm drink with camomile, mint and lavender, and add a spoonful of honey,' she told the maid waiting nervously in the doorway. 'Oh, and a bowl of boiling water and some clean linen.' The girl bobbed a curtsey and disappeared down the hallway.

Gemma pulled up a stool and sat next to Katherine. 'Shush, don't say anything,' she said as Katherine opened her mouth to speak. 'First we'll get you cleaned up, and a warm drink inside you, then you can tell me.' She took hold of Katherine's hands, which were as cold as ice, and rubbed them between her own.

Silence fell, the only sound the crackling of logs as the flames grew larger. Some strands of smoke wafted out of the fireplace, mingling with the darkness around them, leaving a faint scent of pine. The wisps faded into the corners of the room, where the shadows seemed denser than usual. Gemma felt a sense of foreboding come over her, as though once again her life was about to go in a predetermined direction.

The maid entered, carrying a tray. Gemma gestured to a nearby table, then thanked the maid and waited until she left.

'Here, drink this.' She handed Katherine the cup, its aromatic warmth seeping through the wood.

Katherine took a sip, her hands wrapped around the cup, and drank more. Colour appeared in her pale cheeks, and her eyes seemed brighter.

'Can I clean your wound?' Gemma asked. Katherine nodded, but still didn't speak.

Gemma took the cloth and dipped it in the bowl of hot water, then gently dabbed Katherine's head. The cut wasn't deep, and it had already stopped bleeding, but Gemma made sure she cleaned it thoroughly.

'There were some thorns, I got caught up in them,' Katherine said dully.

'It's only a scratch,' Gemma reassured her, 'but I'll put some salve on it when we go upstairs, just to be sure.'

'I feel such an idiot.' Katherine held the cup tightly in her hands, and stared at the fire.

Gemma waited, letting her speak in her own time.

'He promised me–' A tear traced a shimmering path down her cheek, and she wiped it angrily away. 'His promises meant nothing.' Her hand shook as she put the cup down on the table. 'I know you saw me, in the arbour.' She turned and looked at Gemma, her chin held high. 'It wasn't what it seemed.'

'You don't have to tell me anything,' Gemma said.

'He has no intention of marrying me, he never did. I was merely a pastime for him. I had no idea, I thought he loved me, until I begged him to save my reputation and marry me. He laughed in my face and told me to stop being so childish.'

The air in the room hung heavy and ponderous, charged with Katherine's emotions. Gemma opened her mouth, then closed it again, unwilling to say the wrong thing.

'This...' Katherine gestured to her ruined dress, then patted her hair, grimacing at the unpinned curls, 'was his answer when I told him we must marry.'

'Oh, Katherine, I'm so sorry.' Gemma reached out, but Katherine pulled away.

'I don't need your pity.' She stood, swaying slightly, her bruised cheek giving her face a lopsided look in the firelight. She lowered her voice. 'I'm sorry. But I had two options before tonight: either he would tell me he loved me, and my reputation, such as it is, would remain intact, or–'

'Or?' Gemma prompted, after an awkward silence.

'He would refuse. If I stay here, the gossips will spread their malicious rumours and I will no longer be welcome at my so-called friends' houses. My life will be over.' Her face reddened with suppressed anger as she spoke. 'Do you know what it feels like to have everything you created destroyed by one man?'

Gemma lowered her eyes. 'Yes, I do,' she whispered.

'Of course you do.' Katherine gave a short laugh. 'Men. How easily they can break us, with just a snap of their fingers.' She sighed. 'I know what I must do, but I need your help.'

'I can't.' Gemma felt torn. 'I must leave, within the next few days. It's not safe for me here.'

'Leave? Why?'

'The witch hunters are back.'

Katherine thumped her fist against the wall. 'Have they not done enough harm to your family!' Then her face lit up. 'Take me with you.'

'You want to come with me? I don't even know where I'm going! I will have to sleep in the woods, forage for my food.' She couldn't see Katherine living like that for a few hours, let alone weeks or even months.

'It's just like my vision! We can travel together, in my carriage.' Katherine strode to and fro. 'We'll go to England.'

'England?' Gemma stared at her friend, and wondered if the blow to her head had been harder than she'd thought. 'Why all the way to England? We can travel to another town or city nearby, you must have friends–'

'No.' Katherine held up her hand, then lowered her voice. 'I have to leave France.'

'But I don't understand why.'

'I must leave Avignon as soon as possible, before the gossip starts. I have a friend who will... well, never mind that for now. But I need you to come with me. I can't travel alone, not like this. You are the only person I trust.'

Gemma took a deep breath. Her friend stood before her in a torn dress, her body covered in cuts and bruises, declaring her whole future destroyed by the actions of one man. How could they, mere women, survive any encounter with these sorts of men? Travelling with Katherine would be easier, and she could only pray that the witch hunters would remain in Avignon long enough to forget about the green-eyed girl they were chasing. Her anger drained away, leaving Gemma feeling bereft as her dreams of revenge on the witch hunters crumbled to nothing.

Katherine tightened her grasp on Gemma's hands. 'We will be safer together. We can stay with my parents for a while.'

'But why England?' Gemma insisted.

'My vision saw us travelling a great distance together. Do you trust your visions, Gemma?'

Gemma hesitated, then nodded.

'Then please come with me to England.' She leaned forward and grasped Gemma's hand. 'Surely you can see that it will be safer, and easier, for both of us. Where else will you go?'

A sudden memory of cold nights and her stomach cramping with lack of food came to Gemma. Could she really go through all that again? And if she injured herself? There might not be another Jean and Marguerite to look after her.

Gemma squeezed Katherine's hand. 'All right. We shall travel to England together.'

Chapter Nineteen

Tears poured down Gemma's face as she wrapped her arms around Ombra's neck in a tight hug. The mare snorted, then rubbed her nose against Gemma's back.

'I'm so sorry,' Gemma whispered, brusquely wiping the tears away. 'I wanted to take you with us, but Katherine will only travel by carriage, and then there's the crossing by ship…' She had fought fiercely, but Katherine and Leandro had insisted that leaving the mare in Avignon would be the best for everyone. It was only when Katherine had suggested Claude might take care of her that Gemma capitulated.

Claude had gone to her uncle's house as soon as he received her note requesting his help, and they had passed a pleasant afternoon together discussing Ombra's care. When Leandro left the room for a moment, Gemma had taken advantage of their being alone.

'I may not be a witch, but I can see the future.'

'What?' Claude blinked, confused.

'We don't have much time. Give me your hand.'

He hesitated, then held out his hand to her. Gemma took it between hers and closed her eyes. A jumble of images passed through her mind, taking her to unknown places with unknown people, until eventually they ceased swirling. She stood by the stables at the villa, looking out over a field at two horses standing side by side, a foal lying at their feet. Ombra and Lumière, shadow and light.

She opened her eyes and smiled, gladdened by the images she had seen. She knew that, one day, this man would be the one to take her out of the shadows and into the light. 'We will be together again, Claude, this I can promise you.'

'And I promise I will wait for you.' Claude caressed her cheek, then leaned forward. His lips brushed against hers, soft as a dragonfly's wing. Warmth flooded through Gemma, and she kissed him back passionately, her body pressed against his, until her uncle's footsteps in the hallway made them reluctantly break apart.

Now that the day to depart was upon them, Gemma was distraught at the thought of leaving Ombra behind. They had never spent a day apart since the horse had arrived in her life, and had travelled far together. If it hadn't been for the mare, Gemma knew that she would never have made it through the freezing nights in the mountains.

She wiped her face with the back of her hands. 'I promise you I'll come back. I won't leave you here, however long it takes.'

'Gemma, there you are! I might have guessed you'd be with your horse.' Leandro walked along the path, leaning heavily on his stick. He was puffing by the time he reached her. 'Lady Katherine asked me to tell you she is ready.' He put a hand on her shoulder, and spoke through panting breaths. 'Come. Claude's groom will be here soon to take her to his stables. I know how hard it is for you to leave her, but she's in good hands. She'll be treated better than many people.'

Gemma gave one last hug to Ombra, then followed her uncle back down the path, almost bumping into him when he stopped all of a sudden. 'Are you all right, Uncle?' Gemma looked on in concern as he mopped his brow.

'Just one of those days, *mia cara*. I will lie down and rest once you have left, never fear.'

'When I am settled I will search for a cure, or at least something to make you better.' Gemma had grown fond of her uncle, and couldn't bear the thought of him suffering.

'Thank you, I would appreciate that. Now, come along inside so we can say goodbye properly, before the neighbours see us both blubbering like babies!'

Claude was waiting by the carriage, stroking the horses' noses as they stamped their hoofs impatiently. He stepped forward to help, but Gemma shook her head and let Katherine lean on her as she clambered into the carriage.

He pressed a piece of parchment into her hand. 'My address. Write to me when you can, and let me know you are safe.'

She took the parchment. 'I wish I didn't have to go. There are so many things I need to do.'

Claude leaned in and spoke so quietly that only she could hear. 'Our fight against the witch hunters will be for another day. I will be here for you.' He held her hand as she ascended the steps into the carriage. 'Au revoir, ma chérie.'

Gemma sat down next to Katherine and watched him say a few words to the driver. The carriage set off with a jerk, wheels creaking, horses snorting as they strained against the leather harness. Katherine sat quietly beside her and Gemma closed her eyes, grateful for the chance to go through her confused thoughts. Were hers and Claude's destinies entwined, their future already in the hands of fate? Or would it be her choice? Follow the light, or stay in the shadows. Forgiveness or revenge. Claude or the witch hunters. She rubbed her brow, wishing she had all the answers. She was tired; tired of running, tired of chasing, tired of being Gemma Innocenti, tired of everything she had inherited. She no longer had the strength to fight.

Then your mother will have died in vain. Bob's words rang around the carriage, and Gemma glanced at Katherine, afraid the sound had disturbed her. But she remained still, lost in thought, and Gemma realised the voice was inside her mind.

How far must I travel? she replied, her heart heavy. *These last months have taken every ounce of my strength, journeying across the mountains, and now I must do it again. How can I?*

How can you not? You have the blood of the Innocenti, you are a healer. You must accept your destiny, for the cottage, the Grove, and the dragonflies. One day you will return, and these troubled times will be far behind you.

Gemma bowed her head. *I need your help. I cannot do this alone.*

There was no reply.

It would seem I have no choice. She sighed and turned to the window, moving the heavy velvet curtain aside to look out. A blur of colour passed under her nose, and the damselfly landed on her hand. A surge of hope ran through her as she realised she wasn't entirely alone after all. This was Bob's promise that someone would always be there, beside her.

The carriage clattered away from the elegant city centre and back along the narrower, dirty streets that led to the river. People jumped out of its path, shouting and shaking their fists at them, but Gemma barely noticed. Her heart was breaking at leaving Ombra behind, and she could feel the thread between herself and the mare pulling ever tauter with each creaky turn of the carriage's wheels.

She startled as a hand clasped around her arm, pulling her back to the present.

'I know how much it hurts, but you at least will return to Avignon.' Katherine smiled kindly at her, but Gemma noticed her friend's eyes were rimmed with red.

'I have a reason to return.'

'Only one?' Katherine laughed as Gemma blushed. 'I don't. But I will miss the place. Here I was free to do as I wished. Once I am back in England, everything will be very different.'

'You will not return to Avignon with me?' Gemma asked, panic filling her.

'I'm afraid I won't be able to. People have long memories here, they will never let me, or anyone else, forget my mistake.' She opened her mouth as if to say more, but the carriage jerked to a halt, and there was a thud as the coachman jumped down from his seat. A few people waiting for the ferry turned to stare, casting curious glances over the newcomers.

Katherine shook her head. 'We will talk later, when we are alone. Now we must cross the river.'

Gemma stepped down from the carriage, a cool breeze ruffling her hair. She watched the coachman unload their luggage while she waited for Katherine, wondering what her friend had been about to say. Grey clouds loomed overhead, and the ground was soggy after some overnight rain. It seemed a very different place from when she had first seen it only a month earlier. Then it had been bathed in sunlight, full of hope and wonder; now, in the dull grey light, it was easy to see the cracks in its shiny veneer, the corruption and misery below its colourful surface.

A voice called from across the path. 'Milady! The boat is this way.'

'Alberto! I couldn't find you earlier, I thought I'd have to leave without seeing you. I'm glad you're here.'

'Your uncle sent me to help you cross, so I thought I'd say goodbye here.' He grunted as he picked up a box. 'An' don't you worry about that 'orse of yours, I'll make sure 'is Lordship takes good care of her.'

'Thank you,' Gemma replied, her heart a little lighter at his words.

'It should be me thankin' you. Yer uncle's found me work on several houses, an' Paola an' I are thinkin' of gettin' married.'

'That's wonderful!' Gemma clasped her hands together, delighted for him.

'Maybe we'll 'ave some littl'uns by the time you come back, Paola says she ain't gettin' any younger!'

Gemma was about to reply when Katherine came over, holding her skirts off the muddy ground. 'Come on, we have to go!'

'You'll both be back soon,' Alberto said cheerfully.

'I hope you're right,' Gemma replied, sadness in her heart.

'You'll see.' He clapped his hands. 'Now, let's go before Lady Katherine has an apoplectic fit. The carriage has already arrived on the other side, Her Ladyship seems eager to go.'

Gemma smiled, and followed Alberto over to a boat bobbing on the river. Their travelling chests were already inside, tied down securely. She stepped into the boat, her hand lightly caressing the box that held the wooden chest.

England! Every Innocenti knew that Agnes, the first Healer, had come from there, travelling by sea to reach Tuscany. And now she would be retracing her ancestor's footsteps, setting off into the unknown, to a place she had never seen and a future that was to be discovered.

Chapter Twenty

Gemma and Katherine sat silently in the carriage, its rocking motion and the creaking of the wood strangely soothing to the soul. Only now did Gemma begin to relax, with Avignon far behind them. Their journey to Dieppe would take about a fortnight, but there were many roads they could travel, and many ways they could lose anyone who might be following them.

'So.' Katherine's voice broke the silence. The air between them shifted, notes of tension and tendrils of unspoken secrets drifting around their heads. 'We must make plans for our arrival in England, decide where we are to go.'

'Are we not going to your parents' house?' Gemma asked, confused. 'That is where I thought you said we were headed.'

Katherine sighed. 'We are, but I'm not sure how long we will stay there. They have a lot of influential friends abroad, especially in France, and Leandro suggested that perhaps it's best certain people in Avignon don't know where we are. He suggested we go to someone who has no connections there.'

'My uncle said that?' During the short time she had known him, Gemma had thought Leandro to be a little gullible, certainly more trusting of people than he should be.

'He has learned the hard way that not everyone is his friend. Avignon may be more accepting than a small Tuscan village, but people will gossip and say cruel things about a man's preferences or a woman's downfall, or betray you to the witch hunters for a florin. No, we mustn't stay long at my parents' house.' She paused, deep in thought. 'I have a dear friend who once said I could go to her if I'm ever in need. I'm sure her name has never been mentioned among my circle of friends in Avignon. We shall see if she is still so willing.'

'We'll just arrive at her house, unexpected and uninvited?'

'She will understand, she's one of us.'

'What does that mean?' Gemma waited, but Katherine said no more. Hurt and frustrated, she gave voice to a worry that had been niggling her ever since they'd announced their departure. 'How will I manage in England?'

'Hmm?' Katherine seemed lost in a world far away, her mind on other things. 'Sorry. What did you say?'

'I don't speak much English,' Gemma blurted, panic rising in her. 'How will I manage, if I can't speak English?'

Katherine laughed. '*Mia cara*, we have a long journey ahead of us, both across land and sea. By the time we get to Newhaven, you'll speak better English than the king!'

They stopped at small inns, out-of-the-way places frequented by few people who kept to themselves. Katherine's coins secured them a private room, with the coachman sleeping on the floor outside. They usually departed before cockcrow, the carriage well on its way by the time the sun rose, the other guests completely unaware of their presence.

Gemma had to admit, learning English helped pass the time. Their days were spent enclosed in the claustrophobic interior of the carriage, the leather hides across the windows keeping out curious eyes, but also fresh air and sunlight. If she hadn't had the lessons to keep her occupied, Gemma knew she wouldn't have been able to endure the journey. What with the constant jolting over the ruts in the roads, and the sheer boredom of having to hide away, it was hard even with something to occupy her mind.

Katherine was a patient teacher, and by the time they neared the coast Gemma felt more confident about holding a conversation. Her accent, on the other hand, was still as strongly Italian as ever.

'It's a part of your charm, together with those green eyes and your beautiful skin,' Katherine reassured her. 'The English gentlemen will be fighting to kiss your hand at every chance.'

'That's one good reason to not have an accent,' Gemma replied dryly.

'Just because you've lost your heart to a certain Frenchman doesn't mean you can't enjoy yourself in England, my dear. A little harmless flirtation is good for the soul.' Katherine started to chuckle, then fell silent, her brow creased in a frown.

'Is everything all right?' Gemma knew that something was bothering her friend, but Katherine hadn't mentioned it since her attempt at the ferry in Avignon.

'Yes, of course.' Katherine waved her hand in a careless gesture.

Gemma tried again. 'You know, you can tell–' She stopped as the carriage jerked to a halt.

Katherine pulled the piece of leather to one side, and the rich odour of brine filled the carriage. Birds shrieked in the air above them, and shouts could be heard from all around. A strong stench of rotting fish wafted past, making Gemma wrinkle her nose.

Katherine turned, a wry smile on her lips. 'I believe we've arrived in Dieppe.'

Chapter Twenty-One

THE SMELL OF BRINE in the air, the chaos of people shouting and gulls screeching as they circled above their heads in search of an easy meal, their cries like the wailing of lost souls, and the stench of fish entrails and human sweat, brought back unwelcome memories to Gemma as she stood at the entrance to the port. She half-expected to see the witch hunters appear among the crowd, wending their way towards her. People shoved past, eager to see what wares the fishermen had brought, jostling each other in their rush to be first served, and she kept a tighter grip on the wooden chest she was holding.

'Don't worry, our ship lies that way.' Katherine pointed to the other side of the port, away from the crowd milling around the barrels of freshly caught fish. 'I'll go and find someone to take our things, wait here for me.'

Gemma took a deep breath and nodded, feeling strangely alone as Katherine made her way through the throng. After being cooped up in a carriage for days on end, with only Katherine for company, stopping at inns for a quick meal and a night's sleep before leaving again early the next morning, the confusion all around made her feel agitated. A gull landed on the ground nearby and cocked its head, staring at her.

'I haven't got any crumbs for you, it's better you join your friends over by the fish barrels,' she said. The bird blinked once and squawked its indignation, then flew away, wings flapping lazily.

'I see you're getting acquainted with the locals.' Katherine took hold of Gemma's elbow and led her through the entrance and to the left, away from the main crowd of people. 'Over there,' she instructed, turning to two burly men following them, pulling a cart with their luggage.

They grumbled something in a strong French dialect and set off towards the ship, the cart's wheels creaking over the uneven stones.

'Anyone would think I hadn't paid them a florin each for their trouble!' Katherine tutted and shook her head, then took hold of Gemma's hand. 'Come, by this evening we'll be in Newhaven.'

The ship set sail just before noon, amid cheers from the crowds watching from the quay. It was a rare calm day, the ship gliding over the water with a steady rhythm that soothed Gemma's soul. It reminded her of the gentle rocking of Ombra's gait, and she wondered with a pang how the mare was doing without her. She glanced down as something tickled the back of her hand and saw the damselfly there. Even though her heart was heavy, she managed a small smile.

'Thank goodness you're still with me,' she murmured.

'Every time I see you, you're talking to the wildlife,' Katherine exclaimed, coming up behind her. 'That's pretty, such beautiful colours for a dragonfly.'

'Damselfly,' Gemma said automatically.

'I stand corrected. Where does it come from? It's a bit far from land.' Katherine leaned forward and peered at it, then looked up at Gemma. 'It really is an amazing creature.'

Gemma felt a glow of pride, which she tried to quell. Now wasn't the moment to tell her friend about her complicated relationship with her family and the healers. 'How much longer do you think it will take?' she asked instead, steering the conversation away from the damselfly.

'We should be in England by late afternoon, especially if the weather remains like this.'

Gemma looked up at the fluffy white clouds in the clear sky. 'There doesn't appear to be any sign of a storm.'

'We've been lucky,' Katherine agreed. 'The last time I travelled this way the weather was terrible. The waves tossed us up and down as though they wanted to break the ship, I thought we'd never make it across.'

She staggered slightly, and for a moment Gemma thought her friend was going to be sick. Katherine put a hand against a pole to steady herself.

'I-I need your help.' Katherine's hand gripped the wooden pole until her knuckles became white, her face pallid in the bright sunshine.

'Is something wrong? Are you ill?'

Katherine gazed out at sea, her eyes fixed firmly on the horizon. 'Not ill, no.' She sighed. 'I wanted to tell you before we left, but never got the chance. The reason why I came with you – well, one of the reasons – was because I'm–' She gestured helplessly at her stomach.

Realisation suddenly dawned on Gemma. 'Oh. You're with child.' She cringed as soon as the words left her mouth. How had she not noticed before? She'd been so caught up with her own troubles that she hadn't paid much attention to Katherine. What kind of friend was she?

Katherine continued to stare into the distance, her hair whipped around her head by the wind. She placed her hand on her stomach, and Gemma could see the gentle swell beneath her cloak, which she hadn't noticed until that moment.

The memory of the last time she touched her mother's hand came to her, and she saw once again the vision of herself, pregnant, standing on the deck of a ship. Gemma gasped. Was it possible she'd seen Katherine? Had she misinterpreted the vision entirely? And if that hadn't been her own future, but another's, what was to happen to her?

Katherine's voice broke into her thoughts. 'I want you to help me. Y-you know the right herbs to take, I'll be safe if you do it.'

'Are you sure?' Gemma put her hand on Katherine's shoulder.

'No.' Katherine turned to her with a stubborn expression on her face. 'But how can I go home like this? My parents...' She shuddered.

'How far along are you?' From the swell of her stomach, Gemma estimated she was past her first three months.

'I-I'm not sure. I realised in March I hadn't had my courses during the previous two months, so I imagine at least four, if not five.'

Gemma shook her head. 'It's too dangerous. The herbs work in the early weeks, but now... It would be a great risk, for you as well as for the child. You said yourself you're not sure.'

'But what else can I do?' Katherine's hand clenched around the rail, her knuckles turning white. 'I can't go back to England like this. The thought of my parents' smug faces, telling me that they knew I would end up this way, is more than I can bear.'

'I need to think about it.' Gemma glanced at a sailor passing nearby.

Katherine nodded, relieved, and patted Gemma's hand. 'I know you will do what's best.'

Gemma flinched as the images flashed before her, of Katherine lying on a bed in a shadowy chamber, the white sheets dark with blood, her face contorted in agony. She pulled her hand away, rubbing her fingers, and tried to give Katherine a reassuring smile.

'Let's go somewhere quieter,' she said.

They sat in the shade of some crates, the wooden chest between them, Katherine looking out to sea while Gemma thought desperately how to help her friend. The brief vision she'd had – was it during childbirth, or as a result of giving Katherine herbs to lose the baby? She closed her eyes and tried to remember what she had seen: the small bedchamber with sheets covering the window, casting shadows across the room; Katherine writhing as pains gripped her body; the sheets, drenched in bright red blood, so much that Gemma feared for her friend's life. She had to be sure; whatever she decided now would condemn either mother or child.

The scene repeated over and over again in her mind, and each time she concentrated on the smaller details. It wasn't easy; the blood on the sheets kept drawing her gaze, the dark puddle growing larger the longer she stared. But finally she managed to look properly at Katherine's tortured body. When she saw the small, round bump beneath her friend's shift, she knew what she had to choose.

She opened her eyes and drew a deep breath. Katherine turned her gaze upon her, her brow furrowed in an unspoken question.

'It's too late for the herbs.' Gemma held up her hand as Katherine opened her mouth to say something. 'Please, don't ask me to do that. You'll put your life at risk, I can't do that to you.'

Katherine slumped against a crate. 'You saw, didn't you.' It was a statement, not a question.

'When you held my hand.' Gemma put an arm around Katherine's shoulders. 'I'm sorry, it's too late to stop things now.'

'So what do I do?'

'I have an idea. My mother...' Gemma faltered, then carried on. 'My mother once helped a young girl in our village in similar circumstances. The girl went to a town on the coast for a few months, and when she returned, she was a widow with a newborn baby to care for. She wasn't vilified or shamed by the villagers, and became a respectable farmer's wife within the year.'

'I have to get married?' Katherine huffed. 'That's not an option, as I–'

'No one said you have to get married,' Gemma interrupted. 'The girl came back as a widow, with a gold band on her fourth finger. If you go to the town's cemetery, you'll find her husband's grave. But she has no idea who he is. She never met the man.'

Comprehension swept over Katherine's face. 'We *pretend* I was married! Why didn't I think of that? My parents wouldn't be able to say anything.' She slumped against the crate, her excitement gone.

'But they'll ask why there wasn't a wedding, or any news from Avignon. It won't work.'

'You were swept up in the throes of passion, it was a last-minute decision, without giving a thought to anyone else,' Gemma said. 'They'll believe it if you're determined enough.'

Katherine looked down at her stomach, and caressed the small bump. 'You're right. I can do this. I'll *make* it work. Anything to keep this little one.'

Chapter Twenty-Two

Lord and Lady Grey were sitting on velvet-covered chairs in the parlour, talking quietly together, when Gemma and Katherine entered the room. Katherine hurried over and kissed her mother on both cheeks, then curtsied to her father.

'It's lovely to have you home again, dear, it's been far too long,' Lady Grey said. 'You've put on weight, though, your dress is a little tight around the waist.' She glanced at Gemma, who stood nearby, twisting her fingers together and hoping nobody would notice her. 'Who's your friend?'

'This is Gemma, Contessa Innocenti from Tuscany,' Katherine replied, turning her head and mouthing, '*See!*'

Gemma grimaced as she curtsied. Even after everything Katherine had told her about her parents, she'd hoped for a warmer welcome.

Lady Grey shifted on her rose-coloured padded chair, and gestured to the Dante chairs opposite. 'Please sit down, both of you. Katherine dear, tell us your news.'

Gemma perched on the edge of her seat, and observed in silence as Katherine began speaking. Lord Grey had the same nose as her friend, narrow and sharp, giving him a fox-like appearance. His bristly moustache appeared to quiver as he sat, straight-backed, lips pursed, his hazel eyes not missing a thing. Unlike many men of his age and importance, he showed no sign of a paunch under his sombre clothes.

Lady Grey's round cheeks were lightly dusted with brown rouge, while her lips were blood red, in stark contrast to her pale skin. A sapphire-encrusted comb adorned her silver hair, exalting the blueness of her eyes, while her fingers, lightly balanced on the skirts of her dark-blue silk dress, were covered in jewelled rings.

The parlour was as opulent as Lady Grey's appearance; in fact, the whole manor flaunted their wealth in every corner. From what she could see of the view from the window, Gemma imagined the garden was just as ostentatious. But she had seen the villagers as their carriage rattled along the road, with its ramshackle cottages and children wearing rags. *Lord and Lady Grey may be rich,* she thought, *but they are no better than the inhabitants of Avignon, closeted away in their magnificent manor while only a couple of miles away people struggle to survive.*

'As I said, I wanted to spend some time at home,' Katherine was saying. Gemma stopped looking around and concentrated on her friend.

'Yes, we were quite surprised by that,' Lady Grey said. 'You have always seemed so happy in Avignon, even though Cecily says it is a place with a terrible reputation, and she wouldn't set foot there for all the gold in England!'

Katherine's cheeks flushed red. 'My sister would believe anything. The rumours are exaggerated, it's quite a pleasant place to live.'

'So why have you come back?' her father asked, frowning. 'Don't we give you enough money? How long are you likely to stay?'

Gemma suppressed a gasp. Katherine's hands clenched in her lap, before she slowly released them again.

'I have returned to England for good.'

'Really?' Lady Grey raised an eyebrow. 'Whatever for? I thought you had settled in well in Avignon, you told us you would never leave.'

'Circumstances change. I–' Katherine glanced at Gemma, and she nodded in encouragement. Katherine cleared her throat. 'I felt I had to leave, after my husband–'

'Husband? You're married?' Lady Grey interrupted, lifting her eyebrows.

'Yes. I... Robert and I married a few months ago. It was love at first sight, we decided to marry shortly after meeting. It was a quiet wedding, only us, and the contessa, of course.' Katherine gestured to Gemma. 'So now I am Marchioness Fontaine.'

Lady Grey sat up straighter and pasted a smile on her face. 'Oh, how wonderful, darling. What a pity you never told us. We enjoy a good wedding.' Her blue eyes glinted in the afternoon light, her mouth pursed tightly as she stared at Katherine. Then she turned to her husband. 'Do you remember when John came to ask you for Cecily's hand in marriage? He was so nervous, poor man, he could barely get the words out!' She giggled.

'I remember it well,' Lord Grey replied with a smirk. 'A few glasses of brandy soon gave him the courage he needed. Although, I don't think he's stopped drinking since! Not that I blame him, being married to Cecily.'

Lady Grey slapped his arm, but gave him an affectionate smile. 'They are very happy together, as you well know.'

'Much as I love to talk about Cecily and her wonderful family, we were talking about my wedding.' Katherine held her chin high, staring her mother directly in the eyes, and Gemma was reminded of the defiant woman in the paintings, now stored in her uncle's house in Avignon.

'So we were. And where is your husband?' Lady Grey looked around the room.

Katherine lowered her head. 'He died.'

'That was unfortunate.' Lord Grey reached over and poured himself a glass of brandy from a small table at his side. He inhaled the fumes, breathing deeply, then drank, his Adam's apple bobbing up and down as he swallowed.

'*Unfortunate?*' Katherine pulled her shawl around her, her knuckles white against the dark wool. 'Losing my husband was unfortunate? You never change, either of you!'

Her father stood, and crossed his arms over his chest. 'And, it appears, neither do you.' Gemma watched as his cheeks reddened, the blush spreading down to his neck. 'You are such an ungrateful child, always have been. I believe you should leave before you make your mother ill.'

Lady Grey fanned herself with her hand, her face pale as she looked up at her husband.

'You want us to leave?' Katherine stood facing her father, her expression just as furious as his. 'Very well.' She gestured to Gemma, then stormed out of the room.

Gemma curtsied again to Lord and Lady Grey, then gathered her skirts and hurried after her friend.

'I can't believe them!' Katherine slammed the chamber door behind her. She motioned to Gemma to sit on the bed, while she paced around the room, too angry to relax.

Gemma sat down, but said nothing. It had been an excruciating hour, which had made her squirm with embarrassment every time Katherine's parents had spoken.

'Even the fact that I am now a marchioness means nothing to them! They don't care about me. Every time I said something, they talked about my sister, the apple of their eyes.' Katherine tugged her shawl off in fury and threw it on the floor. 'I'm glad we're leaving.'

'But surely once you tell them about the–'

'Don't!' Katherine pointed at the door, and put her finger to her lips. 'I don't think I can, not after today.'

'But...' Gemma stopped. 'What will you do, where will you go? They could help you.'

'Help? Mother has already said I'm getting fat, she'll probably tell cook not to give me any more sweetmeats. They don't care, Gemma. They didn't even give me their condolences when I told them my husband had died.' Katherine snorted. 'No, I've decided. As soon as we're ready to leave we'll go to my friend's house.'

'She won't mind?' Gemma was reluctant to impose on someone else.

'She'll be delighted,' Katherine replied. 'She's like us.'

'Us? Oh. A witch, you mean.' Gemma had tried to insist she was a healer and not a witch, but Katherine wouldn't listen.

'I know she'd love to meet you! Three witches together.' Katherine smiled. 'The perfect number.' She went over to her travelling chest and rummaged among the clothes. 'Where is it? I know I put it in here. Ah, there it is!'

She returned to the bed, holding a small box made of a light-coloured, highly polished wood. 'This box was made from part of a yew tree in the churchyard that fell over during some storms when I was a child.'

Gemma reached over and touched it. A cold, tingling sensation ran through her fingertips, and she withdrew her hand, surprised.

'Open it,' Katherine urged.

Gemma shook her head. She didn't know why, but the box filled her with... not dread, exactly, but a certain wariness. She knew better than to ignore her instincts.

With a tut, Katherine lifted the lid and tilted the box so that Gemma could see inside. It was lined with soft dark-green velvet, on which lay a pearl set in a gold pendant. The opaque surface shone in the afternoon light, the colours of the tapestries on the wall casting shadows over it. But instead of reflecting the images, the pearl appeared to absorb them into itself, the images fading away. Gemma blinked and looked up; the tapestries were still there on the wall, but their reflection no longer showed on the pearl's surface.

'A wise woman gave me this, she told me to only use it in times of great need,' Katherine murmured. 'I've kept it in this box, unused up until now.'

'What would you use it for?' Gemma asked cautiously.

'For darker magic.'

'What? Why would...?' But Gemma knew why her friend would want to use dark magic. She felt it herself, running through her veins, that fierce hatred towards the people who had caused her misery and shame. It had kept her going on her journey from Tuscany to France, only for her to understand at the very last moment that it wasn't in her nature to hurt others, that she would have harmed herself as much as her uncle if she had carried out her revenge. If *she* could change, perhaps she could help Katherine see that there were other paths that could be taken, that hatred and the desire for revenge could be turned into something good and worthwhile.

There was silence in the room, heavy with understanding as they both gazed down at the pearl on its velvet cushion. The sun continued on its journey through the sky, the dappling shadows lengthening across the room, unknown futures and myriad possibilities born and dying with every instant that passed.

'Put it away for now,' Gemma said. 'Perhaps we can make things right, without resorting to... that.'

Chapter Twenty-Three

THE DAMSELFLY RESTED ON the edge of the window frame, its wings folded along its body. Shimmering iridescent in the late afternoon light, it appeared to change its colour as the sun passed behind some clouds, then came out again.

Gemma finished checking through her things and closed the travel chest. The wooden box with the dragonfly carving on its lid was already inside, hidden beneath her cloak. A noise outside caught her attention, and she went over to the window.

A stableboy was crossing the field where the two carriage horses were cropping at the grass. He rattled a bucket of feed and they lifted their heads, ears pricked forward. With a flick of their tails, they wandered over to him, snatching mouthfuls of grass as they went, until he could put their halters on and lead them back to the yard.

'I miss Ombra,' Gemma murmured, blinking back tears. For a moment she could smell the mare's sweet perfume of hay and horse, feel her snuffling nose blowing gently on her hand. 'I will go back,' she said fiercely.

A knock at the door jolted her out of her misery. They were leaving; Gemma had no idea where they were going, but anything would be better than the tense, awkward atmosphere in Lord and Lady Grey's house.

'I'll be right there,' she called. With a final glance out of the window, she pulled her cloak around her and made her way downstairs.

The pattering of rain on the carriage accompanied them during the journey from Katherine's home in Ringmer to a tiny hamlet that Katherine told Gemma, with only a slightly cynical smile, was called Wytch Cross. The rain had stopped but grey clouds hung low in the sky, promising more, as the carriage turned onto the road that led to the manor house. Raindrops dripped from sodden trees, their curved branches drooping under the weight of the water, puddles forming on the ground below. Birds sat among the leaves, drenched and miserable, heads tucked close to their bodies, bright eyes ever alert as the horses trotted down the muddy track.

The manor sprawled before them, its stone walls blending in with the untamed flora, until it was hard to see where the house began and the ground ended. Ivy climbed the worn exterior, vying with water-laden roses for the sunniest spots, spreading its tendrils as far as the timber frame of the roof. Gemma gazed, open-mouthed, as the carriage pulled up to a halt before the front porch.

'The windows are made of glass,' Katherine told her, pointing at the diamond-patterned panes. 'Count Bianchi is very proud of them, he'll probably point them out to you at least a dozen times a day!'

'Count Bianchi?'

'Ah, yes, one of your compatriots. He's a textile merchant... well, was. His son has taken over the business now. He lives in Italy and rarely comes back to visit them. The count met the young Lady Ellen, fell in love with her, and made Wytch Cross his home.' Katherine nudged her. 'Italians are so romantic!'

The coachman helped them out of the carriage, and as they stood brushing the creases out of their dresses, a loud cry came from the manor.

'Katherine!' A young woman came running towards them, heedless of the mud ruining her silk slippers. 'Why didn't you tell us you were coming? What a lovely surprise!'

'That's my friend, Julia-Ann,' Katherine whispered to Gemma, then turned to greet the enthusiastic girl with open arms. 'I'm sorry to just turn up like this, but we didn't know–'

'Don't be silly. You know you're welcome to stay whenever you want. I thought you were still in France.'

'I decided to leave. Oh, and this is my dear friend Gemma. We met in Avignon and travelled here together. I hope your parents won't mind me bringing her.'

Julia-Ann enveloped Gemma in a hug. 'Of course they won't mind! Any friend of Katherine's is our friend too. I'll get some rooms sorted for you both right away.' She suddenly took a step back and peered at Katherine, her eyes wide in shock. 'My goodness, are you... with child? How, I mean, what... who?' Her voice faded as she stared in bewilderment.

'I have some explaining to do,' Katherine said, blushing. She held up her left hand so that her friend could see the ring.

'Oh, how wonderful! Don't tell me anything now, wait until Mamma and Papà are present.'

Katherine glanced at Gemma, and nodded. Gemma gave her what she hoped was a reassuring smile, then followed her as the girl took them into the manor.

Count and Countess Bianchi were as exuberant and friendly as their daughter. They wrapped Katherine in warm embraces, and made Gemma feel a welcome guest. Inside, the manor was as homely and majestic as outside: niches had been created around windows, with comfortable chairs, shelves full of books, and low tables to rest drinks and food on; bright tapestries and paintings of the surrounding countryside lined the walls, while light flooded in through the glass panes, even on such a dull day.

Every room had a fireplace, flickering flames exuding warmth and the delicate aroma of beechwood, a welcome respite to the grey day. Oak-panelled walls lent a sombre air to the house, which felt like a quiet haven of peace and calm.

There was much excitement about Katherine's story of her wedding and ensuing widowhood, then finding herself alone and with child. Gemma knew that the pretence was necessary, but couldn't help feeling guilty about lying to Julia-Ann and her parents.

When talk turned to their journey from France, tiredness crept up on Gemma. She tried to hold the yawn in, but it finally escaped.

'Oh, you must get some rest,' the countess exclaimed. She went to the door and called for a maid.

'No, I'm all right. It's just the heat, after all that rain,' Gemma protested.

'Nonsense. I'm exhausted just listening to Katherine's tales of your travels,' the countess said. She gave Gemma a kind smile. '*Devi essere stanchissima, poverina.*'

Gemma stifled another yawn, then admitted, 'Yes, I am a little tired. Perhaps a short rest would do me good.'

'Alice will take you to your room.' She patted Gemma's hand. '*Riposati bene.*'

The wooden stairs creaked as Gemma followed the maid up the staircase, the curved banister smooth beneath her fingers. They walked along a dark landing, a long rug covering the floor, until the maid stopped at a door at the end of the hallway.

'This is one of the best rooms, milady,' the girl confided as she opened the door and stood aside to let Gemma enter. 'You can hear the doves all day long.'

'Thank you. It looks delightful.'

The maid curtsied and left, closing the door behind her. Gemma opened the window and leaned out. She could hear the burbling of a stream racing along at the end of the garden, and the scents of herbs from the kitchen garden below drifted up to her. Everything was as fresh as newly laundered clothes after the earlier rain, the sun peeking out from behind the clouds and casting its light across the countryside. She smiled as she heard a dove cooing, and caught a glimpse of a dovecote beyond a tall hedge.

A servant had already brought her travelling chest up to the chamber; she opened it, and was relieved to see the box with the dragonfly lid still safely stowed beneath her clothes. Leaving it there, she kicked off her travelling boots and lay down on the four-poster bed. Her body sank into the unusually soft mattress, and her head rested on a feather-filled pillow. Feeling as though she was floating on a cloud, she lay there for a while, her eyes following the curves of the silk canopy draped over the frame of the bed. A bee settled on a flower outside the window, its heavy droning making her drowsy. Days of travel caught up with her, and she succumbed to the sweet song of dreams.

Chapter Twenty-Four

They had only been at the manor for a few days, but Gemma already felt as though she had been there forever. Julia-Ann took them for walks around Wytch Cross when the weather permitted, or showed them around the manor when it was pouring with rain. Gemma was happy to pass pleasant hours with Count Bianchi, the two of them speaking in Italian so quickly that the others merely shook their heads and gave up trying to follow.

After the oppressive stay in Lord and Lady Grey's house it was a welcome respite, and Gemma was delighted to see Katherine blossom under the Bianchi's care. Her pale skin began to glow, and the dark circles beneath her eyes faded as she caught up on much-needed sleep. The manor and its gardens were balm to their souls, healing both their minds and their exhausted bodies.

Gemma was in the library, writing a letter at one of the small tables, while Katherine relaxed in a chair nearby, eyes closed, her hand resting lightly on her stomach, and Julia-Ann sat bent over her needlework at a table by the window.

'Are you writing to the *charmant* Claude?' Julia-Ann asked, without taking her eyes off the embroidery she was working on.

Gemma blushed. 'He asked me to let him know when I arrived. Hopefully we'll still be here by the time he writes back.' She looked at Katherine and raised an eyebrow.

'And of course you want news of your beloved Ombra.' Katherine laughed. 'Poor man! Does he know you only want him for his stables?'

'It's not like that at all,' Gemma retorted. 'I am happy to wait for Claude, until he can join me.'

'And in the meantime, any news of your horse is welcome.' Katherine snorted, keeping her eyes closed.

At times, Katherine's teasing was tiring. Gemma reread the last few lines of her letter, before signing it with a flourish.

Julia-Ann lifted her head and gestured to Katherine. 'Take no notice, she means no harm. I for one am glad he isn't here, so we will have time to get to know each other better. You've been here almost a whole week and I still know barely anything about you! You speak more with Papà about his blessed windows than you do with me.'

Katherine struggled to sit up, wriggling in her chair. 'She means that she has an Italian countess staying at her home, and no gossip to tell anyone.'

'Don't be silly.' Julia-Ann grabbed a cushion and threw it at Katherine. 'I don't gossip.'

Katherine made a face. 'Really?'

'Really,' Julia-Ann retorted. 'Well, not all the time. Not when it matters.' She tutted and peered closely at her embroidery again.

Gemma couldn't help laughing. 'I'm not that interesting.'

Katherine raised her eyebrows. 'A mysterious Italian contessa from Tuscany, whose family's horses are well-known all over Europe, and who knows everything there is to know about plants and healing, isn't interesting?'

Gemma shook her head, her lips pursed.

'Well, I'm tired of sitting here doing nothing.' Katherine got to her feet. 'I've got an idea.'

'What?' Gemma asked warily, knowing that Katherine could propose anything when she was in this kind of mood.

'Come with me and you'll find out.'

Gemma glanced at Julia-Ann, who sighed and put down her sewing.

'You won't give us any peace until we do, will you?' she replied.

'No.' Katherine laughed. 'And you must both bring something that is precious to you.'

Gemma made a face.

'Come.' Katherine pulled her to her feet. 'You won't regret it.'

Katherine pulled the heavy velvet curtains across her chamber window to shut out the afternoon sun. The candles she had lit created small pools of light around the room, flickering in the breeze as though unseen hands moulded the flames into ever-changing shapes.

Gemma looked around, but there was no altar, none of the objects that she had seen at Katherine's house in Avignon. She'd imagined her friend was going to scry again, but it appeared not to be so.

Katherine gestured to them to sit on a rug in the middle of the floor, then brought over three glasses and a bottle of wine. She handed Gemma and Julia-Ann a glass each, and filled it for them.

She sat down with them, and held up her own glass. 'To three friends, bonded for life by secrets untold and hidden desires. Let your soul speak this day, be honest, be true, and be faithful, for the words uttered within these walls will never be spoken to anyone else. And so it will be.' She closed her eyes and drank from her glass.

Julia-Ann shrugged her shoulders, then tasted her drink, tiny sips at first, then continuing until it was all gone.

Gemma held her glass to her nose, breathing in the aroma. It was a light wine, small bubbles popping on the surface, with undertones of something else that she couldn't quite make out. She almost recognised it, the name just out of reach, dancing at the edge of her memory before floating away. The heady scent pulled her in, tantalising, skipping over the surface of her tongue, evoking emotions she had kept suppressed for a long time. Tipping the glass, she drank, holding the liquid in her mouth for a moment, a wave of love, longing, and loss crashing over her, tumultuous sensations flooding through her as she swallowed the wine. She let out a long sigh and drank again, each mouthful evoking different sensations, different memories.

Minutes passed, or days, Gemma couldn't be sure. The candles still cast their flickering shadows around the room, but everything seemed larger, somehow. She could no longer see the walls or the ceiling, just an empty darkness all around them.

Katherine placed a candle in the middle of the triangle they created, sat together on the rug. It was larger than the others, its light shining over each of their faces. She reached behind her and produced a bag, from which she took their chosen objects and laid them on the floor.

Gemma looked down. Katherine's faux wedding ring, a grey lace shawl from Julia-Ann, and a sprig of the silver-leaf plant, which Gemma kept nestled inside the recipe book.

Katherine smiled at them, her eyes glittering in the candlelight. The silence hung around them, soft and velvety, enveloping the three women in its embrace and keeping the dark at bay. Gemma was unsure what Katherine had done, but she felt the incantation weave among them, its wispy strands winding through their hair and touching their fingertips, bringing a promise of friendship and unbreakable bonds. Somehow, she knew what she had to do.

Leaning forward, the wisps of the spell brushing across the hairs on her arms, Gemma picked up the sprig. The familiar aroma was released by her touch, evoking memories she'd locked away, she'd thought forever. A tear rolled down her cheek. She rubbed it between her hands, releasing the plant's oil, then stretched out her arms towards her friends. There was a slight tingle as their fingers touched, and the shadows grew darker around them.

Gemma concentrated on the candle, its flame glowing brighter with every moment. She saw a movement, and peered more closely. The Grove appeared, dragonflies flitting everywhere, the scent of rosemary, sage, and lavender drifting around them. Her mother was there too, tending the plants, putting cuttings in the basket over her arm.

Keeping her eyes on the flame, Gemma told Katherine and Julia-Ann a story. Words spilled off her tongue of dragonflies and healers, of a curse on a family and a grave in the woods, of wounds healed, illnesses cured, women saved from death on their childbed. Emotion filled her every word, so that they weaved among them, above them, around them, soft and feathery, brushing against their skin before nestling in their hearts.

She spoke of love and knowledge, a cottage always open to whoever was in need, of rising at midnight to tend to patients, of helping a loved one's soul move on to a kinder place. And as she spoke, she realised she was the damselfly in Bob's story – even though she felt she was on the outside, a mere observer, she was a part of the healers, just as much as they were a part of her. She may have been far from the Grove, but it was always inside her.

When she spoke of the witch hunters her mood turned dark; the words jumped and jerked, scratching at their skin like the thorns of a blackberry bush. Her voice shook with anger and hurt, but still she continued, telling her tale so that others might understand, so that others could see what men had done to women, what they always had done and what they would continue to do.

She relived the flight through the woods, stumbling after her mother, clutching onto her hand, terrified of falling and slowing them down. The trees loomed above them, branches stretching out to snatch at their clothes, roots ready to trip them as they ran. Fear lent her the strength she needed to reach the villa, to the safety of her grandparents' arms.

She cried the day she learned her mother had been taken away by the witch hunters. Until, a long time after, her despair turned into anger, and fear became determination for revenge. Now her words were barbed seeds, seeking to hook onto clothes to be carried far and wide, spreading their roots in the hearts of women. Thousands had died at the stake, their screams of agony reverberating through the towns and cities and countryside, haunting the shadows and dark places, senseless deaths that would mark the souls of their persecutors forever, and beyond. The wheel of time turned, relentless, unstoppable, but she would remember. She would make sure that all women remembered.

Chapter Twenty-Five

Katherine and Julia-Ann remained silent when she had finished, tears glistening in their eyes, the flickering of the candle reflected in their dark irises. Gemma laid the leaf back down on the floor, next to the candle, and looked at Katherine.

'Your turn,' she said.

Katherine kept her gaze fixed on the gold wedding ring, the metal dulled by age and use. 'It was my great-grandmother's,' she told them in a low, trembling voice. 'I think she would approve.' Hesitant at first, she carefully picked the words as an image appeared in the flame.

He was handsome: tall, blond, with an air of self-confidence that drew people to him. Katherine was no different from the others; she would listen to him talking at dinner parties, or watch him dancing with other women, desire in her heart. The few times he bestowed his attention upon her she was barely able to talk, the words stuck in her throat, overwhelmed by her feelings for this man who had stolen her heart.

There were rumours of romantic trysts, young women spirited away in the dead of night, only to return some months later as hollowed-out versions of themselves, broken, emotionless, married off to elderly widowers before their reputations were shredded. But they were only rumours, started by jealous spinsters who hated seeing the young ladies having fun, and no names were ever mentioned. So Katherine remained in that state of limbo, her heart yearning for something it seemed she could never have, admiring him from afar while he was unaware she existed.

Or so she thought. Until the day he turned his sparkling blue eyes in her direction, with hidden smiles and glances that were only for her, the two of them locked in a secret world that excluded everyone and everything else. The first time they kissed, she thought she would melt. Naïve dreams of chaste kisses were turned upside down when she first experienced the passion he brought out in her. Lips and tongues, hands unfastening buttons and hooks, her fingers running through the silky hairs on his chest, his hands sliding up her stockings, and further, touching, entering, until she shuddered with desire and passion, and let him do whatever he would.

For several weeks, she was his and he was hers. Secret meetings in dark gardens, or deserted corridors, or empty libraries; everywhere and anywhere, their lust insatiable. And then his attention began to wander; a flick of an eye as another woman entered the room, a distracted kiss as they passed in the corridor, a careless fumble where once his fingers had danced over her like a musician with a finely tuned instrument. Excuses fell from his lips as easily as the kisses he had once given her, his tongue used for words instead of pleasure. At the same time she realised there was life growing inside her, he was slipping away, turning his attentions to another.

Katherine used every spell she knew, every charm she could think of, but nothing worked. He spurned her every time she tried to get close, physically thrust her away from him when she insisted they speak, ignored her pleading glances and pathetic attempts to win him back.

The night of the party she had attended with Gemma, she had been so desperate that she'd slipped a potion into his drink. When he turned to her with the smile that had once been for her alone she'd thought it had worked. Together they'd left the ballroom and walked into the garden, away from prying eyes and nosy, all-knowing spinsters, and he'd led her to the arbour where Gemma had come across them.

Sniffing with barely held-back tears, Katherine pointed at the flame, and Gemma recognised the scene. Katherine, her hair falling down, pressed against his body, and him, the unknown gentleman, with a lascivious smirk on his face.

Haltingly, Katherine recounted how he'd taken her in his arms and kissed her with passion, holding her close to him, until she felt his fingers digging into her shoulders, causing more pain than delight. She'd struggled to back away, but he'd kept hold of her, one hand on the neckline of her dress, the other under her skirts, grasping and pinching, his breath hot and stale on her face, a wild expression in his eyes.

When she tried to cry out he'd clamped a hand over her mouth, tilting her head back until she felt as though her neck would snap. He had taken her then, roughly and hurriedly, while she cried out for him to stop, begged him not to harm her or their child. At her words, he'd shoved her away from him, pulling up his breeches as she sobbed.

She'd stumbled out of the arbour, desperate to find Gemma. Humiliated and confused, she'd somehow made her way indoors and found a place to hide, unwilling to let anyone see her in her dishevelled state, waiting until she saw Gemma pass nearby. Hurt and angry, she had taken the opportunity to leave Avignon and return to England, where she could pretend to be widowed and have her baby in peace. But she vowed that she would never love or trust a man again, and could never return to Avignon where the spinsters spread their whispered truths.

Gemma bowed her head. 'If only I'd known…'

'What could you have done? He would have denied it, said it was what I wanted, that I led him on. Who would have believed me?' Katherine swiped the tears from her cheeks, her face fiercely determined. 'I will bring my child up here in England, far from the gossip and hateful insinuations of Avignon.' She caressed her stomach. 'But I will make him pay, have no doubt about that.'

An image of the pearl pendant appeared in Gemma's mind, and she understood why Katherine had shown it to her. And at that moment, she knew she would gladly assist her friend.

Katherine picked up the grey shawl, and it was only then that Gemma noticed the edges were blackened, as though they had been singed.

'Tell Gemma your story,' she said to Julia-Ann.

Chapter Twenty-Six

Julia-Ann took the shawl and held it close to her breast, rubbing the lace between her fingers, breathing in its perfume.

'The woman who this belonged to taught me, and Katherine, everything we know.' She clutched the shawl as the ruins of a shack appeared in the candle flame. Tears ran down her face as she spoke of the two girls, unlike each other in looks and age but so close they were often mistaken for sisters, and of the elderly woman who lived in a ramshackle hut at the edge of the village, among the trees in the forest. With long, curly grey hair and the kindest smile, old Meg took care of any animal that was hurt, or sick, or starving. A crow with only one leg hopped after her wherever she went, squirrels she had tended brought her nuts and seeds, and an old fox curled up on her hearth at night, its nose tucked under its bushy tail.

The old woman's hut held the sweet fragrance of the forest, of wild flowers, and of herbs hung drying from hooks in the ceiling. Salves and tinctures of every kind were stored in crude wooden pots, hewn from fallen branches and whittled by her gnarled old hands till the insides were smooth.

The girls spent many hours in the hut, learning as Meg boiled and steeped and crushed and strained, different herbs for different ailments. Her agile movements belied her years as she flitted about, her eyes bright with joy as she stirred and tasted and sang magical words that floated on the surface of the cures before sinking down into their depths. And the old fox watched, its eyes clouded with age, its grey muzzle resting on its paws, dreaming of its younger days when it would run for miles in search of prey, its withered legs once again strong and sturdy.

The girls sang the words together with Meg, their young voices in perfect harmony with her wavering tones. The villagers grew healthier, crops were abundant, animals mated and gave birth. Even the old fox managed to catch a careless mouse.

The older girl left for adventures in another town, another country, but the younger one remained, her knowledge growing as she became a part of the trees and the flowers and the creatures around her.

And then one night the witch hunters arrived. Galloping hooves thundered through the village, tearing up clods of earth as their horses churned the mud on the village green. Shouts and whistles brought the villagers from their beds, rubbing their eyes and pulling on cloaks as the men demanded answers to their questions. Sleep-muddled and confused, barely knowing what they were saying, the villagers gave them directions to old Meg's hut, then returned indoors, safe in the knowledge that she would help the men.

Warm in her bed, Julia-Ann slept peacefully on, unaware of what was happening in the village. She shifted in her sleep, dreaming of distant thunder and clouds scudding across the sky before a terrible storm broke.

The morning after, the young girl ran to the hut, eager to start the day's magic. The smell of smoke hung heavy in the air as she neared Meg's home, and she slowed to a bewildered walk, a sense of foreboding entering her heart. The creatures of the forest were silent, nothing stirred among the trees. Parting the last branches, Julia-Ann stepped into the clearing. And screamed.

The hut was a blackened shell, the wood still smouldering from the fire that had been raging only a little while before. The herbs were gone, the ceiling collapsed, and the only scent was the acrid smell of smoke and ashes. Silent, she walked across the clearing, too shocked to cry, her steps faltering as she drew nearer to the hut.

The door was gone, burned to nothing, the walls a mere blackened husk. And in the corner, huddled together, lay the crow, the fox, and old Meg. Together until the end, their bodies joined while their spirits had left for another place.

The girl wept bitter tears, her soul aching for the old woman who had taught them so much, anger churning through her for the men who had destroyed what she'd held dearest. She knelt beside Meg's body and vowed she would continue the old woman's work, in secret, until the day she could stand proud and show everyone what she had become.

As she left the hut, Julia-Ann spied Meg's shawl hanging on a nearby bush and took it, wrapping it around her shoulders.

'One day I will stand before the witch hunters, wearing this,' she held her head straight and proud, 'and I will speak against them, in the name of Meg, and every woman who has suffered like her.'

They sat, motionless, while the candles slowly melted, the room heavy with their memories as the flames flickered and finally died. Katherine clambered to her feet, hampered by her belly, and pulled back the velvet curtains. Gemma was surprised to see it was still daylight; she'd half expected to see the moon high in the sky.

Julia-Ann stood, and began collecting the candle holders. She moved awkwardly, her body tense, but Gemma noticed a look of determination on her friend's face. The same determination Gemma felt pulse inside her own body.

'What did we just do?' Gemma asked, looking at the others.

Julia-Ann shuffled her feet and glanced at Katherine, who gestured to her to speak.

'Meg showed us many things that we can't explain. How a silver blade dipped in moonlit water can cure a stye, or how a needle cast with thread woven on a sunless day and then placed under someone's pillow can stop them from telling lies. She had a spell for everything.'

'Such as a spell for telling our darkest secrets?' Gemma rubbed her forehead, still unsettled by her experience.

'It is merely a combination of herbs, suggestion, and the strengthening of a bond that is already there.' Katherine sat down on a stool with a groan and stretched her legs out. 'Meg taught us that much of her "magic" was based on a person's beliefs. She was able to help people who no remedy could cure, people whose maladies were in their humours rather than their bodies, simply because of that belief.'

'That is why we say spells while making the remedies,' Julia-Ann said. 'The villagers have more faith in the cures if they believe there is some magic in them as well. Meg taught us that the words aren't important, it's the mystery that surrounds the ritual.'

'Meg sounds as wise as my mother was,' Gemma said wistfully. 'I wish I could have known her.'

Katherine clasped her hands together in front of her belly. 'We will use what we have learned to help people, and pass her teachings down to our children too. She will not be forgotten, we'll continue to do good in her name.' She hesitated. 'And if we can use the rituals to do good, we can also use them to do harm as well. If someone believes a spell will heal, then what is to stop them believing that it can curse them? I believe this is why our paths have crossed. We three have something to teach the other. Perhaps this is the answer to the fury that rages within each of us. Will you join us?'

The perfume of the candles still hung in the air; purple notes of lavender and hints of red cherry blossom, together with delicate pink brushstrokes of wild rose, threaded their way among the images in Gemma's mind. The world stopped for a moment as myriad paths of the future once again lay before her, demanding she choose her destiny. She closed her eyes, trembling at the thought of making the wrong choice. *Help me*, she cried out in her mind, hoping that Bob would hear her, but she knew that it was her decision to make, no one else's.

Head bowed, she trembled as she fought to choose her path. Centuries of healing struggled against the hurt and destruction the witch hunters had caused. Memories of her father's betrayal, of Tullia standing beside William Hopkins as he tore up the letter of pardon from the Medici women that would have saved Morgana, of her mother's frail body when she last saw her, locked in the prison in Lucca, a mere shadow of the woman she had been before, of Rina returning to her family, destroyed by the nightmares of her imprisonment, all came back to taunt her, prodding at her heart until she thought she would go mad from the pain. There was but one choice she could make, and yet she hesitated.

When she spoke, only a whisper came out. 'I will join you.'

Chapter Twenty-Seven

May-June 1631

Before they could begin to perform any spells, either of healing or curses, Gemma knew she had to take the time to heal herself. During the hot, balmy days that followed the spring rains, there was nothing she liked better than sitting on the bench in the kitchen garden. Birds bathed in the rainwater that collected in the barrel beneath the low-hanging eaves of the kitchen, and dragonflies and damselflies skimmed across its surface. Their brilliant colours flashed in the bright sunlight, their jewel-like bodies a welcome and familiar sight to her.

Few people came to the garden, other than the cook and the kitchen maids, so Gemma could sit in quiet contemplation or gather herbs for some tisanes or simple remedies. The quiet calm of the manor, and the pleasant welcome from Count Bianchi and his family, helped Gemma begin to heal from the traumas of the past months. As the weeks passed she could feel the tension and worry fall from her, giving her the strength to look ahead.

That May morning, as she closed her eyes and breathed in the aromas of lavender, sage, rosemary, mint, and the myriad other herbs from the garden, for a few moments she could almost imagine she was back in the Grove. The sun warming her skin, a light breeze caressing her hair, the sounds of the bees as they flew among the flowers, birds singing from the branches of the trees, all evoked memories of the cottage, and her mother. For the first time in a long time, Gemma felt truly at home.

A rustle of skirts intruded upon her thoughts, and the wooden bench beneath her creaked as someone sat down. She opened her eyes and smiled to see Julia-Ann beside her, and Katherine puffing as she walked up the garden path.

'Gemma, look!' Julia-Ann handed her a brilliant blue feather with black markings. 'It's a gift, to brighten your day.'

Gemma took the feather, caressing the delicate strands. 'Thank you.' She held it by the quill, to keep it safe, then looked at her friends. 'I've been thinking... You asked me to join you, to learn the rituals. You've been kind enough to give me this time to myself, to work my feelings out, and I am grateful for that. But now, I'm ready.'

'A-are you sure?' Katherine asked, still slightly out of breath.

'Yes. I'm sure.' Gemma hesitated a moment when the damselfly settled on her hand, then gave a small sigh of relief when it didn't fly away. '*We're* ready.' The damselfly bobbed its head, as though it agreed, then flew off after a passing mosquito.

'We will begin tonight, after dinner,' Julia-Ann declared. She hesitated, then continued, 'But I feel that you need something more to occupy your days. Tell us something you could do that would make you happy. Perhaps we can help.'

Katherine leaned over. 'Anything at all. When I was younger, this place was wonderful for my soul, somewhere to escape to when life became too much for me at–'

She didn't say the word 'home', but they understood what she meant.

'I miss tending to the villagers,' Gemma said. 'Here, surrounded by all these plants, my hands are itching to pick them and prepare a tisane or salve.'

'So why not do it?' Julia-Ann replied. 'Mamma will be delighted, and I know I would love to learn from you.'

'Really?' Gemma felt her spirits rise at the thought of healing once more.

'Of course. Katherine has told me about your skills. We will need them when the baby comes.'

Katherine made a face. 'That's the thing I'm least looking forward to. Is it really as painful as they say?'

'Every woman is different,' Gemma replied.

Julia-Ann snorted. 'Mamma said she would never go through it again, not even for the king himself!'

Katherine turned pale.

'Like I said, every woman is different,' Gemma said hurriedly. 'The most important thing is to stay calm. I'll be at your side throughout.'

Katherine held out her hand. 'Will you take a look–?'

'No.' Gemma interrupted Katherine before she could say any more. 'You will survive it, just as millions of other women have since time began. I have no need of predictions or visions to know this.'

Katherine spoke again, but Gemma couldn't concentrate on what her friend was saying. A dark cloud passed over the sun, the brilliant colours of the garden becoming dull and drab, and Gemma shivered. She sent a silent prayer to the Healer, but it wasn't until she saw her damselfly flit past that her heart felt lighter.

Gemma learned how to create an altar, made of budding twigs, birds' feathers, odd-shaped stones, empty snails' shells, and other things they found around the garden. Broken eggshells, a solitary butterfly wing, a soft rose petal – everything was precious, everything was saved and taken to Katherine's room.

In the middle of the altar sat the pearl on its velvet cushion. Gemma was still wary, but could sense no evil coming from it. Instead, it absorbed the light cast onto the objects by the candles, as hungrily as a child suckling from its mother's breast. The three women joined hands, creating an unbroken circle around the altar, sealing the light within the pearl, creating a powerful charm for their time of need.

Three women, three hearts beating with the rhythm of the earth, three souls searching for retribution. Sometimes Gemma would awake in the cold hours of the middle of the night, her heart thudding; fearful of what, she didn't know.

Chapter Twenty-Eight

The vicar stood just inside the front door, a tall, imposing man with a straight back and a stern expression. He broke into a smile, his forehead creasing, as Countess Bianchi hurried towards him.

'Countess, I'm so pleased I found you at home.' His voice boomed along the hallway, reaching the parlour where Gemma was peeking out of the doorway, curious.

'Come back and let me finish my story,' Katherine complained, her sewing laying unheeded on her lap.

'Shh, just a moment.' Gemma gestured to her two friends to keep quiet, and turned her attention back to the scene outside.

'Reverend Fairfax, what can I do for you?' Countess Bianchi gestured to him to follow her, but he shook his head.

'I came to plead for some flowers from your gardens, to decorate the church today. The roses at the rectory are woefully inadequate, and blighted by some black fungus. I would be forever grateful.'

'Why, of course.' She turned. 'Oh, there you are, Gemma! Call Katherine and Julia-Ann, and come with me to the garden. Collect some baskets on your way. Reverend, we shall be at the church before lunch!'

Blushing, Gemma returned inside the parlour. 'It appears we must pick flowers for the church,' she told them.

The three girls chattered together as they followed Countess Bianchi through the village. Their boots and the hems of their dresses were soon covered in a thin layer of dust from the dirt track. People stopped and greeted them, exclaiming over the posies they were carrying in their baskets. Gemma felt her spirits rise and her troubles fall away. The warmth of the sun, the clear blue sky, the meadows full of wildflowers and insects and verdant grass, filled her with joy and optimism.

A scream brought them all to an abrupt halt. A dull thud and startled cries came from a little further ahead. Gemma dropped her basket, gathered her skirts and ran down the road, heedless of the clouds of dust she was kicking up. Several people stood in a group, arguing about what best to do, as they stared down at an injured girl lying on the ground.

'What's happened?' Gemma asked, pushing her way through. Her mouth dry, she looked at the girl, desperately trying to think what her mother would have done.

'She was up in the tree, gettin' her brother's ball down off the roof, an' she fell.' A neighbour pointed at a leather-clad ball in the grass nearby, some of the wool and straw stuffing poking out from a burst seam.

Gemma knelt down beside the girl. She sucked in a breath at the sight: one of her arms was sticking out at an odd angle, and her leg was twisted beneath her. Everything Morgana had ever taught her flew out of Gemma's head, and she could feel the panic rising.

Then a hand touched her shoulder. 'Steady breaths, in and out,' came Katherine's voice, soft and gentle in her ear. 'Try to stay calm, you know what to do.'

Gemma wiped sweat from her face, her hands clammy, and nodded. She took a few shuddering breaths and cleared her mind of everything except the girl before her. A flash of blue at the corner of her eye let her know that the damselfly was near. It gave her strength.

'Everything's going to be all right,' she murmured, more for herself than her patient. She could sense Katherine and Julia-Ann standing behind her, their quiet presence lending her the calm she needed.

The girl let out a low moan as Gemma gently ran her hands over her, checking for more broken bones.

'What's her name?' she asked an elderly woman leaning over them, watching intently.

'Elisabeth.' The woman coughed and wiped her nose on her sleeve. 'Elisabeth Osborne. Her mother's a servant at the manor, an' her father is out in the fields. Elisabeth here looks after her little brother durin' the day.'

'Thank you.' Gemma turned to the girl, her hands trembling. 'Elisabeth, can you hear me?'

The girl stirred and tried to move. 'Robbie?'

'Stay still while I see where you've hurt yourself,' Gemma told her. The girl's eyes were open, and although unfocused, they weren't rolling up in her head. 'Your arm is broken, but I need to look at your leg.'

Elisabeth cried out while Gemma moved her as gently as she could. 'You're so brave,' Gemma told her. 'Just a little more… good girl.' She sat back on her heels, her whole body tense with nerves. 'Your leg hurts, but it's not broken. But we need to tend to your arm immediately.' She had seen her mother deal with broken limbs before, and knew that her patient would suffer terrible pain. Leaving the bone to heal by itself would likely mean a permanent disfigurement, perhaps even loss of the use of the arm. She turned to her friends.

'Can you find some men to carry her indoors, as carefully as possible.'

The girl burst into tears. 'I've got to find Robbie!' She sat up, leaning on her injured arm, and fainted.

With her patient unconscious, Gemma worked quickly. A search through the wood pile outside found some wood that was perfect for making a splint, and another villager brought some flax string. While Katherine and Julia-Ann held Elisabeth still, Gemma pushed the bones back into place, then put the arm between the two pieces of wood and securely tied it all together with the string.

Just as Gemma was finishing, a small bundle of dirty rags came bursting through the door and threw itself at Elisabeth with a yell. Katherine caught the boy and held the struggling child in her arms.

'Are you Robbie?' she asked, raising her voice to be heard above his shouts.

He kicked out his legs. 'What're you doin' to my sister?' he demanded, his voice shrill. Clenched fists hammered against Katherine's shoulders.

'That's enough of that.' Julia-Ann put her arms around the boy's chest and pinned his arms to his body. 'We're looking after Elisabeth, she fell off the roof.'

He suddenly went limp, and Katherine gratefully put him on the floor.

'I runned away,' he said, shamefaced.

'Why?'

He burst into tears. 'Th-thought she was dead, she weren't movin'. 'Twas my fault, I threw the ball up there on purpose. She shouted at me 'cause I spilt the milk.' He sniffed, and wiped snot on his sleeve, leaving a glistening trail. 'I just wanted to annoy her, like she was annoyin' me. I didn't mean for her to get hurt.'

Gemma turned and crouched down to his level. 'She's got a broken arm and a lot of bruises, it could have been a lot worse.' His face crumpled up again, and she hastily added, 'She's going to be all right, don't worry. I'll prepare a salve for the bruising and a tisane with herbs for the pain, and bring it here this afternoon.' A bead of sweat trickled down her brow and she wiped it away, thankful that it was over. 'Sit with her now, she'll be awake soon and giving you orders again!' She ruffled the boy's hair and stood up, stretching her back.

'You knew exactly what to do,' Katherine said as they left the cottage.

'I've seen my mother mend broken bones before,' Gemma replied. She clutched onto Julia-Ann's arm as the world spun around her.

'Come, sit down before you faint,' Katherine said, helping her over to a nearby stool. Gemma sat, relieved to rest her trembling legs. 'Your mother would be proud of you, and how you helped that girl today.'

'There can be complications.' Gemma swallowed. 'I might not have set the bones properly, there might be fragments left inside, she might lose the arm or... or worse.'

'But for the moment she is well, and I'm sure you will take good care of her. We'll cast a healing spell to help.'

A group of women stared as they walked past, some whispering behind their hands, then one stepped forward, her cheeks flushed.

'Excuse me, milady.'

Gemma turned to see a young woman, her belly huge with child, a rash covering one side of her face. 'Yes?'

'They says–' She gestured behind her at the other women standing huddled together, and cleared her throat in embarrassment. 'They says you're a healer woman, come from abroad.'

'News travels fast,' the countess said, sounding amused.

'I know some healing,' Gemma replied.

'More than some,' Katherine muttered.

'I... We was wondering if you could help us with our complaints.' The woman hunched her shoulders, clearly unhappy at being the spokeswoman for her friends. She pointed at her face. 'I've had this since I got with child, and Christine there got a thorn in her foot and it's all swollen now, and–'

Gemma held her hand up. 'One at a time! Of course I'll help you.' She hesitated. 'But I will have to think about where I can see you. I need somewhere quiet where you can sit down and I can take my time to understand what's wrong.'

'May I interrupt?' Countess Bianchi moved next to Gemma. 'Julia-Ann told me a while ago about your desire to tend to people, as you did in Tuscany. After speaking with my husband, the count and I would like to offer you one of our barns that is standing empty. I can get the servants to have it ready by noon tomorrow.'

'That would be wonderful!' Gemma hadn't felt so happy since... she could barely remember. A thought occurred, and her excitement waned a little. 'I'll also need some herbs, I don't have any with me. And a place to prepare the remedies.'

'I have a garden full of herbs, you may use whatever you want. And I will tell cook to let you use the kitchen.'

'I-I don't know what to say.'

'Then it's decided.' She turned to the woman. 'Tell your friends to come to the manor tomorrow.'

The woman curtsied. 'Thank you, Countess,' she said breathlessly, bobbing her head. 'Thank you, milady.'

Gemma watched as the woman returned to her friends, their excited chatter drawing other villagers to them. 'Thank you,' she said, with tears in her eyes.

'You may yet regret this,' the countess said with a smile. 'My offer comes with a condition.'

'Anything.'

'I would like Julia-Ann to assist you, so that the village will have another healer when you leave.'

'But I won't–'

The countess held up her hand. 'Don't make promises you can't keep. Do you not have someone waiting for you? That is more than enough reason to go back.'

Gemma blushed.

'Besides, you will need an assistant. I imagine half the village will turn up in the morning.'

'We'll be ready for them.' Gemma smiled at Katherine and Julia-Ann. 'That is one promise I *can* keep.' She saw a flash of brilliant blue dart to her right, and felt a calm descend over her. With the damselfly there, it was as though she had her mother's blessing.

'Good.' The countess pointed at their baskets, left carelessly on the ground. 'Now perhaps we could take these to the church. We are going to be very late, the vicar will not be pleased!'

Chapter Twenty-Nine

Gemma went to check Elisabeth early the next morning. She'd found the girl awake and in some pain, but otherwise well. Her mother was there, a thin, nervous woman who couldn't stand still and chewed on her nails.

'This is a tisane made from willow bark, camomile, and rosemary, it will help with the pain,' Gemma told her, handing her a pouch of herbs and a small wooden spoon. 'Put one spoon in a cup of hot water and let it steep until it's cooled, then make Elisabeth drink it. You can add some honey if she doesn't like the taste.'

The woman nodded. 'And her arm? How long will it take to mend?'

'A few weeks, I'm afraid.'

The woman's face fell, and Gemma thought she was going to burst into tears.

'She can't do any heavy work and must use it as little as possible, so it will mend properly,' Gemma added.

'But what am I supposed to do with Robbie?' the woman wailed. ''E's always getting into mischief, an' I can't look after 'im while I'm up at the manor.'

Gemma turned to the boy, who was sitting on the floor among some dirty rags, making clicking noises with his tongue as he played with a stick.

'Hello, Robbie.'

He looked up at her. 'D'you like my horse?' He held up the stick to show her.

'It's beautiful.' Gemma crouched down beside him and saw that he had a collection of sticks. 'You have a whole herd of horses.' She smiled at him, and was rewarded with a wide smile that made his cheeks dimple.

'One day I'm goin' to have a horse of my own,' he confided. 'A real one.'

'I have a horse. Her name's Ombra.' Gemma thought wistfully of the mare, and wondered how she was, what she was doing, if Claude was taking good care of her as he'd promised.

'Ombra? What a funny name.'

'It means shadow, in Italian,' Gemma told him.

'Italian? Are you Italian, then?' He screwed up his face and peered at her.

Gemma laughed. 'Yes.'

'You don't look Italian. You look exactly like us.' Robbie turned back to his sticks and began playing with them again.

An idea came to Gemma and before she could stop herself she turned to Elisabeth's mother. 'The countess told me that Robbie can come to the manor during the day, if it would help you while Elisabeth is recovering. Perhaps he could help out in the stables.'

The woman burst into tears. 'That would be a weight off my mind.' She leaned back against the wall of the cottage, sniffing loudly. 'With my 'usband workin' away and it just bein' the three of us, I didn't know what to do.'

Gemma held the woman's hand and gave it a squeeze, hoping fervently that the countess wouldn't be angry with her.

The villagers started arriving at the manor shortly before noon. Gemma gently extracted the thorn from Christine's foot and bathed it in a warm bowl with camomile and lavender, before binding it with a poultice of onion, calendula, and yarrow.

'Mrs Mitchell, you must rest your foot and keep it clean,' Gemma admonished, 'otherwise it will get a lot worse.'

Christine chuckled. 'You 'ave seen my brood, 'aven't you?' She gestured to the three young children sitting on the ground beside her, and a tiny baby lay nestled against her breast, thumb in its mouth. 'That's just the 'alf of them, the others are back at 'ome. Rest, she says.'

'Try to keep it clean, then.' Gemma handed her some more strips of linen and a pouch of herbs. 'Take these, and change the poultice every night, before you go to bed. If you come back tomorrow morning, I'll have a salve you can put on your foot as well.'

'Like I've got time to keep comin' back and forth,' the woman grumbled. She wriggled off the chair and stood, tentatively putting her weight on her bad foot. 'Well I never! It doesn't 'urt so much.'

'That's because the herbs I used draw out any nastiness,' Gemma explained. 'If you come back for the salve, you'll see that it will get better in no time.'

'I'll send my Diana up for it tomorrow,' Christine promised. 'Come on, you little beggars, time to get 'ome before this'un starts squalling for 'is dinner.'

Gemma saw the children eyeing up the platter of biscuits cook had made the day before. 'Go ahead, take some. They're for anyone who comes today.'

The children jumped to their feet and grabbed one each, then scarpered out of the barn without waiting for their mother, Mrs Mitchell hobbling after them.

'No rest for the wicked, eh?'

Gemma turned to find the pregnant woman with the rash on her face waiting patiently by the door.

'There's a fair few of us, milady,' she said as she sat down on the bench.

Gemma looked up, and saw a queue of villagers outside the barn, stretching as far as she could see.

'Best we get started, then,' she said.

Her spirits lifted when she saw Julia-Ann and the countess walking towards her, wearing simple linen dresses as she had suggested the evening before. They greeted the villagers, before Julia-Ann hurried over.

'Here I am, ready to help. Mamma asks if she can watch as well. She is interested in seeing what you do.'

'Of course.' Gemma looked around. 'There should be a stool somewhere...'

'Don't worry about that. We'll keep out of your way, just tell us what to do.' Julia-Ann rubbed her hands together, her excitement palpable.

As she worked, examining each person and talking through their ailments with Julia-Ann, Gemma was vaguely aware of the countess's presence nearby, quietly watching while talking to the waiting villagers. When Gemma needed more clean linen, the countess had already prepared some.

'Would you like to help as well?' Gemma asked before thinking. She snapped her mouth shut, worried she had offended the noblewoman. Earlier that morning she'd had to tell her about offering to let Robbie work in the stables, fearing a scolding. However, the countess had told her it was an excellent idea, and that she looked forward to seeing the young boy. Gemma tensed, ready to be told off.

The countess smiled and moved closer. 'I was hoping you would ask!'

Gemma sat on her stool and leaned back against the wall of the barn, every muscle in her body aching. She'd lost count of the number of villagers she'd seen that day. After sending Julia-Ann back to the manor to make sure Katherine was all right, she'd written down everyone's names, their maladies, and her prescribed cures in a journal the countess had given her. All she needed to do now was collect the herbs she needed and prepare the remedies. She sighed deeply, and stretched her arms above her head, trying to relieve the stiffness.

'It's been a long day.' Countess Bianchi attempted to stifle a yawn, without success.

Gemma nodded. 'Thank you for your help. I didn't think so many people would come.'

'We have a physician who passes through the village three or four times a year, but other than him there is no one else. There was a wise woman, but she–' The countess bowed her head.

'Julia-Ann told me about Meg, and what the witch hunters did to her.'

'It was during the first days, when they swept through the area like a plague. We did what we could, but unfortunately by the time we realised what they intended to do, it was too late. She was a good woman, whose only crime was helping people in need.'

'You knew her?'

The countess smiled. 'I asked her to teach Julia-Ann and Katherine. Ever since they were little I saw they could do things, such as seeing the future in a puddle, or making charms from feathers, and I wanted them to learn to use it properly. I knew Meg, everyone around here did, and I sent them to her, so that they would be safe. I made the mistake of telling Katherine's parents – they were so horrified that they forbid Katherine to come here and took her away. Shortly afterwards, the witch hunters arrived. I often wonder if–' She shook her head. 'No, I will not think such things. It is too much to bear.'

'Why do men do these things? What are they scared of?' Tears pricked at Gemma's eyes.

The countess put a hand on Gemma's arm. 'It won't happen again. They will not come back, and in the unlikely event they should, you are under my husband's protection.'

Gemma shuddered. 'I pray that will never happen.' She finished writing up her notes in her journal, closed the book, and lay the quill on the desk next to it, then sighed and rose wearily from the stool. 'I'm afraid I must gather some herbs and make the remedies for tomorrow.'

The countess stood as well. 'May I come with you?'

'Yes, of course,' Gemma replied, delighted to have company.

The evening was cool and fresh, the garden alive with insects ceaselessly flitting to and fro in search of food before the sun set. Birds chirped all around them, and the heady scent of lavender and roses filled the air. Gemma loved walking through the garden at this time of day; its tranquil atmosphere calmed her soul and for a short while she could forget her troubles.

'The villagers have kept you busy today.' Countess Bianchi spoke quietly, her voice full of admiration.

'I remember watching my mother tending to the people of Gallicano,' Gemma replied. 'Some days it seemed never-ending, others she only saw a handful of people. The villagers need my assistance, and I am happy to keep my hands and mind occupied.'

'Even when you can do nothing for them?'

Gemma knew the countess was thinking of the elderly woman she had seen earlier. She had been so fragile that a gust of wind could have blown her over, thin wisps of hair covered her liver-spotted scalp, and her fingers were knotted with rheumatism. But her eyes had sparkled with life, and when Gemma had told her that there were no herbs that could cure the lump she felt in her chest, she had given a toothy smile and shrugged, as though she already knew. Gemma had given her herbs to make a tisane that would help with the pain, and almost burst into tears when the old woman thanked her and gently patted her hand before hobbling away. She couldn't always see a person's last moments when she touched them, as Morgana had, but she could see their future. And Gemma had seen the old woman return to her cottage, boil a pot of water, and tip the herbs into it, adding her own special ingredient that grew in her garden to ensure a painless ending.

'Sometimes the patient knows what is best for them,' she said. 'All I can do is help them on their way.'

The countess thought for a moment, then nodded. 'You have a wise head on young shoulders. Your mother must have been a very special woman.'

Gemma blinked away the tears that suddenly pricked at her eyes, and brushed a burr from her skirts. 'I think I will sit in the herb garden a while, it helps to calm me after a busy day.'

'I will make sure no one disturbs you.' The countess turned to go, then paused. 'Your mother would be proud of you.' She left in a swirl of skirts, the scent of rose water drifting in her wake.

Gemma wiped her eyes and sniffed. The countess's words had stirred up all her emotions once again, the hardened core of her that still wanted revenge for her mother's death vying with her calling as a healer. Confused, torn between healing and hurting, she continued on her way to the kitchen garden.

The cool air outside was a pleasant contrast to the stuffiness inside the barn, and she took several deep breaths before looking around. The garden stretched before her, carefully tended lawns edged with perfectly shaped rose bushes, and the scent of lavender drifted in the air, together with the soft drone of bees as they flew among the purple flowers. Gemma followed the path, stopping to breathe in the delicate perfume of the roses or to watch the bees collect the nectar.

A memory of other bees, deep in the woods surrounding the cottage in Tuscany, popped into her head, but she brushed it away before it could intrude.

Rounding a corner, she entered the kitchen garden, which was filled with every herb imaginable. She crouched down and brushed her fingertips over their leaves, releasing familiar scents of rosemary, sage, marjoram, and mint. Quietly saying the healers' blessing, she picked some sprigs of the herbs she required, then went to a nearby bench and sat down. It was a piece of heaven, she thought; with the aromas drifting around her from the bunch of herbs on her lap, she could almost see her mother once more, bent over the plants in the Grove, choosing the ones she needed for her remedies, tending to the plants, dragonflies flitting over her head as she worked.

Gemma lifted the herbs to her nose, evoking memories both wonderful and sad, looking back on times that were and that could never be again. Rage simmered in her veins, a sudden fury that made her feel lightheaded and sick. She didn't know how to quell it, how to stop her heart pounding with hatred, how to banish the dark thoughts that crowded her mind, and she grew fearful of what she might do.

The damselfly landed on the bench beside her, its thin blue body trembling in the evening breeze. Her breathing settled in time with its movement, the rise and fall of her chest gradually slowing. Her mind cleared, and she thought of Katherine and Julia-Ann, of the promise they had made to each other, of their pasts that bound them together, and the future that awaited, and slowly the anger and hurt faded away. By the time she rose and made her way back to the house, the damselfly had gone.

Chapter Thirty

July 1631

The days slipped one into another and became weeks, and then a month. Gemma spent her mornings preparing concoctions with herbs from the kitchen garden, then tended to the villagers who arrived from mid-afternoon onward. Agatha, the cook, set aside some space on a table for her to work, and made sure there was a pot of water already boiling by the time Gemma came in from the garden, her basket brimming with the herbs she required.

Katherine and Julia-Ann cast healing spells over the remedies, heads bent, hands held above the pots and jars, eyes closed as their whispers conjured up the warmth of the sun, the blue of the sky, the feathery dust of a butterfly's wings, the pollen-brushed legs of a bumble bee, the hushed silence of a meadow at noon, the soft whicker of a curious horse, the deep, vibrating purr of a sleepy cat. Gemma worked as they spoke, a calm stealing over her as the spells hovered in the air, slowly sinking down into the potions she had prepared.

Even Agatha and the kitchen servants worked in silence, hands reaching out for ingredients without turning their heads, unerringly taking exactly what they needed while concentrating on the pots before them. They all moved in harmony, each shifting slightly to let another pass, no words needed as the spells threaded among them.

And then Katherine and Julia-Ann lowered their hands, opened their eyes, and took long, deep breaths as the world returned to normal. The kitchen filled with the sounds of clattering pots and chopping knives once more, and the servants began to talk, quietly at first. Gemma was always the last to break out of the trance, reluctant to leave behind the calmness that, for a little while, took her back to the Dragonfly Grove.

The countess spoke a few words with the last villager to leave, then walked across the barn to where Gemma was sitting and handed her a cup of water. 'I've been meaning to ask, how is young Elisabeth Osborne?'

Gemma smiled. 'She is doing very well. Her arm is almost healed, and is as straight as it was before. She has been very lucky.'

'In particular because you were nearby when it happened.'

'How is her brother doing up at the stables?'

'Paul, the head groom, says he's a willing lad and quick to learn. He's content to clean the stables and feed the horses, he loves being around them.'

Gemma felt the usual pang at the mention of horses. 'They're beautiful creatures. I'm glad he's doing well.' She tidied up her book and quill and stowed them away in a wooden box.

'Will you accompany me to the herb garden?' she asked the countess.

'I would be delighted to.'

The evening was warm, and the crickets chirruped their songs among the tall grasses, occasionally leaping away and startling the two women as they passed. The day was drawing to a close, the sky a blend of orange and red and purple as the sun sank.

They worked together collecting the plants, Gemma pointing out to the countess which ones she needed. After a while, the countess broke the silence.

'The grandson of the Reverend Attersole, a good friend of mine, is fascinated by plants and herbs, and their use in curing people.' She spoke quietly, as though mindful of breaking the quiet calm of the garden. 'Nicholas would like to study medicine, but I'm afraid his grandfather dreams of him becoming a church minister. He wants the boy to go to study Theology at Cambridge next year.'

'I see,' Gemma replied, although she wasn't sure why the countess was telling her this.

'As you have so many patients, I thought that perhaps another willing pair of hands might be welcome.' Countess Bianchi held a sprig of lavender to her nose and inhaled its scent, then glanced across at her. 'Poor Nicholas was distraught when the Reverend forbade him to use the library, and left him only a Bible to read. The boy has an affinity with the natural world, and it is a pity to see him waste his talents. Julia-Ann has learnt much and is eager to help you every day. I'm sure Nicholas would be just as keen to learn.'

Gemma thought of the long hours spent that day with her patients, and at her desk writing up her notes, the knots in her shoulders twinging in sympathy. Even with Julia-Ann by her side, and the countess stepping in to help when necessary, there were too many people needing attention. And soon Katherine would need someone by her side as her pregnancy progressed. Gemma was already worried, as she was larger than normal at this stage.

'Another pair of hands would make things much easier,' she said, still uncertain.

'That's wonderful. I shall send a letter to Nicholas. His father died before he was born, and his mother brought him back to her family home. But she is a weak woman who cannot stand up to her father, and I fear Nicholas isn't happy. The Reverend will not listen to reason but insists on the boy doing as he says. There is already a rift between the two, and I cannot see things ending well. A distraction would be a blessing, for both.' The countess must have seen Gemma's hesitation. 'Perhaps you could try for a few weeks, see how things go.'

'That would be best,' Gemma said, relieved. Julia-Ann was a dedicated student, eager to learn, but Gemma had no idea what Nicholas was like. What if she didn't get on with him?

The balmy days of July melted into August. The sun-scorched ground became dry and dusty, and the plants wilted in the heat. Servants did their best to water the thirsty garden, and Gemma left out bowls of water for the birds and insects. She was standing by the lavender bushes, pouring a jug of water into one of the bowls, when the snap of a twig caught her attention and made her turn round.

A young man stumbled over a stone, managing to right himself as the momentum carried him forward. He took a couple of steps, his face flushed, then noticed her watching him and stopped. She put down the jug, suppressing a giggle.

'My apologies. I tripped over that stone–' He gestured behind him, shaking his head. 'It's not a good first impression, is it?'

Gemma noticed he was holding a short, oddly shaped stick in his hand, smoke rising lazily from it into the sky. He stuck the end of the stick in his mouth and breathed in, then blew out a foul-smelling plume of smoke.

Gemma waved the smoke away, her eyes watering as she coughed. 'What on earth is that?'

'This? It's a clay pipe and tobacco. They're all the rage, you know.'

Gemma frowned. 'I prefer breathing in clean air, if it's all the same to you.' She paused. 'What did you mean, it's not a good first impression?'

The young man put the pipe down on a nearby stone. 'I can smoke later. The countess told me I would find you here. She said you come here whenever you can.'

'It's a beautiful spot. I find it calms me.' Gemma brushed her fingers over the tips of the lavender, releasing the sweet perfume into the air.

He gestured at the herbs all around them. 'I dreamed of using plants to cure people, after I found a book in my grandfather's library. I used to pore over the illustrations and words, I practically learned it off by heart. But it wasn't to be.'

'Ah.' She realised who he was. 'So you're the Reverend's grandson.'

He bowed deeply. 'Nicholas Culpeper.'

'Gemma Innocenti.'

'The Italian contessa. Countess Bianchi told me about you. My grandfather had high hopes that I would become one of the clergy, make something of myself.' He shuddered. 'He's told me I must study Theology at Cambridge – can you think of anything more boring? I want to cure people's bodies, not their souls!'

'I can't, no.' Gemma felt sorry for him. 'The countess seems very fond of you.'

'She and her husband are good friends of my family, I believe they have known my grandfather for many years. They tried to persuade him to let me become a physician, but he insists that I follow in his footsteps. When I received the countess's letter, I came immediately.' He glanced around, then leaned closer. 'She says you know everything about plants. Is that true?'

Gemma held her hands out, her fingers stained with grass and dirt. 'Perhaps not everything, but I know a great deal, yes.'

'Really?' He sat beside her on the bench, his eyes sparkling with eagerness.

'I come from a long line of healers. My mother taught me many things.'

He clasped his hands together. 'The countess said you could teach me. I would like that very much. If that is all right with you.'

Nicholas's eager enthusiasm was refreshing, but still Gemma hesitated. His grandfather would not be pleased if he found out what his grandson was doing. Would he bring the wrath of the witch hunters upon her again? She regretted not having thought it through more before agreeing to teach the boy.

'Look! Isn't it beautiful?' Nicholas suddenly exclaimed.

She glanced to where he pointed, and saw the damselfly resting on a blade of grass, its bright colours twinkling in the sun. She spent a moment contemplating it, then turned to Nicholas.

'It is. All right, I will teach you.' She hoped she wouldn't regret her decision, but she trusted the damselfly.

He rubbed his hands together, and beamed at her. 'I am your eager student, milady. I'm known as Nick to my friends.'

Gemma kept her gaze fixed on the damselfly. 'Well, Mr Culpeper, I hope you are a dedicated scholar, as you have much to learn.'

Chapter Thirty-One

Gemma found Nicholas to be an enthusiastic assistant. He made notes as she explained what ailments she used each plant for, and was quick to memorise the preparation and remedies. When she went to the barn each afternoon she found him already there, talking to the villagers. He suggested putting out blocks of wood they could sit on while waiting, and often pointed out if a patient was stoically hiding some pain or injury.

He paid careful attention as she tended to her patients, and after a few days Gemma began asking him what he would do. At first he was hesitant, unsure of himself, but with her encouragement he used the knowledge he had learned and soon offered suggestions without her having to ask.

'The secret is to treat each person with respect,' Gemma said, washing her hands in a bowl of hot water, the herb-scented soap soothing her aching fingers. 'I remember I giggled once when old Signor Corsi came to my mother for warts on his...' She blushed, then muttered, 'You know, down below. After he left, she sat me down and said, "No matter what these people come for, they've trusted us with their innermost secrets, and the least we can do is behave with dignity. Even if they do have warts in funny places." You didn't raise an eyebrow when Mrs Browne pulled up her skirts!'

Nicholas shrugged. 'Before Grandfather banished me from the library, I read all the books I could about medicine and anatomy. I read about practically every malady a human can suffer from, usually with illustrations!' He shrugged. 'How can people live for years with their problems, carry on their daily lives in such pain? Especially when it can be easily relieved!'

'Even if there was a physician nearby, hardly anyone could afford to pay him for his services,' Gemma replied. 'We are lucky that the countess has given us this space to tend to people.'

'That's true.' Nicholas stood, deep in thought, then sighed. 'If only you could teach everyone about plants and cures, no one would have to suffer.'

The summer passed slowly, each day running into the other. Nicholas was a guest at the manor but passed his free time in the library, studying, or going for a stroll in the gardens. With Julia-Ann taking care of Katherine, who was finding it increasingly difficult to move about, Gemma saw little of her friends. She enjoyed the evenings, when they retired to the parlour after dinner. There they would talk about a variety of topics, until someone yawned and declared they were going to bed.

These were the moments that Gemma felt as though she truly belonged, the count and countess as dear to her as her grandparents in Gallicano, Katherine and Julia-Ann the sisters she had never had, and Nicholas... she was uncertain about him. She tried to regard him as a brother, but sometimes she had feelings for him that left her feeling confused.

One hot afternoon they sat in the shade of a weeping willow, its branches drifting over the pond. Dragonflies swooped, scooping up the midges that swarmed over the surface of the water with their long legs. Gemma watched them, entranced, caught up in memories of the Grove and the white fountain at its centre.

'Tell me about the dragonflies.' Nicholas pinched a sprig of lavender from a nearby plant and crushed it between his fingers. He looked at Gemma, his pale skin dotted with freckles from the summer sun, leafy shadows caressing his face. The feathery beginnings of a moustache coated his upper lip, and grey-green eyes sparkled with curiosity, intense in their stare.

She cleared her throat, embarrassed at the sensations rising up in her, a fleeting image of Claude crossing her mind. Folding her hands in her lap, she fixed her gaze on the blades of grass waving in the light breeze.

'There is a legend that has been passed down through my family, from the first Healer, Agnes, all the way to me, which explains the dragonflies' importance to the Innocenti. I think perhaps your grandfather would not be best pleased at my telling it to you.'

Nicholas looked to his left, then to his right. 'My grandfather isn't here. But I am, and I would like to hear it. Please,' he added, as she hesitated.

Gemma nodded. 'Very well. A long time ago, when the world was forming, dragonflies appeared from a huge crack in the earth...' Her words floated on the torpid air as she recited the legend every healer knew by heart, the tale no less magical even though she'd heard it countless times before.

Nicholas remained silent for so long that Gemma grew nervous, waiting for him to say something. When he did, she was stunned.

'I wish my ancestors had been those who followed the dragonflies,' he said wistfully. 'Will you teach me the prayer you say when you pick the herbs you need?'

'O-of course,' she spluttered, when she'd recovered herself. 'You... believe it?'

'Don't tell my grandfather, but I believe more in the powers of healing from plants and nature than in God,' he replied, his eyes downcast. 'I want to learn everything I can from you, before–' He stopped.

'Before?' Gemma asked gently.

He wrung his hands, his brow furrowed as he spoke. 'Grandfather has arranged for me to go to Cambridge next year. To study Theology, as he has always wanted. And I must begin my studies right away, in preparation.' He huffed. 'I won't be able to assist you so often now.'

'Oh.'

'Oh, indeed. I have no desire to study God and religious beliefs, no more than I would like to become an architect or a farmer! All I want is to learn about plants and healing, and help people who cannot pay for a physician. Is that so terrible?' His voice rose as he spoke with passion, his face twisted in anguish.

'My mother once told me to be patient, that our futures are revealed to us at the right moment. If you are destined to become a physician, then that is what will happen.'

He wiped brusquely at his eyes with his sleeve. 'How did you end up here, so far from your home and your family? What is your future, do you know?'

Gemma shook her head. 'What was it that Bob told me?' She thought deeply for a while. 'Ah, yes. "You will always be a healer, it's in your blood. But you are also more. Your destiny is to take the ways of the healers into the world and teach others, so that they might teach the generations to come."'

'Whoever this Bob is, he seems a very wise man,' Nicholas said. 'Here you are, teaching me. It's almost as if it's your destiny.'

'Indeed.' Gemma smiled. 'And perhaps healing people is yours. Only time will tell.'

He grunted, but his body relaxed as he thought over her words. 'Will you ever go back home, do you think?'

'Yes, one day. I have seen it, I know it will happen.'

'It appears you have much more to teach me, Contessa Innocenti.'

Gemma stood, and brushed off her skirts. 'There are more things in this world than you can ever imagine, Nick. More than I can teach you, and much more than even I can know.'

He smiled. 'You called me Nick. Does this mean we're friends now?'

'I believe it does,' Gemma replied. 'But you can still call me Contessa Innocenti.'

She squealed as he threw a handful of lavender over her, and their carefree laughter danced across the surface of the pond.

Chapter Thirty-Two

October 1631

Gemma missed Nicholas's presence while she tended her patients, and his calm, assured way of dealing with trembling children or injured adults. She missed being able to confer with him about their treatment, but most of all she missed the quiet afternoons in the garden, sorting through the ingredients she needed, explaining how the plants would heal. He had gradually come less and less to help her in the barn until he had told her the week before, barely able to hold back tears of anger, that his grandfather had insisted he remain at the vicarage and study.

She gave a sigh and turned back to Mrs Curtis, sitting patiently on the stool.

'Your leg is doing much better now.' Gemma peered at the wound. Mrs Curtis had come to her two weeks earlier with a horrendous, suppurating cut on her calf, caused by a shovel slipping as she dug her vegetable patch. Gemma had been afraid that the infection was too deep in the flesh for her remedies to do any good, but with perseverance and daily cleansing, the flesh was no longer red and weeping pus. 'The unguent is working, but you must keep putting it on the cut for a week or so.' She wrapped a clean strip of linen around the wound. 'Here's enough unguent for the next three days, and some extra linen. You must clean it every day, just as I've done now, put the salve on it and keep it covered with the linen.'

Mrs Curtis took the proffered goods and stowed them away in her basket. 'I must admit, I thought I was goin' to lose me leg,' she said cheerily. 'I was thinkin' 'ow me 'usband would cope with the littl'uns runnin' rings 'round 'im all day long.'

'You're not out of danger yet, Mrs Curtis,' Gemma admonished. 'Clean hands whenever you change the cloth, including your fingernails,' she pointed at the woman's dirt-blackened nails, 'and clean stockings to wear over it. You mustn't let it get dirty or the infection will come back. It would be better that doesn't happen.'

Mrs Curtis paled, and swallowed nervously. 'I-I'll do me best.'

'I know you will.' Gemma patted her arm. 'Come back in three days and we'll see how it's going.' She watched as the woman hobbled away, then turned to the next villager. 'Ruth, lovely to see you again. How is the cough?'

When she went into the parlour later that morning, Julia-Ann and her mother were already there. The countess sat by the bow window, concentrating on her embroidery. She lifted her head and smiled, then gestured to a tray on a nearby table.

'We saved some lunch for you.'

'Thank you,' Gemma said gratefully. Her stomach rumbled at the aroma of the cut meats and pickled vegetables. She flushed. 'I didn't eat anything this morning, there wasn't time.'

Julia-Ann patted the chair next to hers. 'Come, tell us about today's patients.'

Gemma sat down with a groan, the tray on her lap. 'There were some interesting ones today,' she began, speaking with her mouth full of roast pheasant.

The parlour door burst open and Katherine entered, waddling under the weight of her enormous belly. She headed straight for the chaise longue.

'Ooh, I can't wait until this little one is born,' she complained. 'Look at the size of me, anyone would think I'm carrying a calf in there!' She prodded at her stomach. 'There are feet everywhere, kicking my bladder. As soon as I sit down, I need to use the chamber pot again!'

'There are only a few weeks to go now, it's almost time for your lying-in,' Countess Bianchi observed.

Katherine made a face. 'It's going to be so boring! I insist you all keep me company, otherwise I shall never get through this.'

Gemma put down the tray and went to her side. 'You're a little pale. I want to make sure everything is all right.'

'No, you're eating,' Katherine protested.

'I'll be able to digest my lunch better once I've had a look.' Gemma saw the countess cross the room and close the parlour door, turning the key with a click. She nodded her thanks, and lifted Katherine's skirts.

Her belly was indeed enormous, the skin stretched taut, her belly button protruding. Gemma gently poked and prodded, trying to determine the position of the baby. She smiled as a foot pushed against her hand, its outline clear under Katherine's skin. She ran her hand across the bump, still prodding, until she felt–

'That can't be right.' She frowned, and tried again. She heard the countess and Julia-Ann standing behind her, and blocked out their questions, concentrating on the baby under her hands. 'Oh.' She sat back, stunned.

'What? What is it? Is something wrong?' Katherine demanded.

'No, not at all,' Gemma reassured her. 'It's just... I can feel a foot here,' she placed a hand on the left side of Katherine's stomach, 'and I can feel another one here.' She put her other hand on the right side.

'What!' Katherine struggled to sit up, straining to see.

'Lie down. There's nothing wrong. Only, it's not physically possible to feel your child's feet so far apart.' Gemma bit her lip.

'What do you mean? Just tell me!'

The countess put a hand on Gemma's shoulder. '*Gemelli?*'

Gemma nodded, then looked at Katherine. 'They're *gemelli*. Twins. You're going to have two babies!'

After Katherine had recovered from the shock, Gemma set out her instructions.

'You must stay in bed now until the birth, no more walking up or down stairs. You need to rest as much as possible – the birth could be more arduous than usual, but I will get you through it.'

Katherine stared up at her with wild, frightened eyes, her cheeks pale and drawn. 'Am I going to die?'

Gemma shook her head vehemently. 'No. I won't let that happen to you. But you must do as you're told.'

'Tell me my future,' Katherine whispered. 'Please. I have to know.'

Against her will, Gemma took her friend's hand between her own and closed her eyes. For a moment there was nothing, and then the images rushed in.

Katherine lying on a bed, her hair soaked with sweat, plastered to her skin, her nightgown rucked up as she pushed down with all her might, her face red and contorted from the effort. A baby's cry, piercing and shrill over its mother's grunts, servant girls hastily bundling it in a blanket while Gemma cut the cord. More grunting and pushing, minutes ticking by, sliding into hours, the sun setting outside and the moon rising, and still no sign of the other baby. Gemma, exhausted from worry, urging Katherine to keep pushing, to keep going, until the words all bled into each other and time had no more meaning. And then she heard a voice, a mere whisper at first that gradually grew louder, insistent, telling her to do as it said. Gentle fingertips guided her hands, showing her what to do, until the baby emerged, lifeless and blue.

Gemma blinked as she came to, the parlour bright after the vision. She hugged Katherine, tears pricking at her eyes.

'It will be all right, I know what to do now,' she murmured, stroking Katherine's hair as she held her in arms. 'You will get through the labour. All three of you.'

Chapter Thirty-Three

Julia-Ann placed the bowl on the table, between two candles. Katherine lay in her bed, grimacing every now and then as the babies moved. Gemma hoped the spell they were about to perform would give her friend some relief during childbirth, which, in her opinion, would be soon.

'Remember what we taught you. The words you say aren't important, but the gestures you use are,' Julia-Ann explained to Gemma. 'The white linen cloth over the bowl, which you take off just before saying the spell, the way you hold your hands and move them, your tone of voice, all this is part of the magic you want your patients to believe in.'

'I'll do my best.' Gemma took up a stance similar to Julia-Ann's, holding her hands palm up. The flames on the candles flickered, guttering until they almost went out, then coming back to life again, casting long, distorted shadows on the wall.

Julia-Ann reached over and removed the cloth. The aroma of herbs filled the room, a warm, soothing scent that spoke of innocent childhoods and comforting arms, honeyed milk and sweet treats. She spoke, her voice soft and gentle, a low murmur of words that ran into each other, calming the soul of whoever listened. Gemma followed her lead, reciting the names of the plants in the Grove, her Italian merging with Julia-Ann's English to create subtle nuances of accent and meaning. Heads bowed, they clasped hands over the bowl, their voices rising and falling as the candlewicks hissed and spluttered.

Julia-Ann let go of Gemma's hand. ''Tis done.'

Gemma relaxed her shoulders. She had felt the exact moment the words had become more than a meaningless noise, when the *intent* had left her fingertips and gone into the bowl. At that moment her remedy had become more than just a cure. It had become a spell.

A deep groan from behind interrupted her thoughts.

'Katherine?' Julia-Ann rushed over to the bed.

Gemma turned and saw Katherine contorted in pain, her face pale and sweaty. 'It's time. Call for the countess and her maids, and bring clean sheets and cloths.' As Julia-Ann hurried from the chamber, Gemma went to Katherine's side.

Gemma felt as though she was back in her vision. The darkening room, the groans from Katherine as the contractions grew stronger and closer, her face red as she pushed, hands gripping the sheet until her knuckles turned white.

There was a collective sigh of relief as the first baby slid out. Gemma left the countess and the maids to care for it, and turned back to Katherine.

'I need to help you with the second one,' she said, wiping Katherine's forehead with a damp cloth. 'Julia-Ann, bring me the bowl we prepared earlier.'

Julia-Ann placed the bowl on a table, and Gemma dipped her fingers in it. 'First I'll put some of this unguent on your belly, it will help with the pains.' She rubbed it into Katherine's skin, her fingers massaging the baby beneath. 'I need to move the baby so it can come out more easily. It's the wrong way around at the moment.'

Katherine stared at her, eyes wide open in fear, and shook her head.

'I'm with you, I won't let anything happen,' Gemma said. 'It will hurt a little, but it will save you hours of labour. Do you trust me?'

'I must, mustn't I?' Katherine licked her dry, cracked lips, her voice croaking.

Gemma gestured to Julia-Ann to give her some water squeezed from a cloth. 'We put a spell on the unguent, you saw us do it. Believe, Katherine.' She moved further down the bed, and Julia-Ann took her place at Katherine's head.

Loud, guttural cries filled the chamber, heartrending in their agony. Gemma closed her mind to everything except the slippery skin beneath her fingers, and the strong, steady pulsing of the baby's heartbeat. She could feel her mother guiding her hands, just as she had in her vision, slowly turning the baby.

'Now push, Katherine,' Gemma urged. She placed her elbow at the top of Katherine's belly, behind the bump caused by the baby's bottom, and as Katherine pushed with all her might, Gemma gave it a nudge.

A second baby's wails joined Katherine's triumphant cry. While the maids took care of the newborn, Gemma leaned against the wall, exhausted.

Katherine reached over, her fingertips brushing against Gemma's skirts. 'Thank you.'

She smiled, so weary that it hurt to make the slightest effort. *It worked*, the small voice inside her said. *The spell worked. And that means a curse could too.*

Gemma shook her head to cast the voice out of her mind. She was not that person, not yet.

Chapter Thirty-Four

December 1631

Isfield, 8 December 1631

Dearest Gemma,

First I must apologise for not writing sooner. My grandfather has taken to overseeing my preparation for Cambridge himself, and gives me little free time.

I have come to the conclusion that Theology is a most boring subject – I cannot see myself standing in a pulpit, or tending to my parishioners' souls, for the rest of my life.

Luckily, we have had a few visitors to break the tedium. One was a dear friend who I hadn't seen for some time. I will tell you more about her when we see each other, as she is also fascinated by plants and was genuinely interested in my long discourses about their medicinal purposes (which I held when out of earshot of my grandfather!).

I miss our conversations about the various maladies and problems of the human body, and I count the days until I can return to the manor and assist you once again. As promised, I will search the library here for any information about the curing of the "mal francais" – almost certainly there is a tome hidden somewhere on its shelves that will be of help.

We will be together again at Christmas, and you must promise me a dance beneath the kissing bough.

Your obedient servant,
Nicholas Culpeper

Christmas with Count and Countess Bianchi was an experience Gemma would never forget. From the ghostly tales told in the parlour late on Christmas Eve, the bitter cold wind drifting through the leaded windows to dance among the candle flames, teasing them with its chill breath, making them cast monstrous shadows on the walls, to the magnificent boar's head stuffed with minced meat, the aroma of mustard and herbs mingling with the juices dripping on the platter, followed by turkey, enormous Christmas pies, sweetmeats, and plates brimming over with fruit and vegetables that had been carefully stored for the occasion, Gemma could only watch open-mouthed at the joyful celebrations around her.

When Nicholas arrived later in the week, he brought mysterious parcels with him that he insisted could only be opened on the last day of the year. Then he swept Gemma into his arms and waltzed across the room with her until they stopped, breathless, beneath the ball of mistletoe strung from the ceiling.

'We must talk as soon as possible,' he whispered in her ear, his moustache tickling her skin. 'I am bursting to tell you my news, for I can tell no one else!'

Gemma tilted her head and looked at his flushed cheeks and sparkling eyes. 'Tell me now, I don't think I can wait!'

He placed a chaste kiss on her cheek and pulled her to him, whispering, 'I'm in love!', then let her go again and hurried off to greet Julia-Ann, leaving Gemma open-mouthed at his words. She took a moment to compose herself, then slowly followed him over to her friends.

Katherine sat beside Julia-Ann, head held high, her curves accentuated by the flowing, cream silk dress she wore, a layer of powder hiding the black smudges beneath her eyes. Two maids sat behind her holding the twins, Mary and John. The babies watched the glittering lights and bright costumes in wide-eyed wonder, pudgy fists waving as they tried to grasp at anything they thought was within their reach.

Gemma smiled at the sight of them, so happy in their childish innocence. For the first time in some months she thought of Claude and his promise to wait for her. Guilt for her foolish infatuation with Nicholas washed over her, and she thanked the Healer that it had gone no further.

Gemma and Nicholas sat huddled in a corner of the parlour, a chess board on the low table between them, half-heartedly concentrating on their pieces while the other guests took part in rowdy parlour games. The count liked to have a house full of people during the twelve days of Christmas, and there was no pause in the entertainment all day long.

'You must tell me your news,' Gemma murmured, her eyes on the black knight Nicholas had just moved.

He sat on the edge of his stool, shifting nervously as he glanced around. 'Do you remember the friend I mentioned in my letter?'

Gemma moved her queen out of danger. 'Ah yes, the young lady who is fascinated by your long discourses. You said she is a dear friend?'

He tutted, and edged a pawn forward two spaces. 'You really must protect your bishop better, Gemma.' He took the piece with a flourish, a wide smile on his face. 'My grandfather has known her parents for a long time; I passed many summers running around the countryside with Judith when we were little.'

'Judith? A lovely name.'

'As is she.' He gestured to Gemma to make her next move. 'We hadn't seen each other for a few years, and I missed her greatly. And then one day, there she was, come to visit my grandfather with her parents, no longer the child I knew back then but a woman. A beautiful woman.'

Gemma captured his pawn before it could reach the far side of the board and become a queen. 'I'm intrigued. I imagine her family were pleased to see you.'

Nicholas coughed.

'Is there a problem?'

'Our meeting was awkward, to say the least. They made it clear, on several occasions, that they would not consider me a worthy husband for Judith, should I be mad enough to even think of such a thing.' He sighed. 'They are determined that she will marry someone of their standing, or higher.'

'Oh, Nick.' Gemma could hear the pain in his voice.

'My father is dead, and my mother and I live off my grandfather's charity,' he said bitterly. 'They would never accept me as their son in law. But during the little time we managed to speak in private, Judith told me that she loves me, that she has been in love with me since we were little, and that she will marry no other.'

Gemma leaned forward, as though to look over the chess board. 'What will you do?'

'That is what I wanted to tell you.' His eyes glittered as he spoke, and he shifted with a restless eagerness. 'We will elope.'

'E–?' Gemma cut off her exclamation, and covered her mouth with her hand. 'Have you thought this through?' she said, more quietly. 'You may be ostracised by your families. Judith will have to live in poverty if her parents will not accept your marriage.'

He shook his head. 'They will come around once we are married. Judith is their only child, and they dote on her.' He waited for her to take her move. 'Besides, we have decided. We will meet at an inn near Lewes, then marry in the Netherlands and stay there until it is safe to come back.'

Gemma moved her queen. 'When are you going to do this?'

'As soon as her parents leave for their annual retreat to the country in the spring. She says she will use some excuse to join them later.' He clutched a rook in his hand, his knuckles white. 'Checkmate.'

Dismayed, Gemma looked down at the board, then flicked her king so that it fell over. 'I was a little distracted.' She began picking up the pieces and rearranging them on the board. 'I truly hope it works out for you, Nick,' she murmured. 'I will be sorry to lose a good friend.'

'It won't be forever.' He helped her set up the board, then stood, rubbing his hands on his breeches. 'I will return as soon as I am able, and I hope you'll still be here. I have so much more to learn. Ah, I see the countess is beckoning me over. I must go and pay my respects to our hosts.'

Gemma watched him stride across the room, and felt a shiver go down her spine. Even though she hadn't touched his hand, an uneasy feeling came over her.

'Stop being so superstitious,' she chided herself, and went to find her friends before she became too melancholic.

Chapter Thirty-Five

March 1632

The grass crunched beneath Gemma's feet as she walked through the gardens, her cloak wrapped tightly around her against the morning frost. Despite it being March already, winter clung on stubbornly, reluctant to release its grip on the land. Silver-white leaves glittered in the pale sunlight, and the skeletons of long-dead flowers bowed beneath the hoarfrost's weight. She relished the peace and quiet, alone with her thoughts as she contemplated the day ahead.

Nicholas's first two months at Cambridge had been unhappy and torturous, his anguish palpable in his letters to her. But he had sent her a letter the week before, full of spirits, telling her of his and Judith's plans. She hoped that by now they were together, making preparations for their departure, and that they would be happy together, no matter what happened.

She sent a prayer to the Healer for them, then headed for the shed where she had hung bunches of dried herbs for making her remedies during the long winter months. The first villagers were already arriving, their breath steaming in the cold morning air, and she quickened her pace. There were remedies to prepare and cloths to cut into bandages. It would be a long day.

Gemma watched Julia-Ann walk around the library with Mary, while Katherine sat in a corner, feeding John. Kathcrine's pale face and the dark shadows beneath her eyes were evidence of her babies' demanding natures, but she assured them that she had never been happier.

The count and countess sat with them, keeping up a lively chatter that had them all laughing. They were in the middle of an amusing anecdote when Gemma felt a darkness come over her, and the room appeared to shrink before her eyes. She clung onto the arms of her chair, digging her nails into the wood to stop herself being swept away. The room spun, and she leaned forward with a groan.

'Are you all right?' Julia-Ann put a hand on Gemma's shoulder, concern on her face.

Gemma rubbed her brow, relieved that the sensation was gradually going away. 'I must have worked too long today, I felt faint for a moment.'

Countess Bianchi passed her a glass of wine. 'Sip this. I've added some honey, it will help.'

As Gemma took the glass, the door opened and a servant entered. He hurried over to the countess and spoke urgently in her ear. When he finished, she nodded and gestured for him to leave.

'Come, Gemma, you must accompany me.' She touched her husband's arm briefly. 'I will be back soon.'

Gemma followed her into the corridor, wondering what had happened. The countess walked briskly through the manor, and Gemma had to half run to keep up. To her surprise, they went out of the front door and headed towards the barn.

'Is there a patient?' she asked, puffing out clouds of vapour as she spoke. The night air was cold, and she had only her shawl wrapped around her shoulders.

When they reached the barn door, the countess turned and faced Gemma. 'You must be strong for your friend, he needs you now, more than he's ever needed anyone.' With that, she opened the door and entered.

A lantern hung on the wall at the far end, above a pile of blankets. Hurrying after the countess, Gemma realised that there was someone there. Faint sobs reached her, heartrending sounds muffled beneath the blankets.

The countess crouched down and pulled back the blanket. Nicholas stared up at her, his face blotchy from crying, his eyes red and swollen.

'Oh, Nick,' she said, reaching over and gathering him in her arms. 'I'm so, so sorry. You must stay here with us, for as long as you want.'

'What happened?' Gemma whispered, kneeling beside them.

Nicholas grasped her hand, his breath coming in halting gasps. 'It's Judith,' he managed to say, before bursting into tears again.

The cold dread that had been haunting Gemma since Christmas lay its icy grasp on her heart, and for a moment she thought she'd been turned to stone.

'Judith?'

He haltingly told them how he had been travelling to Lewes in a terrible thunderstorm when his driver had seen the wreckage of a carriage in the middle of the road. A crowd of people stood huddled at the roadside, cloaks held over their heads for shelter from the pelting rain, while others bent over someone lying down. As Nicholas neared, he recognised the insignia on the blackened carriage, jumped down from his coach, and raced over, his head telling him it couldn't be, while his heart already knew.

Heedless of the mud and water, he fell to his knees and cradled Judith's head in his lap, screaming her name over and over. She had been flung from the carriage when lightning had struck it, breaking her left arm and leg, and one of the spokes from a wheel had pierced her side. Barely conscious, she had managed to whisper his name before dying in his arms.

'We were almost at the inn,' he said, his voice empty and desolate. 'She should have been there, safe and warm, waiting for me to arrive. Instead–' He slumped back against the wall of the barn, silent in his anguish.

'I have a tisane, it will help him get some rest,' Gemma whispered to the countess. 'I will go and prepare it.'

The countess nodded. 'I will stay with him until you get back.' She put out a hand as Gemma stood. 'Don't tell anyone yet, let him have this evening to himself. There will be time enough for everything else tomorrow.'

'Of course.'

Gemma hurried back to the kitchen, her mind in turmoil. Poor Nicholas, and poor, poor Judith. Her heart ached at the cruelty of fate, and the wasted years the two lovers could have had together.

'Why must everything be so difficult?' she shouted, furious. 'Why can't people be allowed to live their lives?'

There was no answer. In the distance an owl hooted and a fox yapped, and animals went about their business, unaware of the tragedy that had destroyed Nicholas's life.

Chapter Thirty-Six

May 1632

Gemma watched Nicholas walk among the herbs, stopping every now and then to pick a leaf and rub it between his fingers. He saw her looking and a hint of a smile touched his lips. A scraggly beard covered his cheeks, his greasy, matted hair hanging around his face in clumps. He'd lost a lot of weight, and his once-elegant clothes were now loose-fitting and grubby.

He didn't care anymore. In the first days after Judith's death he'd gone back to his grandfather's house, unable to eat or sleep. The Reverend had berated him for his foolish plan of eloping, blaming him squarely for the accident. His mother had collapsed on hearing what had happened and taken to her bed, refusing to speak to him or even look at him.

Nicholas had returned to the Manor, where Count Bianchi had told him he was welcome to stay for as long as he liked. Trying not to appear ungrateful, he made the effort to sit at the dinner table with them in the evenings, nibbling pieces of dry bread and drinking water. They watched his descent into grief, feeling helpless as he closed himself away more every day.

Gemma often asked him to help her with the villagers, as he used to. He had always refused, until that morning. To her surprise, he'd given a brief nod and gone out into the kitchen garden. She'd left him alone, letting him do what he needed to.

She could see the damselfly hovering over a clump of sage, its blue body bright in the morning sun. Nicholas bent down to pick a leaf, then halted, his hand midway, when he caught sight of the insect. Squinting, he slowly crouched down until he was resting on his heels, and held out his hand. The damselfly flitted away, only to return and hover before him, its dark eyes studying him, while its stick-thin body shivered. Gemma held her breath as the damselfly landed on Nicholas's hand and remained there, immobile. Nick appeared mesmerised, peering into the dark depths of the insect's eyes, his body relaxing.

Gemma didn't know how long they remained there, the three of them. Time seemed to stand still, nothing moving, even the breeze faded away. There was only the warmth of the sun on their skin, the sharp colours of the sky, the trees, and the grass, the distant murmur of the servants working in the kitchen.

The damselfly shook itself then flew away, quickly disappearing among the shrubs. Nicholas blinked and rubbed his eyes, as though astonished to find himself crouched on the ground. Gemma went over to him, holding out her hand to help him to his feet.

'Are you all right?'

'It-it spoke to me,' Nicholas whispered, his eyes unfocused as he stared wildly about. 'The damselfly–'

'They often speak to me,' Gemma said softly. 'I find them a great help in times of need.'

'I-I think I understand now. Everything you told me before, it all makes sense.' He gripped her arm. 'Tell me, can a man become a healer?'

'In the legend of the dragonflies, both men and women were chosen as the first healers.' Gemma shrugged. 'I imagine nothing has changed.'

He remained silent, deep in thought for long minutes. 'You have taught me so much, and I believe I can help people, just as you do. But I want to do something that no one has done before.' He hesitated, his cheeks flushed red. 'I will help everyone who is too poor to be able to call for a physician, those who have to choose between being well or feeding their families. I watch you helping the villagers, giving them your time, and your knowledge, for little or nothing in return. All you want is for them to get better. But what will they do when you leave?'

Gemma opened her mouth, but Nicholas interrupted her.

'You will leave, Gemma. I see the restlessness in you, your desire to return to the cottage in the mountains, and the Grove. Some days I can see your yearning, like an invisible thread that is tugging at you to go back. As is right. You belong in Tuscany, not hidden away in an English village.' He reached out and took a lock of her hair in his hand, running the long brown curl through his fingers. 'I miss her so much. I think about her every minute of every day. I wish I could have been in the coach with her, and we could have died together, in each other's arms. But I am still here, living and breathing, the sun warm on my face, while she lies alone in a cold, dark grave. Some days I feel as though I cannot carry on, but I must.

'My mother is dying, Gemma. She refuses to eat, and drinks only tiny sips of water, while every day she grows weaker and paler. The physician says she has a canker inside her, destroying her, but I know that it is my fault if she is so desperately ill. The shock of my elopement was too much, and now she is suffering because of me.'

'No, Nick.' Gemma tried to hold his hand, but he pulled away from her.

'My grandfather has told me I must return to my studies at Cambridge. We had a heated discussion about it when I visited him at the weekend. He said that if I refuse, I must be an apprentice to the Master Apothecary, Daniel White.'

'That is more in line with what you want to do, is it not?' Gemma asked cautiously.

Nicholas gave a bitter laugh. 'It is exactly what I want. But he made it very clear that if I refuse to return to Cambridge he will disown me. I will be alone and penniless.'

'But happier?'

He nodded. 'While I was contemplating the damselfly, it came to me: the one way I can reach every person in the country.' He took a deep breath. 'Up until now, there have been great tomes that students have studied at great length before becoming physicians. However, they are far beyond the means of ordinary people, as they are written in Latin and cost more than ten years' wages for most.' He leaned forward, his eyes shining. 'My idea is to write a simple booklet, in English, with the names of commonly found plants and how to use them to treat everything from warts to influenza. I will find a way to print it cheaply, so that I can sell each copy for only a few pennies. Everyone in the land will have a copy of my book in their house, that they can turn to for remedies in times of need!'

Gemma gasped. 'That is a wonderful idea! You could add illustrations of plants, so they know what to look for.'

'Will you help me?' Nicholas pleaded, his hands clasped together, imploring.

After weeks of seeing him so deeply melancholic, Gemma sent a silent prayer of thanks to the Healer and the damselfly. 'It will be an honour. We shall begin work on it today, after we have tended to our patients.'

Chapter Thirty-Seven

March-April 1635

It was finally warm enough to sit outside, after a long winter and wet spring spent in front of a smoky fire. The twins charged about, shrieking with joy at the sight of butterflies and bees taking their first outing. Katherine had had her servants put out some benches covered with cushions, and she lay on one, her legs raised to relieve her swollen ankles, while Gemma and Julia-Ann sat opposite.

'I can't wait until this one is born, it's more trouble than the twins ever were!' Katherine grumbled, rubbing her side. 'It won't stay still for a moment, and I'm sure it kicks my bladder on purpose as soon as I lie down to sleep.'

'It won't be long now, only a few more weeks,' Gemma tried to reassure her.

'Then all the fun begins again!' Julia-Ann added, snorting with laughter. She gestured at the twins; John had given a stick to Mary, who was trying to wedge it up her nose.

'John! Don't encourage your sister!' Katherine shouted, then turned with a sigh. A servant rushed over and took the stick away, and the two children promptly burst into tears.

'Remind me again why I thought it would be a good idea to have more children.' Katherine rested her head on a cushion and closed her eyes.

'Because you fell in love with your husband and wanted to give him a child of his own,' Gemma said.

Katherine had met Henry Selwood, a good friend of Count Bianchi, a year earlier, and they had married three months later. Even though they lived in the next village along, any trip with the twins had to be organised months in advance, and Gemma and Julia-Ann had little spare time after tending to their patients. Katherine's spirited contribution to their discussions and her reassuring presence while casting spells were sorely missed, and all three were delighted when they managed to spend a day together.

'Really? What was I thinking?'

'You know you'll forget all this as soon as the baby is born.' Julia-Ann leaned over and patted Katherine's bump. 'And Gemma and I will be with you, all the way through.' She turned, and frowned. 'Won't we, Gemma?'

Deep in thought, Gemma forced herself to pay attention to her friends. 'Yes, of course we will.'

'Is something wrong?' Katherine asked.

'I–' Gemma clasped her hands together, uncertain how to begin. She decided to just blurt it out. 'I've decided to go back to Italy.'

There was a stunned silence. Even the children stopped playing and looked up, curious. No one spoke.

'Please don't look at me like that,' Gemma pleaded. 'I will stay until the baby is born, but then I'll go back to Avignon. I received a letter from my uncle: he is unwell and needs me, although he would never say as much. And afterwards, I will return to Italy, and the cottage.' She took a deep breath. 'You are happily married, Katherine, and you are betrothed, Julia-Ann. You have your families and your homes. I miss my grandparents, I miss the cottage and the Grove, and most of all I miss Ombra. I have to go back, to tend to the plants and the dragonflies, and to live my life where my heart yearns to be.'

'What about the witch hunters?' Katherine asked. 'They're the reason you came to England.'

Gemma nodded. 'My uncle wrote that no one has been searching for a girl of my description for more than a year now, and that in his opinion it would be safe to return. He writes to my grandparents every few months, and they say the witch hunters are gone from Italy. This is the right time for me to return.'

'And what of the people who condemned your mother to death?' Julia-Ann said, raising her eyebrows. 'How will you feel about seeing them again?'

'That is also one of the reasons why I must go back,' Gemma replied. 'There are some things I must do.'

Katherine pulled herself up with some difficulty, puffing as she put a cushion behind her back. 'I'm sure we can help you with that,' she said, winking. Then she became serious. 'And Nicholas? Will you tell him?'

Gemma's breath caught in her throat. She hadn't seen Nicholas for two years, ever since his mother had died and his grandfather had sent him off to become an apprentice to the Master Apothecary. The countess had asked after Nicholas's health, but the reverend refused to speak about his grandson. Gemma and Nicholas wrote to each other occasionally, brief letters that didn't go into any detail. She missed the close friendship they'd had during the time she had taught him everything she could about healing.

'No, I don't want to upset him. He's doing well as an apprentice apothecary, and will soon be able to set up on his own, if his ideas work out. He doesn't need to worry about me. He has enough troubles, with his grandfather's refusal to acknowledge him.'

Katherine nodded. 'As you wish. We have a little time before Henry comes home. Shall we retire indoors? The air is becoming quite chilly now the sun is going down.' She pulled her shawl around her, gestured to the servants to bring the children, and led the way into the house.

Katherine had her baby at the beginning of April, during a terrible storm with thunder so loud that it made the windows and tiles on the roof rattle. Baby Walter made his appearance in the late afternoon, red-faced and squalling, as rain hammered against the glass and the wind shrieked around the walls of the house. While Julia-Ann had seen it as a portent of doom, Katherine had merely shrugged and remarked that her son would go through life much as he'd entered it, angry, loud, and fearless. Gemma would miss them both, but she knew that whatever the future held for her friends, they would face it together, with strength and courage.

The time for Gemma to leave had arrived, and she would return to the cottage, the Grove, and the dragonflies. She packed the last of her things in her bag, then sat on her bed and looked around the room that had been her chamber for four years. She remembered the welcome she and Katherine had received from Count and Countess Bianchi, after the cold reception from Katherine's parents. Over the years, she, Katherine and Julia-Ann had become firm friends, bonded by secrets and witchcraft, and troubled pasts, and it was a friendship she would treasure for the rest of her life.

This would be her last day at the manor, her last dinner with the Bianchi family, her last night sleeping in her comfortable bed. She and Katherine had said their farewells a few days earlier, amid tearful hugs and sobbed promises. They had cried, and laughed, and had sealed their friendship over the flickering flame of a sage-perfumed candle sprinkled with dried fragments of the silver leaves Gemma had carried from the Grove. No matter where she was in the world, she knew that her dear friend would be there beside her, in spirit. Theirs was a bond that would transcend the grave, of this she was sure.

The carriage would depart at dawn, taking her back to the coast. The thought of boarding the ship for France brought another image to mind, of her mother clasping her hand in a damp, dark prison and the vision of an older Gemma standing on the deck of a ship, her hand curled protectively around her swollen belly.

She glanced down at her skirts, pulled tightly in at her waist. 'I may be older, but this is one vision that didn't come true,' she murmured. Perhaps the vision had been about Katherine after all.

A knock on the door and Julia-Ann's voice calling stirred her from her thoughts. She gave a final look around the chamber, then ran to join her friend.

When she opened the door, Julia-Ann grabbed her arm and dragged her along the hallway. Laughing and half-protesting, Gemma let her carry her along, until they got to the top of the stairs. Then she stopped, her hand to her mouth, and tears sprang to her eyes.

'Nick!'

He looked older, his neatly trimmed moustache and beard thicker, with a few lines on his forehead and at the corners of his eyes, as though he spent much of his time frowning. Then he smiled and bowed low to her, and it was as though the last four years had never happened.

A soft whisper of whiskers brushed her skin as he bent over to kiss her hand, and when he looked up at her she could see the sadness in the depths of his grey-green eyes.

'I couldn't let you go back without saying goodbye,' he said.

Gemma glanced at Julia-Ann.

'Mamma and I thought you might like to see each other one more time.' She nudged Gemma, smiling.

'And I couldn't let you leave without giving you this.' Nicholas passed her a small pouch and a scroll sealed with wax. 'For your uncle's malady. After much research, I have found a remedy that will help.'

'But not cure.'

'No,' he replied sadly. 'There is still no cure.'

Gemma held the pouch to her nose and breathed in the peachy aroma of heartsease, blended with other herbs. 'Thank you.' She turned to Julia-Ann. 'And thank you. It's the best gift you could have given me.'

Dinner was a lively affair, full of chatter and laughter. Nicholas told them about his apprenticeship, and how he was determined to use his knowledge to help others as soon as he could. He fell quiet when the countess gave her condolences for his mother's death, but recovered his good humour after a while, telling anecdotes that made the count laugh loudly. Gemma watched him carefully, noticing little signs that no one else would. Her heart ached for him, having suffered so much tragedy already in his life.

'Would you like to go for a last walk in the garden?' Nicholas asked Gemma, while everyone else was saying their goodnights.

'Yes, I would like that very much,' Gemma replied.

The manor was quiet as they walked along the hallway to the kitchen. Most of the servants had already gone to bed, and those that were left were busy tidying up the dining room. The kitchen was deserted, the fire already banked, and the tables were scrubbed clean for the next day.

Outside, the moon hung high above them, casting a silvery glow over the garden. An owl hooted somewhere close by, and a bat flitted across their path. It was a night for magic, the cool air creating a small thrill over Gemma's skin, her senses heightened as they strolled among the herbs.

A snail slid over a stone, leaving behind a glittering trail. Leaves rustled as a beetle scurried away from their feet, the moon reflected in its black shell. The bright eyes of a fox peered out from under a bush at them as the animal crouched, wary, until they passed.

Nicholas stopped by the bench where they used to pass many hours together. 'This place will not be the same without you.' He gestured to her to sit, then sat beside her. 'I have many pleasant memories here; the merest hint of lavender evokes better times.' He sighed. 'How young and innocent we were back then. We thought anything was possible.'

'You must miss Judith so much.' Gemma laid her hand on his arm. 'It will stop hurting, please believe me. With time, your grief will give way to happier memories of her.'

A tear trickled down his cheek. 'Losing Judith, and then my mother, has been hard. Some days I wonder how I can carry on.' He lowered his voice to a whisper. 'I imagine lying down in a cold grave until my soul leaves my body and I can be with her again. But then I can hear Judith telling me that I must stay and continue with my work, that I can help people who are less fortunate than myself, that what I do will be important for them. And so I am still here, bearing the weight of my grief and pain.'

'But not alone, Nick. Countess Bianchi, Julia-Ann, and Katherine will all help you, if you let them,' Gemma urged. 'I know you will finish your book, and many people will have you to thank for saving them, or their children.'

'I will miss you and your wise words,' he said, wiping away the tears.

'Promise you will write to me and tell me all your news,' Gemma said. She leaned over a brushed a lock of hair from his eyes. He caught hold of her hand and drew it to his lips, then gently kissed it.

Gemma felt the whispers of magic all around them, a faint trembling like dragonfly wings in a breeze. The tips of his eyelashes were bathed in silver, shadows cast across his face made him both a stranger and familiar. She held her breath for a moment, an eternity, the cold light from the moon soaking into her skin and travelling through her veins.

And then his mouth was on hers, hungry and passionate, his hands entangled in her hair as he pulled her closer to him. She felt wild and carefree, all restraints abandoned, her spirit floating on the currents of the air, giving her the gift of freedom. As they lay among the lavender and sage, their bodies joined as they gave themselves to each other, she thought for a moment she could see the damselfly above them. Then she turned to Nicholas and lost herself in his arms.

Chapter Thirty-Eight

THE CHILL PRE-DAWN AIR nipped at Gemma's skin, and she pulled her cloak tighter to her body. Two bags with her belongings were on the ground at her feet, the wooden chest resting on top of them.

She had left Nicholas the night before and returned to her room, weighed down by guilt, ashamed of her behaviour. By the time she had reached her room tears were pouring down her cheeks, and she crawled into bed, sobbing. Her dreams had been fitful, Claude staring at her with such pain in his eyes that it was unbearable to look at him, his suffering mirrored in the pain eating her up from within.

When she had awoken in the early hours, tired and fretful, she couldn't stay in her bed any longer. She had taken her things and gone to sit in the garden one last time, trying to quell the turmoil of emotions inside her. As dawn broke, the night before seemed surreal, like fragments of a dream that lingered in her mind, already dissipating in the lightening sky.

Regret hung in the air, along with guilt and a melancholy that she knew would slowly fade as the distance grew between her and

Nicholas. The cord that had kept her tied to Ombra, Claude, and the cottage and the Grove, tightened with every moment that passed, her soul yearning to be with them once more. If nothing else, the night before had shown her the direction in which her future truly lay.

A horse snorted, and a shadow appeared before her, making her jump.

'The carriage is ready, milady. I'll just take yer bags.' The countess's coachman smiled, his few remaining teeth lying haphazardly in his mouth. He hoisted Gemma's bags over his shoulder and stomped back to the carriage.

'Gemma.' Countess Bianchi arrived in a rustle of skirts, looking as immaculate as ever even at this early hour. 'I had my maid wake me. I wanted to say goodbye, and to thank you for everything you have done for us.' She pulled Gemma into a tight hug, enveloping her in a scented cloud of rose water, then stood back, her eyes glistening in the pale light of dawn. 'We will miss you.'

'As will I.' Gemma's voice hitched, the words caught in her throat. 'Remember to give Cathryn Green her tisane every week, and Rachel will need the poultice on her arm changing until there is no more pus, and–'

'I have it all written down,' the countess said gently. 'And you have taught Julia-Ann well – together she and I will take care of the villagers. You leave us richer than before you arrived.' A horse stamped its hoof behind them, and she smiled. 'The journey is long, it's best you go now. The people of Gallicano are fortunate to have you.'

Gemma blinked to keep the tears at bay, but one escaped and rolled down her cheek. She threw her arms around the countess in a clumsy hug, then turned and hurried to the carriage, where the coachman was holding the door open for her. She clambered inside and sat down next to the wooden chest, tears threatening to overwhelm her. The carriage took off with a jolt and Gemma sat facing forwards, determined not to look back for fear that her strength would fail her and she would beg the coachman to return to the manor.

She clutched the pouch Nicholas had given her the evening before, the aroma of the crushed herbs filling the carriage. She could hardly believe she was returning to Avignon, to her uncle, Paola and Alberto, Claude, and Ombra. So much had happened since she had left, and she was no longer the person she had been. Would they accept her as she was now?

With every turn of the wheels, all that she had known and loved for the last four years fell further behind, while her future stretched ahead of her, fragile and uncertain.

Chapter Thirty-Nine

May 1635

Mme Dupuis gave Gemma a thin smile when she opened the door, showing no surprise at seeing her there.

'I trust milady had a pleasant journey,' she remarked, standing aside so that Gemma could enter.

'It has been tiring, it is good to be here at last,' Gemma replied. 'I'm looking forward to changing my clothes and washing away the grime of the coach. But first, I must go to see my uncle.'

'He has not been well these last few weeks, milady. He will be glad to see you have returned.' Mme Dupuis' severe expression slipped slightly, revealing her concern for the count.

Gemma barely recognised the gaunt man slumped in a chair in the parlour. His brightly coloured clothes hung off his once-portly frame, and the skin on his face sagged, creating heavy jowls. Black smudges beneath his eyes, and the deep frown-lines on his forehead, showed that sleep was fitful at best.

She stood in the doorway, hesitant to wake him. His breathing was shallow and laboured, and his body twitched as he wandered the land of dreams. Gemma noticed a mark on his head through the wispy strands of grey hair, about the size of a florin and inflamed at the edges. The illness was taking its toll on Leandro. Nicholas's bag of herbs, and the instructions he had written down for her, were in the wooden chest; as her uncle was sleeping, she thought she would go to the kitchen and prepare the concoction. Nicholas had reassured her that the herbs would alleviate Leandro's symptoms; as he'd said, anything was better than treating him with mercury.

She turned to leave, trying to be as quiet as she could.

'Morgana, is that you?' her uncle enquired, his voice tremulous.

Gemma hurried over to him. 'No, I'm Gemma, Morgana's daughter. Do you remember me?'

He blinked, confusion sweeping over his face, then struggled to sit up among the cushions strewn around him. 'Gemma. Of course. I'm sorry, I didn't mean... The pains are so bad. The physician gave me a cordial, but it makes me muddle-headed.'

'I came as soon as I could, you said you weren't well in your letter.'

'I didn't mean to worry you, *cara*. My health is better some days than others. But just lately the pains are much worse. I don't sleep very well, as they always come at night. Isn't that strange?' He looked down at his gnarled hands, as though seeing them for the first time. 'I always cared so much about my appearance, but now...' He shrugged. 'Now I don't have the energy for anything. Not even to put a wig on.'

'I have a friend who gave me a remedy. It should help to relieve your pains and tiredness. Will you try it?'

He ran his fingers through his wisps of hair and grimaced. 'At this point, I would try anything.'

Gemma patted his hand. 'I will ask Paola to help me prepare it. Get some rest now.'

Her uncle didn't reply, but sank back into the cushions and closed his eyes.

The kitchen was a confusion of riotous noise, clouds of steam, and mouth-watering scents of cooking. Gemma felt as though she had stepped into paradise when she opened the door. After the solemn quietness of the parlour and the rest of the house, it was a pleasant shock.

'Luca, put that down right now!' she heard Paola shout.

A small boy dashed past, an enormous pot in his arms. It was so heavy that he was puffing with the effort, but he seemed determined to carry out whatever mischief he had on his mind.

'Gemma? No one told me you had arrived.' Paola grabbed her son and took the pot away from him, then set him back down on the floor, ignoring his yells of protest. 'Sorry. It's one of those mornings. Luca, stop your squalling, I can't hear myself think!'

'Do you want me to come back later?' Gemma gestured at the tabletops laden with vegetables and meat to prepare.

'Wait just a minute.' Paola took a handful of wooden spoons and gave them to her son, who stopped crying and began bashing them on the floor. 'That should keep him quiet for a while,' she said with a sigh.

'I've just been talking to my uncle,' Gemma said. 'He wrote to me and said he wasn't in good health, but I didn't expect to see him like this.'

'Alberto and I have been worried for a while,' Paola replied. 'He eats hardly anything, no matter what I prepare for him. Either the food is too rich, or too salty, or he isn't hungry, there's always an excuse. He won't go out either, he says everyone will point and stare.'

'I'm glad I came, then.' Gemma took out the pouch. 'If you boil some water, I'll prepare a tisane for him that should at least stimulate his appetite. He must eat, if he is to feel better.'

Paola took the pouch and sniffed it cautiously. 'What's in there?'

'Heartsease, betony, and a few other herbs. Nicholas studied the illness and its effects for years, and swears this will help the symptoms.'

'Nicholas?' Paola said, raising her eyebrows. 'And who would he be?'

'Just someone I met while in England,' Gemma replied, flushing slightly.

'And...?'

Gemma sighed. 'He's a friend of the family I was staying with. He told me he wanted to learn about plants and how to use them to cure maladies, so I taught him as much as I could.'

'I see you have lots to tell me about your time in England.' Paola winked. Luca chose that moment to throw a wooden spoon across the kitchen, almost hitting a servant as she scurried past. 'But now is not the right time.' She passed a wooden cup and a pot of boiling water to Gemma, then picked her son up and sat him firmly on her lap. 'Your father will be here soon, then you'll see!'

'How is Alberto?' Gemma put a spoonful of herbs into a square of muslin, which she closed with a twist of twine before popping it into the cup and pouring water over it.

'He is busy, thanks to your uncle. Many of the nobles have requested his services these last years. He has work for a long time now.'

'I'm glad he's busy, although that leaves your hands full with that little one.'

'And one on the way.' Paola beamed.

'Really? That's wonderful!'

'Yes, although the sickness makes it difficult to work around food sometimes. Here.' She took the dripping muslin square from Gemma and put it in a pail for scraps.

Gemma breathed in the aroma of the herbs. 'With some honey it will be perfect. I'll take this to my uncle and let you get on with your work.'

'I want to hear all about Nicholas,' Paola called after her. Gemma shook her head, smiling to herself.

Chapter Forty

THE TISANE SEEMED TO help. Once Gemma could see that her uncle was fast asleep, his chest rising and falling slowly and steadily, his face relaxed, she tiptoed quietly out of the parlour and closed the door.

Unwilling to face the chaos of the kitchen again, she slipped out of the front door and walked around the side of the house, beneath fruit-laden branches and lavender bushes humming with bees. Her feet took her down through the garden, past the small lily pond, to the stables. The familiar aroma of hay and horse greeted her, and her uncle's stolid old gelding hung its head over the stable door, eager to see if the visitor had brought treats.

Gemma grabbed a handful of grass and held it out to the horse, smiling as its whiskers tickled her palm. She rubbed its ears, and was filled with a heartbreaking longing for Ombra. Her eyes filled with tears, and she sniffed them back, determined not to cry.

'She's being well looked after, milady,' said a familiar voice from behind her.

'Alberto!'

'Paola told me you were back, I thought I'd see if you were here first.'

Gemma gave him a weak smile. 'Am I that predictable?'

'Of course.' Alberto reached over and patted the horse's neck. 'He's missing your uncle, looks out for him every morning. But milord hasn't ridden in ages, not even this old fella 'ere. I take him out if I have time, but that's not very often.' He looked at Gemma. 'Claude is taking good care of Ombra, as he promised.'

'He's a good man. I don't what I would have done without...' Her voice faded as the memory of his kiss came to mind, his lips so soft and warm, filling her with passion. She tried to swallow, her mouth suddenly dry. 'I've missed him,' she whispered. And realised she meant it. Her mind had been focused on seeing Ombra again, while her heart had been yearning for Claude. She coughed. 'Perhaps now my uncle is sleeping, I might go to see her.'

'I'll accompany you.'

'No, that's not necessary. I know the way, and it's not far.'

Alberto shook his head. 'Unfortunately, Avignon has changed since you were last here. There have been some incidents... People from the poorer quartiers have become bolder and sometimes come all the way up here. There have been a number of attacks lately.'

'Attacks?' Gemma said, incredulous. 'What is the Pope doing about it?'

'Nothing.' Alberto's voice became bitter. 'The Pope has run away to Rome with his tail between his legs, and taken all his corrupt bishops and priests with him. Avignon is better off without them, but it can be unsafe for a woman to walk the streets alone.'

'I see.' Gemma sighed. 'When will you have time to take me?'

'We can go now, if you like. Or if you'd rather wait–'

Gemma strode past him, eager to get going.

Claude stood beside Gemma as a stableboy headed into the small paddock to catch Ombra. She looked up at him, breathing in his scent, yearning to reach out and touch his face, his lips, his hair. He turned and smiled, and took her hand in his. There was only time for him to kiss her fingertips before the boy returned to the stable block, but in that moment an eternity passed, their souls entwining as their hearts pulsed with all the love they had for each other. Whatever happened, wherever their paths led them, she hoped they would never be apart again.

For so long Gemma had dreamed of seeing Ombra, of wrapping her arms around the mare's neck and breathing in her sweet perfume. As soon as Ombra saw her, she flung her head up and down, whinnying loudly and stamping her hoof on the ground, sending clouds of dust into the air. Claude stood aside as Gemma ran to her horse.

She had no idea how long she remained there, tears streaming down her face, soaking into the mare's coat, Ombra's whiskers tickling her ears and neck as the mare rubbed her chin against Gemma's head and back.

'Perhaps we can go for a ride?' Claude's voice cracked, and Gemma turned in time to see him wipe a tear away from his eye.

'I would like that very much,' she replied. 'Where's Alberto?'

'He had to go back to finish some work. He tried to tell you, but you were... occupied.'

'I'll see him later.' Gemma threw her arms around Claude's neck, still sniffing. 'I've thought about seeing you and Ombra every day for the last four years. To finally be with you both again, after so much has happened...' Her voice broke. 'You've taken good care of her, she has never looked better. Thank you.'

'She is an incredible horse. I am honoured to have had the privilege of tending to her.' Claude hugged her back. 'And I've missed you too, ma chérie. More than you can possibly know.' He gestured to the various saddles and bridles hanging on the wall. 'Shall we?'

Once they had crossed the bridge and left the crowds behind, they let the horses have their heads. Leaning forward with her cheek against Ombra's neck, the sound of thudding hooves in her ears and strands of mane whipping her face, Gemma had never felt happier.

They took a leisurely walk back, their horses snorting and puffing after their long gallop. Gemma pulled Ombra to a stop and let the mare crop the grass. A couple of magpies flew up into the air, squawking at their intrusion. A myriad of insects crawled among the flowers, and there was the occasional glint of dragonflies' jewelled bodies.

As Gemma dismounted, a damselfly, no, *the* damselfly, flitted past and landed on her hair, its wing gently brushing her forehead.

'Ssh,' she whispered as Claude joined her. He stopped, then jerked back as the damselfly swooped upon him. It landed on his hand and remained there, motionless but for its trembling wings.

He stood still, staring at the creature, a distant look in his eyes. The sun continued its path across the sky, clouds billowed and shrank as the winds tossed them about, leaves on the trees unfurled, soaking up the warmth and light, and all around them the world went about its business. A sigh left Gemma's lips, no louder than a butterfly's wing brushing against a petal, and the spell was broken. The damselfly darted away, and Claude slowly came to, as though waking from a deep sleep.

'It showed me–' He paused, clearly struggling to find the words. 'I saw them all, the healers. Was I dreaming?' He rubbed his forehead, confused. 'Your mother, your great-grandmother, the things they suffered at the hands of others. I'm so sorry.'

'"A healer's task is a thankless one." That was one of my grandmother's sayings, and I never really understood it until the witch hunters came to our village. We have a much easier life than many others, but we have always been persecuted throughout the centuries, thanks to the curse on our family.'

'Curse?'

'There is much you do not yet know about the Innocenti,' Gemma said.

Claude sat down and patted the grass beside him. 'Why don't you tell me?'

Suddenly feeling shy, Gemma sat a little way away and plucked a blade of grass while she gathered her thoughts. Twisting it between her fingers, she quietly began to speak. When she finished, Claude leaned over and kissed her on the lips.

'I love you, Gemma Innocenti,' he murmured, and gently pushed her down onto the grass as they became lost in each other.

Chapter Forty-One

June 1635

Gemma was eating breakfast with her uncle when the letter arrived. He was still pale and weak, but thanks to her tisanes managed to eat at most mealtimes, and keep his food down. Following Nicholas's notes, she had also made a salve to put on his sores, and kept a daily record of the effects of each remedy. She was pleased to note that his symptoms were slowly easing.

'Shall we take a walk in the garden after breakfast?' she asked.

'I'd like that, yes,' he replied, wiping some egg off his chin. 'I enjoy our daily walks, it gives me something to look forward to.'

Gemma looked up as Lucie, the maid, entered the dining room, carrying a folded piece of parchment. 'Milord, this arrived just now, the carrier said it was urgent.' She handed it to Leandro and curtsied, then scurried out of the room.

'Here, you read it, *cara*. Your eyes are better than mine.'

Gemma took the parchment. Her heart stopped when she saw the seal. 'It's from my grandparents!' Her hands shaking, she prised the letter open and started reading.

'"My dear Leandro, I do not wish to burden you with our affairs, especially as your own health is suffering, but I do not know what else to do. Your sister has had to take to her bed due to ill health – unfortunately, our ill-mannered cousins have found out. They have threatened to pay a visit to the villa. I continue to tell them they aren't welcome, as you can imagine, but they are very persistent. I fear that should Isotta become worse, they will not give me a moment's peace.

'There is also another matter of which you must be informed. Yesterday I went to the cottage, as I often do. When I arrived, I found Teo had gone. With the cottage empty, I am concerned for the Grove and its plants. I do not know who else to turn to, so I beg you to return, for your sister's sake if not for mine. Jacopo."' Gemma's voice faltered as she put the letter back down on the table. 'This is terrible!' She remained silent while she thought. 'You told me the witch hunters have left Italy, is that right?'

Leandro put down the napkin he'd been clutching tightly since she started reading. 'The Pope sent them all back to England, every last one of them, when he found out that they had accused his own sister of being a witch.' He snorted. 'He denied all knowledge of them, up until it affected him personally. Now he is back in Rome, and the murdering bastards have gone.'

'Good.' Gemma pushed her chair back as she got to her feet. 'I will pack my things and leave in the morning.'

'You...' Leandro struggled to his feet. 'You want to go back to Italy?'

'You can't travel in your condition. I planned to return when you were better, it appears I will leave sooner than I thought.'

'Wait.' Leandro leaned against the table, panting, until he caught his breath. 'And how do you think you will travel there?'

'I will ride Ombra, as I did four years ago.'

'And how long did it take you? Two months? Three? Come, *cara*, sit so we can plan your journey. It would be better to leave in a few days and arrive sooner, surely, than go through that hardship once more.'

Gemma hesitated.

'And you must speak to Claude before you depart. I've seen how the two of you look at each other – I was certain you would be announcing your wedding soon. I do so love a wedding.' He sighed.

'Oh.' Gemma sank back onto the chair, her heart aching at the thought of leaving Claude so soon. 'It may be a while before I come back. If ever.'

Leandro looked sad. 'It is a hard decision to make. But the cottage and the Grove are your life, and I know that you will do what you must to protect them.'

'I hope Claude is as understanding,' Gemma murmured.

'If he truly loves you, he will be,' Leandro replied. 'I don't claim to have the sight like you and your mother, but even I can see that you are destined to be together.' He patted her arm. 'Everything will work out for the best, you'll see.'

Gemma wished she could stay wrapped in Claude's arms forever, and hide away from all her troubles. With a sigh she stepped back, her hand resting on his chest.

'I will miss you so much,' he said, kissing her forehead. 'I wish you didn't have to leave.'

'I must. With my cousins threatening to take the villa once more, and the cottage empty, I must return as soon as possible.' Gemma clenched her fists at the thought of her grandfather having to deal with their relatives. And if the cottage was empty, it was possible that Tullia would wreak havoc.

'If my father didn't need help with the business–' He broke off with a grunt of frustration.

'I can't wait,' Gemma said. 'My grandfather is in trouble, or he would never have asked Leandro to return home. He knows how ill my uncle is.'

'Even though I will miss you more than words can say, you must return to your family. They need you.' Claude cupped her face in his hands. 'I will follow as soon as is possible.'

Gemma could feel the roughness of the callouses on his palms, his hands those of a labourer rather than a noble. He worked hard, she knew, and never asked his men to do anything he wouldn't. She loved him for it, and wished they could have been married before she had to leave.

'We will be together again,' she promised, but her heart ached at the thought of her lonely journey ahead.

The port of Genoa shone in the distance, bright sunlight reflecting off the white-washed houses shimmering on the horizon. Gemma stood in the shade, agitated at the thought of being in her own country once more. In the four years she had spent away from Italy so much had happened, and she wasn't the same girl who had left in the dead of night on the back of her horse.

The voyage was almost over, and Gemma was grateful. She'd hated shutting Ombra in the hold, even though the mare had coped well with the journey. She wondered if Ombra could smell the scents of Italy in the air, if she knew that she was almost home.

Gemma closed her eyes and thought of Claude, of the last time they had been together before she left Avignon, his gentle kisses that made her shiver with delight, the velvet softness of his skin, the scrape of his stubble against her cheek, and she suddenly yearned to have him there with her. The feeling was so strong that she almost believed she only had to open her eyes and she would see him, standing before her.

She kept her eyes closed, reluctant to break the illusion. And then another image appeared in her mind, accompanied by the familiar scent of rosemary and sage, his smooth, healing hands caressing her skin as they lay together in grief and ecstasy. *Nicholas*.

The air went still about her, the creaking of the ropes stopped, the shouts and laughter of the sailors faded into nothing, and she felt herself on the edge of an abyss. But she wasn't alone. There was a faint pulsing, another soul there with hers, a tiny spark in the enveloping darkness.

Gemma recalled the vision she and her mother had seen, and placed her hand on her stomach. It hadn't been wrong, after all. She was returning to the cottage with the next healer already growing inside her.

Chapter Forty-Two

Before going to her grandparents at the villa, Gemma had one thing to do. She stood in the shadows of the trees at the edge of the clearing, holding onto Ombra's reins, both as still as statues in the twilight gloom. A cool breeze blew through the leaves, a welcome relief after the heat of the day.

Across the meadow, where once there had been the wooden hut where her mother had been held prisoner until William Hopkins had taken her to Lucca, there was now a small stone-walled cottage. Gemma recognised the tree growing next to it; the tiny oak sapling she had planted all those years before now reached the roof of the cottage, its branches stretching towards the grey walls.

There were none of the usual noises coming from the cottage; no pots clattering against a stone hearth, no laughter or chatter, not even the snores of an exhausted labourer. Gemma pulled her cloak around her, prepared to wait as long as it took to find out who lived there.

A sudden movement up among the branches caught her eye. She turned in time to see an owl swoop down, silent as a ghost, to the carpet of leaves on the ground. There was the sound of a scuffle and a small shriek in the quiet, then it flew away with a mouse dangling from its talons.

With a shiver, Gemma peered again at the cottage, then gripped the reins tighter when she saw it. A spiral of smoke wisping up from the chimney, so faint she would have missed it if she hadn't noticed the owl. She tied Ombra's reins to a tree and stroked the mare's nose, whispering to her to keep quiet, then crept towards the cottage, feeling vulnerable without the cover of the trees.

Gemma crouched beneath a window and strained her ears. The shutters were closed, but she could hear someone moving inside. A faint song reached her, a soulful melody hummed in time with soft footsteps as the person... no, the woman, walked around the room.

Straightening up, Gemma risked a glance through the gap between the shutters. At first she could see nothing, then her eyes gradually became used to the candlelight inside. A heavily pregnant woman came into view, holding a young girl in her arms as they swayed in time to her singing. The girl had her arms around the woman's neck, and the flickering candle kept her face in shadow. Gemma squinted, frustrated.

A movement came from a corner, and a man appeared. He wrapped his arms around the woman and the girl, but the girl wriggled free and slipped to the floor.

'Mamma!' She tugged on her mother's skirts, until the woman turned and bent down to her, the man ruffling the girl's hair. All three turned, and she finally saw them.

Gemma legs almost gave way, and she had to lean against the wall for support. Up until that moment she had been holding her emotions in check, but now her fury and hatred returned, threatening to consume her. *How could he?*

The scene she had just witnessed refused to leave her mind, tormenting her with the passion it had stirred up in her. Her father was living in the cottage with Tullia.

Anger surged through Gemma, a blood-red fury that drove all thoughts from her mind except one: revenge. Memories flooded in, of the witch hunters and of the last time she had seen Morgana in the dank prison where they'd kept her, and grief and anger and hatred surged through her. It was unthinkable that her father could be living with the woman who had betrayed his wife and brought about her death. His confession to her outside the walls of Lucca had all but destroyed the last vestiges of love she might have felt for him, but this – this was like a knife to her soul.

Whilst in England she had prepared for this moment, together with Katherine and Julia-Ann. Together, they had created a curse to use on those who had done them ill. With a heavy heart, she returned to Ombra and rummaged around in her travel bag until she found the things she needed.

While the singing and dancing continued inside the house, Gemma sat beside the tree and set everything out. The feather of a crow, a stone reminiscent of an old woman's face, a berry from the belladonna plant, a chip from Katherine's pearl, dust from an ancient grave. And a flower from the silver-leaf plant, carried from Italy to England and back again, dry and brittle, but still perfect for her purpose.

As she went over the curse in her head, she thought about how much she wanted Tullia and Teo to suffer. Not only them, but their children, and their children's children, just as she was suffering, just as her unborn child would suffer, never knowing its grandmother.

Gemma lay her hands on the tree's trunk, feeling the rough bark beneath her fingertips scratching against her skin. She rubbed her hands with the brittle flower of the silver-leaf plant, the bitter aroma making her wrinkle her nose. She picked up each item in turn, whispering the curse as she held the object in her hands. The curse hung heavy and menacing in the air, thick black words that stank of smoke and filth and decay, billowing in the breeze as they drifted towards the tree and wrapped themselves among its branches. The more she spoke, the more hatred she poured into every word, condemning the people inside the cottage to their fate.

She took the curse that she had created with Katherine and Julia-Ann and built on it, adding stone after stone to its crushing weight, sending it up to the highest branches of the tree and down into the soil around the cottage. And when the curse was ready, she called out to all tormented souls and bound them to the tree, entwining their ethereal bodies among the leaves, leaving them screaming and pleading for the soul catcher to release them from their torment.

This time Tullia wouldn't escape her destiny.

Chapter Forty-Three

Exhausted, Gemma and Ombra approached the villa at a slow walk, the mare's hooves stirring up small clouds of dust on the dry track. The heavy oak front door opened and a servant popped his head out.

'Who's there? What d'you want at this time of night?'

She slid off Ombra's back, stumbling slightly. 'Giacomo, is that you? It's me, Gemma.'

'Milady!' He hastily wiped some crumbs from his mouth and hurried down the steps. 'I didn't realise it was you, my eyes aren't what they were. 'Tis good to have you back!'

'It's good to be back, Giacomo.'

'I'll send for a stableboy, then tell your grandfather you're here.'

In no time at all a young lad was leading Ombra to the stables, while Gemma stood in the doorway, brushing the dust of travelling off her clothes.

'Gemma!' Her grandfather's voice was tremulous, but the arms that grasped her in a hug were as strong and wiry as she remembered.

For a moment she forgot all her weariness and troubles as she leaned against him, the gesture still as comforting as it had been when she was a child.

'How is my grandmother?'

'She is no better, but no worse, thank goodness. Did Leandro come with you?'

'He isn't well, either. I told him to stay in Avignon, the journey was too arduous for him.'

'I thank the Lord you were able to come. The situation is a little… delicate, shall we say.' He glanced at the servants standing nearby. 'But it is late. Get some rest, and we shall talk in the morning.'

'Perhaps I should see Grandmother first.' Gemma yawned.

'Isotta is fast asleep for now. We give her something every evening to help her rest through the night at least, even if she can't sleep. And you look like you should be in bed, you must be exhausted.'

'I am,' she admitted.

'Your grandmother will still be here in the morning. Go, get some rest, and tomorrow I will take you to her first thing.'

Too tired to argue, Gemma made her way upstairs to her room, a maid following with her belongings. After a quick wash and a change of clothes, she lay down, pulled the blanket over her, and was soon fast asleep.

Gemma found it hard to believe that the pale, thin woman lying in the bed was her grandmother. Isotta's usually ruddy cheeks and warm, glowing skin were grey and gaunt, leaving behind a pale imitation of the woman she had once been.

'Gemma, is that you?' Isotta opened her eyes and struggled to sit up.

'Shh, don't tire yourself.' Gemma sat on the edge of the bed and stroked her grandmother's cheek. Her skin was cold and papery, coated with a slight sheen of sweat. Gemma had seen this many times before with her elderly patients, and knew that Isotta was at the end of her time. It could be hours, or perhaps days, but the Healer would come to welcome Isotta to her bosom soon.

After preparing a tisane and helping her grandmother to drink it, Gemma watched as Isotta fell asleep again, her breathing shallow. She opened the shutters a little to let in some air and light, then told the waiting maids to leave.

'Have something to eat and drink, and get some rest while my grandmother is sleeping. We will all need our strength later.'

The two women curtsied and left the room, closing the door quietly behind them.

'Come, Grandfather. Sit here next to me.'

Jacopo carried a stool over and sat on it, glancing at Isotta in concern.

'The draught I gave her is strong, we won't disturb her,' Gemma reassured him.

He rubbed his hands over his face and sighed deeply. 'She hasn't been feeling well for a long time now, but these past few weeks...' He gestured helplessly at her. 'She hardly eats, and only sleeps fitfully, as though she is in terrible pain. But just lately I've sensed a presence with us. I like to think it is your mother, come in our time of need, or perhaps her own mother. I know she sees something – she sometimes lies staring at that corner of the room for hours.'

Gemma looked to where he pointed, but could see nothing.

'It's not here now,' Jacopo said, his face glum. 'It comes and goes, although it is here more often of late.'

'Do you know where her pain is?'

He placed his hand on the right side of his chest. 'There is a lump beneath the skin, hard and round as a chestnut. The skin is warm all around it, even when the rest of her is cold.'

Gemma breathed in sharply. She had seen it many times before. 'There is nothing we can do.'

'That is what your grandmother said,' Jacopo replied sadly. 'She thinks it is her punishment.'

'Punishment? For what?'

'There are many things you do not know about us. There are secrets we have kept hidden, things that Morgana told us about your great-grandmother Alessandra, terrible things she did, things that have shaped our future, your future, for good or for bad.'

'Secrets? What can have been so terrible?' Gemma looked at the frail woman in the bed, her heart heavy. After her father's revelations a few years earlier, she had come to dread family secrets.

The dawn sky grew clearer as Jacopo spoke, quietly at first, the words hesitant, then gradually tumbling out more quickly, as though a dam had burst, freeing his emotions and his shame. He told of the boy who almost died at birth, whose future was revealed when Alessandra breathed life into him; of how she had him sent away, and told the mother her son was dead, rather than risk having her family torn apart; and of how the boy, a grown man now, returned to wreak havoc on their lives.

He wept, the tears rolling down his whiskery cheeks, as he told Gemma how Morgana had had no choice but to marry Teo to save the family's reputation. His face crumpled when he said how Teo and Leandro had ruined their wives' lives and brought death to them both, one way or another.

Gemma listened, stony-faced, hardly able to believe the secrets that were being whispered in the room, the words that came out of Jacopo's mouth and swirled all around, insinuating themselves into her thoughts and tormenting her. *If only* tumbled in her head, those two little words that had so much power. So many things could have been different, *if only...* She leaned forward, feeling sick, and her forehead touched her grandmother's hand.

Susurrated pleas tumbled over each other in their hurry to be heard, crashing into one another like tumultuous waves on a beach, shattering on the shore as others took their place. *Please make it stop, make the hurt stop, I can't bear the pain, it burns deep inside me, I am suffering, have mercy on me, Healer, this is my punishment for my mother's sins of the past, I cannot go on, you must help me, please help me, use the belladonna, it will be quick and painless, anything rather than this terrible nightmare that never ends, please –*

Gemma jerked her head back, pressing her fingers against her temples. The pleas stopped instantly. Her grandmother's still body gave no sign of the turmoil within. Hesitant, Gemma gently placed a finger on Isotta's hand. The urgent whispers began again, fainter this time, but just as desperate and chaotic as before.

'You can hear her.' It wasn't a question. Jacopo stared at the floor, his eyes red-rimmed from crying. His face was pale in the early morning light, grey and shadowed as though he had just emerged from a grave. 'I can't hold her hand anymore, her pain is too much for me to bear.' He grasped Gemma's arm, an anguished look on his face. 'The Healer has sent you back to us, you can help her move on, you can take away this pain from her.'

'No. I–' It was too much. The emotions Gemma had been holding back burst to the surface, overwhelming her. She stood and rushed out of the room, tears streaming down her face as she left the room, and her grandparents, behind her. Running along the corridor, she paid no attention to the stunned servants who stepped quickly out of her way, her only desire to leave the house with its tainted atmosphere and ghostly memories.

Her shoulder against the wooden front door, she charged through without looking and crashed into someone standing on the doorstep.

'Watch where you're going!' a voice shouted.

Rubbing her shoulder, Gemma raised her head. The man standing before her reeled backwards, clutching his hand to his chest.

'Morgana?' he whispered. Then, recovering himself, he looked more closely at her. 'No, you're not. But those eyes–' He blanched.

Gemma held her head high and smiled. 'I'm her daughter, Gemma. And you must be my dear cousin Gregorio.'

Chapter Forty-Four

Despite her bravado, Gemma wanted nothing more than to run to Ombra and gallop away from the villa, her dying grandmother, and the trouble her cousin was here to cause. But she knew she couldn't leave her grandfather alone with Gregorio, so she clenched her fist and straightened her chin.

'This happens to be my grandparents' house, I have every right to be here. What do you want?'

'Since I heard about your grandmother's ill health, I have written every day to pay my respects to her. Your grandfather, for reasons only he knows, insists I must not come. So I decided to take matters in my own hands.'

Gemma shook her head. 'He told me about the time he had to throw you and your parents out of his house.' She gestured behind her. 'This very house. I think you know full well why you aren't welcome.'

Gregorio snorted. 'That was my father's fault, the blathering buffoon never had any manners.'

'Had?'

'He died, a few weeks ago.' Gregorio made the sign of the cross, a suffering expression on his face.

'My condolences.' Gemma hesitated. 'But I still can't allow you to enter, I'm afraid.'

'My mother no longer travels, trouble with her legs.' He waved his hand vaguely in the air. 'She wanted me to pay my regards to your grandmother on her behalf...' His voice faded as someone arrived behind Gemma.

'I have told you over and over again that you are not welcome here.' Jacopo folded his arms across his chest, his face red with fury.

'But cousin, I thought we could put the past behind us.' Gregorio put on a placating smile.

'And what of the curse?'

Gregorio's smile faltered.

'Curse?' Gemma asked.

'Rina told us, not long after you left,' Jacopo said to her, not taking his eyes off Gregorio. 'She was there, the day they burned Morgana.'

'Idle threats, from a woman who was about to die and had nothing left to fear.' Gregorio shifted uncomfortably and scratched his cheek, his fingernail rasping against the faint stubble.

'My mother didn't do anything without reason, whether it was threats or promises,' Gemma replied. 'Her healing powers were strong enough to bring someone back from the brink of death – why do you think her curse was a mere "idle threat"?'

Gregorio paled.

'How did Edmondo die?' Jacopo asked, still standing in front of the doorway.

'He – the doctor said it was his heart.' Gregorio wiped some sweat from his forehead. 'He hadn't been feeling too well, and then insisted on carrying my mother's luggage down the stairs instead of getting the servants to do it. He just collapsed, in the middle of the hallway, and never rose again.'

'Where was he going?' Jacopo glared at Gregorio until he tugged nervously at his collar.

'Why here, of course. We had just got the news about Isotta, and immediately decided to visit, so we could help in any way.'

Gemma and Jacopo remained silent. Gregorio stood, shoulders hunched, his brow furrowed.

'You don't honestly think that–?'

'What did my mother say to you?' Gemma asked quietly.

'It was all nonsense,' Gregorio blustered, but he began to edge away from them.

'Rina told me that your parents seemed terrified,' Jacopo said.

'It's strange that your father died while preparing to come here,' Gemma mused, her finger on her lip. 'The curse must be stronger than usual. What did she say would happen to you?'

Gregorio backed away, his arms splayed as he tried to keep his balance. 'No, no! You're mad, the lot of you! There is no curse on me and my family, no one can do that!'

'And yet your father is dead and your mother unwell.' Gemma took a step towards him, making him stumble backwards, and grasped his hand. She closed her eyes and breathed in deeply. 'I see... a darkness all around you, a blackness swirling with the spirits... wait, no, they are demons, come to take you down to the depths of hell with them.' She groaned, her eyelids fluttering. 'The flames are burning in a roaring fire, the demons reach out for your soul, clutching it to their breasts as they drag it down into the abyss, their claws ensnared in your essence as you writhe to free yourself...' With a loud gasp, Gemma opened her eyes wide and stared wildly at Gregorio. 'Go. Please go before it's too late. You might still be able to save yourself, but you must leave now.'

He fell over, a cloud of dust rising into the air, and for a moment Gemma saw the ghostly outline of someone reaching out to grab him.

'Go, now!' she screeched in panic.

Gregorio managed to pick himself up, grimacing as he put weight on his right foot, then half ran, half hobbled down the track to his waiting carriage. He didn't look back, and didn't stop until he reached the carriage and flung himself inside.

Gemma suddenly slumped, tired and weak. Jacopo caught her, and guided her back indoors to the parlour.

'Thank you. I don't know what I would have done if you hadn't been here,' he said, chuckling. 'Pretending the curse would send him to hell. Even I thought your vision was real.'

Gemma sat on a stool and gratefully accepted a cup of water from a servant, her hand trembling. Beads of sweat coated her brow. 'Pretending?'

Jacopo paled. 'You mean...?'

'It was all true.' She leaned forward as her head spun, and Jacopo hurried to pour her a glass of wine.

'Here, drink this.'

She took the cup and sipped at the wine, feeling her emotions calming. They sat in silence, watching the flames flicker in the fireplace. Gemma wondered what her grandfather was thinking, whether he was as scared as she felt, but she didn't dare ask.

All of a sudden, the sound of running feet and brusque orders broke out in the hallway, startling them both. Jacopo strode over to the door and flung it open.

'What is the meaning of this?' he demanded.

The servants froze to the spot, and a young lad spoke, barely able to contain his agitation. 'There's been an accident, down the bottom of the hill. The carriage was out of control, it went headlong into a tree and hit it. The coachman and the passenger was flung onto the road, it looked pretty nasty. I was there, I saw it,' he added, in case no one believed him. 'I came to get help, fast as I could!'

Gemma, standing behind her grandfather, felt the world shift beneath her feet as the boy spoke. She could vaguely hear Jacopo giving orders, sending some servants to find a physician and others to the scene of the accident. But she already knew it would be pointless. The shadows had come for Gregorio, and by now his soul would be theirs. She would not mourn his death, or his father's, and could shed no tears for her devastated aunt.

But she would remember the images she had seen while touching his hand until the day she died. Up until then, she had never imagined the power of a curse could be so strong, and almost felt a hint of remorse for the curse she had unleashed on Tullia. Almost.

Chapter Forty-Five

Gemma knew it wouldn't take long for news of her return to reach Gallicano. By mid-morning the first villagers had arrived, come to gossip over the terrible accident, and at the same time asking when she would be back at the cottage to tend to their ailments. She wondered whether Tullia knew yet.

'Tell them I must look after my grandmother for now, I can't help anyone else at this time,' she said to the servant, biting back the angry retort on the tip of her tongue.

Jacopo grunted. 'You have every right to tell them where to put their damned coughs and broken bones! But they were mere pawns in the Witchfinder's game, doing his will with no thought for anyone but themselves.'

'That doesn't make it right,' Gemma snapped.

'Of course not. And you must do what is best for you. But remember you are a healer, as were your mother, grandmother, and great-grandmother, and no matter what has happened you have a duty, if not to these people, then to their children and grandchildren.'

Gemma lowered her eyes, chastened. 'It will not be easy.'

'I know. But you have so much good inside you, I know you will do what must be done.' Jacopo squeezed her hand. 'Be strong, *cara*. The day is long and Isotta needs you.'

Her grandmother. Gemma knew she had to ignore the plight of the villagers, and of Tullia and her father, until Isotta... She pushed aside the thought, unable to contemplate such an ending.

Isotta lay in the bed, her skin pale and waxy, her breathing shallow. She turned her head when Gemma entered the room and gave her a weak smile. Gemma sat beside her, sadness washing over her.

'How are you today?' she asked, hating herself for asking such a pathetic question. Isotta was clearly in pain; her skin was taut over her bony cheeks, the lines at the edges of her eyes even more evident as she struggled to hide the pain that coursed through her body.

'I'm glad you could be here,' Isotta whispered, her clawed fingers clutching at Gemma's hand. 'I didn't want Leandro to see me like this.'

Gemma placed her hand on Isotta's forehead. 'You're burning with fever! I've got some willow bark, I'll make a tisane.'

Isotta gripped harder. 'Don't. It won't make any difference. I'm dying, child, as you well know. The disease within is too strong, it is consuming me. There is nothing you can do.'

'No!' Gemma fought back tears. 'I'll do everything I can. Perhaps the silver-leaf plant will help...' Her voice faded as Isotta weakly shook her head.

'Many years ago I was like you, trying to do everything I could to save my mother. But each day she worsened, a little at a time, until we both knew nothing could save her. She was old and tired and sick, Gemma, just as I am now, and she begged me to help her on her way. As I am begging you.'

Time seemed to stop as Gemma fought against the shock of her grandmother's words. Morgana's voice came to her then, and Gemma could picture the two of them sat in the Grove, many years earlier, sorting through the basket of herbs.

'Sometimes, when there is no other way to help someone, we must prepare a remedy that will take away their pain forever.' Morgana held up the cuttings of several plants. 'Every healer prays she will never have to use these, but it is a part of life. The toothless old man who can no longer eat, the injured labourer with rot in his leg, the elderly woman whose body is too weak to move; if they do not want to carry on, if life is too much of a burden for them to bear, then we will respect their wishes and be at their side at the moment of death.'

Gemma forced down a lump in her throat, her mouth suddenly dry. 'Tell me how.'

While her grandmother told her where to find the recipe in the book, Gemma sensed the room shrink around her as the shadows slowly appeared. Healers from the past, come to take one of their own back into the fold.

'They are here,' Isotta whispered, her eyes glistening. 'They have come for me.'

'Grandfather,' Gemma called.

He must have been standing outside the door, as he entered immediately. He took one look at Gemma's face and hurried to Isotta's side, grasping her hand in his. Tears rolled down his cheeks and dripped onto the linen pillowcase.

'How long?' he asked Gemma, never taking his eyes off his wife.

'I don't know,' Gemma replied. 'It could be hours.'

Jacopo turned then, his cheeks flushed. 'You can see them,' he said. 'The other healers. Are they nearby, ready to take her soul, or do they hang back while she suffers?'

The shadows were close to the walls, almost indistinguishable from the darker corners of the room.

'It is not her time yet,' Gemma said quietly.

'If you ever loved your grandmother, please put her out of her pain,' Jacopo begged. 'She has borne so much in her life, give her this freedom now.'

The room was silent as everyone awaited her answer. Despite the open window, the air was heavy and cloying, and Gemma could see her grandmother's chest labouring with every breath. She reached out and touched the papery skin of Isotta's arm, feeling the blood flowing through her veins, experiencing every second of pain that her grandmother felt.

She gestured to a servant standing silently nearby. 'Bring me some hot water and a cup.' The girl scurried away, and Gemma felt empty inside at the thought of what she was about to do.

By the time the servant came back with the steaming pot of water, Gemma had prepared the herbs, taken from the bag she always carried with her. The shadows were still at the edge of the room, waiting, watching.

As the herbs steeped and the water cooled, the sun travelled across the sky. The sunbeams stretched over the floor, and the shadows merged into one as the light changed. Gemma strained off the tisane into the wooden cup, then held it to her grandmother's lips and helped her drink.

Side by side, Gemma and Jacopo watched Isotta's face relax as she fell into a dreamless sleep. The healers drew closer, their shadows crossing the room, until they stood all around the bed. There was a moment's hush before the Healer held out a hand. Gemma saw a light rise up from her grandmother's body, a shimmer that became the faint outline of a young woman. The shadows clustered around, gathering her to them, and then they were gone.

Chapter Forty-Six

Gemma couldn't bear to see Jacopo's grief, so profound, so like her own. The hardest thing had been letting her grandmother go, even though she knew Isotta needed to be freed from the unrelenting pain of her illness.

Once arrangements had been made for the funeral, Gemma searched the house until she found Jacopo outside in the garden.

'She loved to sit there,' he said as she approached, his gaze fixed on a marble bench beneath a cherry tree. 'Every season was magical for her: spring, bringing new buds after the long winter cold; summer, with its riot of colours as the flowers bloomed and fruit ripened; autumn's reds and golds, a rich cloak of leaves on the ground; and winter, the time to rest while nature sleeps, so that both body and mind are ready when spring returns once more. Every season she would take some time for herself during the day to come here.'

'I remember she would put blossom in my plaits,' Gemma said, emotional at the memory. 'I felt like a princess, wearing a crown of petals.'

They walked over to the bench and sat down together, side by side.

'I'm going back to the cottage,' she said quietly.

'I thought you might.' He turned and gave her a wistful smile. 'I didn't have a chance to tell you about your father, and who he's–'

Gemma shook her head. 'I know.'

Jacopo gave a resigned shrug. 'Of course you do. Just be careful. I don't trust them, not as far as I could throw them.' He looked at his arms. 'And these days it wouldn't be far at all.'

'I'll be careful. Besides, I have the dragonflies to protect me, and Mamma swore there were ghosts in the cottage. And you are close by. I know I will be safe.'

'I will always worry about you, until my dying day.'

'You will be all right, won't you?' Gemma frowned. 'I can stay if you need me.'

'I will be fine here, with my memories and the servants to take care of me.' Jacopo put his arm around her shoulder and squeezed her in a tight hug. 'My only wish is to see you settled at the cottage with a family that loves you as much as I do.'

'Perhaps one day.' Gemma didn't want to mention Claude, didn't want to utter his name in case she brought bad luck upon them. The child growing within her was all that she needed, if he decided not to come to her. She ignored the niggling voice of doubt that nudged at her mind, insistent, insinuating, full of *what ifs*. The next healer was growing inside her, and that was the only thing that mattered.

Gemma tied Ombra to a tree and approached the cottage on foot. A breeze blew across the clearing, making the dead leaves on the doorstep skitter over the stone with a dry, scratching sound. It looked as though nobody had been living there for a while; when she opened the door, the musty smell of closed rooms and stale air wafted out around her.

Inside, the cottage was exactly as she remembered it: the smoke-blackened fireplace with the hook for the pot hanging in the middle; the aged wooden table, with its myriad marks and scratches, added to over the years as children came, grew up, and left; the pallet in the corner for those patients who had to stay overnight so the healer could tend to them whenever necessary; and her mother's plates, pots, and pans, each one as familiar to her as the backs of her hands.

Gemma walked through to the pantry, where all the herbs were stored in glass jars and earthenware pots. Bunches of dried lavender and sage hung from hooks in the shelves, their fragrance at once welcoming and heartbreaking. She leaned her head against the door frame and closed her eyes, wishing her mother was there to greet her in a loving hug, insisting on learning all her news while putting a pot of water on to boil for a warming tisane.

She held onto the moment for a little longer, so that she could pretend that everything was how it used to be, that her mother was out in the Grove gathering herbs for her remedies, that she would hear Morgana chattering to the birds as she came indoors.

A whinny and a snort brought her out of her reverie. Closing the pantry door behind her, she hurried outside to where she'd left Ombra. The mare stood placidly beneath the tree, blowing softly through her nose as a dragonfly settled between her ears.

'You're right, I should go to the Grove,' Gemma murmured. The dragonfly dipped its wings a few times, then flew away across the garden.

A cat mewed at her feet and she picked it up, delighted when it began to purr loudly. Slow steps took Gemma along the path, past familiar sights such as the chicken coop, where its inhabitants, looking bedraggled and patchy, scratched around in the bare earth; the outhouse, hidden behind a screen of bushes; the chopping block with the axe lodged in it, the blade turning rust-red, the apple tree she had grown from a seed spat on the ground when she was two or three years old. And then she arrived at the gate.

Beyond, the plants were overgrown but healthy. If nothing else, her father had taken care of the Grove, as he'd promised. Recent rains had encouraged vigorous growth, and shoots tangled into each other as the plants sprawled across the ground. Gemma put down the cat, lifted the latch, and stepped inside as the gate creaked open.

Entering the Grove had always felt to her as though she were entering the fairy realm. The colours, the scents, the feel of the leaves against her fingers, the rough bark of the trees and bushes, the perfumes of lemon, lavender, rosemary and a myriad of herbs mingling in the misty morning air, greens and lilacs and pinks and whites and yellows vying for attention as the sun filled them with its energy and light, the soft curves of branches and leaves against the sharp edges of the stone wall at the far end, berries and flowers and leaves for healing and for assisting both life and death.

Gemma took a deep breath, inhaling the magic of the Grove, and turned slowly to take in everything around her. There was work to be done, both here and in the cottage, but for the moment she pushed aside the thoughts that were troubling her and allowed herself to be immersed in the calm and quiet of the Dragonfly Grove.

After so long away, she was home.

Chapter Forty-Seven

Gemma had known he would come. People's tongues wagged, and the gossipmongers spread their news faster than a fire through dry kindling. She knew it would only be a matter of time, and that time was now come.

She stared at the person on the doorstep, her hands on her hips, without saying a word. The cat rubbed its body against her leg, then sat down and began licking its front paw.

He shuffled his feet, coughed nervously and spat a ball of phlegm on the ground, then held out his hands in supplication. 'Daughter.'

'You only have one daughter, and she is back at your home with your... wife.' Gemma couldn't keep the profound hatred out of her voice.

'We're not... I mean, she's not...' Teo's words faded as she glared at him.

'Really? You seemed very cosy together when I saw you a few nights ago.'

He had the grace to blush and turn his head in shame.

'You promised to look after the Grove,' Gemma said, the words painful to speak. 'I left in good faith that you would tend to the plants and the dragonflies.'

Teo jerked his head up. 'I did! I visited the Grove every day, made sure that everything was all right. I came last week – the plants are a bit wild, granted, but they looked healthy enough to me.'

'But you said you would stay here, protect the cottage!' Gemma snapped.

'I...' Teo ran his hand through his greying hair, suddenly looking weary. 'I had to leave, she gave me no choice.'

'Everyone has a choice.' But seeing his face, a feeling of dread crept over her. 'What happened?'

'Can I come in? There are things I have to tell you, I would prefer not to do it out in the open.' He glanced around. 'Even the trees have ears.'

Gemma stood aside to let him enter, then closed the door behind him. Standing with his shoulders hunched, he seemed lost

'It's different without your mother.' Teo gestured to the fire. 'There was always a pot of water boiling there, and herbs strewn over the table. I didn't realise how much–' He put his hand to his mouth and rubbed at his thick beard.

'Tell me what you have to say,' Gemma said, more sharply than she intended. She'd never seen her father so weak, so destroyed by life, and it saddened her, although she would never admit it to him.

Teo sat down heavily on a chair at the table, and clasped his hands together. Gemma saw they were no longer the pale, slender hands of an aristocrat, but the calloused, dirt-ingrained ones of a labourer.

He caught her staring. 'There are many things that have changed since you went away,' he said softly. '*I* have changed.'

'So I see. Now, tell me what you came here to say.' She sat down opposite him, but didn't offer him a drink or something to eat. She wanted him out of the cottage as quickly as possible, away from her confused feelings of pity and hate.

'Where do I start?' He thought for a moment, tapping his fingers on the table. 'So much has happened since you left. I lived here, at the cottage, avoiding everyone, until Tullia came here one evening, her belly huge with child. *His* child.'

'William Hopkins'?'

Teo nodded. 'None of the villagers would have anything to do with her. It was as though she had enchanted them in a spell to make them do her bidding, and when your mother died, the spell was broken.'

Somehow, Gemma managed to bite her tongue and let him continue.

'And when William Hopkins died on the same day as Morgana, they began to regard Tullia with suspicion. They shunned her, and crossed to the other side of the path to avoid her.'

'Why didn't she return to her home? I would have.'

'She didn't want to. Tullia had spent her whole life wanting revenge on the Innocenti, she couldn't stop.'

'My mother died! Wasn't that enough for her?' Gemma shouted, startling her father. The cat, who had been sleeping on a nearby stool, leaped down and slunk away, its tail bristling.

'Tullia's desire for revenge goes deeper than that.' Teo rubbed the back of his neck, then leaned forward. 'Accusing your mother of being a witch was just the beginning. She wanted to take the cottage and the Grove, and destroy them. Take everything away from you, as your ancestors did to hers. She has centuries of resentment buried inside her, and nothing will stop her.'

'But the cottage is still here,' Gemma said, puzzled. 'The plants, the Grove, everything is almost as I left it.'

Teo's body sagged, as though the burden of talking was too much. 'The night she came here, she was intent on destruction. I heard her shouts first, then saw her stride across the clearing with a flaming torch in her hands, heading for the Grove. I ran out and grabbed her, took the torch away, and brought her inside.' His hands trembled as he spoke. 'She sat here, one arm wrapped around her belly, the other ready to strike me as soon as I lowered my guard. The words she said, full of bitter hate, her voice... God, her voice, it seemed to come from Hell itself.'

Gemma looked down at her hands, her knuckles white, unable to say anything.

'Tullia said she would come back, night after night, until she had destroyed me, and then the Grove. She wants the end of the healers, Gemma, she wants to finish the curse Filippo put on your family centuries ago.' He banged his fist on the table. 'She told me she was searching for a silver dagger that Filippo used during the rite when he put the curse on Agnes and Riccardo, that she could use it to destroy the Innocenti forever. I took it as a madwoman's ravings, and laughed at her.'

Gemma kept her face as still as possible, while her mind whirled. All the healers knew about the knife used to spill the blood for the curse, the story was passed down from generation to generation. And on her travels through France she had found a letter tucked away in the recipe book that her great-grandmother had written before she died, which mentioned a dagger – was it the same one?

Her mind focused on other things, she didn't realise her father was still speaking.

'–the curse didn't work centuries ago, so what hope did she have now?' Teo was pale, beads of sweat coating his brow. 'She leaned over and kissed me, and I saw...' He faltered, anguish on his face. 'I saw things that were to come. Terrible things, death, destruction, the livelihoods of the people on the mountain gone, many having to leave while their homes fell to ruin and the animals died in the fields.'

'She has the sight as well,' Gemma said, surprised.

'Tullia is an Innocenti, just like you. After she had shown me those things, she taunted me, telling me how it was all my fault, that I was doomed to lose everything I loved. There was no need to tell me that, I already knew.' He looked at Gemma, his eyes glistening with tears. 'I asked her what would make her stop. And then I knew how truly mad she was. She said that if I wanted to save what I held dearest, I would have to marry her. We would live in a cottage built on the place where your mother was held prisoner, where the witch hunters tortured her. I would fall asleep with Morgana's cries in my ears, and awaken to her desperate pleas every morning, and my dreams would be filled with visions of her death.' He sobbed then, a deep, agonised sound that bore the weight of his suffering.

'You agreed?' Gemma spoke quietly, almost a whisper.

'I couldn't let... those things happen, to any of you. The villagers, your grandparents, you... I had no choice. It was the only way to save the cottage and the Grove.' He thumped his fist on the table. 'This is my penitence for what I did to your mother, and it is my gift to you. I relive my actions every second I am in that cottage, nightmares plague my sleep, but I will carry this burden to my grave so that you may continue your work as a healer.'

Gemma put her hand on his sleeve. 'I can make something that will allow you a deep, dreamless sleep, at least.'

'No!' Teo snatched his arm away. 'I don't want your help. I deserve this, don't you understand? All I ask is that you live your life, as your mother would have wanted, as I want. I have been a terrible, selfish husband and father, I see that now. I don't need your forgiveness, and I won't ask for it. Your mother deserved better than me, she deserved someone who would love her in a way that I never could.' He rose from the chair and wiped his hands on his trousers. 'I've said all I came to say. I won't come again. Live your life, Gemma. I wish you love and happiness, and that you can be safe from all harm.'

He shuffled over to the door, his tread heavy and reluctant.

'Wait,' Gemma said.

He half turned, his hand on the doorknob.

'The first night I came back to Gallicano, I saw you in the house. You, Tullia, and her daughter. Tullia is with child — yours, I presume.'

'I had no choice.' Teo looked down at the floor.

'I–' Gemma stumbled over the words. 'I put a curse on the house. I couldn't bear to see you all so happy there, while Mamma was dead because of that woman. So I cursed Tullia and all her descendants to a life of catching the souls of anyone who dies on the tree that grows there. The tree I planted as a tiny sapling with Mamma when I was little.'

'I know.'

'What?'

'Tullia sensed something was different, and then we heard that you had returned. It wasn't difficult to work out what you had done.

She screamed obscenities in your name, tried to remove it, but it is too strong.'

'It can't be broken,' Gemma said, looking him straight in the eyes. 'Not until one is born who is truly pure of heart, bearing no hatred or ill wishes towards the Innocenti. Only she can break it, but this will not be for many centuries yet. If ever.'

'You are your mother's daughter,' Teo said, and Gemma thought she heard a hint of pride. 'Fare ye well, *tesoro*. We will not see each other again.' He turned the doorknob and stepped outside, a broken shell of the man he had once been.

Chapter Forty-Eight

September 1635

Gemma worked hard at the cottage, getting everything ready before winter arrived. A carpenter from the village built a stable for Ombra, and a small barn to store hay. Jacopo had told her to take Ombra to the stables at the villa, but Gemma couldn't bear to be apart from her for a single moment.

The Dragonfly Grove was tidy again, the plants cut back, most of the weeds gone. Dragonflies swarmed around Gemma while she worked, a whirlwind of bright colours and sparkling wings that swooped and twisted and spiralled throughout the Grove. And sitting on the fountain was the damselfly, as wise as ever, its wings folded neatly along its back as it observed her pulling up weeds.

Her grandfather sent some men to look over the cottage and fix anything that might leak or let in draughts in the winter. Gemma swept and dusted and washed every surface, hung the bedding outside to take advantage of the last days of autumn, and at long last it felt like home once more.

With all the work there was to do, she had no time to visit the grave in the clearing. And if she was honest, Gemma had no wish to go there. She wondered if Bob had known of the fury she had carried in her heart, and came to the conclusion that he had. He knew everything. And yet he had encouraged her to leave, to satisfy her desire to travel and to see more. Had he known what she would do on her return? Or had he hoped that living abroad would quell her thoughts of revenge? Had she done wrong to Tullia? These thoughts and many more constantly filled her mind, and her fear of having brought shame on the healers made her stay away from the clearing in the woods.

Memories of her mother kept her company, as did the shadows in the cottage, although she could never sense Morgana among them. The cat curled up in its place by the fire, tail tucked around its body, filling the room with deep purrs of contentment. And of course, she was never alone: the tiny heart beating within her was a constant promise of better times to come.

Gemma stood on the doorstep watching the rain pour down, little rivulets snaking across the too-dry earth that was unable to absorb so much water all at once. Ombra whickered from her stable, shoving her nose over the half-open door, then shaking her head in disgust as raindrops tickled her whiskers. Gemma had already taken her a bucket of oats, getting drenched as she ran across to the stable.

Having changed her clothes and put her wet things to dry in front of the fire, she had no intention of going back outside.

Her hands wrapped around the wooden cup, the warmth of the tisane seeped through to her fingers. The sweetness of honey on her tongue, together with the gentle aroma of the herbs, brought her a sense of blessed well-being. The peace and quiet of the cottage and the woods around was exactly what she needed to be able to grieve for her grandmother, and her mother. Her life hadn't stopped since the day she left on Ombra's back, and she'd needed this time to heal herself.

The villagers stayed away, whether from guilt or respect, Gemma had no idea. And she was glad of the reprieve, of the opportunity to gather her thoughts and look to her future. She hadn't heard from Claude, but neither had she written to him. A letter had arrived from Katherine, telling her about her children's antics, and Julia-Ann had written to tell her of her marriage. She had replied to both, but she had told neither that she was with child. For now it was her secret.

Across the clearing she saw some branches shaking, and a loud exclamation reached her over the sound of the rain as a man and a horse stepped out from under the trees. Straining her eyes, she tried to make out who it was, but the rain was too heavy. She hoped it wasn't her father, although Teo had kept his promise so far and she hadn't seen him, or Tullia, since the day they'd talked.

'Hello?' she called.

A muffled shout replied from under a hooded cloak. The horse was covered with a blanket in an attempt to keep the rain off, but judging from the way the animal was shaking its head, it wasn't very successful. Ombra whickered from the stable, her ears pricked forward.

Was it one of the villagers? Gemma hoped it was nothing too serious. She was already going over the herbs she had stored in the pantry, ready for any urgent treatment, when the person arrived at the door, pulled back their hood, and smiled at her.

'Hello, Gemma.'

Chapter Forty-Nine

Gemma ushered Claude in. He'd insisted on putting Lumière in the stable with Ombra and drying him off as best he could, telling Gemma to stay indoors and pour him a cup of warm ale. She waited anxiously for him, hardly able to believe he was there, until he stepped through the door, dripping water everywhere.

She silently handed him a piece of linen to dry himself off with, standing to one side as he rubbed vigorously at his head. He peeked out from beneath the damp cloth with a wide grin, which quickly faded when he saw her staring at him.

'Gemma? I thought you would be pleased to see me.'

She held out her hand for the cloth and Claude passed it to her, confusion on his face. Still unable to speak, Gemma shook it out and hung it on a hook near the fireplace to dry, trying to gather her thoughts. His sudden appearance had shocked her to the core; it was as though thinking about the child inside her had conjured him to the cottage. She took a couple of deep breaths, then turned to face him.

'I... You were the last person I was expecting to see! I thought you were a villager, come for help.' Gemma reached out and touched his cheek, the skin damp and chilled, but firm beneath her fingers. 'I can't believe you're here.'

He put his hand over hers, then pulled her to him and held her close. Heedless of the damp seeping into her dress, she wrapped her arms around him, her head against his shoulder, once more in the place where she felt most safe.

'The letters we wrote to each other weren't enough, I missed you too much,' he murmured against her ear, his breath warm on her skin. 'My father grew tired of me pining about the house and ordered me to come to find you, before the horses stopped foaling because of my sour face.' He kissed her hair. 'I arrived in Genoa early yesterday morning, and came straight here.'

'You must be starving!' Gemma lifted her head, and found him gazing at her.

'I was, but now I find that being with you has sated my hunger and left me desiring other things.'

Gemma ran her fingers through his still-damp hair, a deep yearning rising in her. Blushing, she took him by the hand and led him up the stairs.

They lay in bed listening to the sound of rain on the roof, the heavy drops thudding in time with their heartbeats. Gemma snuggled up to Claude, her mind finally relaxing after the constant turmoil since she'd left England.

He turned to her, the warmth from his body banishing the cold chill of the room. The fire was low, mere embers cooling in the grate, but she didn't want to leave the bed to poke it back to life. Her skin tingled as he ran a finger along her side, moving the sheet so that he could travel further down. She suddenly tensed as his fingertip touched the edge of her birthmark.

'Don't, please,' she said, embarrassed. She always took great pains to keep it covered, and her momentary lapse of caution upset her.

'Is this why you had to leave Italy?' Claude leaned over, placing tender kisses along her throat, and down towards the raised red mark.

Gemma shifted. 'It's why my mother sacrificed herself and was burned for being a witch. She knew that if they saw... that,' she gestured sadly at her stomach, 'then there would be no hope for me.'

He lifted his head and laid his hand gently on the mark. 'Your mother was an incredible woman. As are you, Gemma Innocenti.' He wiped away a tear from her cheek. 'Do you remember your vision of the horses? You said we would be together again, that we had a future. Do you still believe that?'

So much has changed since then, Gemma thought. She remembered that night with Nicholas, their souls reaching out to each other, his desperate grief and her need for comfort, however fleeting, merging until they were entwined both in body and spirit. A brief union that, she knew, could have given her a future healer. Its soul was as ethereal as a dragonfly's wings, but she could feel its faint fluttering within her. Either one of these men could be her child's father.

Nicholas hadn't known her truly, not her deepest secrets and fears. She had left Nicholas, too immersed in his own sorrow to hear her own troubles, knowing it was the right thing to do. Theirs would not have been a happy marriage.

Will you accept me? The thought of baring her soul to Claude was terrifying. She had kept so much hidden inside her, locked away in a place where even she rarely went. Her family had a turbulent history, their lives entwined with healing, magic, and curses, and she was so tired of pretending to be someone she wasn't. There could be no secrets in her marriage, she would not live her life as her mother had, hiding what she was, hiding her husband's secrets. Vulnerable and defenceless, she turned to Claude.

'I have much to tell you.'

Gemma could see Claude through the kitchen window, striding backwards and forwards along the garden path, his head bowed. The rain had stopped, leaving behind a sullen grey sky filled with foreboding, the air heavy around them.

He had listened while she spoke, letting her talk uninterrupted. She told him of her great-grandmother, of the events she had set in motion decades earlier; she told him of her mother, and her ability to see a person's death merely by touching their hand; and she told him of Katherine and Julia-Ann, and how the three of them had created the curse she had later put on Tullia. Gemma told him how she had poured all her anger and hatred for the woman into the curse, making it stronger, almost unbreakable, condemning not only Tullia but all her descendants to a life of misery and heartache. She told him how she had seen the shadow of her cousin's death, shortly before his coach crashed. And lastly, she had told him of Nicholas and his tragic grief, and of the baby she was carrying.

She shivered, terrified of what the future held for them. He had listened, that was true, then he had got dressed and gone downstairs, his footsteps heavy and slow as though he carried a heavy weight. By the time she had followed him down, he was already outside.

He turned and headed for the stable, Ombra's and Lumière's heads hanging over the half-open door. Gemma saw a blue blur flit towards him, and the damselfly landed on his arm. Claude faltered, then lifted the latch and went inside the stable, still carrying the damselfly.

Suddenly weary, Gemma sank onto a chair at the kitchen table, and waited.

The back door opened and Claude entered, his face sombre. He shrugged off his coat and hung it on a hook, then joined her at the table, sitting down with a groan.

'Everything you told me... It was a shock.' He ran a hand through his hair, visibly trembling; though whether from the cold or fear, Gemma couldn't tell. 'My grandmother had certain,' he hesitated, 'skills, however they were nothing compared to your family's. And when you told me of Nicholas, and the...' he gestured to her belly, 'I was full of doubt and jealousy. So much so that I wanted to saddle Lumière and leave immediately.'

Gemma couldn't speak. Her stomach twisted at the thought of losing Claude, the one good thing that had come into her life. She bowed her head, her hair shielding her from his gaze.

'And then the damselfly came. It was the same one we saw in France, wasn't it?' Gemma nodded, still not looking at him. 'I don't know how that's possible, but then, I'm starting to realise that a lot of things are possible with you that shouldn't be. I think...' He faltered, and Gemma could see his fists clench on the table. 'I think I fell into a trance. Could that be it? Yes, perhaps. One moment I was looking at the damselfly on my arm, the next I was – how can I say it? Part of an exodus of people travelling somewhere mystical, somewhere beyond this world, it seemed.

'And there were dragonflies, leading the way!' He leaned forward and grasped her hands. 'I saw things that I never believed were possible, Gemma. Things my grandmother told me about, but that I never truly imagined could exist. And I understood that I can bear it all. Your family's burden, their secrets, even my own jealousy, are nothing when I imagine having to live without you. Being here, at your home, seeing the dragonflies in the Grove, and the plants... everything is how you described it to me, apart from one thing.'

Gemma slowly lifted her head, tears sliding down her cheeks. 'What?' she whispered.

'You never told me about the magic.' He smiled then, a tender smile that caressed her soul, full of the same love she felt for him. 'This place, it felt like home as soon as I stepped into the clearing and saw the cottage. And you. Wherever you are, that is where I am meant to be. That is my destiny, to be by your side forever. If you will have me.'

The tears rolled freely down her face as Gemma replied, 'Always.'

Chapter Fifty

April 1637

CHIARA SCREECHED IN DELIGHT as Ombra set off, Gemma's arms wrapped tightly around her. The mare knew to be careful, and the child loved to sit up high on her back. She waved her arms about, and grabbed a fistful of Gemma's hair.

'Ouch!' Gemma leaned over and blew a raspberry against Chiara's cheek, her daughter's skin soft and smooth.

Chiara jiggled her hand, and Gemma carefully disentangled her hair from her daughter's grasp. She had felt a profound love for Chiara the moment she was born, just over a year earlier, the little snub nose so like Morgana's, and vivid green eyes that were just like her own. Chiara's blonde downy hair had a reddish tinge to it in the sunlight, and Gemma wondered if it would turn red or remain brown like hers. Of Claude she could see little, although she had already picked up a few of her father's mannerisms.

The one thing she had taken from both of her parents was her love of horses. From the first time she had seen Ombra and Lumière, she had remained entranced, softly gurgling with glee as Gemma guided her chubby hand to stroke their velvety noses.

Their lives had changed in so many ways since Claude had turned up at the cottage that rainy day. They had talked late into the night, baring their souls to each other, each word binding them closer, until they knew that they would never be apart again. Their wedding had been a quiet affair, without the usual pomp and celebration. Apart from Jacopo and a few loyal servants, the only other person present had been Rina.

The farmer's wife had lost the sparkle in her eyes after her time in prison with Morgana in Lucca, and her once-plump body bore the signs of prolonged starvation. Gemma often went up to the farm when she knew that Fredi, Rina's husband, was out with the sheep, and they would sit and talk for hours. Rina refused to talk about the terrible things that had happened in prison, but would tell Gemma happier stories about Morgana from times when life had been better.

Claude had adapted to life at the cottage, helping her in the Grove as her belly grew steadily bigger, carrying out small repairs, working in the fields alongside her grandfather's labourers. But his greatest moment was when Jacopo asked him to accompany him on a trip to Spain to buy more horses. He had shown an eye for good-quality animals, and Jacopo had gradually let him take on more responsibility, until only a few weeks earlier her grandfather had told Claude that he was now in charge of that side of the business.

'Your papà is a very lucky man, isn't he?' Gemma chanted to Chiara, helping her clap her hands together. 'And very soon he'll be back from Germany, and we can be together again.' She missed him every moment he was away, even though her days were filled with tending to people's ailments and listening to all the local gossip, or preparing various concoctions for their maladies.

As Ombra returned towards the cottage, her hooves churning up the muddy path that was still soaked from the spring rains, a voice hailed them. Gemma smiled as they approached the familiar figure.

'Look, there's Rina!' she told Chiara, who gurgled happily.

After settling Chiara on a rug and giving her some sticks and pots to keep her occupied, Gemma joined Rina at the table.

'I have some cake, if you'd like,' she began.

'Oh no, I can't stay long,' Rina replied. 'Stella is up at the house making lunch, I'd best get back before she burns the place down.' She clasped her hands in front of her, unusually hesitant to speak. 'I was in the village, and bumped into your father.'

'Teo?' His name felt strange on her tongue, the sound foreign to her ears.

Rina nodded. 'He stopped me, said he had a message for you and would I take it to you. I didn't want to, but he looked so desperate. His eyes were all bloodshot, and his beard looked like it hadn't been cut in months, and he looked... haunted.'

Gemma tried to keep her expression neutral, but felt the familiar pang of anguish at the mention of his troubled life. 'Go on.'

'I told him I couldn't promise anything, but he clutched my hand like I was offering him a reprieve for an execution.' Rina grimaced. 'I've never seen him like that.'

'What was the message?' Gemma asked, after a moment's silence.

'What? Oh, yes. It didn't make much sense to me, but he said you'd understand. "Your intentions aren't as impenetrable as you thought, the walls can be broken down. You must find the thing that was given to your mother by your great-grandmother. If you don't, she will use it to destroy you and your family."' Rina folded her arms across her chest and snorted. 'Told you it didn't make much sense. But he insisted you'd know what he was talking about, made me repeat it a few times so as I'd remember.'

Gemma remained silent, deep in thought. It was obvious her father was talking about the curse she had placed on Tullia, but how could it be broken? And what had her great-grandmother given to Morgana?

'Do you know anything about a gift my great-grandmother made to my mother?' she asked Rina.

'No. The old woman died long before I knew Morgana, when she was still a young maiden. Perhaps your grandfather will know.'

'Perhaps.'

'Do you know what it means, the message?' Rina leaned forward eagerly.

Gemma frowned. 'Not entirely. But I've heard enough to understand that yet again my family is in danger.' She glanced at Chiara, playing happily on the rug, and her heart sank at the thought of having to fight once more for her family's safety.

Chapter Fifty-One

Jacopo rubbed his chin, deep in thought. Gemma waited, resisting the urge to shout in frustration. If there was any chance of him remembering, she had to be patient.

'It was such a long time ago, the years are shrouded in mist for me now.'

Gemma thought that he had aged since Isotta's death, and seemed frailer, as though the vitality had gone from his life. As it probably had, she mused. He had been devoted to her grandmother, their love for each other evident to all.

'I was away, on business,' he said, his face brightening. 'That's it. I was down at the coast, when a servant arrived with an urgent message from Isotta. Our cousins were staying at the villa at the time, causing havoc every day. I returned to find them shouting at Isotta and Morgana. I had to threaten Edmondo, then I threw them out, all three of them.' He frowned as he remembered. 'I'm not a violent man, but that day I had no choice. Alessandra was already dead; whatever she gave Morgana, I didn't see it.'

Gemma slumped in her chair. 'So that's it. I'll never know.'

Jacopo shook his head. 'I'm afraid not.'

The kitchen had always been one of Gemma's favourite places to visit when she lived at the villa. The warmth, together with the aromas of freshly baked food, wrapped her in its arms and made her feel safe, for a while at least. Tessa, the jovial cook, was as much a part of the kitchen as its pots and pans. She had often sat Gemma at the table with a plate of biscuits and a cup of warm milk, her grey eyes sparkling as she told the young girl tales about her family.

Tessa's arms were covered in flour up to her elbows when Gemma entered the kitchen, her face red and shiny from the heat of the great fire.

'Good mornin', milady.' She beamed at Gemma, then returned her attention to the dough she was kneading. ''If you're wanting some biscuits, they're in the usual place. Help yoursel'.'

'Do you mind if I just sit here and watch?'

'O' course you can. Where's the young'un? Gettin' up to mischief somewhere?'

'One of the maids offered to look after her. To be honest, I'm glad for a few minutes' peace.'

Tessa stopped kneading and leaned forward, concerned. 'Somethin' wrong? Not 'is lordship, I 'ope.'

'No, no, nothing like that.' Gemma scraped a piece of dough from the table with her fingernail and began rolling it between her fingers. 'I hoped my grandfather could tell me about something that happened when my great-grandmother died, but he said he wasn't here at the time.'

'What d'you want to know? Old Bernica was her maid back then, stayed with her until the end. She has some tales to tell, believe you me!'

'Where can I find her?'

'She 'as a small cottage out near the stables, seeing as her legs can't take the stairs no more. She'll be there, no doubt about it.'

Gemma stood, almost knocking over the stool in her hurry. 'Thank you!'

'Glad to be of 'elp. Come back for some biscuits when you're done.'

The sounds from the kitchen faded as Gemma hurried through the villa to the side entrance that led to the gardens. Through the narrow door, down the stony path, brushing against lavender bushes that released their perfume into the air, the first sleepy bees of spring moving lazily to the side as she passed, then along the dirt track beneath the old oak trees to the stables. Horses stood in the fields, swishing their tails at irritating flies.

The tiny cottages were to the side of the stables, and mainly used by the grooms and stable lads. But when a servant became too old and infirm for working in the villa and had no family to take care of them, they were allowed to stay there to live out the rest of their lives. As Gemma hurried along, she sent a silent prayer to the Healer that Bernica would be able to help her.

'Sit down, milady.' Bernica gestured to the Dante chair near the fire, then settled herself onto a chair opposite. Her face was as wrinkled as a winter-stored apple, and only a few wisps of white hair covered her skull. She pulled her shawl tightly around her, bony fingers clutching at the wool. 'The older you get, the more you feel the cold. Seems like I've been cold forever.' A throaty chuckle turned into a chesty cough.

'I have something for that down at the cottage, I'll bring it to you tomorrow,' Gemma said.

'No need, no need. I can't be doing with all that. The Lord knows when it will be my time, there'll be no running away from Him. Any day soon, I keeps telling myself.'

'Surely not–'

'Hush. When you get to my age, every day is a torture, not a blessing. When every bone in your body aches, when every movement sends pain throughout you, when your mind is sharp but you can hardly move, and you can only eat gruel 'cause you ain't got a tooth left in your head, you don't want to prolong your time on this earth.'

Gemma picked up a blanket off the floor and wrapped it around Bernica, then stirred up the fire. The cosy room became warmer, and she moved her chair away from the fireplace.

'I remember what it was like to be young, just like you.' When Bernica smiled, the wrinkles in her face became deep crevasses. 'I could run up and down those stairs in the villa like a spring hare, and the times I had to catch your mother afore she fell and broke her neck! 'Twas a sad day they burned her, may their unchristian souls rot in hell.' She sniffed, and wiped her eyes.

'You were my great-grandmother's maid, weren't you?' Gemma asked.

'I was, for many years. Until the day she died, in fact. That broke my heart, her going like that, and with those terrible people staying at the villa, just waiting for her to die. But she was determined to go when *she* wanted, without suffering. 'Twas a terrible burden on Isotta, though.'

'Isotta helped her to die?'

''Tis the burden a healer has to bear, isn't it? Alessandra was a good woman, no matter what others might say,' Bernica blurted, the words coming out in a mumbled jumble. 'As was Isotta. They did what had to be done.' She twisted the shawl around her knobbly fingers, her jaw trembling as her watery blue eyes filled with tears. 'They was good people, both o' them.'

'Yes, they were. I never knew my great-grandmother, but everyone spoke well of her,' Gemma said, trying to reassure Bernica. The old woman nodded. 'I'm grateful my great-grandmother had you as a loyal maid, and a friend. Everyone knows how much you loved her. Tessa suggested I speak to you, when I mentioned I wanted to talk to someone about Nonna Alessandra.'

'There isn't no one knows more than me, milady.'

'That's what I'm hoping.' Gemma hesitated, then blurted the question she had to ask. 'Do you remember Alessandra giving anything to my mother, just before she died?'

'Of course.'

'What?' *Could it really be that easy?*

'Alessandra had to pass it on to her, it's every healer's birthright.'

Gemma's heart sank. 'The recipe book?'

The old woman shook her head, then winced with pain. 'My poor neck. No, not the book, Isotta had that and passed it on to Morgana when she married Teo. The box, the one with the dragonfly on the lid. That was what she gave to Morgana.'

'The box? But didn't Isotta have it?'

'She never liked that box, I have no idea why. She left it with Alessandra when she moved to the cottage with Jacopo. So Alessandra gave it to Morgana.'

'I already have the box.' Gemma rubbed her forehead with her fingertips, frustrated. 'There's nothing in there that could help.' She thumped the arm of the chair with her clenched fist.

'Why don't you tell me what you're looking for?' Bernica said kindly.

'No, it's nothing, I'm sorry to disturb you. I have to go.' Gemma rose to her feet, then stopped when she saw a dragonfly sitting on the ledge of the window. 'What on earth–?'

Bernica followed her gaze. 'Oh, him? He comes to visit me every day, keeps me company while I sit here and think about the past.'

Gemma sank back down onto the chair. She knew that the dragonfly was a sign, that she could trust the old woman, so she took a deep breath and recounted Teo's message to Bernica. When she finished, the old woman remained thinking with her eyes closed for so long that Gemma feared she had gone to sleep.

'"The thing that was given to your mother by your great-grandmother." An object that could break a curse.' Bernica fixed her grey eyes on Gemma. 'There's only one thing it could be.'

'Please, put me out of my misery,' Gemma begged. 'What is it?'

'Why, the silver dagger, of course.'

Chapter Fifty-Two

The dagger. Teo had said Tullia was looking for it, and now Gemma knew why. The knife had been used during the curse that Filippo Innocenti had placed on the family, and the blood spilled into the ground to seal their fate. But she thought it had been lost, or destroyed, centuries earlier, and had been certain that Tullia was seeking it in vain. To learn from Bernica that her great-grandmother had had it in her possession, and had given it to Morgana, had been a shock, to say the least.

She hurried back to the cottage and put Chiara to bed, then turned the place upside down looking for it. There were not many hidey-holes where her mother could have hidden the dagger, but her search was fruitless. Gemma even wondered if Tullia had already found it, then cast aside the idea – if she had, she would have wreaked havoc on them already. Her sleep that night was agitated, full of whispering shadows and sneering faces looking down on her as she ran through an endless tunnel of trees.

She was glad when the first rays of sun peeked over the mountains. Chiara stirred beside her, little arms and legs stretching, mouth opening in a wide yawn, and then the first whimpers for food. Gathering her daughter in her arms before the whimpers could turn into howls, Gemma went downstairs.

Once Chiara's hunger was sated, Gemma wrapped her up well against the early morning chill and set off for the Grove. A few cats slinked along beside them, darting into the undergrowth after small animals or a leaf fluttering in the breeze.

Gemma loved the Grove in spring. The long-dormant plants coming into bud, the quiet stillness of winter broken by the first insects, the white blanket of snow finally melting as the days grew warmer. Birds gathered twigs from the ground to build their nests, calling to each other, and all around there were signs of nature's reawakening.

The ground was too damp to lay Chiara on a blanket, so Gemma wrapped her shawl into a makeshift sling and placed her daughter inside, close to her body. Chiara gave a satisfied burp, closed her eyes, and quickly fell asleep.

'Where could my mother have hidden it?' Gemma mused, turning as she looked around the Grove. The fountain was the most obvious place, so she searched there first. There were no loose pieces of marble or holes beneath the base, or even a gap where the knife could have been pushed inside.

Next she searched among the herbs, digging holes beneath the silver-leaf plant and the belladonna, again with no luck. Then she tried the fruit trees, putting her hand inside knotholes in the trunks, or in the gaps beneath their ancient roots. Nothing.

By the time Chiara awoke two hours later, Gemma was hot, sweaty and irritable, and still no closer to finding the dagger. As her daughter's snuffles turned into full-blown wails, she looked to the sky for strength.

'What would my mother do? Who did she always turn to in times of need?' Gemma threw her arms wide in frustration, her head hurting from Chiara's piercing shriek. As she turned to leave the Grove, she saw it. The dragonfly sat on the rim of the fountain, its outstretched wings shimmering in the sunlight, and next to it was the damselfly, wings folded against its stick-thin body. Chiara's wails faded into the background as Gemma stared, mesmerised by the two creatures. And as she stared, the Grove became blurred as she soared into the sky, high above the forest, the canopy of green leaves swaying below her, gentle as waves on the sea, carrying her along until she slowly fell to earth, down towards the forest, down beneath the leaves, down to...

Her feet touched the ground, and she was once more in the Grove. But she knew where to go.

Gemma hadn't been back to the clearing since her return to the cottage. Now, as she stood beside the grave, she murmured an apology before wiping away some moss from the headstone.

She had left Chiara at the cottage with Maria, the young girl who came to help with the everyday chores. Her daughter had been unsettled after the Grove, and Gemma had reluctantly decided to leave her behind.

She ran her hands over the headstone, her fingertips tracing the lettering engraved in the marble. *Bob. Faithful friend, in life and death. 1349.* Bob's blood had been spilled to seal the curse, but she knew nothing about him, only that he had travelled from England to Italy with Agnes. She kneeled on the ground and placed her forehead against the weathered marble stone.

She was in a cluttered room, a ragged cloth hanging at the window, so full of holes that it didn't stop the cold wind swirling around the people inside, who huddled together, shivering. A woman bent over the fire in the middle of the room, her face gaunt and haggard, so thin that her bones showed beneath her skin. Smoke billowed overhead, hanging above their heads, as the children edged forward eagerly, clutching tiny wooden bowls in their grimy hands. When they saw the meagre amount in their bowl, each one moved away, calloused fingers gripping the wood, tears in their eyes but not daring to voice their disappointment.

The woman scraped the pot with her spoon and doled out the last of the stew, then took a piece of stale bread and used it to clean the inside. Pulling a moth-eaten shawl around her scrawny shoulders, she sat on the floor with the wall to her back and began to gnaw on the hard bread, while a baby suckled at her near-empty breast.

A child sobbed quietly, his empty bowl on the ground next to him, licked clean. Gemma had no idea how old he was, but he looked as though he was old beyond any normal years, weighted down with an adult's burden. A girl put her arm around his shoulders, shushing him, and clasped him to her to share what little warmth she had.

Gemma's heart broke as she watched the family settle for the night, the little ones crying with hunger as they slept, the older ones lying wide awake, determined just to get through the night, to see another dawn, to start the whole thing over again. The mother lay so still, her chest barely moving, that Gemma thought she had died, until the woman's body jerked as hunger cramps assailed her. And then Gemma realised that she was trying to conserve energy, that the little she ate wasn't enough to get her through the day, let alone the night. Slowly, surely, the whole family was starving to death.

When the next day dawned, the woman's husband returned, empty-handed. The woman glanced at him with one question in her expression, her face falling when he gave a small shake of his head. Their father's appearance gave the children a burst of energy and they greeted him with laughter and hugs, but all too soon they returned to their lethargic state of merely existing, their bodies no longer capable even of happiness.

Gemma saw the lifeless bundle in the corner before they did. Tears rolled down her face as she realised that the baby had died some time after dawn, when it had had its final feed. The woman's cries filled the room, painfully brief as she sank, sobbing, to the floor, hugging the bundle to her. The children watched in silence, dark eyes sunken in their pale faces, so exhausted they were beyond feeling anything for their tiny sibling.

The man spoke to the woman in a hushed voice, so quietly that no one could hear, not even Gemma. Then he took the young boy and his sister by the hand, and led them from their home. Unable to stop herself, Gemma followed, although she yearned to know what would happen to the rest of the family, looking back until the shack disappeared from view.

He took the children to a farm just outside the village and handed the girl over to a plump woman who had a kind expression. His daughter burst into tears, but he leaned over and whispered, 'Here at least you will eat, and I know they are good people.' The girl sniffed and rubbed at her face, then nodded. Without a word, she followed the woman into the farmhouse.

The boy sobbed as the door closed behind her, but stoically followed his father to the next place. A large manor, set at the edge of the village, with fields as far as the eye could see. The man spoke with several people, but all looked at the boy and shook their heads. His pace slowing, he finally arrived at the stables, where an old man shuffled out to greet them. After a few quick words, the old man leaned over and ruffled the boy's hair with a chuckle.

'Aye, we'll see what he can do. You ever been near a horse, son?'

'No,' the boy whispered, 'but I know which end a foal comes out of.'

'That's good enough for me,' the man said, and led the boy away.

As the boy followed the man, tears rolled down his father's face. He brusquely wiped them away and set off for home, while the boy hungrily crammed a bread roll the old man had given him into his mouth.

Gemma opened her eyes, her body stiff from kneeling for so long. 'What happened to the boy's family?'

Theirs is a story we will never know, a voice whispered along the breeze. *But now you know some of mine.*

'Can you tell me more?' Gemma wanted to know, wanted to *see* what had happened the night of the curse.

There is no time. Nearby, leaves shook as the wind grew stronger. *Someone approaches.*

Gemma spun round, her eyes searching, but couldn't see anything. Then a twig snapped.

'The dagger, tell me where it is, tell me, quickly, before it's too late,' she whispered, frantically trying to see whoever was out there.

The shadows beneath the trees suddenly appeared ominous, dark shapes taking on the form of monsters unknown.

No time, you must hide, you must– Bob's voice stopped in mid-sentence, and only an empty silence remained. Every muscle in Gemma's body was screaming to run, to leave the clearing, to get away from whatever it was that was coming. She ran to the nearest tree and hid behind its trunk, her blood pulsing in her ears, her body poised for flight. The sound of breaking twigs grew louder, the wood snapping loudly with each step.

Gemma froze, listening intently as the footsteps came closer. She glanced at the grave and clenched her fist, then withdrew into the shadow of the trunk as the figure came into view.

Fingers clutched at her arm and pulled her backwards into the forest. Before she could scream, a hand clamped over her mouth, the smell of fresh earth and rotting leaves heavy in her nostrils. She was dragged away from the clearing and the grave, deeper into the forest, the trees closing in and muffling all sound.

She struggled violently, kicking and wriggling, but it was no use. Whoever it was had the advantage of surprise and strength over her, and she couldn't free herself. Suddenly relaxing her body, she caught her attacker off guard. As she slumped, their grip loosened, and she fell with a bump to the ground.

'Jennifer!' she screamed, her eyes wide with fright as she frantically scrambled to her feet. 'Jennifer, run! Leave me, get out of here! Jen–'

We are the descendants of the women they burned.

I have met you at the water where
The dragonflies go,
And climbed up to meet you
Where the branches flow.
Where the meadow meets the sky
In a soft summer night,
Together we dreamt and upon wings took flight.

Imagination by Sarah Northwood
(excerpt taken from *Poetry of the Heart and Soul*)

Jennifer

Chapter Fifty-Three

October, present day

I opened my eyes with a jolt, my breath coming in gasping puffs that hurt my throat.

'Where is she?' I twisted my head, frantically searching for Gemma in the forest.

'Jen!' Francesco held me in his arms, his face almost touching mine. 'Come back, Jen, it's okay, you're with us.'

I stared at him, slowly realising where I was. 'What am I doing here? No, I need to go back, Gemma needs me, oh my God, she was attacked–'

Half-conscious, I could hear Francesco and Agnese talking together. A furry face came into view with a concerned whimper, and I stretched my hand towards it.

'Bella,' I managed to say, before fainting.

From the shadows came whispered words, half-formed sentences fluttering on trails of breath, fading into nothing before I could make out what they were saying. As I slowly emerged from wherever I had been – *the past,* my mind insisted – the shadows merged into the dark corners of the room, taking the whispers with them.

I struggled to sit up, the last vestiges of the dream clinging on. *The forest isn't safe… they're coming… she doesn't know, we must warn her… the trees, it's in the trees… she's in danger… the dagger, they must not find the dagger…*

'Can you hear them?' The room spun, making me clutch at my head.

'Lie back down before you collapse.' Francesco grasped my hand, his face etched with worry. 'You're awake. Thank goodness.'

'Can you hear them?' I insisted, the whispers still echoing in an endless round as they slowly faded away.

'Hear what?' Francesco asked.

I lay my head on the pillow, the confusion ebbing as the whispers ceased. My body felt as though it was made of lead, my limbs too heavy to move. I usually felt out of kilter after my "travels" to the past, but this was worse than anything before.

'What happened?' I couldn't remember anything after seeing Gemma being attacked. Looking around, I realised I was in the bedroom, the shutters closed to keep out most of the daylight.

'You were crying out for help, your whole body was twitching,' Agnese said, pressing a cool, damp cloth onto my forehead. It soothed my mind, calming my still-frantic thoughts. 'When Bella started whining and licking your hand, we knew we had to bring you back.'

'Bella.' The dog heard her name and drew closer, resting her nose on the blankets. I managed to lift my hand and clumsily pat her.

'You're running a temperature,' Agnese said, frowning. 'I think we should call the doctor.'

'No,' I snapped. I took a deep breath to calm myself down. 'Please. I'm fine. I just need some rest.'

Agnese hesitated. 'Okay. But if you're no better tomorrow, or it gets worse, you're seeing the doctor. No arguments.'

I nodded, too tired to fight. 'Thank you.' Just as I started to relax, I suddenly remembered my five-year-old son. 'Edo? Is he all right?'

Francesco put out a hand to stop me sitting up again. 'He's fine. I checked with Zia Liliana a little while ago, he's having a great time with his cousins. *Stai tranquilla.*'

'We'll let you get some rest.' Agnese tucked the blanket around me.

'Don't fuss. I need to write down what I saw—'

'Later.' Agnese's tone was firm, and I knew there would be no getting around her. She was scarily similar to her mother when she wanted to be. 'Now, I need to get back to Malva and Luca, but promise me you'll try to sleep.'

I huffed. 'Okay. But bring Edo up when he comes home.'

'I will,' Francesco promised. 'Now get some sleep.'

They left the room, and I lay as still as I could. My mind was in too much of a turmoil to sleep, but I closed my eyes and tried to relax. Bella jumped onto the bed and curled up beside me, nose tucked under her tail, and I stroked her soft fur, finding the repetitive action soothing.

Bella was getting old now, her muzzle peppered with grey, her joints stiff and achy in the morning. I remembered the first time I'd seen the dog, barking and growling at me while feisty Uncle Tommaso shouted at me to get off his land. I still missed the old man and his brusque manner, and treasured the few weeks I'd had to get to know him.

I thought about how much my life had changed in the last few years. From a desperate, self-pitying alcoholic who destroyed everything I touched, I'd somehow found the courage to leave England behind and start again in my great-grandmother's cottage deep in the heart of Tuscany. Every morning I woke up to stupendous views of the forest-covered mountain, fresh air, and the beautiful Grove, with its plants and dragonflies.

My mother had told me that there was magic at the cottage, and she had been right. It had been nothing like I'd imagined when I discovered it, but it had changed my life forever. The recipes in the book, the silver-leaf plant, and the secrets I had inherited from the healers who had come before me... all this had led me to become the person I was now.

After removing the curse, something hidden away deep inside me had come to the fore, an ability to see beyond the ordinary. It had terrified me at first. I diagnosed illnesses where there were no obvious symptoms, I knew instinctively which remedies were needed for a person's ailments, and I could *see*. Shadows in the cottage that shouldn't have been there, the feeling of a presence when no one was around, rustling leaves guiding me along the paths in the woods. And I could see the future, sometimes. A strange, prickling feeling would come over me, and I knew that what I was seeing would come to be.

I moved, and felt the locket against my chest. I lifted the chain I wore it on and held it before me. It had worked once before, giving Francesco and me Edo when I thought I'd never have a child. Something, I didn't know what, had impelled me to prepare the charm again, to fill the locket and wear it, day and night. I had learned to listen to my inner voice, and to trust it when it spoke to me. As old Anna-Maria once said, 'The wheels of time are turning and no one can stop them. It will happen, come what may. Our lives will never be the same again, for better or for worse.'

The magic of the dragonflies, the Grove, the Healer herself, had given me what I'd always wanted most: a family. This, the most precious of gifts, was something I would never take for granted.

A shiver ran through me, making the hairs on my arms rise. Bella whimpered and snuggled closer, warmth radiating from her, but I could feel an icy chill permeating my body. Something was wrong, I'd known this since the moment Gemma had shouted my name, when present and past had collided in a way that had never happened before. The room became colder, my breath rose in vaporous tendrils, and the tip of my nose tingled as I struggled to move.

A weight on my body prevented me from moving, and hands reaching up from beneath the bed clutched at my arms and legs, trying to drag me down, down into the dark hole below, down into the abyss where I would be alone with my despair for eternity...

With a strangled cry I broke free, thrashing my way to the surface, my arms and legs entangled in the blankets. With a final push I sat up, panting hard, rubbing the gritty sleepy dust from my eyes. Bella licked my face, ears flattened against her head as she growled.

'Did you see it?' I asked Bella, stroking her ears with trembling hands. I had no idea what had just happened, but I knew one thing: I would do whatever was necessary to protect my family.

Chapter Fifty-Four

It took me longer than I'd imagined to recover. Although my fever went down overnight, I felt lethargic for a few days and ached all over, as though I had the flu. When I burst into tears for the third time in an hour this morning, Francesco insisted I get plenty of rest and had taken Edo to Zia Liliana's. Although I protested, I knew that I hardly had the energy to look after myself, let alone a toddler.

Agnese knocked on the bedroom door and entered. 'Morning! How are you feeling today?'

'I think better,' I replied, cautiously stretching out an arm. 'Yes, the aches have almost gone.' I hauled myself into a sitting position, wincing slightly as Agnese opened the shutters. 'Is there any coffee?'

'Definitely better!' Agnese put a cushion behind my back. 'I'll go and make some. Come down when you're ready.'

While she clattered down the stairs, I leaned back against the headboard with a sigh, then forced myself to get up. When Agnese married and moved into Luca's house three years ago, the cottage had seemed quiet at first without her and Malva there. But as we got used to our new routine, I came to relish my time alone with Francesco and Edo, and the chance to live as a family at last.

Most of my relatives popped in regularly anyway, for a chat and a coffee. Giulia brought Beatrice and Antonio, both energetic whirlwinds who loved to run around the garden while we caught up on all the news. Beatrice was thirteen now, and had already broken a few boys' hearts. Giulia regaled me with stories of their turning up on the doorstep to profess their love, while Bea stayed in her room with her earbuds in, completely ignorant of their presence.

And if they didn't come to us, we often went to them. Zia Liliana often invited us over for lunch, which inevitably turned into long days of discussions about politics, Italian celebrities, and more politics. My life had changed completely since leaving England, and although I missed my mum, I wouldn't have swapped it for anything.

Once dressed and sitting downstairs at the kitchen table with a steaming espresso in front of me, I felt more able to face the world.

'Mamma has got her hands full today, she's got Malva as well as Edo so I could come and look after you.' Agnese gestured to a plate of biscuits.

'I'm really sorry to be such a nuisance. If Francesco hadn't had that urgent job–'

'Don't be silly. She's having a great time with her grandkids! And that's what families are for. You stuck up for me when I was pregnant with Malva, and you gave me a home. Just because I don't live here anymore doesn't mean I won't look after you. Actually, it's been lovely having some "us" time, hasn't it? No kids, no husbands, and no people coming at all hours for our remedies.'

'Speaking of which, how–?'

'The pantry is stocked, everything's up to date and labelled, and the lab is spotless,' Agnese interrupted.

'So you're a mind reader too now.' I looked at my empty coffee cup, and Agnese passed me the percolator. 'Yep, definitely a mind reader.'

'Just used to your ways.' Agnese laughed. 'It's good to see some colour in your face, I was a bit worried. What on earth went wrong?'

I drank down her coffee in one gulp. 'I have no idea. One minute I was watching Gemma search for something by Bob's grave, the next she was being attacked. But I couldn't see anyone else there, everything was confused. And then she saw me.'

'What?'

'She stared right at me, and shouted at me to get away, to run.' I rubbed my eyes. 'It was creepy.'

'Are you sure she was looking at you?' Agnese said. 'Maybe there was someone else there, and it seemed she meant you.'

'She called me Jen.'

'Ah.' There was silence for a moment. 'How is that possible?'

'It's never happened before. Every other time, I've watched their stories, been by their sides through all those terrible things, but none of them, not one, has ever given any sign of having seen me. The terror on her face and in her voice haunts me, Agnese. Over and over again I hear her scream my name, and the sounds of her struggling against whoever it is. I don't even know if she survived, or how she got out of there!'

'We can find out.' Agnese grabbed hold of my hand and held it between her own. 'The recipe book will tell us if she survived, and we'll try to track down some more information. Maybe the books here at the cottage – some of them came from the old villa.'

Inspiration hit me. 'Bob's grave! He can tell me, it happened there.' I rose from my chair, but Agnese pulled on my arm and made me sit down again.

'You're not going anywhere,' she said sternly. 'Not until I'm sure you're well enough. Stay there, I'll make some pasta.' She held up a hand as I opened my mouth to protest. 'No. If you eat you can go out for a while, otherwise you can go back to bed.'

I sank back onto my chair, chastised. Agnese was gentle and quiet, but inside she was as fierce as her mother, my aunt Liliana. And both were a force to be reckoned with.

I took Bella with me, her presence a comfort after the events I'd seen a few days earlier. Even though I knew that the things I saw had already taken place in the past, the healers' stories remained with me for a long time after, each event as fresh as if it had just happened.

Lost in my thoughts, it took me a while to notice the dragonfly flitting from tree to tree beside us. The Grove was full of dragonflies, but I knew this one was *the* dragonfly, the one that had been a part of the healers' lives since Agnes's time. It helped to have it there.

The clearing where Bob's grave stood was quiet as usual. It reminded me of a cathedral, with that calm, hushed silence perfect for contemplation, or for hearing the voices of the dead. The weathered marble of the headstone blended into the background, its presence barely noticeable among the dappled light and shadows created by the trees.

I laid my hands on the cold stone, and watched the dragonfly alight nearby. Feeling a little silly, and not really knowing where to look, I started to tell Bob a story.

Chapter Fifty-Five

IN THE END, I told him several stories. Stories I had researched over the years, ever since I'd learned about Agnes and what she had gone through before arriving in Gallicano.

Hesitant at first, unsure if Bob could hear my words, I began to speak. As I spoke, I felt a deep calm settle over me, and I wondered if he was there.

I told him how the plague killed everyone at the manor house, how Agnes tried so hard to save them, but she couldn't. That the village was hit hard too, almost everyone died. How Mrs Smythe's daughter, Betty, was one of the few who survived. She left the village with her two children, a girl and a boy, and remarried a widower living on the south coast. I hadn't been able to find out what happened to her daughter, but Tommy, the son, became a farrier. I remembered how I had sobbed together with Agnes when Mrs Smythe had died, the warm-hearted washerwoman struggling to breathe as the disease ravaged her body.

After Lord Funteyn and his daughter, Elizabeth, were taken by the plague, there was no one to take over the manor or his lands. Upper Fordingbridge was abandoned; no one wanted to live with the tortured spirits of those who had died there. I shivered, a chill running through me at the thought of the deserted houses.

I'd found Constance's family too, her husband and children. They went back to Little Mere, and Simon married Wade Thatcher's widower, Emily. Little Tilly died, as I discovered in the parish records, but the other children all survived and went on to marry and have their own families.

As I talked, a breeze blew through the clearing, stirring the grass around my feet, and carried a leaf onto the grave, where it gently rocked until it settled. I had the sensation that I wasn't alone, that Bob was there with me, listening carefully to everything I said.

I told him about Agnes's fears that Alfredo and John would become like their uncle, Filippo. But they had grown up to become kind, strong men like their father, taking over the running of the villa when Agnes and Riccardo died, and working in the fields alongside the labourers, just as their father did. They both married, and were loved and respected by their children. I knew that Agnes would have been proud of them.

Then I came to the part where I knew I would have to tread carefully. I had found out some of Isadora's past, of how she became the next healer, and her daughter after her. They'd lived at the cottage, and the tradition of the healer's duties being handed to the eldest daughter was born. Isadora learned well from Agnes, and passed the secrets of healing on to her daughter. But there was one secret she kept for herself, a secret I only found out about a little while ago.

'And now I fear that this secret, this one, terrible thing, will be the downfall of our family, if I can't discover where it has been hidden.'

The dagger.

The words were spoken so quietly that I might have thought it was only the breeze blowing through the trees, if I hadn't been waiting for Bob to say something. I knelt down on the grass beside the grave, the damp odour of dead leaves and undergrowth stirring childhood memories of long walks in the woods followed by mugs of hot chocolate, and bowed my head, almost as though in prayer. It had been a long time since I believed in God, but I knew that there was something out there, watching over us and guiding us.

'Morgana knew it was dangerous for the healers – she hid it somewhere near your grave, didn't she? And then Gemma, Gemma came to take it away and hide it in a safer place, but she was attacked, that's the last thing I saw, but she saw me as well, and how was that possible…?' I realised I was getting a bit hysterical and stopped before I scared Bob away.

The dagger was here. The whisper drifted across the clearing, wrapping itself around the trunk of an old oak. *Morgana knew that a healer mustn't touch it, that it would bring only grief and despair. There is a hole at the bottom of the headstone, where it remained for many years.*

I glanced down, but couldn't see any hole, or even a small gap.

Gemma realised that the dagger was here, and came to fetch it before anyone else could get their hands on it. She knew she must destroy it, if the Innocenti were ever to have peace of mind again.

I had a sudden flash of insight. 'Tullia attacked her!'

Tullia believed she could use the dagger to break the curse Gemma had put on her family, reasoning that if Filippo had created it, she could harness the evil within and turn it against the Innocenti once more.

'It didn't work.'

I don't know.

'What do you mean, you don't know? You were here when Gemma was attacked, you must have seen what happened.'

All I can remember is a great darkness, blacker than a starless night, that stopped me from seeing. I don't know who attacked Gemma, or what happened after. I only know that the dagger had gone.

'But Gemma came back, didn't she? Afterwards, I mean. She came back here to talk to you?' My voice was rising in panic; I couldn't bear the thought of not knowing what had happened to Gemma. Bob's next words broke me.

No, she didn't. I never saw Gemma again.

Chapter Fifty-Six

Still in a turmoil, I hurried down to Gallicano to collect Edo from Zia Liliana.

'I'm so sorry I'm late,' I said as I burst into my aunt's house. The door was never locked, and after being told many times that I was one of the family, I didn't knock anymore before entering.

Zia Liliana looked up from the sofa, where she was reading a book with Edo.

'Jennifer! We were wondering where you'd got to! Agnese said you would be along later. Come, sit with Edo while I make us a coffee.' I sat down and flicked through the book while she bustled out into the kitchen, talking non-stop all the time. 'I hope you're feeling better now, Francesco said you had a fever. You probably caught a chill, out in the Grove all day long. It only takes a slight breeze, you know, a *colpo d'aria*, and bam! You are sick with influenza, or bronchitis, or worse... pneumonia!'

Edo giggled, and I smiled at him. He had inherited my British way of shrugging any illness off; I was always reluctant to go to the doctor and waste their time with trivial matters, even though everyone insisted that was what they were there for. Francesco had got used to my little quirks by now, though he often remarked how ironic it was, with me being a healer.

By the time Zia Liliana brought the coffee through, Edo was showing me some drawings he'd done.

'He is a great little artist, that one, he gets it from his great-great-uncle Tommaso,' my aunt said. She put the tray of coffee and biscuits down and gathered Edo in a big hug. 'Have you seen the dragonfly he did this morning?'

'No, I haven't,' I said, watching Edo squirm out of Liliana's embrace.

He dug around among the papers he'd left on the floor, then shyly held one out to me, his cheeks flushed red.

'Oh, sweetheart!' For once, I was speechless. He'd painted the blue dragonfly, the one that had accompanied me to Bob's grave only a little while before, a bold, vibrant swish of colour among a background of plants that immediately took me to the Grove. A dusting of glitter made the wings shimmer in the light, and the bulbous black eyes had depths of wisdom. 'It's beautiful. We'll ask Papà to make a frame for it, and hang it on the wall.'

'And perhaps you could paint one for me,' Zia Liliana said. 'I'd love to have one on the wall here as well. It will remind me of Tommaso.'

'I'll do it right away!' He ran over to the dining table and opened his paintbox.

'Edo–' I started to say, but my aunt interrupted me.

'We have plenty of time. Let him paint, we can chat in the meantime.'

'Won't Zio Dante be home soon?' I was still slightly scared of my uncle. A big, silent man who rarely raised his voice, he was nonetheless an imposing presence in the family. My aunt might have been the typical Italian matriarch, but everyone respected my uncle and listened when he spoke.

'He'd love to see Edo,' Zia Liliana said. She took the empty coffee cup from me and put it back on the tray. 'I would have phoned you later anyway. The couple that are staying in Tommaso's house, they asked if they could buy some of your products to take back to America with them.'

'Of course.' Aunt Liliana rented Tommaso's house out to holiday makers. Situated on the outskirts of Gallicano, it was quiet enough to give tourists a well-earned break, while still being close enough to civilisation for all amenities. Agnese and I had created a line of products, such as shampoos, conditioners, liquid soaps and essential oils made with plants from the Grove, and we left courtesy bottles at the cottage. My aunt usually gave us her guests' orders, and we left the products for her to distribute.

'Would you mind taking them there yourself?' she asked hesitantly.

I looked up, surprised. She walked everywhere, her thin legs used to the steep slopes of Gallicano, and she often put the rest of us to shame with her energy.

'My leg hurts if I walk too far, so I try not to overdo things.' She gave that nonchalant Italian shrug, but I saw the strain in her eyes.

'Would you like me to look at it?'

'No, no, don't fuss, *cara*.' Liliana flapped her hands, embarrassed. 'I have an appointment with the doctor next week. I'm sure it's nothing, but if you could, in the meantime...'

'No problem. Give me the list and I'll take them round tomorrow.'

'Are you sure you're all right?' Zia Liliana squinted at me. 'You look a bit pale. Perhaps some cake–'

'No, thank you,' I replied hurriedly. I loved my aunt's home-made cakes, but I had little appetite.

'There aren't any problems between you and Francesco, are there?' she asked, frowning. 'He hardly spoke this morning, and you seem very tense.'

'We're fine. Honestly. I haven't been very well the last few days, and he's been running around looking after me and Edo. That's all.'

She opened her mouth and I braced myself for another of her concerned but overwhelming speeches, when Edo ran over with his finished picture.

'*Tesoro*, that's beautiful!' Liliana took the picture he'd handed her, careful not to touch the still-wet paint. 'The next time you come, you'll see it hanging on the wall. Where shall we put it?'

I watched as she and Edo chose the best spot to show off his painting, tears in my eyes at the warmth and love between them.

So why do you want to upset the calm by finding the dagger? a small voice whispered snidely in my head. *It doesn't really matter. Gemma belongs in the past – whatever happened to her, she's long dead by now, her bones mere dust in the ground. Let things be, and live your life in peace and happiness.*

But I couldn't let it be. I had to find out who attacked her, and if she'd survived. The silver dagger was the key to everything; I knew that if I could find it, I would have the answers I so desperately needed.

The Innocenti cannot last forever, the day will come when there will be no more healers, the voice insisted, louder now. The room seemed to become darker, day turning to dusk, and a cold chill permeated the room. I shivered. My breath rose in little clouds, barely visible in the dark, and icy fingers touched my arm.

'Mamma?'

I came to with Edo's worried face only centimetres from mine, his eyes wide as he pulled at my top.

'I'm okay, sweetie.' I blinked, trying to clear the vision from my mind. 'Did you find somewhere to hang the picture?'

'Show your mamma where you decided, I think it's perfect.' Zia Liliana gave me a fleeting look, her brow furrowed, but said nothing.

As Edo proudly led me over to the fireplace, I made a silent vow to the retreating darkness. *I* will *find the knife, and there* will *be other healers, for many centuries to come.*

Chapter Fifty-Seven

Wrapped up well in scarves, hats, and autumn coats, Edo and I headed out to Tommaso's cottage with a bag of herbal products for the tenants. The wind was bitterly cold, strong gusts that cleared the last remaining leaves from the skeletal trees. Bella had taken one look at the weather and slunk back to her rug, where she'd curled up with her tail around her nose. I couldn't blame her. Edo was enjoying himself, scarpering about trying to catch the leaves as they whirled past him, his cheeks ruddy and his eyes sparkling.

As we walked down the dirt track that led to the cottage, I again remembered when I'd met my grumpy silver-haired uncle and Bella, one of the ugliest dogs I'd ever seen. In only a few short weeks we had become firm friends, with him helping me out in the Grove until the sad day I'd found him dead in his armchair. Bella, lost and forlorn, had come home with me that day, and had been with us ever since. She became my guardian angel, and I couldn't imagine life without her now. Older, with some rheumatism in her legs, she preferred to stay at home in her warm bed than go on long walks with us, but she still came to the Grove with me whenever I went to gather the herbs I needed.

Edo ran over to an gnarled old tree that stood just outside the fence. 'Mamma, take a photo of me here,' he shouted, stood with his back against the trunk. I smiled sadly, remembering how I'd climbed that very tree to get to the cottage when Tommaso didn't answer the door, and took a couple of photos with my phone.

'There. Come on, ring the bell so we can deliver these things and get back home before Bella needs to pee.'

Giggling, he stood on tiptoes and rang the doorbell. We heard the loud, harsh buzz from inside the cottage, and moments later a large, grey-haired man opened the front door.

'Good morning, Mr Wilson. I'm Liliana's niece, I've brought the products you asked for,' I called.

'Ooh, great! Come on in, I'll get some coffee on and cookies for the kid.'

'No, that's okay–' I began, but he'd already disappeared. 'One biscuit, Edo,' I warned.

'Okay, Mamma.' He shoved the gate open and led the way up the path.

I'd only been in the cottage once since Tommaso's death, when I'd found the wooden chest with the dragonfly carved on the lid, and it felt odd to see how different it was now. Gone was the old armchair with the stuffing coming out, as was the small table and wooden chairs, and the grimy curtains. Zio Dante had given it a lick of paint, and my aunt had filled it with spare furniture from her own house and hung new curtains. It looked fresh and spacious and inviting.

I wondered what had happened to Tommaso's collection of dead insects that he'd kept in a room upstairs, and his beautiful, intricate drawings. I had kept some of his drawings of dragonflies, which now adorned the walls of my cottage, but I'd never asked my aunt what she'd done with the rest.

'Come on through to the kitchen, the coffee's almost ready,' Mr Wilson called. 'I've got some chocolate cookies for the kid... what's your name?'

'Edo. And my mum's name is Jen,' my traitorous son said, running over and sitting at the kitchen table. 'Thank you, Mr Wilson!'

'Oh, call me Mike,' the man said. 'Seeing as we're renting the place from your lovely aunt. How is she?' he said, turning to me. 'And how rude of me – come, sit down. You look exhausted. And give me those.'

I gratefully handed the bag over and sank onto one of the chairs, asking myself how bad I looked if a stranger had noticed.

'Steve will be down in a minute, he's just having a shower.' Mike rummaged through the bag, a satisfied grin on his face. 'We love that blackberry shower gel, and the camomile shampoo. Ooh, and that hand cream works wonders. Steve's prone to rashes if his skin gets too dry, this has been a blessing! How much do I owe you?'

I handed him the receipt, and he dug the euros out of his wallet. 'We'll definitely be back next year for more, we're going to book the cottage before we leave,' he confided.

'My aunt will be pleased you've enjoyed yourselves so much,' I replied. 'My great-uncle Tommaso lived most of his life here, she inherited it when he died.'

'Is he the guy who did the drawings?' Mike pointed up the stairs. 'There's a room up there with walls covered in pictures of all kinds of insects and animals.'

'So that's where she put them!' I finished my coffee and signalled to Edo that we had to go. 'I was wondering where they'd ended up.'

'Drawings?' Edo said. 'I draw dragonflies.'

'You want to see them?' Mike asked him.

'Oh, I don't think–' I began, but Edo was already bounding up the stairs. I sighed, and followed them up.

Tommaso's study had been turned into a spare bedroom. The cabinets and the enormous desk were gone, as were the boxes containing the insects and skulls he'd collected over the years. But Mike hadn't been exaggerating when he'd said the walls were covered in my uncle's drawings.

'Hey, Steve. I was just showing Jen these amazing sketches. She says her uncle did them.'

I was busy staring at the pictures, and hadn't noticed Steve enter the room. He stood next to Mike and put an arm around his shoulders.

'They're fantastic, he should have put them in an art gallery. He could've made a fortune from them,' he drawled.

'I think it was just a hobby of his, he was fascinated by the natural world.' I felt absurdly proud of Tommaso, listening to the two Americans gushing over his sketches.

'Little Edo here says he draws dragonflies,' Mike said to Steve.

'Why dragonflies, kiddo?'

''Cause there's so many of them in the Grove,' Edo said enthusiastically. 'Just like that one!' He pointed at the window, and I saw my dragonfly on the windowsill outside, its wings moving slightly in the breeze.

'Wrong season for dragonflies, isn't it?' Steve wandered over and peered down at it.

'It depends. The Grove's quite sheltered, so we get them most of the year,' I told him.

'The Grove? What's that?'

'The place where I grow the herbs for the lotions.'

'Ah, top secret, then.' Steve tapped the side of his nose and winked. 'Why don't we take a photo of the kid and you together by some of the drawings, it'd be a nice memento for him.'

'Sì, Mamma, please!' Edo went around the room, looking at the sketches, before choosing his favourites. 'Here.'

'Just one, and then we really have to go,' I said. 'Maybe we can ask Zia Liliana if you can have a couple for your room, there are so many here.'

Edo did the biggest smile while Mike took a few photos with my phone. As soon as I could, I made an excuse to get back to Bella, and we left. I'd enjoyed the morning with Mike and Steve, but I was ready to go back to the calm and tranquillity of the cottage.

Chapter Fifty-Eight

The fine drizzle settled on my hair and coat, forming beaded drops that fell to the ground. Edo and Francesco were still asleep, tucked up in their warm beds, and I'd taken advantage of some 'me' time. I stood in the Dragonfly Grove, beside the grave I'd stumbled over some years earlier, feeling displaced.

During my visions I had seen the Grove in its many incarnations over the centuries, from the bare ground that Agnes had first transformed into her herb garden, with the white marble fountain her husband Riccardo had installed, and snow-covered plants deep in their winter slumber, to the grave that now stood at its centre. I loved the tranquillity of the place, the calm atmosphere that helped me in times when I needed to stop and think. Times like now.

It had all started here. One summer night when the dragonfly had appeared and led me to an overgrown wilderness that had become the centre of my life. Here I had tended and cared for the plants, bringing them back to their former glory. Here I'd had the first visions of Agnes, a hint of the traumatic events that had led to blood being spilled and a curse being put on the family. And here I had cast a spell that had broken the curse one moonlit night, and opened my heart to truly becoming a healer.

But now it seemed I had one more thing to do. I loved my life, I loved being a healer and preparing remedies that would help people, I loved having a family, and I finally loved being me. After years of despising myself, of losing myself in an alcoholic haze, of pushing away anyone who tried to help me, I loved being me.

'I. Love. Being. Me,' I repeated out loud. My words were swallowed up by the light rain and borne down to the ground, where they melted into the land of my ancestors.

I had watched as Filippo had drawn the dagger across Bob's throat, the boy falling to the ground, his blood soaking into the earth as the life left him. I had seen Riccardo and Filippo fighting within the circle that Agnes had created, a fight that only one of them could survive. And I had seen the spirits come, at the end, to take Filippo's soul away to whatever dark, torturous place existed.

The dagger. It all came back to the dagger. The moment it had spilled Bob's blood, it had become intrinsically entwined in my family's history, and had lain dormant until Tullia used it to stir up the curse again to bring tragedy to the Innocenti. I *had* to find it.

'What are you doing?'

I looked up from the pile of books strewn around me, and fixed a smile on my face. All the excuses I'd prepared faded away, suddenly ridiculous even to me.

'Erm...' I gestured pathetically at the empty bookcase. 'I hoped to find something – I don't know, a diary, or a scroll, or... something. Anything that tells me what happened to Gemma.'

Francesco crouched down next to me. 'Jen, it's in the past. Gemma lived almost four hundred years ago; whether she survived the attack or not, she's long dead now.'

'You don't understand–' I began.

'I understand that you're not sleeping or eating well, and that I'm worried about you.' He put his arm around me, and I leaned my head on his shoulder. 'You can't do all this by yourself, so Edo and I are going to help you search the cottage. But if we don't find anything, you have to promise me that you'll stop, before you make yourself ill.'

I shook my head. 'I don't know if I can.'

'Well, at least don't keep it bottled up like you usually do.' He sat down with a bump next to me, and pulled me closer. 'You know you can talk to me.'

In the six years we had been together, he had proved time and time again his love and support for me. I looked into his blue eyes, so serious, tinged with worry, and knew that I was no longer alone. His stubble was rough beneath my fingers, but his lips were soft as I kissed him.

'Mamma, Papà.' Edo stood at the top of the stairs, his hair standing on end, his face still puffed up from heavy sleep.

'Coming, Edo.' Francesco helped me to my feet and gave me a quick kiss. 'Put the coffee on, then we'll start searching.'

We looked everywhere, Bella enthusiastically putting her nose in every nook and cranny. I flicked through the books on the shelves, in the hope that I would find a piece of paper inside, but there was nothing. We went through the kitchen cupboards, the wardrobes, even the cabinet in the hallway, searching methodically for any hidden compartments or long-lost gaps. Francesco took down every jar in the pantry, handing them to me to clean, before putting them all back again. Nothing.

By the afternoon we were dusty, tired, and grumpy. Edo, on the other hand, wanted to keep playing the game.

'The woman in the corner over there keeps pointing towards the Grove,' he said, pouting.

I sat up with a jolt, and looked over at the shadows in the corner. *Was there a woman's figure?* I leaned forward, but couldn't see anything.

'Edo, if you want to go outside, just say,' Francesco said, standing up with a groan. 'Don't make up silly stories.'

Wrapped up against the cold, we made our way to the Grove. Bella followed us, nose to the ground as usual as she sniffed out the trails of various creatures.

'Where do you think we should look, Edo?' I swung my arms up and down, trying to keep warm. Our breath was visible in the chilly air, it wouldn't be long before winter set in.

Edo turned round, frowning as he peered at the plants. 'She said there was a fountain.'

A chill ran through me that had nothing to do with the cold air. 'What?'

'The woman at the cottage. She said there's a fountain.' He shrugged. 'I can't see a fountain.'

Francesco gripped my arm. 'Didn't there used to be a fountain?' he whispered.

I nodded. 'Exactly where Malva's grave is now.'

He raised his eyebrows. 'What else did the woman say, Edo?'

My son bit his lip, his brow furrowed as he thought. 'Nothin'. She just said there's a fountain, and to go there.'

'What did she look like?'

He shrugged. 'I couldn't actually see her, Mamma, she was all dark like the shadows.'

'Of course. Did she say what we had to look for at the fountain?'

'Don't think so.' He scuffed his feet through a pile of fallen leaves, kicking them up into the air with a giggle. 'She seemed scared of it. But there's nothin' scary here, is there, Mamma?'

'Of course not,' I reassured him. 'There's no place safer than the Grove.' I turned to Francesco and spoke quietly, so that Edo wouldn't hear me. 'Morgana said there was an evil presence here; she had to fight it until she managed to send it back beyond the veil.'

'Do you think it's come back?'

'I'm not sure.' I stepped towards the grave, and placed my hand on the weathered marble of the headstone. 'This is where I had the visions of Agnes.'

Francesco put his hand on mine. 'I remember.'

We stood quietly for a moment, each lost in our own thoughts.

'Can you sense anything?'

I knelt and put my palm on the ground. Everything fell dark, as though someone had closed my eyes, and my head spun as a distant shriek grew ever louder. I clasped my hands over my ears, my teeth aching at the high-pitched scream, every nerve in my body taut as it reached an unbearable volume. Tears poured down my cheeks, damp rivulets that I could barely feel as I fought to keep myself in the real world. A gossamer veil opened before me, its once-golden threads now bedraggled strands of grey, and a bony hand reached out to pull me through. Long, blackened fingernails scraped my skin, leaving a burning, red trail.

'Mamma!'

Edo's scream broke through the vision, pulling me back to reality, while Bella tugged on my sleeve with her teeth. The dark silence was gone, and I found myself sitting on the ground next to the grave, my arm burning.

'Bad thing gone, Mamma, it's gone now,' Edo said, putting his arms around my neck and hugging me tightly. I hugged him back, still crying.

Francesco picked him up and helped me to my feet. We made our way out of the Grove, arms wrapped around each other, Edo safely between us. Bella barked twice at the grave before following.

The memory of what had just happened was already fading, the tears drying on my cheeks. But I had a feeling that I knew who had tried to drag my soul beyond the grave, desperate that I wouldn't find the dagger. Tullia.

Chapter Fifty-Nine

It was a Saturday, so Francesco and Luca took Malva and Edo out while Agnese and I worked side by side in the laboratory. The sweet perfume of herbs hung in the air, pots bubbled on the stove, and we chatted while preparing the remedies.

'Mike and Steve sound like fun!' Agnese carefully strained the herbs that had been boiling for the last hour into a stainless-steel bowl.

'They were lovely. It was a bit strange seeing other people in Tommaso's cottage, though.' I poured some melted wax into a glass jar, making sure the wick stayed up straight in the middle. The rose petals I'd added were visible through the glass, creating a floral pattern. Placing the wick between two sticks so that it would stay upright, I stepped back and looked at my masterpiece. Once the wax had cooled and hardened we would add a waterproof paper lid decorated with our dragonfly logo, and tie it on with a piece of string.

'I kept expecting to see him stomp into the room and demand to know what those "bloody Americans" were doing in his house.'

Agnese laughed. 'He was impossible, but we all loved him. I helped Mamma redecorate the place, it was sad seeing all his stuff being taken away.'

'Do you know what happened to his insect collection?'

'Mamma gave it to the museum in Lucca, they were interested in it. Did you see his drawings? We thought we'd put them on the wall, it was a shame to hide them away.'

'Edo loved them.' I took out my phone and brought up the gallery. 'Look, they took some photos of us under his favourite ones.' I swiped across until I found them.

'I'm sure Mamma will let him have a few if he wants them for his bedroom,' Agnese said. 'Ah, that was one of my favourites too.' She pointed at a drawing of a praying mantis, each tiny detail painstakingly drawn in pencil. 'Look at Edo's big grin! It's a pity he never knew Zio Tommaso, they'd have got on like a house on fire.' She flicked through the other photos.

'I had to climb that tree to get over the fence, the day he died.' I pointed at the old oak, its lower branch hanging over the fence. 'Bella was barking her head off, I knew something was wrong.' I peered at the photo, smiling at Edo's happy face. The branch jutted out over the garden; if it had been a foot longer it would have tapped at the window. My eyes followed the direction it was pointing in, and I saw a rose bush planted on a mound near the house.

A memory flitted into my head, niggling at me. A thunderstorm, branches tapping against the stone walls of a house, a woman in a shawl standing in the rain, arms raised, head tilted up to the sky–

'The soul catcher!' I stared at the photo on my phone, hardly able to breathe.

'Jen, are you okay?'

'Look!' I stabbed my finger at the screen. 'Tommaso's cottage is at the edge of the village, with no neighbours, and the tree... look where the branch is pointing!'

Agnese stared at me, with either pity or concern, I wasn't sure which.

'That rose bush. The mound it's on, that's where the tree was.'

'Which tree?'

I sighed heavily. 'The Hanging Tree!'

'What? How can you be sure? They cut it down, didn't they?'

'Yes.' I tried to order my thoughts, frustrated at the chaos in my mind. 'Anna-Maria had the tree chopped down before she died. She was the last soul catcher, the one pure enough to break the curse on Tullia's family. I saw it, the tree, so many times. I know that's her house.'

'Okay.' Agnese held out a placating hand. 'But hers was a one-room cottage, which Tommaso's isn't. Is there anything else that could confirm it's the soul catchers' house?'

'It's been added to over the years.' I enlarged the photo to see the stonework more clearly. 'See. Here and here, couldn't that be where the house has been extended?'

Agnese peered closely. 'It does look like it. The whole top floor is different to the ground floor, which makes sense. There wasn't an upstairs when Anna-Maria lived there.'

'The Hanging Tree was close enough to the house that its branches tapped against the walls when it was windy.' I pointed at the rose bush. 'Imagine a tree there, just like the oak I photographed, with a branch reaching out like that.'

Agnese stared at me. 'I think you could be right.'

'So you know what this means?'

'I... erm, no.'

'If it's the soul catchers' house, this is where Tullia lived. If she took the dagger, it could still be there!'

By the time Agnese left, we'd agreed to go to the house on Monday, when Mike and Steve would be gone. Agnese had told me to try and keep calm, even though we both knew that would be impossible.

I hadn't told her about my dreams of Gemma, and how she haunted me every night. The not knowing what had happened to her was torture, and I was determined to find out, somehow. But for the moment I kept quiet about it. Agnese and Francesco would suggest I travel back to the past using my great-grandmother's fruit juice, but I had a reason for not wanting to do that.

I pulled out the necklace I always wore now, and held the locket in my hand, the sweet perfume of the herbs inside drifting over me. I could feel the strength of the charm within, the subtle magic making my skin tingle. I had watched the healers from the past as they had become aware of the very moment that life sparked into being inside them, and had never understood how that could be. Until now.

I pulled up my jumper and t-shirt and placed my hand on the bare skin of my stomach, shivering slightly at my cold fingertips. I closed my eyes, and concentrated. There. A tiny spark, deep within me, pulsing in time with my heartbeat. My daughter.

Chapter Sixty

Anna-Maria shuffled across the room, her hand on her hip as she grimaced in pain. A cat lay in an empty drawer, her kittens strewn around her, all sleeping deeply. The old woman went over to a deep wooden coffer in the far corner and slowly lifted the heavy lid. It rested upright on its hinges, and she placed a stick to keep it propped open.

The coffer was full of pots and pans and embroidered linens, and a myriad of other things that she took out and put on the floor. The thing she was searching for was right at the bottom, underneath a faded tapestry. Bright sunshine streamed in through the only window of the cottage, but somehow the room grew darker, smaller, as Anna-Maria took a step back, a bundle of rags in her hand. She began to unwrap the bundle, a glint of silver barely visible, but then she suddenly pulled the cloth around it again and hobbled over to fireplace.

Sweating slightly, she leaned against the fireplace, then crouched down, grunting loudly as her stiff joints protested. The walls of the *fireplace were black with soot, and she glared at the cold grate before stepping into the chimney.*

Flakes of soot fell around her. She reached up and struggled with something, wincing and grunting, then raised the bundle of rags in her other hand. When she lowered her arm, the bundle was gone.

Anna-Maria turned and looked directly at me, then winked.

The weekend seemed to last forever, but eventually Monday arrived. Agnese and I stood outside Tommaso's cottage, suddenly apprehensive. I glimpsed the rose bush from the corner of my eye and turned. For a moment I saw a gnarled old tree, its twisted trunk entwined with ivy, with two figures dangling from a branch, swinging gently in a non-existent breeze. I jerked my head back round, but not before I heard the screams of a thousand tortured souls spiralling up from the tree, until they faded into the pale-blue sky. I glanced at Agnese, but she didn't seem to have noticed anything. My jaw clenched, I tried to concentrate on what she was saying.

'I feel like we're breaking and entering.' She giggled nervously.

'Me too.' I tried to smile reassuringly at her, but it was more of a grimace. The screams still reverberated in my head, and I knew they would haunt me for a long time. 'Shall we go and find out if it really was Anna-Maria or just my over-active imagination?' Ever since I'd told Agnese and Francesco about the dream, we'd been trying to figure out if it had really happened. And if it had, how had the past and present collided again? was the question I kept asking myself.

I half-expected the front door to creak as we opened it, but it slid silently on well-oiled hinges. The hallway led to a living room and cloakroom, with a stair going up, and a door at the end took us through to the kitchen.

I turned around, looking at the small room. 'It's hard to believe this was the original cottage, where Anna-Maria cooked, ate, and slept.' Zio Tommaso's old armchair had taken up most of the space in front of the fire and even now, with no other furniture than a dresser, a small sofa, and a coffee table, the room seemed cramped.

'At least the fireplace is still the original one,' Agnese said. 'Whoever built onto the cottage kept its original features, thank goodness.'

I walked over and touched the grey stonework around the fireplace. 'I saw this when Gemma came back to Tuscany from her exile. She crouched outside that window,' I pointed, 'and peeked in to see her father with Tullia.'

'It must have been heartbreaking for her,' Agnese said softly.

'She was devastated. It was then that she placed the curse on Tullia and her descendants, condemning them to a life as soul catchers.'

'After what Tullia did to Morgana, I don't blame her,' Agnese replied, her cheeks flushed. 'To think her family carried the desire for revenge in their hearts for centuries!'

'Sometimes I feel sorry for her,' I admitted.

'What!'

'I saw how Anna-Maria suffered. She was tormented by the souls, day and night; she could hear their screams and feel their anguish. It was a just punishment for Tullia, but to make generations after suffer that way was cruel.'

Agnese frowned. 'I see what you mean. But perhaps it was the only way to protect the Innocenti, other than removing the curse from the dagger.'

We fell silent. I stared at the fireplace, putting off the moment I would have to poke my arm up the chimney and find the hidey hole that Anna-Maria had shown me.

'Go on, Jen,' Agnese urged, as though reading my thoughts.

I crouched in the fireplace and peered up. The chimney was black with centuries of soot, and I knew I was going to get grubby. For a moment I envied Francesco, back at home with Edo, but knew that waiting, not knowing what was happening, would be worse. I tried to remember Anna-Maria's exact position from my dream, and stretched out my arm.

Soot fell around me as my fingers dislodged the grime on the chimney walls, but I couldn't feel anything. I gritted my teeth and reached higher, half-standing in the fireplace.

'If a spider falls on me, I'm going to run out screaming,' I warned Agnese.

'Don't be so pathetic,' she replied, giggling.

'Do you want to do it?' From her silence, I took that she didn't.

The brickwork was rough beneath my fingers, and I hoped I wouldn't cut myself. And then I felt it. The edge of a brick jutting out from the others, so slightly that I almost missed it. I prodded and pulled, scraping the skin off my fingers.

'Have you found the hiding place?' I heard Agnese call.

'I think so. Just a moment–' I felt the brick shift, dust, soot and debris falling on my feet. I got a better a grip on it and pulled, jumping to one side as it crashed into the grate. Agnese gave a little scream. My fingers found the hole, and I slowly put my hand inside, dreading what I would find. When I touched something soft I almost yelled in fear, thinking it was a dead rat or mouse, then remembered that the dagger had been wrapped in rags. With my heartbeat thudding in my ears I grabbed hold and dragged it out.

'Your face,' Agnese said, trying to suppress her laughter.

I looked down at my clothes, which were barely visible beneath the layer of soot. 'I'd better go outside, Zia Liliana will kill me if I get anything dirty.'

Agnese couldn't hold her laughter back anymore. Tears streaming down her face, she helped me outside, where I brushed off my clothes, hair and skin the best I could.

'I need to go home for a shower,' I said forlornly.

Agnese was still giggling. 'Let's at least have a look at it before we go.'

I picked up the bundle of rags from the ground. Grubby from the centuries of dirt, the cloth looked innocuous enough. I gently unwound the rags, and we found ourselves staring down at the cursed dagger.

Chapter Sixty-One

Francesco peered at the dagger on the stainless-steel worktop. Agnese and I waited patiently for him to speak. Edo was tucked up in bed, Bella on the rug beside him, and Malva was at home with Luca. We were in the laboratory, the damp chill of evening coming through the open door.

'So Anna-Maria really was telling you where to find it in your dream.' Francesco shook his head. 'These things never cease to amaze me. But now that you have it, what are you going to do?'

'Remove the curse, if I can.' I felt helpless. How could I do it when Morgana hadn't been able to?

'Do you know how?' Francesco asked, reading my thoughts as usual.

'No. That's the problem.' I sighed. 'We've gone through the recipe book I don't know how many times, but all we can find is the few words of advice from Isadora. And they don't really help. Morgana worked out that the flowers from the silver-leaf plant hold the answer, but she didn't understand how. When she drank the potion she made from them, she managed to send the darkness out of her body and back into the earth, back beyond the veil. But the knife still remained cursed, and in the end she hid it beneath Bob's grave.'

'Where Tullia found it,' Agnese added.

Francesco unfolded the cloth around the dagger, deep in thought. 'You'd have thought Isadora would've left clearer instructions.' He rubbed at a tarnished mark on the metal. 'This is good-quality linen; considering how old it is, it should fall to pieces in my hands. And someone's embroidered it. Look.'

He held it out to us and I peered at the elegant stitches. 'Almost looks like they could be–'

'Words!' Agnese finished for me. She picked up the cloth. 'It's too dirty to see properly. D'you think we can wash it?'

'We're not going to be able to read them if we don't. Be careful, though. Use cold water, and the gentle soap.'

We all stood over the sink, tense with anticipation as Agnese carefully washed it in the soapy water. As the water turned a muddy brown, the linen took on a light beige hue. She rinsed it through several times until the water remained clear, then smoothed it out on the draining board.

'Bloody hell,' I whispered.

Zia Liliana had helped us transcribe the recipe book, especially with the older entries. Now she frowned at the piece of cloth on her kitchen table, then looked at us.

'You'll have to fetch my glasses if you want me to read that,' she said.

Agnese got them from the dresser and gave them to her mother. Edo pulled out a chair and clambered up, eager to see what was going on.

'You'll fall, young man,' Liliana admonished, then perched the glasses on her nose and peered at the linen.

Francesco stood behind Edo, holding onto him.

'Papà!' Edo complained, trying to dislodge his father's hands from his waist.

'Your aunt's right. You don't want to fall and miss all the fun, do you?'

Edo squirmed in protest, but he stopped speaking when Zia Liliana held up her hand for silence.

'I can hardly hear myself think! Agnese, I can only just read it, so make sure you write it all down.'

Agnese nodded, pen poised over a notepad. I found myself leaning in, as eager as Edo to hear what was written.

'"The silver-leaf plant has been entwined with the fate of the healers from the beginning. Their leaves, so sweet of perfume, cure all ailments, and their berries will help in others. But it is the flowers that are the most precious of all, despite their unpleasant aroma. Oft discarded, instead they must be preserved and dried."'

Agnese stopped writing. 'But didn't Morgana already try that?'

Zia Liliana pursed her lips. 'Do you want me to continue? There's a bit more.'

Agnese nodded, chastened.

'Right then. "Finally, I have found the incantation for the cursed dagger. But the blade is lost, and I am sorely angry with myself.

This is what must be done, should it ever be found: For three days and three nights the flowers must steep in moon-bathed water in a shallow silver bowl, after which pound the flowers into a paste to smear over the blade."'

'Morgana did that,' I blurted. Zia Liliana glared at me, then turned back to the embroidered cloth.

'"Immerse the knife in the water and set on a windowsill in the midday sun. Light must replace dark, good will replace evil, the wheel of life continues to turn while you speak the words of the spell."' She put the cloth down and looked up at us expectantly.

'Is that it?' I asked. 'What spell?'

'There is nothing else written here,' Zia Liliana said, peering at the cloth again.

Agnese slumped in her chair. 'I really thought this would be the answer.'

'Can I see the notepad?' She passed it to me, and I read through her notes.

'Mamma?' Edo tugged at my arm.

'Just a moment, sweetie.' Something was niggling at me, I almost had it. I bit on my lip, concentrating on the words.

'Come with me for a moment, Edo,' Francesco said. 'We'll get a biscuit. Mamma will give you a cuddle when she's finished.'

Barely taking any notice of everyone else, I grabbed a pencil and translated the lines into English. '"*La luce deve rimpiazzare lo scuro, il bene rimpiazzerà il male, mentre la ruota della vita continua a girare*. Light must *replace* dark, good will *replace* evil, as the wheel of life continues to turn,"' I muttered. 'Rimpiazzare, not scacciare. Replace, not drive away.' I slammed down the pencil, making Agnese jump. 'It makes more sense in English,' I said triumphantly.

'Isadora called the flowers *scaccia maledizioni*, curse snatchers, in the recipe book, but here she uses different words. Morgana followed the spell in the book, but it was incomplete. Isadora must have written this later in her life, but she no longer had the knife. It was too late for her to perform the incantation.'

'But what does it mean?' Francesco had come back into the living room, followed by a sticky-faced Edo.

Agnese leaped to her feet, her eyes sparkling. 'It means that it's impossible to remove a curse. Even though we're talking about magic, there are still rules to follow, and certain things that have to be done.'

'I see you've been studying,' I said, smiling.

'I picked up a book in an antique shop last week, I've been meaning to show you.' She sat back down, her face flushed. 'I haven't read much, but in the introduction the author speaks about keeping a balance in the universe so that the forces are aligned and there isn't too much of one thing and too little of another.'

'That's interesting. From Isadora's embroidery, I'm guessing she reached the same conclusion. We can't just remove the curse and leave the knife... empty, for want of a better word.' A thought occurred to me and I looked at Francesco. 'When I performed the incantation in the Grove, the blood came up from under the ground and was replaced by water. Do you remember?'

'There was a small stream coming up out of the earth, and the bowl was full of blood.' He grimaced.

I could still see it if I closed my eyes; the blood forcing its way up to the surface of the ground, carrying the ancient curse with it, clear spring water gushing into the grooves it left behind.

'When we pick a leaf off a plant, we say a prayer to encourage it to grow more, to replace the one we've taken. Everything we do is in symbiosis with the world – we can't take something without replacing it.'

'"Good will replace evil."' Zia Liliana looked down at the cloth on the table, her fingers trembling as she traced the embroidered letters. 'So to get rid of the curse, you must replace it with... what?'

I shrugged. 'A lucky charm, perhaps, or a spell of protection, or wellbeing, or love.'

'Ugh, love!' Edo snorted, making us laugh.

'Don't mock it, son, it's not that bad,' Francesco said, winking at me. 'So, do you think you can do it? Turn the knife into a force for good, once and for all?'

Zia Liliana neatly folded the cloth and slid it across the table. 'I hope you can. This family needs some peace, after all these years.' Her hand trembled again and she pulled it back, but not before I noticed.

I frowned, but before I could say anything she stood abruptly. 'We've got a silver bowl that'll be perfect, I'll fetch it for you,' she called as she hurried into the kitchen.

'Is she okay?' I asked Agnese.

'I think so. Why?'

'Nothing.' I made a mental note to come back and speak to my aunt when she was by herself.

'Here you go. It needs a bit of a polish, but it should do.' Liliana handed me an oval bowl, perfect for laying the dagger in.

'Thank you.' I glanced at the others. 'We should go, we've got lots to do.'

As we walked back to the cottage, Edo sitting on Francesco's shoulders, chattering happily about anything and everything, I was busy making my own plans for breaking the curse on the knife.

Chapter Sixty-Two

31 October

EVER SINCE THE NIGHT I removed the curse from the Grove, I'd become aware of the shadows in the cottage. They didn't scare me; indeed, their presence was a comfort. Knowing that the healers from the past were watching over me helped me in times of need.

Because sometimes, in those dark hours of the night when my mind was too busy to rest but my body fought for sleep, I still had cravings. I would lie beside Francesco, listening to his deep, regular breathing, trying to push back the urge for a glass of wine. Over the years it happened less, but I was always terrified of giving in, of Francesco seeing me at my very worst. In those long, tormented hours, the shadows would gather around me, enveloping me in a circle of love and compassion, soothing me until my head calmed and I fell asleep.

And now, as I placed the silver bowl with the silver-leaf flowers steeping in 'moon-bathed water' on the kitchen table, I could feel them nearby, full of curiosity at what would happen next. I was just as curious, and a bit apprehensive. The dagger was on a plate, still wrapped in the embroidered linen cloth.

I'd sent Francesco and Agnese down to Zia Liliana's with Edo and Malva, telling them I'd wait until they got back before doing anything. But I had no intention of waiting. The gate was locked, and a protection spell created another barrier to keep them away. I was terrified that something would go wrong, that I would unleash something evil, as Tullia had four centuries earlier. My dreams were filled with dark entities dragging me down to the depths of hell, and I could no longer tell if they were premonitions or manifestations of my fear. Either way, I wanted the cottage empty when I performed the incantation. Bella and the healers would protect me, I hoped, and the baby growing inside me.

A blur of colour at the window caught my eye, and I looked up to see the dragonfly settling on the windowsill outside. Its presence gave me courage, and I silently thanked it for being there. Bella lay on her rug in front of the fire, her eyes closed but her ears twitching, ever alert.

I picked up the fine sieve I'd prepared and strained off the flowers, putting them in the mortar. With the pestle, I mushed them to a thick paste, coughing at the pungent odour coming off them.

'It's all right for you, with no sense of smell,' I muttered, glaring at the shadows in the corners. I thought I saw a ripple go through them, and imagined them laughing at my plight. The dragonfly twitched its wings, its gaze concentrated on me as I moved around. Bella whined, and moved further away.

My eyes watering, I took the mortar with its stinking, pulpy mess and placed it next to the knife. When I unwrapped the cloth, I stopped and stared at the silver blade shining in the sunlight. It had brought devastation on my family over the centuries: it had spilled Bob's blood and left a curse in the ground, it had driven an old woman to fake the death of a child in order to save the Innocenti from shame and exile, and even when it had saved the life of Rina, it had condemned Morgana to death as a witch.

As I smeared the paste over the blade, myriad thoughts ran through my head. Who was I to think that I could drive the evil out of it and use it for good? Would there be a price to pay? I hesitated, fearful for my unborn child, but also fearful of what could happen if I didn't break the curse.

I repeated over and over the words Agnese had written down, trying to convince myself it was what I had to do. "'Immerse the knife in the water and set on a windowsill in the midday sun. Light must replace dark, good will replace evil, the wheel of life continues to turn while you speak the words of the spell.'"

With dread in my heart, I placed the knife in the silver bowl. The water covered it, shimmering in the light dancing over the surface as I carried it to the windowsill. Five minutes to go. The sun streamed in through the kitchen window, sparkling on the silver surfaces, so bright that I could hardly bear to look. It was almost time, and I was too scared to move.

A hand rested on top of mine, shadowy and tremulous, barely there, but I could feel the love and strength emanating from it. I turned to my right and saw her. Gemma. Her hair was a muted chestnut brown, a mere shadow of its vibrant hue when she was alive, but her green eyes pierced through the darkness, kind and reassuring. She gestured to my other side, and when I turned I saw another woman. Pale skin, blonde hair, a willowy figure not yet changed by childbearing. I recognised her immediately.

'Katherine,' I whispered.

She nodded, and took my left hand in hers. Another shadow appeared, and Julia-Ann completed the circle. I shivered, suddenly in awe of these women from the past; witches, mothers, and friends, they shared a bond that not even death could break. And they were here, now, to help me.

Together we stood in a circle around the bowl, the walls of the cottage no barrier to the three ghostly women. As a church clock struck midday, its chimes audible in the distance, I lifted my face to the sun and closed my eyes. The incantation flowed from me, unrehearsed, unknown; centuries-old words given to me as a gift, never to be uttered again.

Three times I spoke the incantation, and each time I sensed the other shadows in the cottage moving closer. Luisa, Morgana, Sara, Alessandra, Isotta, and more, all the healers from all the centuries. And Isadora and Agnes were there too, watching over me, their pride and love flowing through my heart. I hadn't opened a window or door, but somehow the dragonfly was there as well, hovering above me, emanating its calm wisdom and quiet fortitude. As the darkness in the blade pushed back, fighting for its place in the world, they lent me their strength and goodness, until the darkness subsided into nothingness.

And then we filled the blade with light and warmth and love, pouring every ounce of our energy and spirits into it. I chanted spells for protection, for love, and for health, not only for my family but for everyone in Gallicano and the valley. For the people who had loved us, defended us, come to us in times of need, and even for those who had betrayed and hurt us. I poured all the love and compassion I had into my words, until the blade glowed and I knew it was done.

The shadows fell back, merging once more into the darker corners of the cottage. I caught a glimpse of their faces, those healers I'd known so well, and others I'd never met, before they faded away. All except three.

Katherine, Julia-Ann and Gemma guided me over to the sofa, where I gratefully sat down. I hadn't realised how much my legs were trembling until the adrenaline wore off. I smiled at them, and at the dragonfly landing gently on my hand.

'We did it.'

Gemma touched my cheek. *You did it.* I heard her voice in my mind, a shadow of the voice I knew so well, at once familiar and comforting.

'The baby?' I asked, suddenly terrified that I'd hurt my daughter in some way.

Gemma lay a hand on my stomach. *She is well, safe and warm and snug. She will be a strong healer, just like her mother.*

'I don't feel strong. I'm so tired.' Relieved she was okay, I lay my head on a cushion, drowsy. 'Please stay with me.'

Sleep, and I will tell you a story, Gemma said.

The room faded, and my eyes closed.

Chapter Sixty-Three

April 1637

Gemma froze, listening intently as the footsteps came closer. She glanced at the grave and clenched her fist, then withdrew into the shadow of the trunk as the figure came into view.

Fingers clutched at her arm and pulled her backwards into the forest. Before she could scream, a hand clamped over her mouth, the smell of fresh earth and rotting leaves heavy in her nostrils. She was dragged away from the clearing and the grave, deeper into the forest, the trees closing in and muffling all sound.

She struggled violently, kicking and wriggling, but it was no use. Whoever it was had the advantage of surprise and strength over her, and she couldn't free herself. Suddenly relaxing her body, she caught her attacker off guard. As she slumped, their grip loosened, and she fell with a bump to the ground.

Gemma scrambled to her feet and ran, following the half-hidden paths she knew so well. She could hear no sound of anyone running after her, no cracking twigs or muffled footfalls, no imprecations as branches snagged unwary pursuers, but still she ran.

Bob had been afraid. He was never afraid; indeed, he was the one who usually gave courage to the healers when they needed it. She had sensed the darkness at the clearing too, the smothering, suffocating presence of whatever entity Tullia had evoked.

Because Gemma knew that it had been Tullia there. She had caught the scent of rhododendrons, the overpowering perfume evoking memories of that long-ago night when she had eaten the poisoned honey. Only Tullia would have followed her there, to the clearing. And Tullia wanted the dagger. She had to get home.

The cottage stood in the gloom of dusk, a lantern at the window welcoming her home. Standing outside the door, Gemma could hear Maria singing softly to Chiara, and her arms ached to hold her daughter.

A hand grasped her shoulder, making her jump, and she turned to see her father there.

'Gemma,' he said, before falling to the ground with a groan.

She saw the blood soaking into the dirt beneath his body, and only then did she notice the wound in his side.

'Papà? Who did this?' she asked, already tearing a strip of cloth off her skirt to staunch the bleeding.

His breathing was laboured, but he managed to say, 'Tullia.'

His wound tightly bound, Gemma ran into the cottage, startling Maria and making Chiara burst into tears.

'My father is injured. I need boiling water, a needle and thread, and as many clean cloths as we have. Oh, and the jar of mixed herbs on the first shelf in the pantry.' She dragged the pallet out from the corner over to the fire, and grabbed a couple of blankets. 'Quickly now, please,' she snapped, as Maria stood gawping at her. 'Put Chiara in her cradle and fetch my things.'

While Maria dashed about, Gemma went outside. Teo groaned as she pulled him up to a sitting position, careful not to jolt his wound.

'I need to get you indoors, near the fire. Can you stand?'

He grunted as she lifted him, but used his legs to help her. Staggering under his weight, she guided him over to the pallet and lay him down. The wound was bleeding again, and she placed more clean cloths around it.

Beads of sweat coated his brow and his face was pale, even in the firelight. Gemma forced herself to remain calm and assess the situation. The wound was deep, too deep for her to be able to save him, she feared.

Feeling helpless as she listened to him gasp for breath, all she could do was wet his lips with a cloth soaked in cool water. She heard Chiara grizzling in the background, then Maria began singing a lullaby. The quiet melody floated around the room, the notes soothing, blending with the scent of the sweet herbs that Gemma had put in the pot of hot water.

'Tullia,' her father whispered.

'Shh. Stay still, don't try to talk.'

Teo lifted his hand, grimacing. 'I need... to tell...'

'No,' she repeated. 'You have to rest, get better.'

'I don't have... long.' His breath was laboured. 'You have to listen.'

Gemma opened her mouth to deny his words, but she knew he was right. She leaned forward. 'I'm listening.'

'Tullia h-has the dagger.' Teo had to force each word out, and Gemma could only imagine the effort it took him. 'She... I was meant t-to kill you, but...' A tear rolled down his cheek. 'You must stay a-away from her. Sh-she threatened to d-destroy the grave in the forest.'

'Bob's grave?' Gemma whispered.

Teo nodded. 'Sh-she will s-stop at nothing to break the c-curse you put on her.' He closed his eyes and groaned in pain. 'Stay away from h-her and the g-grave. Sh-she will leave as s-soon as she is free of the curse.'

Gemma bowed her head. 'She will never be free,' she said fiercely. 'Only someone pure of heart can break the curse. If she tries...' She clenched her fists. 'It will rebound on her.'

Teo opened his eyes and looked at her with such sadness that she wanted to cry. 'Then both your l-lives will be wasted in h-hate and v-vengeance.' He gasped, and his hand clutched feebly at his side.

A pool of blood spread on the pallet, instantly soaking through the cloths that Gemma had pressed against the wound. She could do nothing to stop it, could only watch as the life ebbed from him. She took hold of his hand, and his eyelids fluttered.

'Mamma! Papà!' he cried, lifting his head and staring at the darkness beyond the firelight. He smiled, his face relaxing. And then he screamed, a deep, guttural scream that made Gemma shiver with fear. His hand gripped hers, fingers scrabbling at the blankets, before his head sank back down, his body limp.

Gemma sat beside her dead father, her mind and body numb as Teo's blood soaked into the blankets.

Chapter Sixty-Four

People's memories were long, their feelings of guilt even longer. Teo's name reminded the villagers of Morgana's trial, of how few of them had defended her innocence, of her humiliation at the Witchfinder's hands. No one mourned his death, no one offered to help his widow and children.

The priest kept the ceremony as brief as possible, his sombre voice intoning the ritual while Chiara wriggled in Claude's arms, Gemma standing beside them, pale and dry-eyed. There had been no sign of Tullia since the night of his death, which made more than a few tongues waggle.

Only Gemma knew why. The day after Teo died, she went to the cottage where he had lived with Tullia. The young girl she had seen before sat outside on the doorstep, crying bitterly. Gemma stood beneath the trees, unsure whether to approach. Her father had warned her to stay away, but she wanted to see if Tullia had indeed broken the curse.

A woman screeched inside the cottage, and the girl immediately stopped crying. She wiped the tears and snot on the sleeve of her tunic and glanced fearfully behind her at the closed door, half-crouching as though to run away.

The sound of crockery smashing on the floor came from the cottage, followed by several other shrieks. The girl flinched, and began sobbing again.

'Laura, damn you, come here!' Tullia's voice was harsh and rasping, filled with mad fury. More crockery crashed to the floor and a baby started wailing, adding to the growing cacophony. 'I said, get inside *now*!'

The girl hesitated, her feet poised to run into the forest, and then her shoulders slumped and she opened the door. A hand reached out, grabbed hold of her tunic, and dragged her inside, the shrieking voice colliding with the baby's screams in a confusion of rage and noise. Tullia leaned out and slammed the door shut, but not before Gemma saw her face.

Tullia's hair was white as snow, her once-beautiful features wizened and aged like an old crone, her once-full lips dried and cracked. As she turned to go back inside, she stared sightlessly at the forest, cloudy white cataracts covering her eyes.

Gemma had her answer. Tullia had paid a heavy price for stealing the dagger and attempting to break the curse: her youth and beauty were gone, leaving behind the aged, blind shell of a woman, suddenly without a husband, and two small daughters to bring up on her own. Her life would be hard, Gemma knew, made even harder by the fact that everyone nearby would shun her. Gemma had a sudden vision of Tullia, driven to madness by the curse, hanging from one of the branches of the oak tree, her neck broken, her soul whispering among the leaves, searching, always searching.

She shook her head to rid it of the image. The wheel of life would continue to turn, and Tullia and her daughters, and their daughters after, would have to live their own lives as best they could. There was nothing Gemma could do.

She turned and left the cottage, and its cursed inhabitants, behind her as she made her way back through the forest to her own family.

Chapter Sixty-Five

June 1667

The years have been kind to me, Gemma mused as she sat on a bench and looked around the Grove. Claude stood under an apple tree, his blue eyes twinkling in his weathered face, deep in animated conversation with Chiara about how to best cut back its branches.

The cat sunning itself on the bench next to her stretched out, lazily batting a paw at a passing dragonfly, too sleepy to do anything more. Gemma let the dragonfly settle on her hand, its legs tickling her skin, its wings spread out wide.

Every day her bones ached a little more, every day it was harder to get started in the morning and harder to get to sleep at night. She remembered when her bed had been the frozen ground of the mountains, her only warmth coming from Ombra. How young she had been! Now, if she tried to lie down on the ground, she would never get back up again. She chuckled.

Even thinking of Ombra no longer hurt, not as much as it did in the first years after the mare's death. Gemma's faithful companion through the most eventful years of her life, the horse had lived to the ripe old age of twenty-seven. Claude's stallion, Lumière, had died two years before Ombra, and was buried in the clearing in front of the cottage. They had laid Ombra to rest with him. The two horses lived on in their offspring, colts and fillies whose blood had enriched the Innocenti's world-renowned stables.

Gemma sighed. Almost everyone she had ever known was now dead. Jacopo, Leandro, Nicholas, Katherine, Count and Countess Bianchi, all were gone. Everyone she'd ever known, except for Julia-Ann. Slightly older than Gemma, she and her walking stick were feared by everyone around her, as she delighted in writing in her letters. They arrived less frequently nowadays, but every one Gemma received took her back to those enchanting days where curses were real and witches were her best friends.

And there was Claude. Her husband, her friend, her soul mate, was always by her side. He'd comforted her when their son had died at just a few weeks old, and again when she'd lost a baby before the moon had completed its cycle three times. They had been blessed with Chiara, and they treasured their fortune while mourning their loss.

Yes, she had lived a good life and had some incredible experiences. She had fond memories of her time in France and England, even though her heart had longed for the cottage and the Grove. Sometimes she wondered how her life would have been if she'd stayed in England, if she had married Nicholas, but the curiosity soon passed. Her life was here, in Gallicano, tending to her patients and teaching her daughter to be the next healer. At certain angles, and in a certain light, if she looked closely, she thought she could see some of Nicholas in Chiara's features. Then she would tell herself not to be such a stupid old woman, that nothing could be further from the truth.

Claude looked over and waved, shrugging his shoulders as Chiara continued to talk. Gemma waved back, and made herself more comfortable on the bench. She was content to wait, however long it took.

The dragonfly flew away and the damselfly took its place. Gemma smiled down at it, peace in her heart. The warmth of the sun on her face, the delicate perfume of the plants all around her, a breeze cooling her skin, were all she wanted. Her soul was part of the Dragonfly Grove, and the Grove was a part of her. And as she looked into the dark orbs of the damselfly, she knew that her time had come.

Peacefully, quietly, with the sounds of her family's voices in her ears and the scents of her beloved plants all around, she succumbed to the damselfly's gaze. Her hand rested on the cat's sleek fur as her breathing slowed and the healers welcomed her into their open arms.

Chapter Sixty-Six

Present day

I SLOWLY CAME TO, feeling a peace inside me that I hadn't felt in a long time. Bella sat beside me, her head resting on the sofa, her nose against my arm. The shadows were gone, the room bathed in light, and the clock on the wall told me it was after midday. I sat up and stretched, then walked over to the table.

I half thought it had all been a dream, but there was the knife, still smeared with the bitter-smelling paste, lying submerged in the silver bowl. I leaned over and peered at it, then hesitantly poked it with a finger. There was no dark vision, no nightmarish figure trying to drag me underground; there was nothing. I picked it up and used a cloth to wipe away the paste. And then it happened.

The sunlight caught the blade, the ray so bright that I had to turn my head, temporarily blinded. When I could see again, the knife glowed in my hand, a deep orange glow that looked like fire at first, flickering tongues of flame shimmering up and down the blade. I dropped it on the table and stepped back. Bella stood beside me, her hackles up, but she wasn't growling. Instead, her tail was wagging gently as she pushed her muzzle into my hand.

It wasn't until the dragonfly landed on the handle of the knife that I realised what was different. The darkness was gone, banished by the incantation Katherine, Julia-Ann and I had recited, replaced with love, peace and wellbeing. And I knew that I could use it, together with our remedies, to heal the people I loved.

The feeling of peace didn't leave me, not even when Francesco and Agnese came home and were rightly upset to find I'd already performed the incantation.

'We should have been here, anything could have happened!' Francesco glared at me, his concern etched on his face.

'But it didn't,' I replied, holding my hand up as he started to speak again. 'Bella was with me, and the dragonfly, and Gemma–'

'Gemma?' he interrupted, incredulous.

'The shadows in the cottage.' I gestured all around us. 'Have you never noticed them, Agnese?'

My cousin shrugged, then nodded reluctantly.

'They're the healers from the past, our ancestors, keeping watch over us. They were here, protecting me, and helping me. I was never at risk.' I'd almost forgotten my own fears, and felt a little guilty.

'You did it then?' Francesco asked gruffly.

I was startled to see tears in his eyes. 'Yes, I did it. The curse is gone, replaced by light. And,' I couldn't keep the eagerness out of my voice, 'I learned the rest of Gemma's story.'

'What?' Agnese glanced over at Edo, playing with Bella on the rug, driving his cars over her body while making 'brroom brroom' sounds. 'You have to tell us everything!'

'Make a coffee and I will,' I replied, smiling sweetly at her. 'But first, I have something else to tell you.'

I made sure that they were both sitting down, then showed them the charm I wore around my neck. Agnese understood before Francesco, but it wasn't long before all three of us were crying and hugging, while Edo looked on, bemused.

Chapter Sixty-Seven

One year later

I picked up the bundle of papers and tapped it lightly on the desk until they all aligned perfectly.

'I can't believe it's finally finished,' I said, sighing.

'"A History of Healers",' Francesco read over my shoulder. A shrill cry came from upstairs. 'Sounds like you finished printing it just in time.'

I put down the papers and stood with a groan. 'It's a miracle it got written at all. Coming, sweetheart.'

Francesco gave me a quick hug. 'I'll go and sort out madam, if you keep an eye on Edo.'

I glanced at my son over on the rug, playing with some Lego. 'Deal.' I smiled as Francesco took the stairs two at a time, then my shoulders sagged with relief as Chloe's screams ceased.

Edo looked up, then returned to building the Lego car he'd been working on all morning. 'I've almost finished too, Mamma.'

'I can see. That's a cool car,' I told him.

'It's for chasing dinosaurs.' He gestured to the pile of plastic dinosaurs nearby. 'We're going to round them up and catch them, then use them to ride about on!'

I ruffled his hair and left him to it. He hardly noticed I'd gone, although he briefly glanced up as Francesco came downstairs with a wrapped-up bundle in his arms.

Chloe scrunched up her little face as soon as she saw me and let out a tremendous wail.

'She's a bit hungry,' Francesco said.

'Oh, so that's why she's crying.' I carried her over to the sofa and soon she was lost in a world of warm, tummy-filling milk, her pudgy hand laid on my skin. As soon as we officially knew she was going to be a girl we decided on her name. Chloe. Symbolic of new beginnings, growth and fertility, it was the perfect choice.

I never thought I'd have moments such as these, I'd told myself that they were things only other women would experience. Every time I looked at my children, every time I breathed in the warm perfume of their skin, every time they smiled at me, I was overwhelmed by the love I felt for them. As Chloe snuffled, I closed my eyes and cleared my mind, letting my thoughts drift wherever they wished, happy in the warm embrace of my family.

That afternoon, I watched as Francesco searched the chimney in our cottage for a similar hidey-hole to the one in Tommaso's house. We had put it off for too long, so many other things had seemed more important. With the rain pouring down outside, Chloe fast asleep in her pram, and Edo watching his favourite film, it had seemed like the best time to do it. I sniggered as soot fell into the fireplace, but then I heard the familiar sound of stone grating on stone, and gasped when he emerged, covered in soot and dust, holding a box in his hand.

'Told you,' he said triumphantly, and sneezed.

'Outside and get cleaned up,' I ordered, taking the box from him.

'Don't open it without me,' he called over his shoulder.

I examined the wooden box, intrigued. A dragonfly motif had been burned into the lid, and I wondered who had made it.

Francesco came back inside, his clothes cleaner, the soot gone from his hands and face. I handed him the box.

'Seeing as you did the dirty work, you can open it.'

He raised an eyebrow, but said nothing as he prised the lid off. Inside there was something wrapped in a thick cloth. I recognised the scent of the silver-leaf plant before I saw the crumbled remnants of dried leaves fall out, and peered closely as Francesco removed the cloth and the contents were revealed.

'Oh.' I was speechless.

'"The English Physician by Nicholas Culpeper",' Francesco read. He gave a low whistle. 'Printed in 1651. Better you put some gloves on before handling it.'

I went to the dresser and took out a new pair of cotton gloves I'd bought for working in the Grove, and put them on. Carefully, terrified of destroying the book, I opened the cover. The pages were pristine white, as crisp as if the book had just been printed. Awestruck, I turned the page.

'There's an inscription! "To my dearest friend and teacher, Gemma, without whom this book would have remained but a dream. May I one day see the dragonflies and walk among the flowers in the Grove, and breathe the Tuscan air with you. Your faithful servant, Nicholas Culpeper."'

I sat down with a thump, my legs shaking. 'This is a first edition.' My head spun.

'Gemma must have put it there for safe keeping. It's a miracle it's still intact,' Francesco said, wonder in his voice. 'What are you going to do with it?'

'Read it. And treasure it.' My hands shaking, I wrapped it back up in the cloth, together with some fresh leaves from the silver-leaf plant, and gently put it inside the box. 'I'll keep it in the dragonfly box Ted made, together with the tapestry, where it will be safe for our grandchildren, and their grandchildren too.'

During my research for my book, I'd found out that Nicholas had never come to Tuscany, and that Gemma hadn't seen him again. He had died in 1654, unaware that his book would still be in use four hundred years later. Was Chiara his daughter? Or was she Claude's? I had no idea, and imagined that we would never know. But whoever's blood ran in our veins, we were richer for them both having been part of our history.

I had hidden the knife away in the pantry after performing the incantation, the glow still emanating from it, charging the jars of herbs on the shelves with its spells. It was our secret, one that would never be revealed, one that had already helped Zia Liliana over the past year and would, I knew, help many more.

I couldn't quite believe that my travels to the past were over. Sometimes I found myself drifting away and would tense, ready to be transported to another time, another healer's life. But it never happened. With Gemma's story, I knew enough of my family's history to become the healer I was always meant to be.

Agnes, Sara, Morgana, Gemma, Luisa, and their daughters, had shown me the strength and resilience every woman has inside them, no matter how dire the times or how desperate the situation. They had helped me from the path of self-destruction and led me to a future I could never have imagined all those years before, when Umberto Bini, my friendly taxi driver, brought me to the gates of the cottage.

I remembered the desolation I had felt when I'd first seen the state of the cottage, and how my family had all pitched in, even pregnant Giulia, to help make it a place fit to live in. Zio Dante and Zia Liliana had welcomed me with open arms, and had shown me love and acceptance when I couldn't love or accept myself. Slowly, surely, they had made me believe in myself.

Even Mark had served as a lesson. Lonely, still in the grip of an alcoholic's cravings, with little to no self-esteem, I had clung on to the first person who showed the slightest interest in me, only to realise that I was worth more, that I didn't have to settle for second best, that I didn't need a man.

And then Francesco came into my life. I might not have needed a man, but I found my soulmate, someone who would give me the love and support I was searching for. He held me when I cried after seeing what my ancestors went through, and he encouraged me to write their stories down.

Agnese and I began a new tradition when we both took over as healers, and we hoped that Malva and Chloe would carry it on. Perhaps Edo would help them as well, and another tradition would be born. With the magic of the cottage, and the blessing of the dragonflies, anything was possible.

My mother had insisted that there was magic at the cottage, and every time she came to visit I was delighted to tell her she'd been right. But even she hadn't imagined that there was so much magic here, so many possibilities. The dragonflies, the Grove, the silver-leaf plant, began here more than six centuries earlier and became a part of the Innocenti.

And now we were a part of their story. Mine and Agnese's names were written in the book, where Chloe and Malva, and Edo, would also write their names eventually. The cottage would become theirs, they would tend the Grove, and the dragonflies and shadows would protect them, as they had protected us all. And out in the woods they would find the grave, and hear precious words of advice in their moments of need.

In time, our children would learn the magic of the healers. This was our gift to them, this was the healers' legacy.

THE END

If you enjoyed reading this book, please consider leaving a review. Even just a few words can make all the difference, and will make the book more visible to others who may enjoy it as well. Thank you.

Author's Note

First of all, I would like to thank you, the reader, for sharing this journey with me. It started in 2017, when I came up with the idea of a young woman finding a baby's skeleton in her garden, and travelling back in time. This idea changed, as most stories do when you actually sit down and write them, and when Luisa insisted that her past be told, I realised that I had to let the characters take over and go wherever they took me.

I've loved writing these books. Each one is a labour of love, with many hours spent on researching even the most basic things. I know I've got things wrong, I know that historians are probably shaking their heads at scenes I've written, but I hope that the magic and love in these stories help make up for any errors.

Nicholas Culpeper lived from 1616-1654, and he wrote *The English Physician*, later known as *Culpeper's Complete Herbal*, which you can still buy. There isn't much information about his life, but he did fall in love with heiress Judith Rivers, and she did die when her coach was struck by lightning the day they planned to elope. After reading his book and learning about his life, I knew I had to introduce him into the story somehow!

Although I said there would be two more books after Morgana's story, this is the last one. I felt that I had to finish the series on a high, before people got bored and started saying, 'Not more dragonflies!'. Writing 'The End' to this book was a bitter-sweet moment for me –

while I'm sad to part company with Jennifer, Francesco, Agnese and all the healers, I have other projects I'd like to work on, and more books waiting to be written. I hope you will be there to accompany me on my journey.

As a special thank you, there's an exclusive Healer short story at the end of the book. I hope you enjoy it!

Acknowledgements

I HAVE A FEW people to thank, so please bear with me!

First of all, my loyal readers and supporters who cheer me on through my Facebook page, Twitter, and my secret group on Facebook – you really are the best! Thank you for reading, reviewing, and telling others about my books; you have no idea how much I appreciate you all.

A special mention goes to Christine Petrone-Curtis, who came up with the title. It's perfect!

A huge thank you to my dear friend and talented fellow author Annette Spratte, without whom this book would have been a mere shadow of itself. After I finished the first draft, I needed someone to go over it who had read all the books, and wouldn't be afraid to tell me exactly what was wrong with it. Annette and I have been friends for a few years, and she was what the book, and I, desperately needed. She confirmed my doubts about certain parts, and boosted my ego on others. Several rewrites later, and with quite a lot of cursing, the book you have just read was the result.

Special thanks to Kayleigh and Sarah for their friendship and support. We have been on an incredible journey together, with highs and lows, and there is no better feeling than knowing that they are always there, no matter what.

I am honoured that Sarah Northwood gave me permission to use two of her poems in my book. She writes poetry that reaches inside you, to those emotions you keep hidden away, and touches your soul.

If you're still here, thank you for reading the whole book. I'd love to hear what you think of it, whether you write a review, or let me know via social media, or through my newsletter.

As usual, the last thank you goes to my husband, Ivan. Your support and love mean everything to me, and always will. *Ti amo. Sei la mia luce, la mia anima, il mio amore.*

You can also follow me on:
Facebook
Blue Sky
Bookbub

On my blog:
https://pinkquillbooks.wordpress.com

You can sign up for my newsletter at:
https://sendfox.com/lp/1knl41
for up-to-date information on my books, behind the scenes details, chat about life in Italy, and freebies/promos of other authors' books I think you may like. I only send my newsletter out once a month or so, unless I have any exciting news to share with you!

Also By Helen Pryke

<u>Short Stories</u>
Autumn Sky (a short story)
In Dark Places (a collection of 13 chilling short stories)

<u>Suspense</u>
The Lost Girls (Maggie Turner Suspense Series #1)
Right Beside You (Maggie Turner Suspense Series #2)
The Secrets That Bind Us (Maggie Turner Suspense Series #3)

<u>Historical Fiction</u>
The Healer's Secret (The Healer Saga #1)
The Healer's Curse (The Healer Saga #2)
The Healer's Awakening (The Healer Saga #3)
The Healer's Betrayal (The Healer Saga #4)
The Healer's Legacy (The Healer Saga #5)

Walls of Silence

<u>Children's Books</u>
(under the pen name Julia E. Clements)
Dreamland (also available as an audiobook)
Adventure in Malasorte Castle
The Last of the Guardians (a short story)
Unicorns, Mermaids, and Magical Tales
(written with Sarah Northwood)

About Helen Pryke

HELEN PRYKE IS A British author who has been living in the north of Italy for more than 30 years, learning everything about Italians, their culture, and their way of life. She now considers herself more Italian than British, even though she has never lost her British accent. Addicted to coffee and chocolate, she has also developed a passion for good food, having married an Italian who is a wonderful cook!

Author of the popular Healer series set in Tuscany, Helen writes emotional women's fiction as well as suspense novels. She also writes middle grade fiction under the pen name Julia E. Clements.

The Dragonfly Grove

Prologue

ONCE UPON A TIME, when the world was young, an enormous swarm of dragonflies emerged from a huge crack in the earth and completely covered the ground. The people came out of their houses, wailing, "What are we going to do now? We can't plant our crops or feed our animals, how will we live?"

The dragonflies rose in the air and spoke to the people. "Fear not," they said. "We are here to help you, not destroy you. Listen to our wisdom, and you will learn much from the knowledge we have to give you."

But the people were afraid and grew angry. They threw stones at the dragonflies and tried to drive them away. The dragonflies were sad, but understood why the people reacted that way. "We will help those who ask us for help," they said, before taking to the skies and disappearing.

Some people followed them, curious to see what the dragonflies could teach them. They journeyed to a gushing spring at the far ends of the earth, this group of people eager to learn. The dragonflies greeted them with joy, delighted that they wanted their knowledge.

"We will teach you many things, things you can use to spread our wisdom among your people, without causing fear or anger," they told those gathered before them. "You will leave us as different people, with a connection to other worlds that exist without your knowledge. The fairies and sprites, elves and gnomes, all will become your friends and allies, helping you in times of need. You will be able to speak with spirits from the other world, people who are dear to you, others who have a message to pass on. You will learn to adapt to this new world we will introduce you to, it will change your vision and fill you with joy.

"As you explore these new realms, it will become clear what is an illusion and what is real, in all aspects of your life. Your emotions, your empathy, your sense of being will change, and so will you. This knowledge will remain inside you and be passed from generation to generation, never to be lost, an oasis of hope among the rest of humanity."

The people clapped their hands in delight and were eager to begin their lessons. But the dragonflies had a warning for them. "There will be some among you who will use this knowledge to gain power, to gain control over others. This is inevitable, it is a part of human nature, as we sadly know. You shake your heads, but it will happen. And when it does, we have faith that the others will make sure they do not succeed. And those others shall be called healers."

Forest Brook, England
January 1253

THE CRONE WALKED ACROSS the clearing, her cloak wrapped tightly around her shoulders, and pulled her hood up over her head. A cloud of dragonflies hovered around her, their wings fluttering in the breeze, then scattered as she disappeared among the trees of the surrounding woods. Stepping slowly and carefully, her shoulders bowed as though she bore the weight of the world, she followed the almost invisible trail that would lead her to her destination. Someone, somewhere, was dying, and she could feel the soul calling to her.

The gentle murmur of a nearby river accompanied her, and she caught glimpses of it every now and then as moonlit ripples shivered across its surface. Silently, she walked through the woods, following the curve of the land, her mind intent on the seeds in her pocket. A fox barked in the distance, its cry echoing among the trees, and an owl glided swiftly in front of her, its talons out-stretched as it plucked its cowering prey from where it hid, quaking, beneath a bush. Tiny squeals faded into nothing as the owl flew away into the night, searching for a place to enjoy its feast. Nature was beautiful, but it could also be cruel. The crone knew this only too well.

The slumbering village lay beyond the meadows, the houses becoming visible as she crossed the bridge. The rooftops shone with moonglow, but the windows were all dark, not a light to be seen.

Except one. In a small cottage near the far end of the village, a mother tended her sick child, pressing a damp cloth to his fever-sweaty forehead, her heart breaking at the sound of his feeble whimpers. The crone knew that the boy, Lucan, would perish before sunrise but she carried on towards the cottage as fast as her legs would take her. Emmeline, the mother, needed what little comfort she could give.

Emmeline jumped at the rap on the door, not expecting anyone at this late hour, and hurried to open it. Lucan wailed, and she jiggled him gently, shushing him as he lay in her arms.

'Yes?' she said, her anxious face pale in the gloom. The infant snuffled, scrunching his fists in pain.

'May I come in?' the crone asked.

Emmeline was about to refuse, but the crone pulled back the hood of her cloak, a beam of moonlight revealing her worn face etched with the wisdom, and suffering, of centuries. 'Of course.' She stood to one side, rocking her son, and closed the door after the crone entered.

'Please, sit down, Mother.' She gestured to a wooden stool near the fire.

'You're not asleep yet, lass.'

Emmeline glanced down at her son, her eyes filling with tears. 'I don't believe I will get much sleep this night.' She sighed.

'Are you here alone?'

'Hob, my husband, went to the market yesterday, he won't be back until tomorrow evening.' She hesitated, then dared to ask, 'Can you do anything to help him, Mother?'

The crone held her hands out towards the dying embers in the grate, her heart heavy at the answer she had to give. 'He is very sick, lass. I think you know as well as I there is little that can be done.'

'No!' Emmeline dropped to her knees, clutching Lucan to her chest. 'Please, you must help him! He is only a few weeks old, he has seen nothing of this life, only these four walls and the muck out back where the pigs live. He can't die, not when he has seen so little of life.'

The crone stroked the young woman's hair, tears rolling down her wrinkled, weathered cheeks. 'Every child who comes to me is precious and loved, and I nurture their souls as their mothers nurtured them when they were alive. This is his time, lass, I can do nothing to stop Death.'

'So what was the point?' Emmeline cried, scrabbling to her feet. 'Why give him life when he would live so little?'

'Does every life have to have a purpose?' the crone said sadly. 'Perhaps he was only meant to bring you joy for this short time, perhaps that was his purpose.'

'I want more for him,' Emmeline sobbed. 'Why did you come if you can't save him? Please, don't let him die like this.'

The crone shook her head. 'I cannot defeat Death, lass. I can heal some things, but when one is marked by Death himself, I cannot interfere.'

Emmeline looked down at her son in her arms. His lips were blue, his chest barely rising. 'Make it worthwhile, please,' she whispered. 'Give me some solace for his death.'

The crone stood and held out her arms for the infant. Emmeline passed him to her, fearful, yet hopeful. Lucan looked so small and frail, too weak to fight the illness devastating his body. She crossed her fingers and prayed to every god she could think of. But the crone's next words shattered her hopes.

'I cannot save you, little one, this is beyond my gifts. But you will save others.' The infant whimpered, his tiny fingers clutching on to her gnarled ones. ''Tis his time,' the crone murmured, gently passing him back to his mother.

They sat on the floor together, the child nestled in Emmeline's arms.

'What did you mean, he can save people?' she asked.

'His final breath can give life to others,' the crone replied.

'How?'

'With magic, lass.'

Emmeline's eyes widened as she realised who was sitting before her, and she felt a shiver run through her. Countless tales spoke of the crone, under many different names, and she had heard them all throughout the years.

'I come in many guises,' the crone said. 'Where Death comes knocking, I try to arrive before him. Sometimes I do, other times I am too late. Your son may not live a full life, but he will help many others do so. May I?'

Emmeline nodded, unsure what she was agreeing to. She glanced at Lucan, his skin grey in the gloom.

'Be strong,' the crone said softly. She reached under her cloak and took a leather pouch from a bag tied around her waist. Something rustled inside, a gentle susurrus like a field of corn in a summer breeze, and Emmeline thought she could smell the sweet perfume of freshly picked herbs.

Huddled over the infant, the crone opened the pouch. As he took his last rattling breaths, she placed the edge of the pouch against his lips. His last breath left him with a sigh, and Emmeline looked on, too stunned to move, as the pouch filled and a golden, shimmering light filled the air.

'Rest well, little one,' the crone said, as the child's limp body lay in his mother's arms.

They remained together until dawn. The room grew cold as the embers died down and eventually extinguished, but neither the crone nor Emmeline stirred from their vigil over the infant.

When the cock crowed, the crone stiffly got to her feet, brushing the dust from her skirts. 'You know what to do now,' she said.

Emmeline nodded, sniffing back tears. 'Lucan *is* at peace, isn't he?' she asked, fearful. Like everyone else, she knew the stories of vengeful gods and couldn't bear the thought of her son suffering for eternity. The crone was kind in the stories, but this wasn't a child's bedtime tale.

'He is in the arms of the Goddess, don't fear.'

'And the magic?'

'Now we must wait, lass.' The crone smiled and hobbled towards the door. As she opened it, she turned to Emmeline. 'You will have a daughter, lass, a beautiful, strong girl who will live a full and rewarding life.'

Emmeline stood gawping after her as the crone hobbled back into the forest.

Seven years later
June 1260

THE NIGHT THE CRONE returned, there was a full moon. It was the summer solstice, and Emmeline had been agitated all day, unable to settle at one chore before starting another. Her husband had grumbled that the stew was overcooked, the meat stringy, and vegetables were too mushy. She apologised, distraught.

'Yer actin' like a horse with the wind up its tail,' Hob said. 'Everythin' all right?'

'Of course,' she replied, blinking too rapidly.

'Maybe yer with child again,' he said hopefully.

Emmeline looked at her daughter, Margaret, who was diligently chewing on a hunk of bread. Her heart ached for her lost son, as it did every day, but she always thanked the Goddess for the gift of another chance.

'Maybe,' she replied, although she knew it wasn't so. 'Meggy, shall we go for a walk after dinner? We can go up the hill, see if the fox cubs are playing.'

Meggy nodded, her eyes alight with joy. She swallowed the last of the bread before speaking. 'I'd like that, Ma.'

'Just be quiet when you get back, the pair o' yer, I'll be asleep, I 'spect.' Hob stretched his legs out towards the fire, his belly finally full.

Their chores done, Emmeline and Meggy set off along the path. The night air was cool after the stuffy heat inside the cottage. An owl hooted from a branch above their heads, and something large moved in the undergrowth nearby. Meggy clutched her mother's hand.

'It's all right, don't be scared,' Emmeline said calmly, trying to reassure the child. 'You see that oak over there?' She pointed at an ancient, gnarled tree, its branches twisting around each other as they fought to reach the sky. 'Quercus, the guardian of the forest, has been here since the beginning of time. He will protect us.'

After a few minutes of silence, Meggy asked, 'Where are we going, Ma?'

Emmeline smiled at her. 'We'll know when we get there.'

They came upon the clearing while following the path through the woods – a path that Emmeline had walked many times without ever coming across any clearings. She stopped, surprised, under a silver birch, almost afraid to step out into the open.

'Come, lass,' a familiar voice called.

Emmeline blinked, and saw the crone sitting on a rock, her silver-white hair glowing in the moonlight.

'I'm glad you are here, for the time is right.' The crone took a worn leather pouch out of the folds of her cloak and placed it on her open palm.

Emmeline sagged under the weight of the memories of that fateful day so many years before. She could hear again Lucan's pained cries, his snuffly whimpers, and the final, heavy silence as death came to claim her son.

'What's that?' Meggy asked, her eyes wide with curiosity. 'It's sparklin', Ma, can you see it?'

Emmeline looked more closely, and saw a faint haze of golden dust around the pouch. She put her hand to her mouth, her grief too great for her to be able to say a word.

'This, child, is the legacy left by your brother, seven years ago. I made your mother a promise, and tonight it will be fulfilled.' The crone beckoned them over, putting a finger on her lips. 'Now you must keep quiet, until I tell you to speak.'

Meggy nodded, too excited and terrified to question why. The old woman stood with a groan, and gestured to them to follow.

Across the clearing was a stream, flowing through the grass and flowers, gently burbling as it disappeared into the forest again. The crone knelt by the water's edge and bowed her head. As she knelt, hundreds of dragonflies flew up from the grass, so many that their wings created a shushing whisper all around the three women. Silver wings shimmered in the moonglow, as the creatures darted about.

'Bless these seeds, Goddess and Sister. Make them grow into strong plants that will heal, and ward off evil, and enable our healers to walk beyond the veil. Make them grow where and when they are needed, and bless the healers who will learn the ways to use them.' She dipped her hand in the stream and raised it, water dripping from her fingertips into the open pouch.

'I thank you, Goddess, for your blessing this night, and renew my vows to follow your wisdom always.' The crone stood and lifted the pouch above her head. Eyes closed, she whispered, 'Dea Luna, blessed be those who live their lives only to do good, now and forever.'

A moonbeam shone through the trees, striking the pouch the crone held aloft. Emmeline had to pinch herself to stop from crying out as misty wisps weaved around the crone's hand. A cloud passed in front of the moon, and just like that darkness surrounded them again, as quickly as the snuffing of a candle.

All was quiet for a while, as the crone remained kneeling, head bowed. A dragonfly settled on her arm and she came to, as though stirring from a deep sleep.

'Come,' she said, and Emmeline and Meggy went to her side. 'Hold out your hands.'

Meggy obediently stretched her hand out, palm up. The crone upended the pouch and tipped the seeds onto her hand. The girl stared at the shimmering sliver seeds in fascination.

'Take them and plant them around the glade,' the crone told her.
'Where?'
'Anywhere you want. And as you plant each seed, say these words: From a dying breath let come forth life, for now and for always, in times of strife.'

Meggy laughed and ran a little way across the clearing before throwing herself to the ground and digging small holes for the seeds.

The crone quirked an eyebrow at Emmeline. 'Will you help?'

Emmeline thought of the night Lucan died, and the magic that had surrounded them as he breathed his last breath. 'Of course,' she said, and held out her hand.

As the moon began to pale against the dawn sky, the three finished their work. With soil under their fingernails, smudges of dirt on their pallid faces, and dragonflies in their hair, they stood together in the centre of the clearing, shivering slightly in the cool breeze.

The Crone, the Mother, and the Maiden had cast their spell by the light of the moon, under the watchful gaze of the Goddess Luna. Now it was the turn of the sun to give its blessing to the new life in the clearing.

Meggy gasped and pointed. 'Look!'

Tiny shoots were already pushing through the earth, their tips turning silver as they reached towards the sky.

'Come,' the crone said, and led them over to where Meggy had planted the first seed. A small, fully formed plant had grown, its leaves shimmering sliver in the early morning light.

The crone muttered a blessing, then picked a leaf and rubbed it between her fingers. An aromatic perfume filled the air, enveloping them, heightening their senses. A quiet calm came over them as their blood surged in their veins and their hearts pulsed in time with the beat of the earth. They felt the roots of the trees, the grass, and the plants, pushing down into the soil in a never-ending quest for nutriment and water; worms burrowing through layers of decaying leaves and plants, churning up the earth and replenishing its goodness so that more would grow; tiny seeds cracking open, hair-thin shoots burying themselves in the earth, spreading a network of gossamer roots, each one becoming a part of the woods around them, each one separate but connected.

The crone smiled, her worn face crinkling with joy. 'This plant we shall call Lucan's Breath. It will have many names in the times to come, but it will come to be known simply as the silver-leaf plant.'

A dragonfly settled on the back of Emmeline's hand, its brilliant blue body shining vibrantly as its delicate wings stretched out. A gold dust shimmered over it, making the dragonfly look like a precious jewelled brooch a noblewoman would pin to her cloak. She gasped, and remained still as she stared at the creature.

'This is my second gift to you,' the crone said. She held out a gnarled finger, the knuckles swollen with age, the skin as dry as leather. 'This dragonfly and your son's soul are now entwined, and will be for all time. It will never grow old, and never die. So it will be, today and forever.'

As tears coursed down Emmeline's cheeks, the crone bent down until her head was level with Meggy's. 'One day, your great-great-great granddaughter will discover this grove and her journey will begin. She will travel to distant lands and battle a terrible evil, in order to become the first of the Healers. It will be hard, but she will have help, from the plants and from the dragonflies. They will all have help, throughout the generations.' She stood up straight and smiled, and her face changed. Faces that would become known to the Innocenti women in time, Matilde, Anna-Maria, Rina, Katherine, all appeared one after the other, so quickly that

Emmeline and Meggy thought they were dreaming, until eventually she was the Crone once more. She was almost as old as time itself, so many lives lived behind her, so many more to come.

'Agnes will be the first of many. Their lives will be hard, cruel sometimes, but they will remain true to their calling. They will be known as healers, and they will always be there for people in times of need.' She turned in a circle, her cloak swaying around her. 'This place shall be a part of them, their place of solace when times are too hard. Wherever they may be, they will always have the Dragonfly Grove.'

THE END

Printed in Dunstable, United Kingdom